THE SINGING

Alison Croggon is an award-winning poet whose work has been published extensively in anthologies and magazines internationally. She has written widely for theatre, and her plays and opera libretti have been produced all round Australia. She is also an editor and a critic. *The Singing* is the fourth and final of the Books of Pellinor and follows on from *The Gift*, *The Riddle* and *The Crow*. Alison lives in Melbourne with her husband Daniel Keene, the playwright, and their three children.

For more information about the author, visit:
www.alisoncroggon.com

Books by the same author

The Gift
The Riddle
The Crow

The Singing

ALISON CROGGON

WALKER BOOKS

First published 2008 by Walker Books Ltd
87 Vauxhall Walk, London SE11 5HJ

This edition published 2012

2 4 6 8 10 9 7 5 3 1

Published by arrangement with Penguin Books Australia Ltd

This book has been typeset in Palatino and GoldenCockerel

Printed and bound in Great Britain by Clays Ltd, St Ives plc

British Library Cataloguing in Publication Data:
a catalogue record for this book
is available from the British Library

ISBN 978-1-4063-3877-5

www.walker.co.uk

FOR DANIEL

A NOTE ON THE TEXT

I vividly remember when I finished my translation of the *Naraudh Lar-Chanë*. I looked up from my desk, which was covered in reference books, scribbled notes, facsimiles of scrolls, Post-it notes and all the other necessary detritus of the hapless translator, and realized that it was a fine spring day. I sat there for some time, savouring the moment, as a great weight fell off my shoulders. My task – perhaps the most challenging I've taken on in a long career of scrying ancient scripts – was done. I felt all the relief of completing a long and difficult labour; yet at the same time, I already missed the world of Edil-Amarandh. My work on what are now known as the Books of Pellinor occupied me to the exclusion of almost everything else for more than a decade, so I suppose it is not surprising I should feel such contradictory emotions. A long, often difficult, but always intensely rewarding relationship was now at an end.

Many readers have told me that they felt much the same mixture of sadness and joy when they reached the end of the epic. And here I want to thank them for their enthusiasm for these books, which buoyed me through many difficult times over the years. When I encountered an untranslatable phrase, or agonized over how best to express a fiendishly complex concept, I thought of the readers who wrote to bolster my instinct, back in 1999, that this story deserved a wider audience than a tiny academic coterie. Indeed it does; and as it has found its audience, so my labours have been repaid.

The Singing is the climactic fourth act of the narrative, which brings together the stories of Hem and Maerad, as described in the earlier books. In *The Gift* we follow Maerad's adventures as she meets the Bard Cadvan of Lirigon, learns her Gift and true identity as a Bard and journeys to Norloch, the great citadel of the Light in Annar, discovering her lost brother, Hem, on the way. In the second volume, *The Riddle*, Maerad travels with Cadvan to the frozen wastelands of the north in search of the Treesong, a mysterious text linked to the immortal Elementals. *The Crow* shifts the focus to follow Hem, who travels with the Bard Saliman to the southern city of Turbansk and becomes embroiled in the great battles in the south, where the Nameless One marches on the Suderain and lays siege to Turbansk. By the end of Book Three, both siblings have discovered different halves of the Treesong, and now they must reunite them.

In the course of the books, we encounter some of the diverse cultures of Edil-Amarandh and learn about the place of Barding in this society, details of which I have endeavoured to fill out for the interested reader in the appendices. I have always considered this story more than just a mine of archaeological information – it is a treasure as much for its delights as its usefulness – but as the ever-growing field of Annaren Studies illustrates, the history remains of abiding interest.

Here I'd like to briefly answer a couple of the most common questions that have come from readers. Many people have asked for Maerad's Elemental name. This will never be known, since Maerad didn't possess her Elemental powers long enough to learn it. However, the question of Cadvan's Truename, another very common question, is more happily dealt with, as after his death it was, as was the tradition among Bards, his most common appellation. His Truename was Inareskai, which means "Stormcloud" in the Speech. Many people have also asked if Maerad and Cadvan ever married. This is a puzzling question, as although they are often referred to as a pair in the

Annaren texts, it is never with the formal pronoun that indicates a married couple. However, we do know that they had children together, and shared their homes at various times during their lives. Equally as often, as was sometimes the way with Bards (perhaps because of their longevity), they also led independent lives and were apart from each other for long periods of time.

I owe thanks to so many people that I do not have the space to acknowledge them all here. Firstly, as always, I want to thank my family for their patience and help over the years while I was working on this translation – my husband, Daniel Keene, for his support of this project and his proofreading skills, and my children, Joshua, Zoë and Ben. I am again grateful to Richard, Jan, Nicholas and Veryan Croggon for their generous feedback on early drafts of the translation. I owe a special debt to my editor, Chris Kloet, whose sharp eye and good advice has improved my own work beyond measure; it has been an unfailingly pleasurable collaboration. My debt to the generous and creative contributions of my colleague Professor Patrick Insole, now Regius Professor of Ancient Languages at the University of Leeds, is also beyond measure. Equally, I would like to thank my many colleagues who have so kindly helped me with suggestions and advice over what have been many years of delightful conversations; they are now too numerous to name, and I am grateful to them all. Their help has been beyond price, and any oversights or errors that remain after such advice are all my own. Lastly, I would again like to acknowledge the unfailing courtesy and helpfulness of the staff of the Libridha Museum at the University of Querétaro during the months I spent there researching the *Naraudh Lar-Chanë*.

Alison Croggon
Melbourne, Australia, 2012

A NOTE ON PRONUNCIATION

MOST Annaren proper nouns derive from the Speech, and generally share its pronunciation. In words of three or more syllables, the stress is usually laid on the second syllable: in words of two syllables, (eg, *lembel*, invisible) stress is always on the first. There are some exceptions in proper names; the names *Pellinor* and *Annar*, for example, are pronounced with the stress on the first syllable.

Spellings are mainly phonetic.

a – as in *flat*. *Ar* rhymes with *bar*.

ae – a long sound, as in *ice*. *Maerad* is pronounced My–rad.

aë – two syllables pronounced separately, to sound *eye–ee*. *Maninaë* is pronounced Man–in–eye–ee.

ai – rhymes with hay. *Innail* rhymes with *nail*.

au – ow. *Raur* rhymes with *sour*.

e – as in *get*. Always pronounced at the end of a word: for example, *remane*, to walk, has three syllables. Sometimes this is indicated with ë, which indicates also that the stress of the word lies on the vowel (for example, *ilë*, we, is sometimes pronounced almost to lose the *i* sound).

ea – the two vowel sounds are pronounced separately, to make the sound ay–uh. *Inasfrea*, to walk, thus sounds: in–ass–fray–uh.

eu – *oi* sound, as in *boy*.

i – as in *hit*.

ia – two vowels pronounced separately, as in the name *Ian*.

y – *uh* sound, as in *much*.

c – always a hard *c*, as in *crust*, not *ice*.

ch – soft, as in the German *ach* or *loch*, not *church*.

dh – a consonantal sound halfway between a hard *d* and a hard *th*, as in *the*, not *thought*. There is no equivalent in English; it is best approximated by hard *th*. *Medhyl* can be said Meth'l.

s – always soft, as in *soft*, not *noise*.

Note: *Dén Raven* does not derive from the Speech, but from the southern tongues. It is pronounced Don Rah–ven.

Contents

THE DEAD

EPILOGUE

APPENDICES

One is the singer, hidden from sunlight
Two is the seeker, fleeing from shadows
Three is the journey, taken in danger
Four are the riddles, answered in treesong:
Earth, fire, water, air
Spells you OUT!

Traditional Annaren nursery rhyme
Annaren Scrolls, Library of Busk

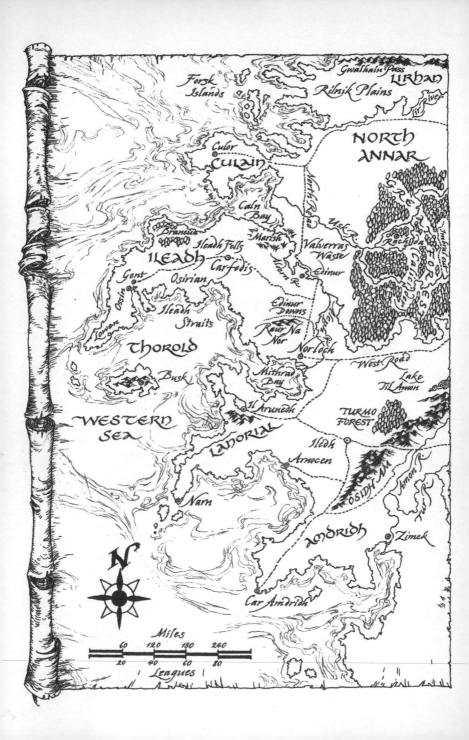

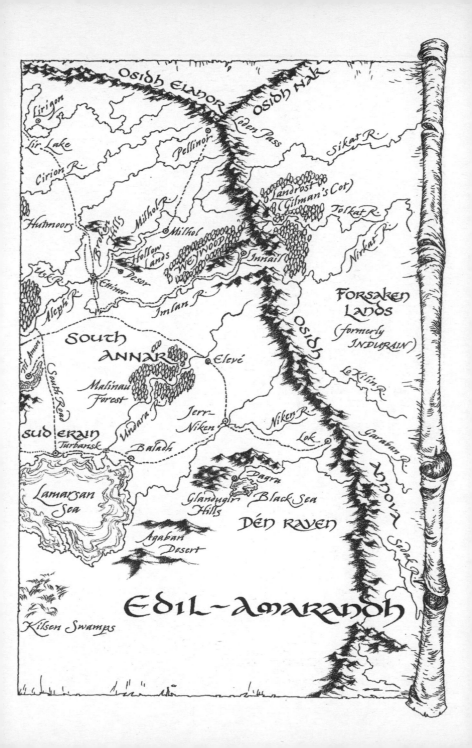

RETURN

I am the Lily that stands in the still waters,
   and the morning sun alights on me, amber and rose;
I am delicate, as the mist is delicate that climbs with the
   dawn; yea, the smallest breath of the wind will stir me.
And yet my roots run deep as the Song,
   and my crown is mightier than the sky itself,
And my heart is a white flame that dances in its joy,
   and its light will never be quenched.

Though the Dark One comes in all his strength,
   I shall not be daunted.
Though he attack with his mighty armies, though he strike
   with iron and fire, with all his grievous weapons,
Even should he turn his deadly eye upon me,
   fear will not defeat me.
I will arise, and he will be shaken where he stands,
   and his sword will be shivered in the dust,
For he is blind and knows nothing of love,
   and it will be love that defeats him.

From *The Song of Maerad*, Itilan of Turbansk

I

WOLF

A SHEPHERD was gathering firewood by the old Pellinor Road when a strange sight caught his attention. A horseman dressed in black, mounted on a magnificent black horse, was trotting briskly along the disused course, a clear, small figure in the pale winter sunshine.

To see a stranger at all was noteworthy. Since the sack of the School of Pellinor ten years before and the bad times that had followed, few travellers came this way. The days when Bards and merchants had ridden easily to Pellinor, making the road bright with their fine clothes and singing, had vanished so completely they now seemed like a time of legend. But the sight of a stranger, even one so ominously cloaked, was not what made the old man clutch his bundle of faggots to his chest and step warily behind a thicket of brambles, fearfully making the sign against the evil eye. His eyes were fixed on the beast that accompanied the rider: a large, white dog. If it was a dog, that is. It was like no dog the shepherd had seen. It was taller than a calf, and seemed bigger because of its thick winter pelt, which stood out around its head like a ruff. It kept pace effortlessly with the horse, running at an easy lope that revealed the strong muscles of its shoulders and haunches. If it hadn't been with the rider, the old man would have thought it a wolf; but he had never heard that a wolf would run with a horse.

As the strange trio came nearer, the shepherd's heart chilled and he crouched down behind the brambles, his hands trembling. His eyesight wasn't what it was, but he knew a wolf when he saw one. He began to regret having strayed so close to the road, even on so fair a day, and all the rumours he had heard of uncanny events, of evil creatures and dark sorcerers crowded into his head at once. If anything should happen to him, his wife would never know; and she would be quite alone, as their son had left the hamlet looking for a better life. The shepherd crouched closer to the ground, hoping he would remain unnoticed, and held his breath as the hoofbeats came closer and closer. To his alarm, they slowed to a walk; and then they stopped altogether.

"Where is he, Maerad?" A man's voice rang clear on the cold air, although he spoke in a low voice.

Even though he was so frightened, the old man was confused: to whom was the stranger speaking? He had seen no other with him. Did he converse, as the black witches were said to do, with spirits of the air? The shepherd held his breath, clutching his bundle of faggots so tightly to his chest that his knuckles were white.

"Over there, you think?"

The shepherd heard the man dismount and begin to walk towards him. In his agitation, the old man dropped his firewood with a clatter that to him sounded like thunder. He turned to run, but tripped over a tussock and fell over. As he scrambled onto his hands and knees, he found himself face to face with the wolf, and groaned in terror. Instinctively he hid his face in his hands, so he should not see his own death.

But he did not feel the wolf's teeth meeting in his neck, as he had expected. Instead, the stranger was speaking to him. At first the shepherd was too terrified to hear what he said.

"I beg your forgiveness," the stranger was saying. "I swear by the Light that we mean you no harm."

Slowly, the shepherd took his hands from his face. There was no sign of the wolf, and instead the stranger was standing before him, offering his hand. He helped the old man to his feet and gently brushed down his jerkin. Then he silently picked up the firewood and carefully heaped it in the shepherd's arms. The old man regained his breath. The stranger had a kindly look; but there was something else about him, an air of grace, that reminded the shepherd of better days. It had been a long time since his kind had been seen here.

He thanked the stranger gravely, in the formal way he once would have thanked a Bard who did him some healing or said the spring rites over a crop, and the other gave him a sharp look.

"It's been many years since I've seen a Bard around here," said the old man. Now his fright was over, he wanted to talk.

"There is little reason to come," said the stranger. His eyes met the old man's, and they both looked away at the same instant, as if reading in each other's face a sadness they didn't wish to name.

"Does this mean that the School of Pellinor will come back? Will there be Bards again?"

The Bard hesitated. "I don't know," he said.

The shepherd shifted the firewood, as it was getting heavy. "I am hoping that they do," he said at last. "It's hard with them gone. The winters bad and the lambs born awry and all else gone wrong."

"Aye," said the Bard. "Much else, and not only here. These are hard times for many people."

The shepherd nodded, and sniffed unhappily. But the stranger reached forward and touched his brow briefly, and for a moment it was as if a soft sun bloomed in the old man's forehead, and spread its golden warmth through his whole body.

"The Light go with you," said the Bard.

"And with you," answered the shepherd, in the proper way. He watched as the stranger walked back to his horse, which stood patiently on the road awaiting its rider. The white wolf sat on its haunches by the horse, looking no more dangerous than a big puppy. The Bard mounted, raised his hand in farewell, and rode away. It was only then that the old man realized that he hadn't asked his name.

He didn't stay to watch the horseman vanish in the distance. His wife would be waiting. The warmth from the Bard's touch still ran through his veins, and he hummed an old song as he walked home. His step was light: for the first time since he could remember, hope stirred in his heart.

"You almost made that poor old man die of fright, Maerad," said the Bard, glancing down at the wolf.

I didn't mean to, Cadvan. The wolf answered him in the Speech. She was silent for a time, and then added: *He did smell of fear. But if he planned to attack us, he would have been frightened anyway…*

"I suppose so. It's as well to be wary, but I think we were lucky his heart didn't give way." Cadvan shrugged. "No harm done in the end. I hope. Still, it worries me that he saw through the glimmerspells and was hiding from us. He should have seen only an empty road. He knew I was a Bard, you know."

I heard him. Did he have the Gift?

"A little," said Cadvan. "Not the Gift of a Bard, but enough to have a little Bardsight. I imagine that he's good with beasts. Probably he runs the healthiest flock in the district. Or did once, anyway, when this was a populous and pleasant region. It oppresses my heart, Maerad, to ride through it now."

He sighed and looked ahead, over the hills before them. It was not long after Midwinter Day and, despite the sunshine, there was little sign of spring. The wild was reclaiming the land, and leafless brambles and other weeds crept over what had once been stone-fenced fields.

The trio travelled swiftly, and the sun reached the height of its short day and began to descend to the horizon. Every now and then they saw an abandoned farmhouse, and once passed through a deserted village where doors hung off their hinges and pans left many years ago by the side of the overgrown paths rusted in the mud.

The wild no longer seemed desolate to Maerad, as once it had: a landscape untamed by human hands had its own meanings. But here the land was neither tame nor untamed. It just felt abandoned and sad and eerie. Her questing nose picked up the scent of old sorceries: evil had been done here, evil had driven these people from their homes. Perhaps it still hid among the crumbling farmhouses and overgrown orchards, watching as they passed, waiting for the shadows to fall and its powers to grow strong. At the thought her hackles rose, and she gave an involuntary growl.

I do not like it here, Maerad said, speaking directly into Cadvan's mind.

Nor I, replied Cadvan in the mindspeech; his earlier words had seemed too loud. *It has a deathly air.*

Darsor, Cadvan's mount, seemed to agree; although he said nothing, he quickened his pace to a steady canter. They continued in silence, and Maerad remained alert and uneasy. Towards sunset the sky clouded over, and a thick mist began to rise from the ground, muffling her sense of smell. This bothered her more than the darkness; she depended more on her nose than her eyes.

They didn't stop until it became too dark to move on. Cadvan found an overgrown copse where he might conceal a fire easily with a little magery, and unsaddled Darsor and rubbed down his rough coat. Maerad watched him as he worked, her eyes glowing. She had eaten the day before and was not hungry, but the water rose in her mouth as Cadvan cooked himself a meal and ate it. He glanced at her.

"You should say if you want something," he said.

Maerad was slightly offended and turned her head away. She would not ask; it was up to him to offer. Cadvan laughed.

"I swear, Maerad, you behave more like a real wolf every day. I can't always remember wolf etiquette. Would you like a bite?"

Maerad stared over his shoulder, ignoring him, and he shrugged and finished his meal. When he had cleaned the pot, he glanced at the wolf again. She lay on her belly, just at the edge of the circle of firelight, her massive muzzle resting on her paws, and watched his every movement. Her ears flickered back and forth, but she betrayed no other sign of uneasiness.

"I worry that you will forget that you are human if you are too much wolf," said Cadvan. "I know nothing of these powers. Are you ever afraid that you will forget how to become Maerad again?"

Maerad's ears pricked up, but she did not answer. Her gaze turned inward as she pondered Cadvan's words. She had travelled in wolf form for a week now. The ability to transform was part of her Gift, an Elemental power that was outside the usual capacity of Bards, and she knew that Cadvan was not wholly at ease with it. Her human self was present inside her, but it was true that the longer she stayed in wolf form, the more distant it seemed, like a dream she had once had. But she dared not change into the young girl she was, not so close to the mountains.

I don't think I'll forget, she said at last. *But even so, I can't change now. The Winterking would find me at once.*

Cadvan nodded, and seemed about to say more, but checked himself. Instead he asked Maerad if she would take the first watch. They had travelled hard since they left the burned ruins of Pellinor on Midwinter Day, heading south to haven in the School of Innail, and he ached with exhaustion. He wrapped himself in his cloak and a thick blanket against the deep chill of the night, and fell asleep at once.

Maerad was tired, but not unpleasantly, and she didn't feel the cold at all. She seemed to doze, but she was by no means asleep: her keen senses registered the smallest twitch of a twig, the tiniest shift of the air currents. She thought about Arkan, the Winterking, the Elemental being who had captured her in his mountain fortress and from whom she had so recently escaped. The reason she dared not change into her human form was not because she feared Arkan – although she did – but because she didn't trust herself. The thought of him opened a hollow inside her, a mixture of fear and desire. If Arkan said her name, she thought with contempt, she would even now turn and run to him. She didn't understand him – he was as beyond her understanding as the mountains themselves – and she didn't even like him; but something burned inside her that she couldn't control or ignore. Perhaps her desire for him was her Elidhu blood surging within her, like responding to like; perhaps her fear came from her human self. At this point, she shifted impatiently. It was always confusing thinking about her different selves.

It was simpler to be a wolf.

The night deepened. Maerad smelt rain coming, perhaps the next day. The clouds were heavy overhead, and neither moon nor star lifted the utter blackness. The damped-down fire gave out little light, and even that only illuminated the curls of mist that gathered between the tree trunks: but sight was only one of Maerad's senses. She heard an owl hoot in the distance, and the soft swirl of its wings as it swooped on a small night creature which squeaked briefly and was silent. A light wind soughed through the bare branches, rattling the dead winter leaves that still clung to them, and she heard Cadvan's soft breathing, and Darsor as he shifted while he slept; but there was little other sound. There seemed to be nothing amiss, but she felt more and more uneasy. She stood up and prowled noiselessly around the copse, her muzzle tilted upwards, tasting the air.

There was nothing to smell, nothing to hear, nothing to see; but still the hair stood up on her spine. Some other sense prickled her alarm. She paced restlessly back and forth, waking Darsor, who put his nose down to hers and blew out of his nostrils.

Something is wrong? he asked.

Yes. No. Now she was bristling all over. *Yes, but I don't know what it is.*

Darsor lifted his head and sniffed the air, and a shiver went through his skin. *There is someone approaching,* he said. *Someone well cloaked. You must wake my friend.*

Maerad nosed Cadvan and he was alert at once, his hair ruffled with sleep, reaching for his sword. *What is it?*

I don't know, said Maerad. *Darsor says someone is here. Someone cloaked.*

Cadvan was already standing. *Darsor would know,* he said.

His stillness and intensity told Maerad that Cadvan was listening with his Bard hearing. She felt a sudden frustration: the sharpness of her wolf instincts were matched by the dimming of other senses. While Cadvan could feel the working of magery, or the presence of the Dark, Maerad's abilities were blunted.

Do you think it's a Hull? A red flash lit Maerad's eyes at the thought: Hulls were Bards who had allied themselves with the Dark, giving their power to the Nameless One in return for endless life. They filled her with a mixture of contempt and fear.

Most likely. I hope it is, because if it isn't, it is probably something worse. I wish that you were a Bard right now.

Maerad paused, and then asked: *Should I change?*

Cadvan studied her thoughtfully for a moment, and then shook his head. *No*, he said. *I think we don't need to risk calling down more trouble on our heads and attract the Winterking as well. In any case, you're dangerous enough as you are.* A ghost of a smile fleetingly lit his face, and then he turned away from the fire and was swallowed in shadow.

For some time, nothing happened. The moments passed with agonizing slowness: the approaching menace neither grew nor lessened. Perhaps, thought Maerad, whatever approached knew that they were aware of its presence. Her hunting senses were fully alert, and she didn't move a muscle. Nearby she heard Darsor shift his weight and breathe out heavily. She wondered fleetingly how many times she and Cadvan had stood in just such suspense, waiting to be attacked: it was more often than she liked to think.

Then something infinitesimal seemed to shift, although her acute senses couldn't trace what it was. She glanced quickly at Cadvan, and saw his hand tighten on his sword. Then a blast of light seared across the clearing where they were camped, hitting a tree behind Maerad, which burst into instant flame. Darsor didn't even flinch, but Maerad crouched low to the ground, growling in her throat, the shadows from the flaming branches flickering over her coat. Cadvan didn't strike back; he swore instead, and she turned in surprise. It was a moment before she understood why. It wasn't a Hull attacking them, after all: no Hull used white fire.

That was a Bard, she said. *Or Bards.*

No, only one, I think. Cadvan sighed heavily, and strengthened his shield. *I would say, not a particularly powerful Bard. It explains the cloaking charm. It takes a powerful Hull to cloak its presence so thoroughly; Bards find it easier to hide themselves. But even if this Bard desires to kill us, I do not desire to kill any Bards. Though what a Bard is doing around here, I cannot begin to imagine...*

They probably think you're a Hull, said Maerad. *You should stop wearing black…*

At that moment, another blast of white fire flashed above them. It followed the last almost at once; their conversation had passed between them as swiftly as thought itself.

The white fire had broken the Bard's cloaking charm, and now Maerad could sense exactly where their attacker was. He was a few spans from them, just outside the copse; he was definitely a man, and definitely a Bard, and alone. But there was something wrong, all the same: even Maerad's muffled Bardic instincts could tell that there was something amiss in his magery.

Can he harm us? she asked, as another bolt of white fire flashed over their heads.

I don't believe so. Though he may be holding something in reserve.

Shield me, said Maerad. *Perhaps I can overpower him without hurting him.*

Cadvan nodded, and she felt the prickle of magery in her skin as he cast a shield of magery to protect her. Then he lifted his hand and sent a blast of white flame over the Bard's head to distract him, as Maerad began to move noiselessly out of the trees, circling behind their attacker so she could stalk him. Before long she was behind him, readying herself to pounce: his silhouette jumped out briefly, black against another flash of white fire. She felt her puzzlement deepen as she watched him. He reminded her of nothing so much as a boy throwing stones at a tree, and his attack was about as effective. It made no sense at all.

She mindtouched Cadvan to warn him that she was about to attack, readied herself, and then leapt upon the Bard's back, knocking him to the ground and winding him. He was taken so completely by surprise he could do nothing to defend himself, falling without even a cry. He lay struggling for breath beneath Maerad's weight as she pinned him to the ground.

Within moments Cadvan had joined Maerad. He froze the Bard with a charm, rendering him utterly unable to move or to work magery. Maerad lifted her paws from his shoulders and sat on her haunches nearby. Now there was no danger, she was overwhelmed with curiosity.

Cadvan waited until the Bard had stopped gasping, and then roughly sat him up and loosened the charm so he could speak, setting a small magelight before his face for illumination. It was difficult to tell how old he was, even given the difficulty of estimating a Bard's age. He looked like a man in his late fifties, but he was skeletally thin and his face was so seamed with suffering it made any guess impossible: he might have been much younger. He had a grotesque tic, so that he seemed to be always grimacing, and his flesh shone white through the rents in his filthy clothes. Although he must have known it was no use, he struggled violently against the freezing charm.

Maerad looked once into his eyes, and then turned her head away, battling an overwhelming animal panic. *He's mad*, she said to Cadvan.

Cadvan said nothing. He seemed to be bracing himself.

"It is no use trying any magery against us," he said to the Bard. Although he spoke harshly, Maerad could hear the pity in his voice. "And I don't recommend it."

The man stopped struggling and met Cadvan's gaze. His eyes glittered with hatred.

"Kill me then," he said, and spat.

"I do not wish to kill you," said Cadvan. "That's the last thing I want to do."

"Then I will kill you." The Bard's face twisted. "Get your monstrous beast to tear me to pieces. I will kill you if you do not kill me. So kill me."

"I don't want to kill you," said Cadvan again. "And you can't kill me." He paused. "What is your name?"

The Bard cackled, and Maerad jumped. It was a horrible sound, an expression of such despair that she went cold.

"Name? You ask my name? I don't have any name. What's yours, you spawn of the Dark? I know that such as you have no name either, so why do you ask me?"

"I have a name," said Cadvan. "And so do you." A halo of starlight began to bloom gently about Cadvan's form, and he leaned forward and pressed his palm against the man's forehead. After a time, Cadvan sighed deeply and took away his hand, and Maerad looked again at the Bard. His face slowly relaxed as the pain and hatred ebbed from his expression.

"Now," said Cadvan calmly. "What is your name?"

There was a long silence before the Bard answered, as if he had to search through his memory before he could find the right answer. "Hilarin," he said. "Hilarin of Pellinor."

Cadvan's face went white. "Hilarin of Pellinor?" he repeated.

Do you know him? asked Maerad.

I have heard his name, said Cadvan. *Hilarin of Pellinor was a famous singer, once.*

"My friend, what has happened to you?" Cadvan spoke with a grieving gentleness and took his hand, but Hilarin snatched it back, rubbing it with his other hand as if the touch had soiled him. "It was thought that you were dead. Where have you been?"

"I don't know. I've been – I've been hunting…" Hilarin's words were confused, and Maerad saw the shadows gathering in his face again. Even Cadvan's magery couldn't keep his madness at bay for long. "There was a School here once and it has been taken and hidden. But I know where to find it. It's buried beneath the earth. They took it, those dark ones, the dark ones like you, I'll kill them all, you disgust me, you traitors…" He trailed off into a string of obscenities, and then began to weep helplessly. Maerad looked at Cadvan in bafflement.

What does he mean?

Cadvan's face was grim and sad. *Not much, I fear. Nonsense. I guess that the sack of Pellinor drove him mad. Or perhaps something else.*

Maerad stared at Hilarin. This man, she thought, had once been a proud Bard of Pellinor. This drooling, broken man. She wondered how he had survived. She suddenly wanted to be sick.

What can we do with him? she asked at last. *We can't leave him like this.*

She felt the agony of indecision in Cadvan's mind. *No,* he said. *But neither can we take him with us. Our quest is too urgent to risk it with a madman. I wonder what happened to him...*

A vivid image rose in Maerad's mind: she saw again how her mother Milana, also a proud Bard, had been broken by Enkir, the First Bard of Annar, during the sack of Pellinor. It was Enkir, a traitor to the Light, who had led the assault on Pellinor when Maerad had been a small child. What he had done to her mother was one of Maerad's most painful memories. She thought she knew what might have happened to Hilarin.

Can you heal him? asked Maerad.

Healing this is beyond my Knowing, said Cadvan. *I can but offer a little relief, a little rest. And perhaps set a thought in his dreams, to lead him where he might find some respite. Lirigon would be the closest place...*

He sat down next to Hilarin and began to weave a charm, murmuring words from the Speech in a low voice. The Bard at once sank into a deep sleep; but that was only the beginning of Cadvan's magery. Maerad watched him for a while, and then, realizing that he would be some time, she wandered back to the fire.

Darsor was a seasoned warrior: knowing that the skirmish was over, he had already fallen asleep again. Maerad didn't wake him. She lay with her nose to the fire, as deeply depressed as she had ever been. She wasn't sure if she had seen anything more pitiable in her life. Hilarin of Pellinor was a famous singer, once. And now...

Cadvan returned later, his face grey with weariness, and laid his hand lightly on Maerad's pelt.

You should sleep, she said, turning to him as he sat down beside her.

Soon, he answered.

Will Hilarin ever heal?

I don't think so, he said. *Something is so deeply broken in him that I think it will never mend. I have done what I can; he will sleep for a long time, and I have shielded him so he will be safe. And when we are far from here, he will wake up and make his way to Lirigon, where there are healers who might be able to soothe his suffering, if nothing else.*

What happened to him is like what has happened to this country, said Maerad.

Aye, said Cadvan. *It is. The Dark does its work thoroughly.*

What can we do against such wills that work these things?

Cadvan picked up a stick and stirred up the embers of the fire, and sparks flew up into the night. *We do what we can*, he said.

But is there any hope?

Cadvan said nothing for a while. When he spoke, his voice was harsh. *There is always hope*, he said.

II

INNAIL

MAERAD and Cadvan arrived in Innail in the late afternoon, just as the high pale blue of the winter sky was darkening towards a frosty, moonless evening. The sight of the white walls in the distance, glimmering under the stars that burned huge and still in the clear sky, made Maerad's heart beat painfully in her breast.

When she and Cadvan had left Innail, just under a year ago now, she had thought that she might never see it again. To be in a School again after all their hard journeying was for Maerad the best part of bliss, but Innail held a special place in her heart. It was here, in this centre of Bardic learning and making, that she had first found what it meant to be a Bard. And it was here that she had first encountered the meaning of human kindness.

Cadvan would not let her change from her wolf shape until they were well inside the School, and as a result he had argued at Innail's gate for some time. Cadvan would not identify himself and the guard didn't recognize him. Aside from that, the guard was very dubious about letting in a wild animal, especially one as big and powerful-looking as Maerad. She had tried to look as docile as possible, all but rolling on her back in her efforts to show how harmless she was. Finally, on Cadvan's insistence, Malgorn the First Bard himself appeared and, after a hurried consultation with Cadvan, sternly informed the wolf in the Speech that she was welcome, but that she was not to chase or eat any of the hens or ducks or other domestic animals.

Maerad flashed an ironic glance to Cadvan as Malgorn ordered the gates open, and he winked solemnly as he led her and Darsor inside.

"By the Light, Cadvan, what are you doing with a wolf?" asked Malgorn, as he hurried them through the outer streets. "Where am I going to put it? I can hardly place it in the stables; the horses would go mad, no matter how tame it is."

"The house will do fine, old friend," said Cadvan. "Surely you have a spare bedchamber?"

"For a wolf?" Malgorn boggled briefly and then, clearly deciding that Cadvan was either joking or out of his mind, dropped the subject. They went to the stables, where Cadvan saw Darsor comfortably housed and well fed, and then turned their steps towards Silvia and Malgorn's house. Maerad stuck close to Cadvan, fearing that she might, after all, be housed in the stables: what she wanted above all was a bath and a good supper. Malgorn watched her warily but made no comment, even when she entered his front door and followed the Bards into the music room. Maerad thought he seemed reserved, even stiff. He stood in the doorway uncertainly, as if he were trying to think of what to say.

"How about one of your marvellous brews?" asked Cadvan, flinging himself on the couch. "I tell you, Malgorn, I have a well-earned thirst. And I am a mort tired."

"Of course," said Malgorn, almost with relief, and hurried to get some wine.

Something is wrong, Maerad said. *Is it because he is nervous around wolves?*

Malgorn? I think not. Remember, the lore of animals is his Knowing, Cadvan answered. *In any case, you can change now.*

Maerad sat on her haunches and grew still, seeking that deep inner place where the names fell away and she was no longer Maerad nor Elednor nor anyone else. She felt herself become clear and empty, the still point of transformation where all possibilities opened. *Be Maerad,* she told herself. *Be Me.*

There was an ease about her transforming that almost astonished her, as if she had been shapeshifting since she was a baby. But always before she did it there was a moment of dread, a fear that ran through her veins like cold water. To reach that point of being no one, she had to forget everything she knew about herself, and this was more frightening than she cared to admit. As she transformed there was that flash of pure agony, as if, for the briefest moment, she had been thrown into a fire. And then she wasn't a wolf any more.

"I don't think I'll ever get used to your doing that," said Cadvan mildly. "I have never seen anything so strange."

Maerad shook her head as if she were shaking her thick winter wolf's ruff, and stretched out her arms. There was still something wolfish about her gestures.

"That's so much better," she said, sighing. "But, you know, Cadvan, I think you're right: I have been too much wolf."

Cadvan opened his mouth to reply, but at that moment Malgorn bustled in with a carafe. He stopped in the doorway, his mouth open.

"Maerad!" he said. "Where did you come from?"

"Greetings, Malgorn," said Maerad. "I'm sorry I couldn't say so before. Cadvan didn't want anyone to know that I was here."

Malgorn plumped down on the couch next to Cadvan, holding the carafe like one in a daze. Cadvan gently removed it from his hands.

"Allow me to pour a drink, my dear friend," he said to Malgorn.

Malgorn didn't answer. He was still staring at Maerad.

"Cadvan, what black magery is this?" he said at last. "What have you brought into this house?"

Malgorn was flushed with anger, and Maerad glanced nervously at Cadvan. Were they to be thrown out of Innail, after all? But Cadvan looked unperturbed.

"Malgorn, you know Maerad. Maerad of Edil-Amarandh, if you want her proper name these days. I know it's astounding that she can change her shape, but that doesn't make her a wer nor any creature of the Dark."

"Cadvan, these are perilous days … are you mad? Have you any idea what is happening here? And you dare to bring a creature of the Dark into my *house*?"

Cadvan leant forward and clasped Malgorn's hand.

"My friend, if ever you have trusted me, trust me in this. I know well that these are dark times. None know better than I do. But I swear to you, by the Light itself, that neither Maerad nor I have any dealings with the Dark. And I would never endanger the safety of those I love as well as you and Silvia by inviting the Dark into your home."

Malgorn held Cadvan's eyes a moment, and looked over towards Maerad. Maerad, hurt and offended, met his gaze, and Malgorn flinched and looked down at his feet.

"My tale since we last met is a strange one," said Maerad. Her voice was cold with anger. "I have faced death and seen the death of some I love. I have spoken with the Elidhu. I have found the Treesong. I have risked so much, suffered so much, as part of our struggle against the Dark. And then you say…"

Her voice broke, and she turned away and looked of out the window.

There was a heavy silence. Cadvan stood up and took some glasses from a shelf on the far side of the room, poured some laradhel into one of them and handed it to Malgorn. He then poured out another measure and gave it to Maerad.

"Old friend," said Cadvan, filling another glass for himself and sniffing its rich smell. "If we do not trust each other, we are already defeated."

Malgorn sat up and sighed. He lifted his glass to Maerad and drank it down in one gulp.

"I am sorry," he said. "Maerad, I am sorry. These are fearful times, and fear does not make us wise."

Maerad turned to face him and tried to smile. "I know," she said. "We have all suffered…" She studied Malgorn's face, noting for the first time how tired and strained he looked, and a terrible thought occurred to her. "Malgorn, is Silvia … is Silvia well? Is she…?"

Silvia, Malgorn's wife, was probably the main reason Maerad had longed for Innail these past harsh months. Her kindness had opened Maerad's eyes to another world, a world very different from Gilman's Cot, the brutish slave settlement in which she had spent her childhood. Maerad could not have borne it if something had happened to Silvia.

"Aye, aye, she's well," said Malgorn hastily, seeing the look on Maerad's face. "You mustn't worry. She's busy, but I've told her that Cadvan is here, and she will come as soon as she can. She asked after you, Maerad…"

Maerad sighed with relief, and sat down on the couch, cradling her glass. Suddenly she felt exhausted. Malgorn and Cadvan began to talk and she listened idly, with no desire to participate in the conversation.

Shortly afterwards, when Silvia still did not appear, Malgorn disappeared to organize beds for the two travellers. To her delight, Maerad was given the same chamber she had slept in last time she had been in Innail. A friendly woman whom she did not know gave her clean clothes. Maerad dumped her pack on the floor and immediately repaired to the bathroom where, with a feeling of inexpressible bliss, she lowered herself into the hot water and washed off all the grime of travel.

She avoided looking at her left hand as she washed. The two fingers she had lost to frostbite made it an ugly claw, and she felt ashamed whenever she caught sight of it. She was getting used to compensating and could now do most things without too much difficulty, but she tried to keep it out of sight whenever possible. With a hand so maimed, she could no longer play music whenever she wished; and every time she glimpsed her missing fingers, she remembered her loss anew.

Finally she dressed in the clean clothes, sighing for the sheer pleasure of the soft fabrics against her skin, and made her way to the music room. It was now full night and the lamps were lit, casting a soft glow. For this brief suspended time, she pretended nothing was wrong: that she was just an ordinary Bard, that she had never heard of the Nameless One, the Dark power who now made war on all Edil-Amarandh. Tonight she would eat a delicious dinner, and tomorrow she would resume her studies...

She curled up on a red couch and waited for Cadvan. Right now she was very content to be alone. This room was her favourite in the house. Though her bedchamber was her favourite room as well ... and she loved the bathroom too, with its deep stone bath and bottles of scented oils and endless supply of hot water. Her gaze swept lazily across the pale yellow walls with their stencilled flowers, the musical instruments stacked casually against the bookshelves, the mullioned window, and returned to the fire in the grate which burned brightly against the cold winter evening.

It felt like an age since she had last been here, although it had been less than a year. Would that shy girl who had arrived last spring, ashamed of her rags and tangled hair, ignorant of Bards and Schools and Magery, recognize the Maerad who sat here now? Perhaps she would have gazed in wonder at her as at a figure out of legend: Maerad of Edil-Amarandh, the Fire Lily, who had spoken with the Elemental Ardina, Queen of Rachida, Daughter of the Moon; the same who had travelled to the very north of the world and seen cold curtains of light dancing in the sky, and had escaped the clutches of Arkan, the Ice Witch, himself. Maerad the Shape Shifter, who could become a wolf at will. Maerad the Chosen, the Fated, the One, whose destiny was to save Edil-Amarandh from the Dark.

Maerad the Unpredictable, she added, thinking of an old joke of Cadvan's. *But I am really quite predictable. I don't want any of these fine names. I don't want these mysterious powers that frighten good people and make the Dark hunt me down. I just want to stay where I am and to sleep in a bed with clean linen sheets and a warm coverlet. And I don't want to be cold or hungry or sad ever again.*

Although, for as long as she could remember, Maerad had always been sad.

Her thoughts were interrupted by the entrance of Silvia, who stopped dead in surprise when she saw Maerad and then, when Maerad stood up, came forward and embraced her hard, kissing the top of her head.

"Maerad!" she said, standing back and earnestly examining Maerad's face. "What a relief! When I was told only Cadvan had arrived, I feared the worst ... but here you are!"

Maerad smiled with pure happiness. "Here I am!" she said. "And it's so good to be here. Innail is as beautiful as I remembered."

"Aye. But things have changed since last you were here." Silvia's clear brow briefly darkened, but she shook her head, putting those thoughts aside. "But – wasn't there a wolf? Malgorn said Cadvan had lost his mind and insisted on bringing a wolf into the house."

Maerad laughed. "That was me," she said. "Cadvan didn't want anyone to know that I was here."

Silvia stared at Maerad for a time without speaking, her face expressionless. "You?" she said at last.

"Yes." Maerad gazed back at Silvia with a stab of sadness, feeling again the gulf that lay between her and those she loved. "I can shapeshift. It's one of the things I have found out about myself." She wondered whether she should tell Silvia about her Elemental self, those inborn powers that made her different from other Bards – but she couldn't, for the moment, face the thought. Bards deeply distrusted the Elidhu, the Elemental entities whose ways had long been sundered from humankind, and Maerad felt she couldn't bear to see the doubt it would raise in Silvia's face. Another time. "It's part of – part of my Gift."

"I can see that there's an interesting story to tell," said Silvia. "We can do that over dinner. Malgorn's arranged it, so it's sure to be good – even in these hard times, we in Innail take pride in our table." She smiled, reaching for Maerad's hand, and went still with shock. Blushing, Maerad pulled back her hand and concealed it again in the folds of her dress, where she had kept it hidden from Silvia's eyes. Very gently, Silvia reached out and took her maimed hand, pressing it between both of her own.

"Oh, Maerad," she said, her voice hoarse with sorrow.

"It – I lost some fingers in the cold," said Maerad awkwardly. "It's all right. I can do most things."

"But you can't play your lyre with your hand like that!" said Silvia, putting her finger straight on the deepest wound. "My dear. I am so sorry... Oh, this world!" she cried with sudden passion, her eyes brimming with tears. "It is filled with such hurts!"

Maerad, her face averted, had nothing to say. But Silvia

gathered her into her arms and hugged her again. Then, her voice muffled by Maerad's hair, she said, "And it is full of such joys, and we must not forget those. I thought of you every day, and feared I would not see you again. I am so glad that you are back. Now," and suddenly she became brisk, "I think that both of us need something to drink. Or at least, I do. I'm pretty sure there's wine in here somewhere..."

She went over to a table by the window, where a carafe stood next to some glasses, and poured two drinks. She handed a glass to Maerad, lifted hers in salute, and took a long draught.

"It has been a hard year, Maerad," she said. "And we have had our own losses. But I doubt that my year has been as hard as yours."

"It has been hard," Maerad answered, thinking back. "But I'd rather hear about what has happened here."

Silvia sighed, and looked down at her wine, swirling it thoughtfully in her glass. "We lost Oron," she said, naming the First Bard of Innail.

Maerad drew in her breath, remembering Oron's stern, iron-grey head, her straight back, her kind authority. "How?"

"A battle near Tinagel. Innail has been much afflicted by bands of marauders down this side of the mountain, men mainly, but also some wers... They mounted a big assault on Tinagel, attacking the townspeople at night. They weren't entirely unprepared, but it was a hard battle. Oron went to help the defence, with many other Bards. They destroyed the attackers. But Oron did not return." There was a slight catch in Silvia's voice, and she sighed. "She is sorely missed. Malgorn is First Bard now, which doesn't sit easily on him. He worries overmuch. Not that there isn't much to worry about." She smiled crookedly. "Alas, I am trying to think of good things to tell, but none will come to me."

Looking at Silvia closely, Maerad saw that her face had lines of care that hadn't been there last spring. She hunted for something to say that might be comforting.

"We're still here!" she said at last.

"Yes, despite all. Though we have not reached the worst, I think." Silvia shook her head again, like a dog shaking off rain. "Maerad, almost I have forgotten lightness. Is that the worst thing?" Suddenly she smiled, with a spark of her normal mischief. "Of course, you are right. We are here, and the fire is bright and this room – well, this room is as beautiful as it has ever been. And we are about to eat, I am quite sure, a delicious dinner. That should be enough for any of us."

Dinner was as tasty as Silvia had promised: roasted wild duck basted with almond oil and butter and stuffed with fresh herbs and nuts, carrots flavoured with honey and rosemary, and fried cabbage with butter melting into its green and white and purple folds. That was followed by a rich latticed pie made out of the last of the winter apples. Maerad resisted the urge to gobble it all down, and savoured every mouthful. She couldn't remember when she had last eaten such food: it must have been when she was in Norloch.

By unspoken consent, all the Bards spoke about distant or pleasant things – memories of Cadvan's and Malgorn's youth, or funny stories that Silvia remembered from her childhood in a village nearby, or arguments about the relative merits of favourite songs – until they had finished eating. They returned to the music room holding glasses of an apricot liqueur of Malgorn's concoction like amber jewels in their hands, and settled in the comfortable red couches by the fire.

Malgorn could not conceal his gloom, although he tried his best to be a cheerful host. At first, they did not speak about Maerad's and Cadvan's travels over the past year; Cadvan, hungry for information, wanted to know what had happened in Annar over the past few months. There was, it seemed, no good news anywhere. Bands of soldiers from Norloch, claiming to be under the orders of Enkir, the First Bard of Annar, were, it was rumoured, roaming the land, press-ganging farmers and tradesmen and acting like brigands.

"Enkir grows in his strength," Malgorn said. "Still many Schools support him, and none dare oppose him openly. Yet. People are more afraid of the Dark than they are of what Enkir is doing. I fear both of them, equally... As ever, the greatest resistance is in the Seven Kingdoms."

"Enkir demands clear and unambiguous fealty from every School," said Silvia. "As if a First Bard has ever demanded such a thing! Only the Kings have dared to do this, and we know what that led to – war and ruin in Annar. But we all fear that he plans to march on Til Amon, which lies most open to him. They have not, as yet, returned their pledge. As we have not. And others."

"It's hard to keep in touch," added Malgorn, frowning. "Roads are no longer as safe as they were, and no one dares to trust letters, lest they fall into the wrong hands. And so we sift gossip and rumours, trying to discern what is true and what is not, what is likely and what is impossible..." He fell silent and stared at the table.

"We hear news, all the same," said Silvia. "And Bards have not completely given up travelling. The worst, of course, is the Fall of Turbansk..."

Maerad looked up sharply. Silvia could not know that her brother, Hem, was in Turbansk with their friend Saliman.

"Turbansk has fallen?" Cadvan said, glancing anxiously at Maerad. "What news of that?"

"Little, and bad," said Malgorn heavily. "We hear that the Black Army, led by the sorcerer Imank, marched on Baladh, and sacked and burned the city, and then on to Turbansk, where it laid siege; and at last the city fell to the Dark forces. Now there are rumours that Imank marches north, while others say that he is moving westward to Car Amdridh. Many have fled northwards to Til Amon, seeking refuge. I heard that Juriken, the First Bard there, is dead. But from this distance, it is impossible to know the truth of the matter: we have bird news at best, and that is always sketchy."

"But some got away," said Maerad quickly. "Surely some people escaped."

"Always some escape," Silvia answered. She had noticed Maerad's anxiety, and attempted to comfort her. "Saliman is a resourceful Bard, and a powerful one, and no mean warrior. I am sure he would have as good a chance as anyone."

That was cold comfort indeed. For a time the only sound was the sleepy popping of the fire.

"When did you hear this news?" asked Cadvan.

"Only a fortnight ago," said Silvia. "It is a heavy blow. We can look for no help from the south, and can only hope that Amdridh holds against the Black Army."

"Turbansk has never fallen before," said Cadvan. "Not even through all the long years of the Great Silence. It must be a vast army."

"I saw it," said Maerad suddenly. The Bards gravely turned to look at her. "I saw the army in a dream. A huge army, stretching further than the eye could see, with monstrous soldiers made of iron... And I saw Turbansk laid waste and all its towers and walls crumbled." She suddenly wanted to weep. "My brother is there."

Now Silvia was astonished. "Your brother?"

"My brother Hem. Well, Cai is his proper name, but he only calls himself Hem. We found him, Cadvan and me, in the middle of the Valverras. The Hulls kidnapped him; I think that's why they sacked Pellinor, because Enkir and the Hulls wanted to find him. They thought he was the One, not me. We took him to Norloch. And then, when Norloch was burning, Saliman took him to Turbansk, to join the School there. And now..." She felt tears gathering like a hot ball in her throat, but she didn't want to cry. "Now, I don't know where he is."

"Silvia is right, Maerad," said Cadvan gently. "If anyone could make sure that Hem is safe, it is Saliman."

"Yes," said Maerad harshly. "But we don't know if Saliman is alive. Do we?"

There was a long silence. Malgorn, looking at Maerad sympathetically, wordlessly filled everyone's glasses. It did seem strange, Maerad thought suddenly, to be speaking of war and death in such a comfortable and beautiful room, drinking out of delicately blown glasses. Nothing seemed to be quite real.

At last she broke the silence. "I think I would know if Hem was dead," she said. "It's as if there's a ... a kind of thread that binds me to him. I don't think I imagine it."

"Sometimes," said Silvia gravely, "it is like that between people. I do not doubt you, Maerad."

Maerad looked up into Silvia's gentle, dark eyes, now filled with a deep sadness and love. She looked away swiftly, because kindness really would make her weep, and she did not wish to weep here, among people who had also suffered deeply. "If Hem is still alive," she said, "then so are other people. Saliman too."

"I hope you are right," said Malgorn.

"I have to find him." Maerad already felt light-headed, but drained her glass anyway. "I have to find him very soon."

Malgorn almost smiled. "In all of Annar and the Suderain, you seek your brother?"

"It's a Knowing I have." She stared fiercely at Malgorn. "I know it's important. Beyond wanting him and loving him; of course I want to find him because of that. But it's more important even than that. I don't know why."

Such was the passion and certainty in Maerad's voice that no one in the room disbelieved her. Malgorn nodded gravely. "Well, then, you must seek him," he said, with a special gentleness that she had not heard in his voice before. "But first, I think you must sleep."

Maerad woke late to another clear winter day. The pale sun spilt through the casement, and she lay idly, listening, as she had almost a year ago, to the noises of the School: musical instruments tuning up; a dog barking; pigeons cooing outside her window. Her room was warm, and it was no punishment to leave her cosy bed and wash herself and dress.

She wandered downstairs to see what she could get for breakfast. She met Cadvan in the corridor, on the same errand.

"We're up a bit late," he said. "But there will be something. I'm ravenous!"

"Something" turned out to be meat pastries, warmed up for them by the Bardhouse cook, fresh rye bread, white cheese and fruit. They took their bounty to the small dining room where they had eaten the night before, and set to with pleasure, talking over their plans for the day. Maerad wanted to wander around in the sunshine and visit her favourite places in Innail, and perhaps to see the swordmaster Indik and others she had met on her last stay here. Cadvan, his brow creased, was already planning further ahead.

"What shall we do, Maerad?" he asked, pushing back his plate with a contented sigh. "I believe you utterly when you say that we have to find Hem. But how do we go about that? He could be anywhere in Edil-Amarandh. And travelling, as Malgorn said last night, has become perilous: Annar is already at war. It would be good to have some idea of where to start, at least."

Maerad studied Cadvan gravely. Unlike Silvia and Malgorn,

he was little changed from when she had first met him, aside from a thin white scar that curled around his cheekbone and left eye, the mark of a Hull's whiplash. He had always had a certain grimness about him. Perhaps, thought Maerad, he was a little more careworn; yet she often had the sense that his grimness was a veil, and that underneath it welled a brilliant fountain of joy. Her thoughts made her feel strangely shy.

This was the first time he had asked her what they ought to do next. Always it had been Cadvan who made the decisions, who led the way. It made her realize again how she had changed in the past months. And perhaps Cadvan had changed as well. He was prepared to go with her, unquestioningly, on a dangerous quest which most people would dismiss as mad and futile.

"I think we have to go south." Maerad frowned, pondering her ignorance of Annar. All she knew was that the Suderain was south of Annar, and that Turbansk was – had been – in the Suderain. And that, if they were lucky, Hem would be heading north. If he had survived. "I mean, Hem would likely be coming north – maybe."

"What do you *feel*, though?" Cadvan stared at her intently. "Maerad, I trust that you are correct, that your Knowing speaks true in you. I remember when we first found Hem, how your Knowing guided you then, against my better judgement." Cadvan unconsciously rubbed the scar on his cheekbone – meeting Hem had led to the battle with the Hulls that had nearly killed him and that had marred his face. "I think perhaps we can use that sense to guide us. But you must be certain: you must not let the Knowing be muddied by your hope."

Maerad paused a while before she answered, searching inside herself for her truest feeling. She knew exactly what Cadvan meant. In Gilman's Cot, when she had been a slave, there had been a saying: "Hope shines in the dying man." The more desperate you were, she thought, the more danger there was of being misled by your hopefulness.

She missed Hem with every fibre of her being. He was the only family she had left. Her mother and father were dead, killed by the Dark. Her brother's thin, mischievous face rose up in her mind's eye. She thought with a pang that he probably looked different now. When she had last seen him he had seemed to her, for all his toughness, to be mostly a little boy. But boys his age, in the awkward space between childhood and manhood, changed so fast…

She sighed, and tried to focus her thoughts. Or, more precisely, tried not to think at all, so that whatever was in her mind would rise up and speak. She waited, with a relaxed attention, for what she knew to reveal itself.

"I think it is south," she said at last. "Some kind of – tug – that way. I don't know anything else."

"South it is, then," Cadvan said. "As soon as we can. But for now, I would dearly love to rest in Innail. It has been a difficult winter, and I doubt that spring will be any easier."

Maerad felt a huge relief, as if she had passed some test she had not been aware she was taking. Cadvan's implicit trust moved her deeply: she doubted herself so fiercely. A sudden tenderness washed over her, and she almost reached out to brush back the lock of hair that dropped over his forehead as he leaned across the table towards her; but she checked herself, and again looked down at the table, a slight flush rising in her cheeks. She and Cadvan had been close companions for many months, but their intimacy was hedged with many unspoken barriers.

"I need a new sword," she said, changing the subject. "Arkan took Irigan when he captured me."

"And a horse. Unless you want to run south wolfwise," said Cadvan.

"I think I have been too much a wolf lately." Maerad loved

the strength that went with her wolf-self, the sense of freedom, the vivid and exciting sensual world of smell and taste and instinct, but even before Cadvan had raised the possibility, she had begun to be secretly afraid that she might forget how to turn back into herself.

"Well then, we can mix business with pleasure today, and ask Indik about both mount and sword," said Cadvan, standing up to gather their plates.

"I wish I had Imi." Maerad thought sadly of the mare who had carried her the length of Annar, and who had been her dear and gentle friend.

"She's with the Pilanel. They are good with beasts, especially with horses, so you must not worry for her. It would be some detour to go north over the mountains to get her back."

Maerad knew that was only sense, but still regretted the loss of her horse. For months it had been the four of them, Cadvan and Maerad, Darsor and Imi. It would be strange to have another mount.

Cadvan still wanted Maerad's presence in Innail to be known as little as possible, and he insisted that she leave the Bardhouse heavily hooded. Maerad didn't protest: although it was sunny outside, the air was still and cold.

Their first stop was to visit Indik, swordmaster and horse-master of Innail. On her last visit, Maerad had almost hated him. He had taught her the rudiments of swordskills with scant patience. Even as she had cursed him, she had given Indik her grudging respect; if he was harsh, it was not without reason. Later she had seen another, warmer side of him, and now thought of him fondly.

Indik's house was at the outer rim of the School, and for Maerad it was sheer pleasure to walk through the paved stone streets, greeting the buildings which now seemed so familiar to her, although in truth she had lived here only briefly. The gardens were wintry, the trees not yet coming into leaf, but Innail was still beautiful. She felt as if she were breathing the beauty in, as if she had been starving for it.

"It's strange," she mused to Cadvan. "In the north, I saw so many things that I will never forget. I saw the Hramask snow-lands under the winter sun, and the seas of the north with their bergs of ice, which are like the most outlandish castles you ever saw, and their islands of ice and fire. I saw the heavenly dancers in the sky. But this ..." She gestured at a house they were now passing, with wide, shallow stone steps leading up to a door carven with leaves. "... this is different..."

Cadvan glanced across at her. "There is a beauty that humans make that answers to our need," he said. "A need for home, maybe."

Home. Maerad rolled the word on her tongue. Yes, coming back to Innail was like coming home. "I don't have a home," she said. "Pellinor was my home, and that was lost to me a long time ago."

"These are still your people," said Cadvan. "Innail is not so far from Pellinor. And it is the place where you first came into your own, Maerad. It is not surprising that you should love it." He looked around him, his face alight. "One day you must come to Lirigon, my birth home," he said. "There the houses are built of dark stone and have clay red tiles. The marketplace of Lirigon is famous for its pottery. There is good clay near the Lir River."

Maerad did not answer. At first her heart lifted at the thought of visiting Lirigon with Cadvan, but its mention also raised a dark memory. On the road to Lirigon, as she and Cadvan had made their way northwards, a lifetime ago it seemed, Maerad had killed a Bard, Ilar of Desor, who was travelling with a Lirigon Bard, Namaridh. She and Cadvan had become bitterly estranged afterwards, and that had led to disaster.

"I do not think I can ever go to Lirigon," said Maerad at last. "There is a black crime on my soul."

Cadvan looked at her in surprise. They had not spoken of the murder since they had reunited, such a short time ago; it had been too painful to essay. "There is, Maerad," he said. "You will have to answer to it, if you have not already."

"How could I have answered already?" asked Maerad, with an edge of bitterness.

Cadvan reached for her gloved left hand, but she flinched away. "You have suffered much since then," he said. "And I think that suffering has made you wiser. It doesn't always do that, you know. Suffering can destroy the soul; it can make people mean where once they were generous, small where once they were great. It can turn people mad. Remember that half-mad woman we saw in Edinur?"

"Her name was Ikabel," she said softly, remembering the woman's broken face.

"That was done to her. And things at least as bad have been done to you, Maerad. But you have not broken. You entered your suffering, and it has made you better understand the suffering of others."

Maerad listened in silence, her face averted. "I cannot undo it," she said. "And I wish I could."

"No, you cannot undo it. When all this is over, when peace returns to Edil-Amarandh, we will address this question. Only then can you answer to Ilar's people, and hear justice. For the moment it must be put aside. But Maerad," and now Cadvan's voice was urgent, "remember this. It is only through understanding the darkness in yourself that you can understand the good, for the stars do not distinguish between good and bad as people do. There is much light in you. It shines more brightly than it ever did. And by the laws of the Balance, the light in you must be weighed in the scales, as much as your crimes."

They walked on for a while in silence, and Cadvan added: "I do not mean that there will be nothing to answer."

"I know that," said Maerad. Her voice was so low he could barely hear it. "I do not seek to escape what justice is owed me."

"If our labours bear fruit, it will be just," Cadvan answered. "If the Dark succeeds, there will be no justice anywhere."

Maerad nodded again. "I know that too," she said.

She was thinking of how she had felt when she had killed other beings – those of the Dark, the wer and the kulag, or the Hulls. She had always felt that the act had marked her. She could justify it: they were evil, she had to save her own life. And yet, all the same, it seemed to her that killing the murderous creatures of the Dark had led, subtly but inevitably, to her killing of Ilar. Whether she liked it or not, whether she thought her assailants were evil or not, she was dealing out death, and she couldn't still the voice inside her that said that it was wrong. She reflected, not for the first time, that it wasn't so easy to know whether or not your actions were right. "Sometimes," Cadvan had said to her once, "there is no choice before you, except between bad and worse."

III

A FAREWELL

THEY tracked down Indik in the saddlery, where he was overseeing some young Bards and apprentices who were polishing the saddles, bridles and other equipment. The room was filled with a quiet hum of industrious activity and a delicious smell of linseed oil and leather. Maerad sniffed appreciatively.

Indik glanced up when they entered and, despite himself, smiled broadly. He was a stern-looking, stocky man, the severity of his face exaggerated by a savage scar that drew the skin around his eyes into a squint.

"I'll be leaving you scoundrels for a while," he said to his students. "If I find that any of you have been lazy while I'm away, a price will be exacted. Don't think that I won't notice. I will. That includes you, Rundal," he said, turning his fierce gaze onto a young man whose undisciplined hair framed his face with a mass of curls.

Rundal, an imp-faced lad of about fifteen, looked up and nodded seriously. As Indik turned away, he winked slyly at his friend next to him. Maerad was quite certain that Indik saw this, but he gave no sign as he greeted them.

"So you're still alive," he said gruffly to Maerad, unable to entirely conceal his pleasure. "Amazing. I think that deserves a wine, don't you?"

Bards, Maerad reflected, as she and Cadvan followed Indik to a nearby tavern called, predictably enough, the Horse's Mane, thought every occasion deserved a drink. Even if there wasn't an occasion, they would invent one. So different from the thugs at Gilman's Cot, where she had been a slave; there they would gulp down the voka, an eye-stinging spirit distilled from turnips, until they vomited or fell senseless to the ground. Maerad had very seldom seen a drunken Bard, and had never seen Bards drinking themselves into a stupor. For them, drinking was all about pleasure: winemaking was considered one of the higher arts, and skilled winemakers were greatly revered.

Once they had their wine, and were seated by a fire at a low table looking out through a mullioned window on a day that was rapidly clouding over, Indik began to talk about the recent events in Annar. Unlike Silvia or Malgorn, he seemed enlivened; a cold light burned in his eyes as he spoke of the battles that had taken place.

"I've felt it coming," he said. "Like you, Cadvan, I knew something was happening these past years – a gathering. And now the storm breaks, no?"

"Only its outriders, I fear," Cadvan answered. "The storm itself is yet to hit."

"Yes, well. I heard about Turbansk." Indik was briefly gloomy, staring ahead, pulling at his lower lip. "That is bad, certainly. Very bad. And all this scheming from Enkir. That's bad too. If Norloch has gone to the Dark without a sword being raised, we are in desperate times indeed."

Maerad glanced swiftly at the shrewd old warrior. No one else, even in Innail, had spoken of Norloch as being in alliance with the Dark; it was thought that Enkir was acting on his own black counsel.

"Enkir is with the Dark," she said. "I have no doubt of it. Though many others do, obviously. I suppose no one wants to believe that of the First Bard of Annar." She tried to keep the scorn from her voice, but it was difficult; she felt a particular hatred for Enkir. It was Enkir who had set fire to Pellinor, who had betrayed and killed her parents, who had destroyed her childhood.

"Difficult to get people to believe you, huh," Indik snorted. "It's obvious enough to me. I never trusted that dried-up old fish. People like Enkir need power to cover up their weakness; they are afraid of who they will see if they are left without its trappings. Some puny unmuscled thing, I imagine, all covered in sores. Those people have worms for souls. Hulls in almost every respect…"

The contempt was thick in his voice, and he nearly spat. Cadvan smiled grimly. "How right you are, old friend," he said. "And how do you read things here?"

"The attacks on us are all from the mountains, mainly at the east end of Innail Fesse. Westwards so far is basically untouched. But they are directed with a chill intelligence, and we have suffered some bad losses. You heard, of course, about Oron… The only walled towns in Innail are Innail School and Tinagel; most people live in villages. But many villagers are now behind walls in Tinagel or here. Some stay and fight. One thing, those who say the valley dwellers are soft have it sadly wrong… Most attacks have been murderous raids on the villages, aside from the big assault on Tinagel itself. We fought them back that time. But there is a will, Cadvan, a will; something leads these wers."

"Not Hulls?" said Cadvan.

"No. Wers, hundreds of them. Foul, evil creatures. And men, too, fighting for spoils. Mountain dwellers. Rough warriors, decent weaponry, cunningly led … they kill any male, of any age, and the women and girls…" He screwed up his face. "You don't want to lose those battles."

"The Landrost, I suppose," said Maerad. The Landrost was a powerful Elidhu allied to the Dark, who had once held Cadvan captive.

"Innail is still far from the Landrost's home, on the other side of the mountains," Cadvan said musingly. "All the same, it seems possible to me. He is most certainly in the thrall of the Nameless One, and does his bidding here."

"I fear it may be so," said Indik, "though few people agree with me. There is a strange sorcery in some of these attacks that is not one we know of from the Dark. And weathercraft. Unless it is just chance that attacks only happen in thunderstorms." He pulled at his lip again, his scarred face dark with thought. "I guess you are not staying, Cadvan. We could do with one of your abilities here."

"Maerad and I have other tasks," said Cadvan. "Much as we would stay to help defend this place we love."

"Yes." Indik looked between the two. "I won't ask," he said. "I will find out, I expect, and I have enough to worry over. Still, I am sorry you can't fight here. If it is the Landrost we face – and that is our best guess – then we have a formidable foe. We won't get any help from Annar, that's for sure. But Innail has always stood on her own." He grinned, his scarred face becoming a savage mask, and Maerad thought what a terrifying warrior Indik would be. There was something in him that loved battle for its very peril, a kind of finely judged recklessness, an utter ruthlessness. *He* would have no qualms about killing Hulls...

"I've a favour to ask," said Cadvan. "We will have to leave Innail soon, and Maerad needs a horse and a sword. Do you have any that would suit?"

Indik looked sternly at Maerad. "It goes hard to lose a horse," he said. "Imi was a good mount."

"She didn't die," said Maerad, with a shade of indignation. "She's with the Pilanel in Murask, and we can't get her back right now."

Indik's eyebrows rose. "You have wandered far in your

travels," he said. "And the sword?"

"Arkan took Irigan when he captured me. I don't know what happened to it." Maerad thought of her sword regretfully; it had been one of her few possessions, and it was precious to her.

"Arkan? The Winterking?" Indik glanced over to Cadvan for confirmation, plainly flabbergasted, although he covered it quickly. "Well, then. To lose arms when you are captured is only to be expected."

"Don't be such a dry old stick, Indik," said Maerad teasingly. "I wouldn't just leave my sword in an inn, would I? But I do need a new one. I can't be a wolf *all* the time."

"Now you are talking in riddles," said Indik, rubbing his chin and directing a piercing look at Maerad. Suddenly she was conscious that she had been gesturing with her left hand, and that he must have noticed her missing fingers. He had said nothing: Indik was no stranger, after all, to wounds and scars. It was, Maerad realized, the first time she hadn't felt ashamed of it.

"I am chiefly wondering," said Indik, "what happened to that shy, charming Bard I met last spring. What did you do with her, Cadvan? Who is this bold young warrior?"

"I'm not sure. I ask myself the same question," said Cadvan, smiling.

"I'm the same person," Maerad said, lifting her chin. "Maerad of Pellinor, at your service."

"You're still too thin," said Indik. "But I somehow think that you don't drop your sword any more."

With Darsor's freely given advice thrown in, Maerad chose a new horse shortly afterwards. Indik had three of the same hardy cross-breed as Imi, two mares and a stallion. As far as Darsor was concerned, the fine-looking bay stallion was out of the question (although Maerad rather regretfully turned her eyes from him). There was also a black mare, and a strawberry roan with a broad blaze down her nose. Maerad examined both of them carefully, under Indik's deceptively casual gaze, and picked the roan. She knew she had chosen well by Indik's barely perceptible nod of approval.

"That's Keru," said Indik, patting the mare's neck. "She'll carry you far. A little flightier than Imi, but just as tough."

The mare reached her nose forward and sniffed Maerad's hand.

Will you carry me? asked Maerad in the Speech.

You smell good, said Keru. *And you're very small. You're a friend of Darsor's?*

Yes, said Maerad. *But we will be travelling hard and far and fast.*

Good. I'm bored here. I will bear you. The mare turned away to snatch some straw from a manger, and Maerad missed Imi all over again. She saw at once that Keru was a good, strong horse, and she had been polite, but the companionship Maerad had with Imi would be hard to replace.

Well, she thought. I suppose we can't be friends all at once.

Indik gave her a sword that he had forged himself. "It was supposed to be for a young woman in Tinagel," he said. "She will have to wait a few days longer; she has not your urgency. It is well made: I laid charms in every tempering. Make sure you are less careless with this one." He drew it from its light leather scabbard and handed the hilt to Maerad. She tested the balance, feeling it light and apt to her hand.

"Thank you, Indik. I'll take good care of it, I promise."

"What will you name it?" asked Cadvan.

Maerad examined the sword. It was beautiful, with a straight, short blade of blue steel and a silver hilt shaped like a leaf and cunningly enamelled with green. "*Eled*, I think," she said after a while. "Lily. It is a lily, like me."

"Eled is a good name. It was meant for you, I think, although I did not know that when I made it." Maerad looked up and met Indik's eyes, and saw there the well-guarded gentleness that burned like a quiet flame inside him. "May you bear it to good fortune."

Maerad felt the blessing in his words. Indik said things sometimes that resonated through her being; if he wasn't a Truthteller like Cadvan, he was very nearly one. She realized afresh how much she liked this ugly, harsh, honest man.

"I hope so," she said fervently. "For all our sakes."

After they left Indik, Cadvan went off on some business of his own and Maerad made her way to the centre of the School, bending her steps to the Library. She wanted to visit Dernhil's rooms. Dernhil of Gent was a Bard – a great poet, Cadvan had said – who had taught her how to read and write, opening up the world of books to her astonished pleasure and delight. She was still very slow at both – she had not had much time to practise in the past year – and the hunger to learn more ached inside her; but Dernhil's promise that he would teach her all the lore of Annar and the Seven Kingdoms would never now be kept. He had died last spring, when Hulls had secretly entered Innail in search of Maerad. The small illuminated book of poems Dernhil had given her was one of her most treasured possessions; she kept it in her pack, wrapped in oilskin.

She remembered the way through the maze of corridors without difficulty, nodding to the Bards she passed, and halted outside the familiar door, suddenly feeling a little foolish. What if someone was in there? She hadn't asked anyone's permission to come, and it wasn't as if it was Dernhil's room any longer. She knocked hesitantly and, when no one answered, slowly pushed open the door.

She had expected to find the room changed, filled perhaps with the belongings of another Bard. And it was different, but not for that reason. What had once been a cheerful room, full of clutter and work and warm light, was now empty and forlorn and cold. The air smelt musty and stale, as if it had not been opened for a long time. Dernhil's furniture – a huge wooden desk and two chairs covered in azure silk – was still there, but the books that had filled the shelves were gone, leaving behind a litter of dusty oddments. A chill winter sun shone through the casement, casting a silver light over the dusty desk and chairs. Clearly no one used the room now.

Maerad entered the chamber and shut the door behind her, filled with a sudden and overwhelming sense of bereavement. It was as if she hadn't really believed Dernhil was dead until this moment. Some secret part of her had still thought that really he was waiting here, at work in his room, that she would knock on the door and he would glance up to greet her with that quick, ironic smile and clear a space for her on the chair beside his.

He died in this room, Maerad thought. That's probably why no one took it over. She wandered around the room, looking at the shelves, and found a broken pen she remembered Dernhil using lying forgotten against the wall. She picked it up and closed her fist around it; she would keep it with Dernhil's book, and the beautiful pen he had given her for her own use, as a memento. Then she walked over to the desk and sat down. The desk that she remembered as scarcely visible under a clutter of books, writing materials, parchments and scrolls was completely bare, covered in a thin layer of dust. Into her mind, unbidden, came the chant Cadvan had sung for Dernhil, after they had heard the news of his death:

Where has he gone? His chamber is empty
And bright are the tears in the high halls of Oron
Where once he stepped lightly, singing deep secrets
Out of the heartvault and into the open...

I didn't know him long enough, Maerad thought, to feel this sad. But even as she thought this, she knew it to be nonsense, a denial of a deeper knowing. *I know he loved you*, Cadvan had told her, long ago it seemed now, in another life. *He was one of those who can see clearly into another's soul, and his feelings were true. Such things have little to do with brevity of meeting.* All too brief, all the same: when we parted, there was promise of so many things, of deep friendship, of learning; and now all that promise is frozen in the past, like those strange animals I saw deep in the glacier... Is that what I am really mourning? All the conversations we never had, the books you will never read to me, the lovers we will never be. If you kissed me now, would I hit you?

In her mind's eye, Maerad could see Dernhil as vividly as if he stood before her. He was tall and slender, his brown hair falling carelessly over his forehead, his expression intelligent, mobile, amused. He was, she realized, very handsome. She hadn't really noticed that when they had met. No, she thought, I would not hit him now.

What would you say to me if we met now? Would you say, like Indik, *where is the shy, charming girl I met last spring*? Would you still want to kiss me? I have changed so much. But I am still Maerad...

"I wanted to tell you—" she said, and jumped, because she had spoken aloud. But who would hear her? She dug her nails into her palms to stop herself from crying. It was important that she say at last what she wanted to say, even if there was no one there to hear it.

"I wanted to tell you that your poem saved me when I was captured by the Winterking and held in his palace," she said. "I read your poem, and it reminded me of everyone I love. Including you. It reminded me of why we are fighting so hard. It reminded me how much beauty there is …" – Maerad stared down at her hands lying on the desk, one whole, the other maimed, and bit her lip – "… how much beauty there is in the world, and why it matters. It reminded me that even if we die, it doesn't mean that everything we do is useless. That even though you are dead, you are still speaking to me. I hear your voice every time I read your poems."

She paused, taking in a long breath. "But it made me feel sadder than ever, Dernhil. Reading your poems is not the same as talking to you. My Cousin Dharin will never come back. I'll never see my mother or my father again, no matter how much I want to. Maybe all of us will die in this battle. And I know I'm just talking to empty space, I know you are not here. I think that perhaps, somewhere, in some other place where time is different, you might hear what I say and smile, and that comforts me a little. I know that's a stupid thought, but I think it all the same. Maybe it's not so stupid. I don't know… I just wish, with all my heart, that you were here and that I could talk to you and tell you these things."

Maerad fell silent and sat for a long time at the desk, with her head in her hands. Finally she stood up and went to the door, turning for a last look at Dernhil's empty room. "Farewell, my friend," she whispered, and closed the door behind her.

When she returned to her room, Maerad emptied her pack and laid out all her possessions on her bed. As a slave, she hadn't owned anything beyond the clothes she wore and her lyre, and she still felt a faint disbelief at her comparative riches, even if they could all be put into one bag. The objects laid out on her bed were like a tangible diary of her life.

Most precious of all was her lyre, lying snugly inside the leather case that Cadvan had given her. She put Dernhil's book next to it, and then her new sword, Eled. There were oddments like her kit for the horses, and a water bottle, and a flask of medhyl, the herbed drink that Bards used to ward off weariness when travelling. There were her spare clothes, now newly washed and folded. Some of her possessions were gifts that she wore: the white stone that hung from a slender chain around her neck, a present from Silvia; and the exquisite golden ring that the Elidhu Queen Ardina had given her, which she wore on her right hand; also from Ardina was a rustic reed flute; a small fish carved of ivory was a gift from the Wise Kindred, whom she had visited far in the North, seeking knowledge of the Treesong from their wise man, Inka-Reb; she put next to that the blackstone she had taken from a Hull in Thorold. The blackstone was a strange object made of albarac, a mineral valued among Bards because it could deflect or absorb magery. She stroked the stone's surface with her fingertip: it was more like the absence of something than an object, neither cold nor warm, rough nor smooth. It was attached to a silver chain, but she felt there was something uncanny about it, and she never wore it. She wondered if she would ever use it.

There were things that were missing, because she had given them away: a little wooden cat that she had given to Mirka, the old woman who had cared for her in the mountains when she had nearly died; and the silver brooch with the arum lilies, the sign of the School of Pellinor, which she had given to Nim, a young man who had been one of her Jussack captors, and who had been kind to her. That had been a princely gift: the brooch had been given to her by Oron herself. But, somehow, Maerad was sure that Oron would have understood: Innail was a School that set great, unspoken store on kindness.

She studied her possessions for a while, and then, one by one, put them back in her pack with the pen she had taken from Dernhil's chamber, wondering if she would ever have a room of her own in which to keep them. Innail was the first place, in almost a year of travelling, to which she had returned. Cadvan and she would be off any day now, and perhaps she would never see it again. She felt as if she had been travelling for ever. Perhaps, when all this was finished, if she survived it, she could begin to make a home…

She pushed that thought away. If she followed it, she would end up wallowing in self-pity. Tonight, she knew, Malgorn and Silvia had invited some other Bards from the First Circle for a meal, and she should bathe first. Maerad's habit was to have a bath whenever it was possible; sometimes in Innail she bathed twice a day, to make up for the months of scrappy washes in cold streams when she was travelling. Sighing, she stood and made her way to the bathroom.

That evening was a merry one in the Bardhouse. No one spoke of the troubles in Innail, putting them aside for the moment. Maerad noticed that the Bards, perhaps warned by Silvia that Maerad could no longer play her lyre, had not taken out their instruments after the meal as was their custom.

"I can play my lyre," she said firmly. "If you don't mind me glowing."

Indik glanced at her with something like approval, as she drew her lyre out of its case. She paused to gather her power, and as her magery began softly to illuminate the room, she looked down and saw her hand was whole, a hand of light. Silvia smiled with joyous surprise, and took down her own lyre from the wall, and the other Bards disappeared briefly to get their instruments. They began with an instrumental piece in a minor key, beautiful and melancholy, and then Cadvan and Maerad sang the duet of Andomian and Beruldh, which they had sung when they had first met. The other Bards listened in absorbed silence and burst into applause when they both finished.

The Bards made music together long into the night, and Maerad felt something in her fill up, as if she had been starving. Music, she thought, is like meat and drink for the soul, a necessity. For these few enchanted hours she felt entirely happy.

Music, Cadvan had once said to her, *is my home*.

Waking late the next day, Maerad felt stronger than she had in a long time. Her life might be hard and full of sadnesses, but she counted herself lucky; it had also granted her moments that she would not have missed for the world. She lounged lazily, feeling no hurry to rise; life would be tough again soon enough, so why not enjoy a comfortable bed while she could?

Eventually, after her ritual bath, she made her way downstairs to break her fast. She grabbed a pastry from the kitchen and ate in the corner, where she was out of the way. Normally, Silvia would have been in the kitchen at that time, but she was out again; she was kept busy looking after the flood of people who were seeking refuge in Innail from the attacks in the valley. Then, at a loose end, Maerad began to look for Cadvan. Although nothing had been said between them, she knew that they would be leaving soon: perhaps the next day. Against her desire to stay in Innail was an even stronger sense of urgency; somehow she knew that time was running short.

Although he had said little, Malgorn had clearly thought Maerad was mad when she announced that she was looking for Hem, who could be anywhere in Edil-Amarandh, if he was alive at all. And Maerad couldn't pretend that she didn't have her own doubts. On the other hand, she had journeyed across the frozen wastes of the north in her quest for the Treesong, with little more than hints to guide her; she felt more confident now of her own intuitions. Cadvan's trust in her Knowing was comforting.

It was raining, with a hint of sleet: winter was back with a vengeance. Maerad wrapped her cloak tightly around her and hurried head-down through the rain-lashed streets to the stables, where she guessed Cadvan was most likely to be. She guessed aright: he was sitting on a feedbin, deep in conversation with Darsor. He looked up as Maerad entered, and smiled.

"Darsor was just letting me know that he rather likes the idea of a warm stable on a day like this," he said. "Good weather, all the same, for those who wish to travel unnoticed."

"It was raining last time we left." Maerad sat down next to Cadvan, and let Darsor nuzzle her neck in greeting before he attended to a mash of oats Cadvan had made for him. The great black horse looked none the worse for his recent travels, his muscles rippling beneath his rough winter coat.

"Yes, I remember." Cadvan looked at Maerad sidelong. "But not much else is the same, I think. Not least you, Maerad. Being here reminds me of the waif you were then. You barely dared to open your mouth."

"It was terrifying. I thought they'd throw me out when they discovered I wasn't a proper Bard."

"You're not a proper Bard," Cadvan said, smiling. "You're something altogether strange."

"I suppose I am." Maerad picked up some straw and twirled it around her finger meditatively. "I can't help wishing I was a normal Bard, though. I can think of nothing better than staying here, learning the Three Arts properly, reading all the lore of Annar, just being ordinary..." She couldn't keep the raw longing out of her voice, and Cadvan was silent for a time.

"I wish all that for you, Maerad," he said at last. "You don't know how much. And I begin to think, too, that I am tired of my restless life. I wonder how many steps I've walked since my youth… I suppose I never felt that I had the right to stop anywhere for long."

Cadvan had never said anything like that before, and Maerad glanced at him, surprised. He was staring at the floor, his face reflective and a little sad. In the dim light of the stables he seemed younger, not much older than she was.

"You probably earned the right years ago," she said.

"It's never a question of what others think," Cadvan answered, with an edge of harshness in his voice. "The hard thing is always to forgive oneself."

"Then you're simply being selfish."

"Do you think so?" A smile quirked the edge of Cadvan's mouth. "A little self-indulgent, perhaps?"

"I think so. Definitely. If others forgive you, what right have you not to forgive yourself? It's just vanity."

Cadvan almost looked offended, but then he started to laugh. "Ah, Maerad," he said. "I think I will keep you as my conscience. I fear that you're painfully right."

"I've had quite a bit of time to get to know you," she said, smiling. "They're not wrong, those who accuse you of pride."

"Or arrogance. No, they're not wrong. Maybe only you know how hard I work to keep these things at bay."

"But you wouldn't be you without them, all the same."

"It's a question of the Balance. As always. I wish it were not the case that our faults are so often the other side of our virtues." He stood up and stretched. "Well, I don't know about you, but I'm hungry."

"I just broke my fast," said Maerad. "But I only had a pastry. I wouldn't mind eating again."

"We could go to that tavern. The food looks like good Innail fare."

Over their meal, they discussed their immediate plans.

Cadvan thought they should leave Innail the following day, heading south. "I think our best bet would be to make for Til Amon," he said. "If Hem and – I hope – Saliman have fled Turbansk, they would, I imagine, have gone there. And – I suppose – we'll just follow your nose."

"I hope it's working properly," Maerad said dryly. "Obviously Malgorn thinks we've taken leave of our senses."

"Maybe we have," said Cadvan, grinning. "Perhaps not. The Way of the Heart is not, after all, so mad; and it's something the Dark does not understand. I think we follow that way now. Although I do not know where it will lead us."

"No." Maerad turned her face away, and Cadvan, sensing her discomfort, began to talk of practical things: the food they would take, whether it would be safe to stay in inns in the valley, how dangerous the road might be.

Early the next morning, they farewelled their friends and trotted through the main gate of Innail. The rain had stopped, leaving in its wake a biting wind straight off the mountainside; Maerad had dressed in several layers of clothes to ward off the cold, and still felt the chill. Their leavetaking had been quick and sombre: Maerad had embraced her friends, feeling as if she were about to jump into an abyss. Suddenly all sense of urgency had vanished: she just wanted to stay where it was safe and warm, amid the beauty of Innail. But she knew better, and bit down the tears that threatened and turned her face determinedly to the road.

They set off at a leisurely pace. It was still dark, and the road glimmered faintly beneath them. Keru, Maerad's mare, was clearly wishing that she was back in a warm stable, although she said nothing; she carried Maerad as she had promised she would, but there was no willingness in her step. Maerad thought of Imi, and hoped that she was happy in Murask. No doubt she was safer than she would be with Maerad, but Maerad missed her all the same.

After a while the sky lightened to a faint grey, but the day brought no relief; the wind lifted and it began to rain. They quickened their pace: they planned to stay that night at an inn in Barcombe, a hard day's ride from Innail, and both were anxious to get there as swiftly as they could. The countryside was bare and wintry, and gave them little incentive to dawdle. Maerad's hands were freezing, even though she was wearing thick silk gloves, and her face began to turn numb. The further they rode, the colder it became: soon it became unbearable. Maerad hunched miserably on Keru in a futile attempt to retain the little fugitive warmth in her body.

Cadvan pulled Darsor up, and Keru drew to a halt beside him. "I like not this cold," he said. "The wind has an unnatural taste."

Her wits slowed by the cold, Maerad stared at him, missing his meaning.

"Weatherworking, I think," said Cadvan. He was scanning the sky anxiously. "And powerful weatherworking, too. It must be the Landrost. Maerad, I am thinking it is a bad time to be out in the open."

Maerad turned Keru around, looked up at the sky and swore viciously. They had been riding uphill, and the valley slanted down in front of her back towards Innail. The School itself was hidden in the murk, but Maerad could see black clouds building to the east of them in the distance beyond Innail. Even from this far it was clear that they were veined with strange lightnings. There was a faint tang in the air, like the smell of burnt metal, that left a sour taste in her mouth, and an oppression in her mind. She wondered why she hadn't noticed it before.

She and Cadvan had discussed the risk of being caught on the road during one of the Landrost's attacks. All previous attacks had been at night, and near Tinagel, and they had judged they ought to be reasonably safe if they left early and travelled fast. Fighting alone in the open against the Landrost's wers was the worst possible chance: they would have very little likelihood of survival.

"We can't stay here," she said. "Stormont is not so far – perhaps we could ride there…"

"I'm thinking that Stormont will be no shelter against an attack like this," Cadvan answered. "But that storm looks as if it is heading for Innail, Maerad. Indik said that he was expecting an attack on the School very soon. And the Landrost knows that if he can destroy Innail, the rest of the vale is his."

For a moment they stared at each other, the same thought in both their minds. Then they pushed the horses on so sharply that Keru stumbled, and began to ride for their lives back to Innail. The road was straight before them, and Darsor stretched flat into a full gallop. Keru began to fall behind.

Faster, Keru, Maerad cried to her mare.

I'm – trying, Keru said. *I cannot run as fast as Darsor—*

If we do not reach Innail very soon, we will die. Do you understand?

Keru didn't answer: she plunged forward, her ears flat against her skull. Now they were bolting down the road; Darsor was still ahead of them, but the gap between them was not growing. Perhaps Cadvan, seeing that Maerad had fallen behind, had slowed Darsor down. Maerad leaned forward in the saddle, the wind of their speed lashing her hair into her mouth, all thought of the cold forgotten. How long had they been riding since they left Innail? An hour? Two hours? For much of that time they had ridden slowly because of the dark; they couldn't have come too far. And how hardy was Keru? Maerad didn't know how far her mare could be pushed. She urged her on, checking the sky when she could. Visibility was poor, as the rain was getting heavier and turning to hail, and she could no longer see the clouds in the east. Perhaps they would be too late, perhaps they would find themselves outside the walls of Innail when the Landrost's forces attacked, caught between the hammer and the nail.

She concentrated on keeping Darsor and Cadvan in sight and staying on the road; the sleet drove into her eyes, but she strained to see ahead, knowing she had to guide Keru, who was running blind. Huge rolls of thunder boomed in the distance, and she could feel the mare panicking beneath her.

It's all right, my beauty, she said to the mare. *Just keep on. We're getting there...*

I hope, Maerad added silently to herself. I hope we're getting there. It felt as if it was taking too long. Her maimed left hand had been aching with the cold all morning, but now it was really hurting her. She began to worry that they had taken a wrong turning; but they had passed no forks in the road – there was no wrong turning here... There were evil voices in the wind, she was sure: screams and howls that came from throats. It was rising all the time, with powerful gusts that sometimes threatened to push them off the road, and the mingled sleet and hail and rain stung her face. She could feel Keru tiring beneath her.

At last Maerad saw a light burning through the veils of rain. She would have cried out with relief if she were not so breathless: Innail was in sight. Keru saw it too, and put on an extra burst of speed, catching up at last with Darsor. They were going so fast they almost slammed into the heavy oaken gates.

The gates were shut fast, and Maerad's Bard sense told her that they were held with powerful magery as well as iron bars; the wards almost made her head buzz. Of course they were shut: after her initial shock, Maerad realized that they would hardly be open if Innail were under imminent attack.

Cadvan stood up in his stirrups and thrust his arms high in the air, making a blinding light around him, and shouted in a great voice: *"Lirean! Lirean noch Dhillarearean!"*

Maerad thought there was little chance that anyone could hear him above the storm; and even if they did, would they open the gates? She began to shout with Cadvan, fighting the panic that assailed her at the thought that they might be trapped outside the walls.

She had almost given up hope when the gate suddenly swung inward. Behind it a cloaked figure was waving them in; whoever it was shouted too, but their words were torn away by the wind. Darsor and Keru didn't have to be told to go inside: as soon as the gap was wide enough, they pushed through. The gate slammed shut behind them, and half a dozen people heaved the heavy iron bars back into place.

It suddenly seemed very quiet.

Maerad swung off Keru, who stood with head down, her chest heaving, wet and trembling all over.

Well done, Keru, she whispered in the mare's ears, patting her neck. Then she turned to thank the person who had let them in, and saw it was Silvia.

"Thank the Light," said Silvia, clutching Maerad to her breast and then embracing Cadvan. "I told them it was you. I knew soon after you left that it had been a mistake…"

Maerad hugged her tightly, and then stood back, because she was as wet as if she had jumped into a pond. "I'd better put Keru in the stables," she said.

"And I must see to Darsor too," said Cadvan. "Silvia, we'll take care of the horses and change our clothes. And maybe then we can work out how we can be of best use to you."

"Malgorn is in the Watch House. Meet us there, as soon as you can. I have to hurry – there are too many things to do…" Silvia drew herself up and Maerad saw with a small shock that underneath her cloak she was wearing mail. She had never thought of Silvia as a warrior. "This is the attack that we all feared was coming. I can't pretend that we don't need all the help we can get. I'm grateful you're here, Cadvan."

Cadvan clasped Silvia's shoulder, and she nodded at both of them and left. They stood for a moment, listening to the howls of the wind.

"Well," Cadvan said, picking up Darsor's reins. "Once more into the storm, Darsor; but at least this time there's hay at the end of it." He turned to Maerad. "Better here than outside," he said. "But still, I have a feeling it's going to be a long day."

IV

WEATHERLORE

THEY rode the short distance to the stables at a gallop, fighting the wind all the way, and one of Indik's apprentices, looking pale, took the horses in hand. There they threw on some dry clothes from their packs in one of the empty stalls: there wasn't time to run to the Bardhouse. That morning when she had dressed, Maerad had only thought of warmth: it had been foolish, she reflected, not to put on her mail coat. Now she slipped it over her head with a shiver. While she rummaged in her pack, her hand clasped the blackstone, sliding across its strange surface. She didn't like touching it, and dropped it at once. Then she picked it up, more slowly, and put it around her neck.

Maerad peered out of the stable door into the chaos beyond: even in the short time they had spent in the stables, the storm had worsened. It was now almost as dark as night, although it couldn't have been much past mid-morning, and the air was bitterly cold. Torn branches and other objects were skidding down the narrow roads between the buildings. It looked dangerous simply to step outside.

"Shield yourself, Maerad," said Cadvan in her ear. "We're going to have to make a run for it, and you don't want to be knocked over by a flying tree."

She paused for a moment, shielding herself with magery, and then she and Cadvan left the warm refuge of the stables and began to run to the Watch House. The shield protected Maerad from the storm, and the light of the magery made it a little easier to see, although it was disconcerting when leaves and other debris blew straight at her face and then slid past. Rain, hail and sleet were driven so violently by the wind that they spurted horizontally from the eaves of the buildings. Maerad heard a crash behind her; a tree, probably, falling onto a house or a wall. She didn't look back. Even with her shielding, the storm was terrifying. Such a storm could only be summoned by the Landrost. This, Maerad thought, was why Bards distrusted the Elidhu: this blind, amoral power, turned to utter destructiveness.

They were almost at the Watch House, a small stone tower that rose over the gates, when a terrible shriek sounded almost in Maerad's ear and something hit her shield from behind. Even protected as she was, she was almost knocked sprawling, and she called to Cadvan as she leapt sideways, backing up against a wall and drawing her sword. She couldn't see what had hit her, but she had felt a deathly cold push past her like a wave. It was of a different quality from the freezing air.

Up, said Cadvan into her mind. *Did you not see the wings?*

I didn't see anything, Maerad said. *And my hearing doesn't work in this noise.*

Wers, I think, said Cadvan. *And flying... they must have come over the wards.* He was squinting into the sky. *With this magelight, we're clear targets. I can't see anything up there, but that thing came down out of nowhere. I'd barely sensed it when it was gone...*

Maerad was surprised to find that she wasn't afraid. *The Watch House isn't far,* she said.

Cadvan nodded, and they made a final dash, zigzagging down the street like rabbits dodging an eagle. Two guards stood by the door, sheltered very minimally by a porch, and let them in without comment.

"There are winged wers out," Cadvan shouted over the wind as they entered the door. "Beware."

One of the guards nodded to indicate he had heard, but he didn't look alarmed. He was probably too cold, Maerad thought; the skin on his face looked blue.

The door swung shut, and the sound of the storm was suddenly muted. Maerad sighed unconsciously with relief: the screaming of the wind was almost as unbearable as the cold. They stood in a small, bare room of undressed stone lit by a single lamp, but it seemed almost homely after the chaos outside.

"I expect Malgorn will be at the top," said Cadvan, gesturing towards a flight of stairs. Maerad nodded, and they wound their way to the top room. Like everything else in the Watch House, the room was without decoration, save for the horse emblem of Innail carved in relief on the wall above the wide hearth, where a fire burned. The storm rattled the shutters of the windows, and Maerad suddenly felt claustrophobic. What was going on outside? In the middle of the room was a broad wooden table surrounded by chairs, and the Bards of Innail's First Circle were gathered around it, deep in discussion.

Malgorn turned as Cadvan and Maerad came up the last steps and waved them over. "Wise of you to come back," he said.

"The weather took a turn for the worse," said Cadvan. "And I have some bad news. A winged wer swooped down on Maerad as we came over here."

"A wer?" Silvia looked up, her face pale. "Malgorn, I told you the wards were not enough…"

"The warding spells worked well enough in Tinagel," said Malgorn sharply. Their conversation had the air of an old argument. "And it's all we can do. We're stretched thinly enough as it is."

"Aye, we are." Indik looked grim. "This is a different attack from Tinagel, Malgorn, the weatherworking has an ill feel about it. This is no mere storm, though the Light knows that was bad enough at Tinagel. There's the smell of sorcery in the air. And I sense something approaching that I haven't felt before. I like it not."

Maerad blinked. Indik was right: there was a presence, a sense of menace she had only noted subliminally, that grew in intensity with every moment. It was unsettlingly familiar...

"I recognize that presence," said Cadvan. "I remember it all too well. It is the Landrost."

A sudden appalled silence fell over the table. Of all the Bards, only Indik looked unmoved.

"I thought the Elementals could not leave their place," said Kelia, a short Bard who sat to the left of Malgorn, her dark brows drawn into a fierce frown. "I thought that the Landrost was bound to his mountain..."

"They don't like to leave," said Maerad. The Bards turned to her, listening gravely. "Arkan – the Winterking – told me that it is to them like losing their being. But that doesn't mean that they can't."

"Would he be weaker for being away from his mountain?" asked Indik dubiously, pulling at his lower lip.

"I don't know." Maerad looked helplessly around the table. The six most powerful Bards in Innail sat before her. In battle, each of them was worth a rank of soldiers; and yet she felt her heart quailing within her. "But – there's a taste like sorcery in the air. The Elidhu are not sorcerers."

Indik flashed her a sharp glance.

"You think that there's some Hullish business here too?" he asked. Maerad shrugged. "There have been no Hulls in any other attacks. It's the one thing I've been grateful for. Well..."

He straightened himself, and looked around the table.

"Clearly, the wards have been breached by wers," he said. "I think they should be maintained, all the same. I sent out scouts early this morning, as soon as I smelt the weather, and they tell me there is an army of mountain men marching this way; they will be here soon. And there will be wers on the ground, to be sure." Suddenly his eyes went blank, as if he were listening to something no one else could hear. The other Bards watched him in silence, waiting courteously; Indik was mindtouching, in silent conversation with a Bard on the walls. At last he looked up. "Kelavar tells me that outriding forces have been sighted outside the east wall. They can't tell how many, visibility is very poor... but the flying wers are playing havoc in the town. Not much damage, but a lot of panic. Again, they don't know how many. He thinks five wers have been killed."

Malgorn frowned and stood up, and walked over to the fireplace. Maerad watched him anxiously. She liked Malgorn, and recognized his strengths; but she suspected that he was not a Bard of war. She looked inquiringly at Cadvan.

"The weakest place, as ever, is the gate," said Cadvan. "If the Landrost himself marches with his forces, he will lodge his fiercest attack here. Still, we must give thought to the rest of the wall..."

"We lack an army," said Malgorn. "Farmers who use swords as if they're cutting hay are no match, no matter how brave ... and yes, we have great Bards here. But too few..." He said this almost in a whisper.

Indik's face darkened. "Malgorn, we have no time now for lamentation or regret," he said. "The Light knows that we may have plenty of time later... Yes, we have not enough soldiers, not enough mages. It seems to me that the Landrost aims to crush us utterly. The Dark marches with him. I admit, things do not look hopeful for us. So let us bend our thought to how best to use the strengths we have."

He glowered around the table, and the other Bards nodded. Malgorn flushed, and looked down at his hands and Silvia glanced at him, her face unreadable. She was very pale, but her jaw was set and determined. There was a steel in Silvia, thought Maerad, that Malgorn lacked, and she wondered why Silvia had not been made First Bard. For the first time since she had entered the Watch House, Maerad felt a sudden focus of energy, a surge of purpose. As Indik began to outline how he saw the battle before them, she felt, despite the grim picture, a small flicker of hope.

Indik had a realistic notion of what Innail was up against. He had set captains at intervals around the walls of Innail; they communicated with him through mindspeech. Each was in charge of varying numbers of Bards and soldiers, and bands of volunteers drawn from the valley population. There were too few of them, as Malgorn had said, and too few skilled or hardened warriors. They were armed with swords and bows – although in the chaos of the storm, arrows were next to useless – and vats of tar and boiling oil and stones to throw on the heads of the attackers. Indik had a select band of highly trained warriors, both horsed and on foot, whom he kept by the gates.

He had encountered the mountain men before, and he knew them as hard fighters, ruthless, cunning and unafraid. He was more worried than he liked to admit about the probability that the Landrost was exploiting both Elemental powers and Dark sorcery. He could calculate the odds of battle as well as anyone, and he had measured the strength of wers in other battles in the valley; he figured that even if the wers had breached the wards that he and Malgorn had set in the walls, Innail still had a fighting chance. The presence of the Landrost was an imponderable; until they met him in battle, they wouldn't know his strength. Indik was one of those who believed the Landrost was the same figure as Karak, who in the Great Silence had laid waste to the lost realm of Indurain. If he was correct, they were up against one of the most powerful of the Nameless One's allies.

When he thought about it, Innail didn't stand a chance. But Indik was stubborn; the worse the odds, the harder he would fight. While he still breathed, Innail falling to the Landrost was something he was not prepared to contemplate.

Like Cadvan, Indik reckoned that the major force would be brought against the gates, but he thought their strength of soldiery should be deployed along the walls. "There we will most likely face siege ladders," he said. "And if the town is not to be razed behind our backs, we will need to fight them off. The wards will help, but I am not sure whether they will be enough, especially if the wers can simply fly over them... I am very disturbed that they are already breached. I don't understand why they haven't flown a whole wer army over the walls already."

"Perhaps only the powerful wers can break the wards?" suggested Maerad. She was thinking of the first battle she had ever faced, against wers in the wilds of the Indurain: Cadvan had made a barrier then to protect them, and the wers had changed their wolf shapes in order to fly over it. "Or are they waiting?"

"The former, I think," said Malgorn. "We are not stupid: we know that wers shapeshift, and can become winged. These wards were set when Tinagel was attacked, and they do not work like walls. Not even a hostile bird should be able to pass them."

Indik nodded. "I think we should concentrate our strength of magery at the gate. If the Landrost breaks the gate, the wards will fail also. Maerad, do you know how to fight an Elidhu?"

"No," said Maerad.

"That's not quite true," Cadvan said impatiently. "You held back the Landrost even before you were in your full powers."

"I've never fought an Elidhu," said Maerad. "I don't know

how." Indik's question made her feel sick with panic; she saw that she was his main hope. Suddenly a major part of the responsibility for defending Innail was on her shoulders, and she didn't know if she would be any help at all. She met Indik's gaze; he was studying her, his face inscrutable, weighing the odds. With a slight shock, she realized that on his face was the same expression as when he tried a new sword: he was calculating the merit of a weapon, testing its temper and edge.

"Maerad, you know much more about the Elementals than any of us; none of us have even seen one," said Indik. "I don't expect you to strike the Landrost down single-handedly, but I will be relying on your sense of him. Especially any sense you have of weakness. And you too, Cadvan: you were his prisoner for a time. In the coming hours, the smallest detail might swing things in our favour."

"The first thing is the storm," said Malgorn, frowning. "I've had all the Bards I can spare weatherworking since the clouds were first seen, to no avail. The winds will not hear us. Cadvan, I know you can weatherwork; perhaps you could lend your powers there? It would free me up."

"Of course," said Cadvan. "It may be an idea for Maerad to help it here too. Maerad?"

Maerad had never done weatherworking in her life, and pointed out that if the Bards of Innail couldn't turn the winds, she had little hope of being any use at all. Despite this, Malgorn detailed both of them to the task.

There was a briskness among the First Circle now; they knew that there was very little time, and that the Landrost's army was almost at the gates. They departed to various destinations around Innail, embracing sombrely as they took their leave. Silvia kissed Maerad lightly on the forehead, and to Maerad's surprise, smiled warmly. "While there's breath, there's hope," she said. "I'm still breathing!" She was in charge of a section of the walls to the east of Innail, and Maerad watched her go, sadly wondering if she would ever see her again.

Maerad and Cadvan left with Indik and Malgorn: weather-work had to be performed in the open, and the Bards were gathered on the walls above the gate, near where Indik and Malgorn had their command.

As she stood up, Maerad glanced at Cadvan, taking a deep breath. She had never been in a real battle before, and her insides felt hollow. Cadvan's expression was stern, but his face softened as he perceived Maerad's anxiety. "Silvia's right," he said. "We have a chance, Maerad, as long as we stand fast."

"We don't have any choice, do we?" said Maerad, forcing a smile.

"There's always a choice," Cadvan answered. "As I have told you many times before. None of us will yield our souls, should the end be even as bitter as we fear. Now, for the sake of the Light, let us go and defend what we love!"

It was hard walking out into the storm again. A walkway led from the top floor of the Watch House to the outer keep above the gate, and it was a wrestle even to open the heavy door and keep it from immediately slamming shut. Without her magery shielding her, Maerad would likely have been blown straight off the bridge. The shrieking of the wind was so loud it hurt her ears. Although her shield protected her against the wind and the rain, it did not keep out the bitter cold, and Maerad gasped with the first shock of it; it went into her bones like the deep cold of the northlands.

But that doesn't make any sense, she thought. If it were that cold, everything would be ice...

When they reached the keep, a fork of lightning stabbed down so close to them Maerad could smell it, a sharp smell like the sea, followed by a massive crack of thunder that made her involuntarily duck. In its brief illumination, she saw the battlements were crowded with people. A few pitch torches lit the walls, but otherwise there was very little light; a silver glow a short distance away showed where the Bards were weatherworking.

Maerad realized at once that this was no easy task. For one thing, it wasn't possible to work weather from within a shield, and the eight Bards assigned to the task were huddled against the outer wall, trying to stay out of the worst of the tempest. The sheer cacophony of the storm was a constant assault, making it impossible to talk.

Maerad, said Cadvan into her mind. *You remember how to meld your powers? I know you've never done it with so many Bards before, but really there is little difference.*

Maerad nodded. She was afraid that she might fail – the last time she had tried to meld with Cadvan, when they were attacked in the mountains, it hadn't worked at all – but she said nothing. It had to work.

She didn't know the Bards they were to work with; there were faces she vaguely remembered, but she had never been long enough in Innail to meet everybody. They looked up, their faces grey with strain, as Cadvan and Maerad entered their circle and let down their shields.

There was no time for introductions, though a couple of the Bards cried out gladly when they recognized Cadvan. To her relief, when Maerad opened her mind she could feel the joined powers of the other Bards. Tentatively she put out her own to meld with them. It was a little like a vine putting out tendrils to tangle with another plant, she thought, a process at once delicate and chaotic and individual to itself. As soon as she had joined with the other Bards, the storm began to bother her less; despite the extremity of the situation, she found herself fascinated by touching so many minds at once, intrigued by the forces they were weaving together. It really was like trying to puzzle out a tapestry of deep, abstract intricacies, only its pattern was constantly changing. Or, more accurately, it was constantly being torn up and then being rewoven.

The magery was coloured by the Bards' emotions; she immediately felt both their fear and determination. As she sensed her way into its pattern, she saw it had a formal shape. She couldn't read it; she didn't have the training, she supposed, and it was as if she were looking into a book of poems in a language she didn't understand. She could perceive the grammar, the syntax, the recurring words, the shapes of the verses, but its meaning was beyond her.

At this point, Maerad felt like giving up: she was obviously going to be useless, as she didn't have the experience. But she was still deeply intrigued, and kept on feeling her way in. Even as she did, she felt with a shock the magery being torn apart by the forces of the storm; its tendrils broke and whipped apart, although the Bards' melding stayed firm. Maerad found herself admiring their strength: she felt as if she had been punched, and gasped aloud.

Patiently, the Bards began again, and this time Maerad thought she could see what they were trying to do. She was staggered at the size of the spell. They were attempting to weave a charm around the borders of Innail, which would keep the air calm within its walls, and leave the storm raging without. But, as Malgorn had said, the wind would not listen, and raged against the magery.

They're making it worse, she thought. The storm would not be harnessed in this way. It was driven by the dire rage of the Landrost, but it was not the Landrost himself. The fell voices on the air, which Maerad had thought were wers, were Elemental creatures, not creatures of the Dark.

Speak to them, Maerad said suddenly. *We must speak to them.*

One of the Bards, whom Maerad thought was the leading mage among them, turned sharply towards her. He was soaked to the skin, his hair plastered over his forehead, and his eyes were set in deep hollows; he looked exhausted and angry.

In case you haven't noticed, he said, ice in his voice, *we have been trying to do just that for some time.*

Just as he spoke, the Bards rocked back as their magery tore apart with a new violence and a fork of lightning hit the stone parapet near them, splintering the rock. Maerad had a nightmare glimpse of a man falling, his mouth open in a scream she couldn't hear, his hair on fire. One of the Bards gave Maerad a look of such rage that she almost withdrew from the melding in fear and shame, as if it were her fault. But then she felt Cadvan's voice, calm amid the growing panic of the Bards.

What do you mean, Maerad?

I mean – you're not speaking to it in the right way ... it's like – it's like a baby, or something – but very angry and strong – what you're doing isn't, well, crude enough...

It was hard to explain, even in mindspeech, which didn't use language as it was normally used, relying as much on a current of empathy between minds as much as words to communicate. So Maerad thought it might be easier just to do it.

Something like this, she said. *I don't know if this will work...*

She paused briefly to focus, and then began to croon a string of nonsense words. The other Bards kept their melding strong, preparing to attempt their own magery again in a moment, and she could feel their scepticism and even a thread of savage mockery. Maerad first used the Speech, trying to feel her way into some rhythm that she felt she could almost hear, and as she became more sure, slipped imperceptibly into the language of the Elidhu. Now she felt incomprehension around her, rising to anger, and tried to ignore it; she was fumbling, trying to sense something by feel, something strange, and she needed to concentrate. For a moment she felt she nearly had the key, but it slipped by, and almost at the same time she heard the same Bard who had turned on her in rage seek to stop her.

Don't, said Cadvan. His voice was gentle, but it held something implacable. The Bard halted. *Listen instead*, said Cadvan. *Listen well...*

Maerad kept mumbling, not knowing what she was saying, concentrating so hard that she lost almost all sense of the others, and of the storm itself. And then she caught a feeling that was like a melody, something recognizable, and then another. She matched them together, repeating them with variations as she went, and found something else yielding. Gradually a pattern of enormous complexity opened up before her, and she could see the relationships between its different parts, its infinite variations and repetitions. Then – *Ah!* – she saw the Landrost within it, like a black spiral, churning and churning the pattern.

Just as she perceived this, she felt the Landrost jolt into awareness of her probing. He struck back blindly, a black bolt of energy that sent her reeling. But she had the pattern now. She looked around, blinking, and found she was still held in the meld of the Bards, who were now paying close attention.

I found it, she told them. *Now, I will need you to follow me... if you can. I'm not sure I'm strong enough by myself, though I'll try. I don't know how to shape the charm around Innail. I will need you to do that. And the Landrost knows I'm there, so be careful.*

She felt a shock reverberate through the Bards at the mention of the Landrost, and realized that they hadn't known what they were dealing with. No wonder their magery had been useless. But she didn't have time to explain. She re-entered the patterning, cautious now, but more confident, avoiding the maelstrom at its centre. It was a question of finding a shape and then, patiently, reshaping it, slowing and stilling the outer edges. Almost immediately she felt a difference; but it was so tiring.

The Landrost felt her there and was seeking her. The black spiral grew twisting arms that snaked out to catch her, and she felt the chill malevolent presence she remembered from so long ago, like a dank breath on her skin, and she shuddered with disgust.

She bit her lip, willing herself on. For all his strength, the Landrost was nothing like as powerful as the Winterking. She realized she was not afraid of him breaking her. But the Landrost had the endurance of rock, and she was only a woman; she already felt the weariness in her mind, like the ache that steadily grows in muscles that are overtaxed.

And then there was someone else there, with her. Cadvan. Tears of relief started into her eyes; suddenly the burden was not quite so heavy. Soon, other minds joined hers, keeping up the repetitions and freeing Maerad to find new variations, new shapes. The whole thing was so immensely complex, so very big... Shortly afterwards, she became aware of the Bardic charm being woven into the new pattern she was making.

She could feel the blind anger of the Landrost boiling around her. The more she undid his making, the more savage his responses became. But although he could feel what was happening, he couldn't trace her; Maerad was slipping like a tiny fish in and out of the currents of his wrath, untouched by them. It was like trying to set a trap; he did not know what they were trying to do, and she wanted him to remain ignorant until the last piece was in place and the whole structure could snap shut.

She had lost all sense of time, and even of urgency, and was utterly absorbed in the delicacy and intricacy of what she was doing. Bit by bit, with infinite care and patience, she and the Bards worked together. They could not afford one mistake. They would probably only get one chance.

At last she felt a pressure of assent from Cadvan: the charm was prepared, and the Bards awaited her signal. She poised herself like a fisherman standing with a spear above a river, waiting for a fish to glint beneath the surface: things shifted all the time, wavering and changing, and it had to be just right...

Now! she said, and she heard the words of command explode in her skull, and a blaze of white fire seemed to pour up into the clouds and boil against them, although Maerad didn't know if she really saw it, or if it was something that only happened in the strange world inside her head. The charm, meticulously shaped to the walls of Innail, snapped into place.

And suddenly, it was quiet.

Maerad was so exhausted that she would have pitched forward onto her face, had Cadvan not put his arm around her shoulders. She realized that she was cold to her very marrow, and that she was shaking all over.

"Well done," Cadvan whispered into her ear. "Oh, that was well done. Maerad, ever you repay my faith in you..." His words were echoed by cheering from the soldiers on the walls.

The eight other Bards looked almost as weary as Maerad. The man who had been angry with her, a tall, heavy-set, fair-haired Bard, smiled awkwardly and offered his hand.

"My gratitude, whoever you are," he said. "Am I right in guessing that you are Maerad of Pellinor?" Maerad nodded. "I am Isam of Innail. I had heard rumours, of course, but I had no idea..." He shook his head. "The Landrost himself attacks us, eh? Well, at least we've put a spoke in his wheel."

"One spoke in one wheel," said Cadvan. "Sadly, he has many more... Maerad, can you make any guess how far he is from our walls?"

Maerad pondered. She could sense the baffled anger of the Landrost, but it was difficult to locate it. "Not really," she said at last. "He is not quite here. But he is very close."

The relief of no longer being battered by the wind was

indescribable, and that numbing, bitter cold was also gone. Maerad looked up at the sky, blinking at the pale winter daylight that now poured through the gap in the clouds. What the Bards had done was effectively to place Innail in the eye of the storm. Within the walls, there was an eerie stillness; a strange pressure of the air made Maerad's ears pop. Outside, the tempest still raged.

"I expect the Landrost will still the storm, once he understands it disadvantages him," said Cadvan.

"If he can," said Maerad. "He may not be able to command it any more."

Cadvan glanced at her in surprise. "Do you think so?" Maerad shrugged. "Well, it would help us beyond measure if it were so. In any case"– he looked around at the weary Bards – "perhaps we should see Malgorn and Indik, and find out how we can best be of use."

Isam sighed heavily. "Right now, the thought of doing anything other than sleeping for uncounted hours is almost unendurable," he said. "And I know this is only the beginning." He stretched his arms wearily. "But you're right."

They wound past lines of Bards and fighters who were busily drying themselves and their equipment and looking about them with wonder. Malgorn was in the Watch House above the gate. He was openly delighted at the success of the charm, and when Isam told him of Maerad's part in it, embraced her with a new warmth. Then he held her back from him, studying her face.

"Maerad, you are the colour of snow," he said. "Are you all right?"

Maerad nodded. "I'm – tired. That's all."

Malgorn looked dubious. "I've seen people that colour when they are dead," he said. "You have done too much. Perhaps you ought to rest."

Maerad looked up and met his eyes. "So should you. So should all the other Bards who helped with the weather working. But Indik was right: I could help with the Landrost. It worked with the storm. Of course I'm staying here."

"Perhaps some medhyl wouldn't go astray," said Isam, producing a small stoppered bottle from a bag. "It is made to stay exhaustion. Especially of the kind that comes from magery."

Maerad sipped it gratefully, and it took the edge off her weariness at once. She still could have slept for hours, but she no longer felt dizzy.

Malgorn watched her steadily until some colour came back into her face. "That's better," he said. "Maerad, if you are to be our major weapon against the Landrost – an idea I like not at all – I would prefer if you didn't kill yourself. But I thank you. We have a chance now, I think. It does mean that we can't see the enemy, and that is a problem for us. They are cloaked by the storm. But on the other hand, those without sorcery shielding them will scarce be able to draw a sword or a bow with that wind howling about their ears. They can barely see a handbreadth in front of them."

"Maerad thinks the Landrost is close," said Cadvan. "If he plans to assault the gate, it won't be long now."

Malgorn set his jaw and stared at the outer walls, as if his sight could pierce the darkness beyond them. "Let him come," he said. "He shall not take our home as easily as he thinks."

Isam and the other Bards were sent to various points around the walls of Innail, but Malgorn asked Maerad and Cadvan to stay with him. There was no sign of Indik, but Malgorn was kept busy with a constant stream of people entering and leaving the keep. For the moment, Maerad felt no interest in what was happening out in the streets: she was too cold. She huddled by a brazier in a corner, trying to dry off. She had no idea how long she had been out in the rain, but it had been long enough to soak her through for the second time that day. She wondered what time it was: her departure that morning from Innail seemed as if it had been last week. Steam rose up from her cloak, and her mail grew uncomfortably hot, but she huddled close, feeling her body thaw. Once she stopped shivering, she realized she was hungry.

"Is it time to eat yet?" she asked Cadvan.

A young Bard nearby laughed. "We balance on the edge of doom, and Maerad of Pellinor demands the noon meal!" he said. "Mistress Maerad, you must be more used to peril than some of us." He bowed flamboyantly, and Maerad found herself smiling. "I confess, I have no appetite at all."

"Maerad is a seasoned warrior indeed, Camphis," said Cadvan. "And like all old soldiers, thinks chiefly about a comfortable bed and a good meal. It is not long after noon, Maerad. I'm sure there'll be food up here somewhere. This is Innail, after all…"

Camphis took some smoked fish, cheese, bread and fruit from a cupboard, and spread them on a table with a flask of wine. "Will this do?" he asked. "I assume you have your own knife."

"I lost mine," said Maerad, feeling a little foolish.

"You can borrow mine, then." Camphis handed over a wooden-handled clasp knife, and Maerad smiled her thanks, sat down and set to. She was ravenous: the morning's ride, the scramble back to Innail and the charm casting had worked up a keen appetite. Cadvan joined her, and Camphis picked at some dried plums to keep them company, chatting idly. Maerad could see that, underneath his lightness, he was very frightened, and admired how he hid it. It seemed that he had but lately become a major Bard. He was one of Silvia's students.

"My true interest is herblore, not swordcraft," he said, regarding his armour with distaste. "Although of course I know how to use weapons; Indik bullies us all into some kind of competence. I'd die for Innail. I only hope I don't have to." He smiled a little crookedly, and Cadvan patted his shoulder.

"We all hope that," he said. "Never fear, we have Maerad on our side. One never knows what she might do. She could turn all the enemies into rabbits."

Camphis looked his astonishment, and began to laugh again.

"She did it once to a Hull, you know," said Cadvan, enjoying himself as Maerad blushed next to him. "She even sang a lullaby to a stormdog."

"These are strange tales," Camphis said. "I hope one day you will have the time to tell me them in full."

"The strangest thing about them is that they are true," said Cadvan. He winked at Maerad. "She is perilous company, to be sure, but you can't say she's dull."

"Is it true that you take the form of a white wolf?" Camphis asked, fascinated.

Maerad looked over at Cadvan before she nodded. Clearly there was no point in hiding her presence in Innail now.

"And other forms as well?"

"I don't know. I haven't tried."

Their conversation was interrupted by the sound of wild yelling. It sounded uncomfortably close and the Bards started up, feeling for their swords. Almost immediately, Indik strode into the room.

"It has begun," he said. "The outriders are at our gates. And already we have beaten back two attacks on the eastern walls."

Maerad saw Camphis turn white, although his mouth was set and hard. He was much more frightened, she realized, than she was. And the Light knows, she thought, that I am afraid enough...

"Maerad," said Indik. "Can you tell if the Landrost is close to us, or not? So far we face mountain men and some wers, but it is hard to tell precisely what assails us."

"I do not think he is at the gate," said Maerad, unwillingly dragging herself back to consciousness of the shadow that oppressed her mind. "He seems a little distant to me. Though I could be wrong…"

Cadvan glanced at Indik, his face serious. "What will you have of us?" he asked.

"At present, I want Maerad to stay in mindtouch with me." Indik looked across at her. "If you could tell me the moment you feel any change, any – tensing – as if he prepares to leap – you know the kind of thing. Cadvan, Camphis, I could do with some help with any wers. Malgorn, are there any other Bards to spare?"

"No," said Malgorn. He paused and listened intently for a few moments. "Silvia is asking for more hands as well. I've placed all the Bards as evenly as possible around the walls. We are spread thin as it is. There is no sign of wers within Innail. Either they fled when the charm was set or they have been killed."

"We'll have to make do with what we have." Indik's face was expressionless. "I wish I could clearly see what is out there. But all reports seem to indicate that a great force is gathered in that darkness. And Innail is not a fortress, after all. I am glad of the wards; magery will have to make up for what we lack in stone."

"Do you need me there?" asked Malgorn.

"I'd rather you stayed out of the fighting," said Indik. "It is hard to keep mindtouch with many people in the midst of battle, and we need one Bard at least in constant contact with everyone – I will send if we need you." He nodded at the other Bards, and marched out.

Maerad glanced quickly over at Cadvan. "I'd like to come with you," she said.

"Why not?" said Cadvan. "You can keep an eye on the Landrost just as well on the outer wall as here."

Maerad hesitated, and then, on impulse, drew the black-stone over her head and held it out to Cadvan. He looked at her inquiringly.

"I don't think I'll use it," she said. "I don't like it. I know it's not from the Dark, but there's – there's something about it – and it might be useful to you."

Cadvan reached out and took it, and held it in his hand, weighing it.

"They are strange to use, I know," he said. "It's as if they numb the magery inside your skin. But it might be handy, all the same. Are you sure?"

She nodded, and Cadvan stroked the stone's strange surface, which seemed to absorb all light as if it were a hole instead of a solid stone, and put it around his neck.

They left the keep and climbed a flight of steps to a broad area behind the battlemented wall. Here they were directly above the gate, and it was bustling with activity: archers were posted thickly around the battlements and there were knots of grim-faced soldiers, ready to repel any attackers who raised ladders. They had the same contained, disciplined air that Indik possessed, and although there was a tension among them, a palpable sense that the attack would happen at any moment, they were relaxed: some were playing dice, others were joking with the young boys and girls who stood ready to tip cauldrons of boiling pitch or to throw stones onto the heads of any who threatened the gate itself.

Maerad was shocked to see children so young up on the battlements; most were no older than Hem. Indik caught her expression.

"I didn't think children fought in Innail," she said to him.

"All volunteers," he answered shortly. "We need every hand we can get. These ones know what they face if we lose. Some have already seen their homes destroyed, their families killed."

Maerad said nothing. It brought home to her, as nothing else had, the violence that had already occurred in the gentle valley of Innail. She felt a deep anger smouldering inside her.

Here on the battlements, she could see the full strangeness of the weathercharm she had helped to cast. The air was still here, even a little stuffy, but the noise of the wind was very loud. Winter sunlight fell on her shoulders, but only a few spans away was a great shadow in which light faltered and died. Through the gloom, she could make out a boiling mass of figures on the ground before the Innail gates, holding flaring torches that hissed and spat in the rain. She could hear the rhythmic twang of bowstrings, and she realized that archers were picking off any attackers foolhardy enough to venture into bowshot.

Indik was right: it was very hard to see what the army was doing, or how far back it stretched into the gloom. But there seemed many, many more soldiers than were stationed here at the gates. Maerad wondered if the forces were this thick all the way around the walls, and drew in her breath. She didn't know if it was worse imagining their attackers or seeing them with her own eyes. On the whole, she thought, it was better to know the worst. But now she was very frightened indeed.

Remember, said Indik into her mind. *I rely on you to keep track of the Landrost. And stay out of bowshot… I don't want any stray arrows putting you out of action…*

Maerad nodded, as if Indik – who was out of sight – could see her, and gathering her wits, moved back from the battlements. Without losing awareness of her present surroundings, she delicately felt her way back into the net of magery that she had woven with the weatherworkers. She knew the Landrost was in there somewhere, and she could feel his presence more accurately if she let her mind touch its strands, as if he were a spider in the centre of his web and she a fly on its outer edges, sensing his presence by subtle vibrations.

From her post, Maerad could see the outer wall better. Although at first it had seemed chaotic with activity, now she saw there was an order in it. She had little experience of fortifications, but even she could see that compared with Norloch, Innail had minimal defences. A high stone wall, reinforced with wards woven into the stone to keep out creatures of the Dark, seemed the thinnest tissue against the forces she had seen swirling below.

Even as she thought this, the clouds before her seemed to explode, and Maerad reeled and almost fell. Before she even knew what was happening, she had automatically drawn her sword, shaking her head to rid herself of a dizziness, as if something had struck her head, although nothing had come near her. The air seemed to be full of black, wet, leathery wings. Wers, she thought, in some cold part of her. They've broken through the wards…

The wers landed swiftly, their claws raking the stone and striking sparks, and began to transform almost immediately into man shapes: tall figures with shoulders of brutal strength and black broadswords. Maerad heard, as if from a great distance, Indik shouting orders, and the screaming of the children, and already the clash of weapons. Almost without thinking, she lifted her arms and said the word for white fire, noroch, and a silver ball shot from her fingertips and caught the nearest wer on its shoulder, as it raised its arm to strike at a Bard. The flame stuck and burned, flaming through its hair, and the wer screeched. The sound went through Maerad's head like a knife. As it writhed on the ground, flames blackening and withering its body, the white flame leapt to another wer close by, and

Maerad saw more wers behind and stretched out her hand to send more white fire: but it was already over, all the wers were dead, either hacked by the Bards and soldiers or burned by the white flame.

The orderliness of the outer wall was now splintered into chaos. Maerad saw that one of the children had been killed, and averted her eyes; another body lay limp close by. She rushed over to see if she could help, her heart in her mouth, and turned the body over; it was a Bard she didn't know, and she still breathed. A bruise was already turning purple over her temple.

"Quick! Over here!" cried a voice at her shoulder, and Maerad turned in surprise. It was Camphis, who laid a hand on the Bard's face, over the bruise, and briefly glowed with magery. Yes, he would be a healer, Maerad thought, drawing back so she wouldn't be in the way. Indik had already arranged Bards in a fighting line, which was just as well, as the attack was almost immediately followed by another. Camphis stayed with the injured Bard until men arrived with a stretcher to carry her away, protecting her even as a wer rose on its haunches and struck out at him with its savage claws. He shore off its head with his sword, and the thing collapsed heavily to the ground, and smoking blood spurted across the stones and over Maerad's feet.

Maerad had no time to feel disgust: she sent out white flame, hitting every wer she could see, wondering why other Bards were not following her example. All of them except Cadvan, she saw, were fighting with weapons, not magery. In a very short time – or perhaps the time only seemed short – the wers were again all destroyed. The ground was littered with their foul corpses and smirched with their blood. One of the cauldrons of pitch had been spilt and a pool of molten tar was spreading slowly over the stones. The stench made her gorge rise. Indik was shouting for men to throw the corpses off the wall, and in twos they flung the heavy bodies over the battlements. And then it happened again. Cadvan was scorching the wers with white fire as they landed so they flared up like living torches and collapsed, wrecks of burned leather and bone; but still no one else seemed to be using magery.

Maerad, said Indik into Maerad's mind. *Do not forget to track the Landrost. This is meant to distract us...*

In the confusion, Maerad had forgotten entirely about the Landrost. She hastily began to explore, feeling for his presence. She drew back as far as she could from the fighting, trying not to look: to witness these savage acts was somehow worse than to perform them. Again, the fighting was over quickly, but there were more bodies on the ground this time: a young girl with her neck at an awful, unnatural angle, another Bard whom Maerad saw, after a quick glance, was certainly dead. Then there was a wave of attacks, one after the other, so that Maerad lost count, but this time more Bards could use the white flame. The children had scrambled down the steps into shelter after the first couple of attacks, and the soldiers were now fighting steadily. No one else was hurt, and it began to turn into a systematic, sickening slaughter. Some wers, seeing the carnage, swerved back over the wall without even attempting to fight. Maerad concentrated on staying out of the way of the skirmishes, following the malevolent pressure that signalled the Landrost, trying to feel him without letting him become aware of her.

Cadvan was suddenly next to her; she hadn't seen him approach, and started in surprise. His face was grim, and splashed with blood, and his sword was black with it, but he seemed unhurt.

"Out of trouble here?" he asked.

Maerad nodded abstractedly; she didn't want to lose the thread she was following.

"I thank you for the blackstone," he said. "You were right: it came in very useful. The Landrost somehow broke the wards and staved off our magery at the same time. The blackstone prevented him from affecting me, but everyone else was disempowered… His little revenge, no doubt, for that weathercharm. Maerad, if you could find out how he did it, it would help us… It costs the Landrost far less to lose ten than for us to lose one."

Maerad turned to him. "He couldn't block me either," she said. "I told you I didn't need it."

"I know. Maerad, you are key to this…"

"Are these attacks happening all over Innail?"

"I don't know. Probably."

Yes. Indik's voice sounded harshly in Maerad's head: she had forgotten she was in mindtouch with him. *We have been hard pressed. But the wards are remade, and are stronger now. I think they will not try that again.*

For a moment, Maerad panicked: in the intimacy of mindtouching, she could feel the anxiety that Indik otherwise concealed, and she knew that Indik was depending on her in their battle with the Landrost. And she was already so weary… If Innail fell, it would be her fault. Cadvan caught the tenor of her thoughts, and took her hand.

"Maerad, yes, much is hoped of you," he said. "But like all of us, you can only do your best, and no one will blame you if even that is not enough. We all have our parts to play in this, and our own responsibilities." Cadvan grimaced. "We are all tired. And it is not as if the wards were completely ineffective even though they were breached. It cost the wers to break them; they used a large part of their native powers, and were slower and less deadly when they attacked us. The Landrost is sending them to be slaughtered. I suspect there will not be many more of these attacks."

"Indik thinks he won't try that again," said Maerad.

"Well, then. We have won at least some respite."

"What next, then?" Maerad studied the scene before her: already the wers' bodies had been flung over the walls, the wounded fighters taken to the healers, and reeds and sand scattered over the blood that smeared the stone. For the moment everything seemed orderly again, although all swords were drawn and the defenders were wary, prepared for assault at any moment.

"I don't know," said Cadvan. "The Light grant us strength to meet it."

In the other part of her mind, Maerad tensed: she was now very close to the Landrost, and she could feel him brooding. She sensed a miasma of doubt colouring his presence, a bafflement: he had met resistance where he had thought to find none. Shifting cautiously, Maerad attempted to move closer to his thoughts. No, he was nothing like the Winterking, who was subtle and complex as well as powerful. The Landrost was a creature who thought only in crude patterns of power, seeking to overwhelm like a landslide. And yes, there was great and frightening power in these forces, but surely, also, a weakness. A landslide could only go in one direction, after all...

She froze. She had become too absorbed in her contemplation, and the Landrost had become aware of her. Just as she could read him, her mind could be open to his. For a vital moment, she was too terrified to move. The Landrost lashed out with a blast of energy, and she felt the shock of it go through her, a malevolent pulse of chill darkness that left her numb and stupid. In that moment, the Landrost perceived her. As if she could see a reflection of herself in another's eye, she glimpsed for the briefest moment how he saw her: a glowing figure in the darkness, very small and very bright, pulsing with an unknowable power. Now she was trapped in his gaze, as if his perception pinned her beneath a crushing weight; she could neither move nor think. She felt his astonishment give way to a gloating triumph, and she felt his mind flex. The Landrost would squash her flat as if she were a beetle, and there was nothing she could do. Panicking, she struggled in his grip, but he held her fast.

From very far away, at the edges of her mind, she heard a voice. She was so frightened that she didn't recognize who it was; her whole being was infused with darkness and impotence.

Elednor Edil-Amarandh na, said the voice. It was cold too, colder than the Landrost, and glittered with an icy brilliance. *This creature is nothing compared to you. Are you really so weak? Is the pebble really less than the mountain?* And, bizarrely, it laughed. Its laughter was like ice falling on her skin, cutting her open, waking her from the impotence of nightmare.

There was no time to think. The pressure was unbearable, and already the Landrost was blotting out her whole being: only the smallest light remained of herself. With her failing consciousness, she latched fiercely onto the idea of the pebble: in the landslide, a pebble would not be destroyed. She stopped resisting the Landrost and let herself sink into the darkness, hard and round and small and herself. The wave of blackness tossed her an immeasurable distance, through realms of vacant space where stars rolled in their inscrutable dance, through clouds of blinding colours more vast than she could even imagine, where time itself was squeezed and stretched by colossal forces. She was lost, lost... but still she arced through her trajectory, a tiny star.

She didn't know any more who or where she was; everything went through her, faster and faster. And then, quite suddenly, time seemed to start again, and someone called her name. Blindly she reached towards it, to whoever knew her and called her. At last she rolled to a halt, dizzy and breathless. She was a body of flesh and blood and bone, and she could hear her own breathing. She gasped, feeling the air rush into her lungs, a hard surface pressing against her legs, something soft around her. Someone was stroking her face and saying her name.

She opened her eyes and found herself looking straight into Cadvan's eyes. He repeated her name again, a question in his voice, and she nodded, still stunned.

"Are you all right?" He was pale, with deep shadows under his eyes, and the scar around his eye stood out lividly against his skin.

"No," said Maerad. She waited until the dizziness began to dissipate, and then pushed Cadvan away and was sick. Wordlessly he handed her a cloth. She wiped her mouth, and then he gave her some medhyl. Maerad took a long draught and sat down next to him, her back against the wall.

"He saw me," she said at last. "The Landrost. He almost destroyed me."

Cadvan nodded, his face expressionless.

She twisted around so she could look Cadvan in the face. "Was it you who laughed at me?"

Cadvan looked puzzled. "No, my dear. I could not laugh at you in such a place. I called you home. You were so very far away…"

"Someone laughed at me. He saved my life, just as I thought I was going to be crushed. No, it wasn't your voice…" Maerad frowned and took another sip of the medhyl. Her heart was no longer pounding so painfully. "I wonder who it was. It was a cold voice, very cold…"

She gasped: of course she knew who it was. The knowledge gave her the feeling that she was standing on a very high cliff.

She wanted to be sick again, but at the same time she felt as if she were full of light, a strange, thrilling buoyancy.

"Was it the Winterking?" asked Cadvan, after a long silence.

Maerad nodded. "Yes," she said. "Yes. It was."

V

THE CARAVAN

HEM was tired of walking. Every day, for what seemed like the past fifty years, he had slept on the ground, woken cold and stiff with the first light of dawn, and then spent all day walking. It wasn't just ordinary walking, either. He and his companions, Saliman of Turbansk and Soron of Til Amon, stumbled through a rough, marshy landscape, and they were constantly weaving charms – glimveils, shadowmazes, shields – to help keep them hidden from any Black Army scouts or patrols. It was exhausting, skulking like this. He was tired of eating dried nuts and fruits and salted meat. He was tired of everything.

He vented his feelings to Irc, the white crow perched on his shoulder who was his constant companion, using mindspeech. Aside from being the only way to speak to Irc, it had the advantage that the others could not overhear and rebuke him. *When we get to Til Amon*, Hem said, *I am going to sleep all day. No, first I will eat. A big, big meal. A lamb roasted on the spit, with all the juices dripping, and roasted turnips and carrots and onions. And some spiced apples.* His mouth watered just thinking about it. *And then I will sleep. And no one will wake me up until I want to wake up.*

Irc cocked his head and fixed him with his eye. *You're lazy,* he said. *It's not so bad. Though some fresh meat would be good.*

You had a squab yesterday, said Hem. *And you didn't share it!*

Irc looked unrepentant. *You would have spoiled it by putting it in the fire,* he said. *Anyway, it was very scrawny. There was only enough for me.*

Oh, you wouldn't understand, said Hem. *You're just a bloody crow. Go away. You're too heavy.*

Irc ruffled his feathers, a sign of offence. *I am a very clever crow,* he said. *I am the King's Messenger. I saved you from Dagra.*

That doesn't stop you from being the most annoying bird I've ever met, said Hem.

Irc gave Hem a sharp nip on his ear and took off, soaring into the sky. Hem sighed impatiently, immediately regretting what he had said. *I'm sorry!* he called. *I didn't mean it, Irc. I'm just tired, that's all.*

Irc didn't answer. Hem watched him until he was out of sight. He'd be back later, probably having done a little hunting, and might have forgiven Hem by then. Or not, depending.

"Have you offended that bird?" said Saliman, from behind him.

"He takes offence if you don't bow to him all the time," said Hem irritably. "I wish every day that Ara-kin had never made him a messenger. I've paid for it ever since."

Saliman, a black-skinned Bard of Turbansk and Hem's mentor, laughed. "You and every bird he meets," he said. "Mind you, life would be far more tedious if you didn't have Irc to squabble with. Be of good cheer, Hem. We're not so far from Til Amon." He pointed to a mountain rising before them. "A few days at most, I'd say, the Light willing. We've been lucky. I think we have far outstripped the Black Army, if they are indeed planning to march on South Annar."

Hem nodded. Saliman was right, he knew; they had been lucky.

After he and Irc had stumbled out of the Glandugir Hills to Sjug'hakar Im, the nightmarish camp where child soldiers had been trained for battle, he had met Saliman and they had briefly returned (to Irc's deep displeasure) to the Bards in the caves at Nal-Ak-Burat. There Hem had endured an uncomfortable

session with Hared, who – despite the outcome of his diso-
bedience – was furious with Hem for disobeying orders at
Sjug'hakar Im. After everything he had been through, especially after his gruelling journey across Dén Raven in a fruitless
attempt to rescue his friend Zelika, Hem was in no mood to be
told off.

"I found out things you wouldn't know otherwise," he said
sullenly. "Even Saliman said he wouldn't dare enter Dagra.
And I couldn't abandon Zelika. Perhaps you don't know what
it means to have a friend."

Hared's face, hard at the best of times, closed at that jibe,
and he said nothing more. After that, he had treated Hem with
a warier respect. A few days later, after several long and cir-
cular arguments, Hem, Soron and Saliman left Nal-Ak-Burat,
heading in the first instance for Til Amon. Soron was itching to
return home, and Hem wouldn't be budged from his conviction that he had to find his sister Maerad, who he was sure was
somewhere in Annar.

Hared had wanted Saliman to stay in Nal-Ak-Burat with the
other Bards of the resistance, to fight the Black Army. "Saliman,
I will be frank," he said, during one discussion. "Movement
has been easier this past fortnight, I grant you, since Imank
vanished and the Black Army has been in disarray. But once
Sharma organizes himself – which I foresee will not take long
– those forces will no longer be divided. I have no doubt it will
get much more difficult here, and the Light knows it is difficult
enough. And to lose a Bard like you to a wild goose chase – it
goes hard, Saliman. It goes hard."

This was as close as Hared came to begging, and Saliman
knew it was a measure of his desperation.

"Hared," he said gently. "I understand, my friend. Believe
me, I understand. And I cannot say that I am not torn... It
is always possible that I am mistaken. I know it looks like

madness to you. But I cannot go against my Knowing. I knew from the beginning that Hem had some part to play in this. So far, he has not proved me wrong. And it is very clear to me that we have to find his sister."

Hared heard the decision in Saliman's voice and knew better than to argue, but he shook his head sadly. The following day, Hem, Soron and Saliman left the safety of the caves of Nal-Ak-Burat, heading west through Nazar, and crossed, at some peril to their lives, the Undara River into Savitir, until they reached the edges of the Neera Marshes. There they turned north, keeping the Neera Marshes to their left.

In all this time they had seen no one else; Saliman guided them away from roads and tracks, and they avoided all villages. The landscape they crossed was lonely: at dusk they heard the melancholy cry of the curlew calling in the night. Occasionally they came across a burned byre or the remains of slaughtered goats or other signs of war, but these were all cold, remnants of a violence now well past, and there were few signs of sorcery. Still, they kept vigilant, and it seemed to Hem that the landscape watched them warily, as if eyes noted their presence and waited anxiously for them to pass. They travelled swiftly: aside from the urgency of their quest, the strange emptiness of the land gave them no desire to dawdle.

At last they arrived at the northern reaches of the Neera Marshes and again turned west to meet the South Road. Here they doubled their precautions: if the Black Army had scouts or, worse, was marching northwards to South Annar, this was where they would most likely encounter problems. They travelled north with the road to their left a good distance away, their passing muffled by shadowmazing and shields so they would be invisible to the naked eye. Irc had investigated the road at regular intervals. Nothing, he said, moved on it, as far as his eye could see.

The worst that could be said of their journey was that it was dull. Soron perked up the closer they came to Til Amon, his birth home. It had been a long time since he had last seen it.

"It is, of all Schools, the most beautiful," he told Hem one night as they huddled in their meagre blankets for warmth, having decided against lighting a fire.

"It has some rivals," said Saliman. Hem could hear the smile in Saliman's voice. "Have you travelled to Il Arunedh, the mountain of roses?"

"Aye, aye. And you remember, I lived in Turbansk for many years, and count it one of the fairest cities I have ever seen." He paused briefly, perhaps seeing in his mind's eye the ruin of Turbansk's beauty. "But beauty, Saliman, is in the heart as well as the eye, and Til Amon will ever hold my love."

"One cannot argue with love," said Saliman gravely.

"You have to concur all the same that for the natural beauty that surrounds it, Til Amon cannot be surpassed. It stands, Hem, on the shores of the Lake of Til Amon, and its towers rise high over the waters. On still days you see the city reflected in the lake, rippling at its own feet. From its walls spread the gentle meads of Amon, orchards and groves and vineyards and fields, from which come some of the finest fruits and wines in all Edil-Amarandh. It is, Hem, a cook's dream... And across the lake rise the Osidh Am, majestic and high."

"They are lovely mountains," said Hem. "Saliman and I rode through them on our way to Turbansk."

"That would have been somewhat south of us," Soron said. "Here the mountains are higher and harsher. They are not so easy to cross! But to wake in Til Amon on a still morning, and to see the white-tipped peaks before you, trembling in the blue lake – ah, that is a sight that takes your breath away."

"Why did you leave?" Hem rolled over to look at Soron's face, but it was hidden in the dark.

"Why did I leave? At first, I wanted to learn of the cooking of the Suderain. There was much I wished to know. And then I became the chief cook for the School. And, somehow, I stayed in Turbansk. I made many friends there, and I came to love the city. As I think you might understand, Hem: there was much to love about it. And so, after a while, you realize that many years have passed without your noticing. But Til Amon is still my home. I am sad that I haven't thought to travel there these past years, since my family died, and even as we come closer, my fear rises that it will already be ashes and rubble, trampled beneath Enkir's army."

The yearning in Soron's voice pierced Hem's heart, and he asked no more questions. I don't have a home, Hem thought. I don't remember Pellinor at all, and will never feel that way about it. Turbansk might have been a home for me, but it all lies in ruins. Where will I make a home, once all this is over? If it ever is? Will I ever find Maerad again? Have I already lost her, or is she still alive, looking for me? He was convinced she was alive, although he had no good reason for it; some sense of her presence touched the edges of his mind and assured him, in quiet moments, that she was alive and thinking of him. But how could he trust his feelings, when he had been so wrong about Zelika? He had been so sure that Zelika was alive among the child soldiers; he had chased her trail to the very fortress of the Nameless One, only to find that she had been killed weeks before. Perhaps his feeling about Maerad was as deceptive. He flinched away from the thought.

Maybe Zelika has found home, he thought. He thought of her as he had first seen her in Turbansk, an orphan who had fled the ruins of war in Baladh, desperate to revenge herself against the Dark. Maybe through the Gates she had found everything she desired. On this side, she had lost everything: her home, her family, hope... Maybe that was why she threw her life away...

Thinking of Zelika opened a rift inside Hem that was so deep and raw he could barely comprehend it. He could see her delicate face and wild hair as clearly as if she stood in front of him. He still couldn't quite believe that she was dead, that he would never see her again: sometimes he still found himself expecting to see her at his shoulder, an ironic smile on her lips, and caught himself with a pang.

Until he had lost her, he hadn't realized how deeply Zelika had wound herself into his heart. The knowledge of her death was still too recent: his body still bore the fading bruises from his hopeless, mad quest to save her, the terrible march through Dén Raven to the dark city of Dagra, where he had witnessed things that frightened him more than his worst nightmares. He hadn't had much time to come to terms with what had happened to him in the past few months, but he knew that his failure to save Zelika hurt him more than anything else he had been through.

Hem lay on his back looking up into the clear winter sky, where the stars burned cold and white in the darkness, and it was a long time before he slept. The wrenching ache in his breast persisted through his dreams that night, and coloured his mood the following day. Hence, he thought, his argument with Irc.

He hadn't seen Irc for some time now, and was feeling anxious: the bird wouldn't answer any of his summonings. He had clearly decided to punish Hem thoroughly. Hem sighed impatiently. If Irc disappeared for hours, he couldn't rid himself of his anxiety that something had happened to him; but still, it wasn't worth worrying unless he didn't turn up for dinner.

Irc reappeared later, as the first edges of dusk began to draw over the land and the travellers were looking for a likely campsite. He dropped from the sky and landed heavily on Hem's shoulder with no forewarning, so that Hem jumped. The crow wiped his beak on Hem's shoulder and nipped his ear gently in greeting, as if they hadn't quarrelled at all. Hem's hand automatically went up to tickle Irc's neck, even though he had sworn not long before that he would break his scrawny legs if he dared to show his beak again.

There are humans, said Irc. *Not far away.*

Hem halted in surprise. *Humans?*

They don't seem like soldiers. Or spies. They are very strange. Hem could hear the curiosity in Irc's voice. *They keep shouting at each other. They have swords, and they try to hit each other, and then they stop and begin to argue.*

Are they Bards or Hulls? asked Hem.

No. Though at first I wasn't sure.

Hem looked around, but he could see no sign of people. *Where?*

Ahead of us, not far, said Irc. Hem knew that Irc had little idea of distance: "not far" could mean anything between a hundred spans and a league. *They have horses and a big wagon.*

"Irc says there are people ahead of us," said Hem, turning to Saliman and Soron. "But he doesn't think they are soldiers or spies."

"People?" Saliman's eyebrows shot up.

"He says they are behaving very strangely. They seem to be fighting with each other. And he says that they have swords."

Soron frowned. "The last thing we need is trouble," he said. "Anyone wandering through this forsaken land is bound to be trouble."

"Like us, you mean?" Saliman laughed. "Well, we shall just be cautious. It should be easy enough to avoid them."

It became evident that night that the strangers were not, in fact, far away at all. They saw a camp fire burning through the scrub, and were close enough to see dark figures passing in front of it. Whoever these people were, they were clearly enjoying themselves: the sound of conversation, laughter and even singing drifted over the night air towards the three Bards.

"Don't they know that the Black Army could be marching up this road any moment?" asked Hem in wonder, as he lay sleepless in the cold, staring up at the bright winter stars.

"Clearly not," said Soron. "I wonder who they are?"

"Minstrels, by the sound of it," said Saliman sleepily.

Hem sent out his listening, the acute hearing that was a special ability of Bards. He could hear a dulcimer and a flute, and maybe a lyre, but he didn't recognize any of the songs. They were singing in Annaren, he thought, and they sounded cheerful and unafraid. He was suddenly full of yearning for some plain good fellowship.

"I think I'd like to talk to them," he said. "They don't sound dangerous at all."

"Go to sleep," said Saliman.

Hem sighed and huddled into his blanket. The ground seemed particularly hard tonight.

The people in the wagon were moving northwards as they were, and so they followed them at a judicious distance all the next day. Irc was beside himself with curiosity, and spent most of the day observing them and bringing back reports. It seemed that there were three, two men and a woman. He was quite sure that they were neither Bards nor Hulls. Most interestingly, to Irc anyway, their wagon was made of gold.

Gold? said Hem.

And they are carrying a great treasure. Hem could hear the acquisitive greed in Irc's voice. *Jewels and golden things.*

You didn't go inside the wagon? asked Hem, aghast.

Irc didn't answer the question, and he ignored Hem's worried warning to stay out of the wagon. Irc couldn't resist bright things: he had a particular weakness for spoons and in Turbansk

Hem had had to continually raid Irc's treasure stores to replenish the dining hall's supplies.

Puzzled, Hem discussed Irc's observations with Saliman, who burst out laughing. "If the caravan is made of gold, I feel sorry for the horses," he said. "But I think Irc has discovered a group of players. The gold will be paint, and the jewels will be made of glass. Not that that would worry Irc... The Light alone knows what they are doing wandering through the wilderness in the midst of war."

"Players?" asked Hem. "What are they?"

"Have you never seen them? Turbansk has some fine players... I mean, it did..." Saliman paused for a moment. "They are people who tell stories. Plays."

"I've heard storytellers," said Hem. While in Turbansk, he had once heard a legendary storyteller, Nakar, in the market-place, who had enraptured him with a tale of the lost love of the first Ernani of Turbansk, who had been kidnapped by water Elementals. The crowd at his feet had been silent and breath-less, hanging on his every word. Although Nakar was not a Bard, Hem had thought the powers he held were very like those of Barding, although he couldn't have said why.

"No, these play out the story. They dress up as kings or lovers or villains and pretend they are the people in the legends. They travel from city to city, and make their living that way. There are some very good players in the Suderain, but mostly they are Annaren."

Hem fell silent, trying to imagine it. "I'd like to see that," he said at last.

"Perhaps, if our friends are heading for Til Amon, as seems likely, you will," said Saliman, grinning. "But you are not allowed to run away with them."

"Why would I do that?"

"People do," said Saliman.

Irc was gone for a long time, and Hem began to fear that he had been stealing from the players and had been caught. But when he returned, he had very different news: from high up, he had seen dust on the South Road, many leagues in the distance. He had flown down the South Road as far as he dared, and had seen a great army moving north.

How far did you fly? asked Hem, his heart plummeting into his feet.

A long way. Very far through the marshes.

Hem relayed the news to Saliman and Soron, who received it grimly.

"I think they are marching for Til Amon," said Soron. "If they take it, they have a good base from which to attack South Annar. If Enkir, too, marches on my city, I do not like our chances."

"Armies move slowly. We can at least warn Til Amon and give them some time to prepare."

"What about the players?" asked Hem. "If they don't hurry, they might be caught. We should warn them too."

"You just want to see the wagon of gold," said Saliman, with a faint smile.

"If they don't know, the army might catch them up," said Hem. "Maybe they don't even know what's happened in the Suderain. And you know they would be killed."

Saliman looked across at Hem and smiled. "It seems fair to warn them," he said. "So we shall. But we must make good speed now."

"Tonight?"

"Perhaps before. They are travelling slowly, and I think we must move as swiftly as possible."

The players must have quickened their own pace, because the Bards didn't catch up with the caravan until nightfall. The players had stopped in a hollow that protected them from a sharp wind that cut through the scrub of the plains, and had

lit a fire, over which an iron pot suspended from a tripod bub-
bled promisingly. Hem, who had not had the luxury of hot food
since they had left Nal-Ak-Burat, felt his mouth fill with water
and Irc nipped his ear with excitement. Despite the bird's pref-
erence for raw meat, he had developed a taste for well-cooked
food in his time with the Bards and was certainly not averse to
eating it.

The Bards hesitated outside the circle of firelight, looking in
from the darkness: it seemed astounding to them that anybody
could be travelling through the wilderness so casually. Not only
had the players made no effort to conceal themselves, no one
was even keeping watch.

The caravan was bigger than Hem had expected, and it was
indeed gold or, more accurately, a kind of shabby gilt: it had
clearly seen better days, and in several places the paint had
flaked off. A picture of heroic battle was painted rather crudely
on its side, framed by much superfluous ornamentation,
and a tattered crimson curtain hung over the door. Two hob-
bled horses cropped grass nearby, and a lean yellow dog was
propped on its haunches by the fire, its nose twitching at the
aromas from the pot. As soon as Saliman saw the dog, he told
it silently to be quiet: he would rather announce himself when
he chose.

There were three people, clearly all Annarens, at the campsite. A fair-haired young woman was seated cross-legged by the
fire and two men, one in his twenties, the other perhaps twenty
years older, were practising swordcraft. They were fighting with
wooden swords which made loud cracks when they connected,
and were arguing hotly at the same time.

"No, no, no, no!" cried the older man, stopping and leaning on his sword. "My dear Marich, what are you doing? You're
supposed to be losing."

"Yes, in the end," said the other. "But it's more exciting if

I look as if I'm winning and then you overcome me. Then you look even more heroic."

"You forget that you are the weak, evil villain," said the first. "And that I am the nobleman. The audience should be in no doubt of my strength and superiority. You should fall, here, and then wriggle out of the way – that's much better. The most important thing, my dear Marich, is the story…"

"The important thing is that everyone doesn't get bored and heave themselves to the nearest tavern. Honestly, Karim, the way you're playing it we'll be lucky if there are three people left at the end."

"I think…" said the woman; but Hem, who had no idea what they were talking about and was following the argument with fascination, never heard what she thought, because at that moment Saliman stepped into the firelight. Hem started and followed him, with Soron at his shoulder.

"Greetings, travellers," said Saliman, bowing courteously. The woman hastily stood up, and the two men, alarmed, dropped their wooden swords and drew knives from their belts.

"What do you want?" asked the one called Karim. "We have no money here."

Saliman spread out his hands to show he was not carrying a weapon (and to silence Hem, who was about to protest indignantly at the suggestion that they were bandits). "We do not wish you any harm," he said. "Like you, we travel in peace through Savitir. We simply wish to warn you to hurry."

"Do you not know that you travel through a country that is threatened by war?" asked Soron abruptly, incredulity raw in his voice. "The Black Army marches on the South Road behind us even as we speak. Do you think wooden swords and toy daggers will protect you from the forces of Sharma himself?"

"The Black Army?" asked the woman. "What do you mean?"

Hem glanced at Soron and Saliman. Their faces were polite masks, sure signs that they thought the players were fools. The two men, looking a little embarrassed, put their knives back in their belts.

"I cry you mercy for any discourtesy," said Karim, drawing himself up with dignity. "We have been long out of human contact. We made a wrong turn some way out of Elevé, and only lately found the South Road. It is long since we had any news."

"Of anything," said the woman. She was looking narrowly at the three Bards. "Why should we believe you? We have seen no sign of war."

"No reason," said Hem, who was still feeling offended at being mistaken for a bandit. "Except that it might save your lives."

"I should have said who we are," said Saliman. "I am Saliman of Turbansk. With me are Soron of Til Amon and Hem of Turbansk. We travel urgently to Til Amon, to warn them that they are likely to face attack, and thought to let you know, since we have been aware of you for the past day, that you are in mortal peril unless you, too, hurry."

Karim opened his mouth, as if he wanted to say something, and then shut it. The woman glanced swiftly at the two men as if in annoyance, and stepped forward, holding her hand out in greeting.

"I thank you for your kindness, then," she said. Her voice was beautiful, low and clear. "My name is Hekibel, daughter of Hirean, and with me are Karim of Lok and Marich, son of Marichan. Believe me, we have spoken to no stranger for the past two months, and have heard nothing of this; there was no news of it in Elevé when we left. What is the news?"

"The Black Army has invaded the Suderain, and Turbansk and Baladh have fallen," said Hem. "Many have fled to Car Amdridh, which we hope to defend. Now the Nameless One is marching on South Annar. We think most likely they seek to lay siege to Til Amon."

"Turbansk? Baladh? Fallen?" said Marich falteringly. "Is this true?"

"Aye." Saliman's face was expressionless, but Hem knew the disbelief in the faces of the players made him feel his grief anew, as if he himself had heard the news for the first time.

"Well." Karim looked stunned. "Well. I had heard that times were black, but I didn't know... Well."

There was a brief, uncomfortable silence. Saliman opened his mouth to take his leave, but Hekibel turned to Karim.

"Perhaps we could invite our guests for a bite to eat?" said Hekibel. "That is, of course, if you have time, given the urgency of your errand."

"Yes. Indeed. Friends, please, you are welcome to partake in our humble repast." Karim made a flourish with his hands, as if he were inviting them to a king's table. "It is the least we can offer, as our thanks."

Hem looked pleadingly at Saliman, whom he saw was about to refuse, and Saliman hesitated. The stew smelt very inviting.

"I thank you," said Saliman. "That is, if there is enough to share with three strangers. We need not stand on courtesy here: we are all poor travellers."

"Oh, we've got plenty of supplies," said Hekibel. "And Marich caught a wild goat yesterday, so I've made a big pot."

Soron, Hem saw, was not too pleased with the idea – he still seemed outraged, even angered, by the players' ignorance of the war – but Hem was delighted. After their cold fare of the past few days, a plate of stew seemed luxurious beyond comparison.

The players turned out to be good company, and even Soron was soon mollified. Hekibel, seeing Hem's curiosity, had shown him inside the caravan. (Irc was on his shoulder bristling with inquisitiveness, but was sternly told to behave himself.) Hem felt a sudden pang as he bent his head to enter: for a short time he had been taken in by a family of Pilanel, and he had vivid memories of their cosy caravans. They had been very kind to him. But that memory called up images he would rather forget.

This caravan was very different from the Pilanel's. It was big enough to be divided into three sleeping compartments with thick red curtains, although they were now drawn back, lending the interior an air of faded splendour. Hekibel showed him how the whole of one side of the caravan could be let down and turned into a stage, using the red curtains as a backdrop. The opposite wall was lined with cupboards where robes, masks and other props were neatly put away. The back of the caravan was basically a well-stocked larder: it included rice, pulses, spices, flour, various oils, nuts, dried fruits and smoked meats.

"It's beautiful," said Hem, enraptured.

"Try living in it with Marich and Karim for a year," said Hekibel dryly. "It loses some of its charm."

"And you just travel around, pretending to be people in stories?"

Hekibel laughed. "Yes, I suppose that's exactly what we do."

"And people pay you?"

"They give us what they can. We had a good season in Elevé, but all the flour and the lentils came from a little village. They didn't have any coins."

"I'd love to see something like that." Hem was flushed with enthusiasm. "I never have before."

"Sometimes it can be magical," said Hekibel. "And sometimes it's just plain awful. I love it and I hate it at the same time.

I can't say it's an easy life. But look, we had better go back to the others, or the stew will burn." They could hear Karim's voice raised outside, and she turned sharply. "And it's been a while since Karim has had an audience. I fear he might be boring your friends."

Karim was standing silhouetted by the fire, his arms outstretched to the sky. He was declaiming a speech by a king who was dying of a mortal wound, having lost his kingdom, his children and his life through his own folly and greed. It was, Hem thought as he listened, like a beautiful poem. Karim's voice rang out in the night air, caressing the words, and Hem, entranced, felt the king's regret and sorrow as if they were his own. Finally Karim clutched his breast, and fell to one knee, bowing his head in sorrow. There was a short silence, and then the others, including the players, started clapping. Karim's voice was as spellbinding as any Bard's.

"The great Lorica," said Karim, in a hushed voice. "It is always a privilege to speak her words."

"It is," said Hekibel. "But now, we should eat."

For most of the dinner, they avoided speaking about the Black Army or the war in the Suderain. Saliman had told Hem that they were to conceal that they were Bards; they were refugees from the south, fleeing north. Which, Hem thought privately, was not so far from the truth. The stew was delicious compared to the marching fare they had been eating since leaving Nal-Ak-Burat, and respectable even by Soron's standards; and Karim brought out some surprisingly good wine.

"Why stint oneself?" he said, as he gnawed the last morsels of meat off a bone. "We are like migratory birds, always on the wing, but should we suffer for that? It only takes a little organization. Admittedly, our stocks were getting low – it was a relief to find the road again—"

"If we'd stuck to the road in the first place, we would never have got lost," said Hekibel, turning to Saliman. "Always these short cuts."

"One never knows when one will find a lone village or isolated hamlet, eager for our art." Karim threw his bone away with another flourish.

Karim's gestures fascinated Hem: he had never seen anyone, even the stateliest courtiers in Turbansk, speak with so much decoration, and his voice was rich and full, like that of the best singers. Marich, in contrast, was plain-spoken and tended to the taciturn, although soon he was deep in conversation with Soron about the pleasures of the table. Hem saw that Marich was shy, and he thought it strange that someone who performed in front of strangers would be shy. Irc approved of Marich and Hekibel at once, because they were generous with titbits.

"He's a charming pet," said Hekibel, laughing as Irc danced in front of her, begging for more food. "You've trained him very well. Where did you find him?"

Hem bit back his protest that Irc was not a pet, and told how he had rescued him from attack by some of his kin when he was a fledgling. "He's a white crow, usually," he said. "He looks a bit bedraggled at the moment because we had to dye him, and it hasn't quite come out of his feathers yet."

"Yes, I can see that he would be very handsome with white feathers," said Hekibel. Irc, conscious that he was being talked about, preened himself.

"He is very vain, I'm afraid," said Hem fondly. "But loyal and true, for all that."

Karim seemed to talk mostly about himself. Like the other two players, he was a fair-skinned Annaren, with a greying beard cropped close around his chin. He hailed originally, he told them, from northern Annar, but had travelled to Lok when he was a young man, where he had learned his craft. He had been working with Hekibel and Marich for the past year, and they had been making their way across South Annar. Now they were heading, like the Bards, for Til Amon.

"We formed the company in Lanorial, at last year's spring gathering," he said. "When I find raw talent, such as shines in these two, I like to pass on the fruit of my rich experience in this craft, and, youthful though they are, they are grateful to sip from the chalice of age. I like to think that our humble company does not disgrace our profession."

"I'm certain that you represent it well," Saliman said politely. "It is an ancient and honourable art."

"Indeed," said Karim, looking narrowly at Saliman. "I see you are a man of culture. No doubt you were once a person of importance in Turbansk. Well," he said, and sighed with an air of tragic melancholy, "we have all seen better days."

Hekibel looked embarrassed and hastily offered more wine, but Saliman refused. A full moon had risen over the plains, and Saliman and Soron wanted to move on while it was light enough to see. Even Hem felt anxious about how visible they must be, although he had enjoyed the feast and the conversation, which had lightened his heart. The Bards thanked their hosts and prepared to leave.

"If I were you, I'd move north as fast as you can," said Saliman. "And I'd light no more fires. It is unlikely that the army would overtake you, but there will be scouts and out-riders along the road."

"I thank you for your advice," said Karim. "Perhaps we will meet you in Til Amon. As always, we will perform there in the Inner Circle."

"We'll keep an eye out," said Soron. "May the Light shine on your path."

Karim bowed deeply. "And on yours, my good sirs."

"Goodbye," said Hekibel, smiling. "I hope our paths cross

again. I should like to use your crow in our plays; I'm sure we could find a part for him."

Irc squawked a faint farewell from Hem's shoulder. He was stuffed full of food and was half asleep.

"I hope they're all right," said Hem, when they were out of earshot. "I should hate anything to happen to them."

"Somehow I think they will be," said Soron. "Hekibel seems like a very sensible woman. In any case, we have done what we can."

VI

TIL AMON

THE next few days passed in a blur of tiredness. Whereas before they had been moving cautiously and steadily, now they relied on heavy glimveils for concealment, and stayed as close to the road as they dared. They began before light and stopped well after dark, keeping up a punishing pace.

Irc flew back along the road to check the Black Army morning and evening. He reported that it was falling further behind them. By the time they had reached the fork in the road that led to Til Amon, curving back southwards around the Osidh Am mountains, the Black Army was only just past the Neera Marshes. The clear winter days had given way, and now they strode on through heavy rain. It pleased Saliman – he thought it would slow the Black Army even more, and it made the Bards less visible on the road – but it was certainly miserable.

"The question now is, whether the army turns off towards Til Amon, or marches straight into South Annar," said Saliman, staring down the Til Amon Road. "I fear it makes most sense for them to take Til Amon, and make a base from which to attack South Annar through Lauchomon or Lukernil."

Soron looked grim. "It is my thought, too," he said. "And if Enkir marches also, Til Amon will be caught between the hammer and the anvil. Still, it is a hard place to take: the lake enfolds it. They will have to besiege the city." He sighed, remembering perhaps the siege of Turbansk and the slaughter and destruction that had followed, and the other two nodded in sombre silence and pressed on.

It was about twenty leagues south to Til Amon from the fork in the South Road, and they covered it in three days. The mountains swept up to their left: grey, naked edges of rock, their peaks hidden in thick cloud. On the first day they reached the Lake of Til Amon, a huge body of water stretching south before them, iron grey under the grey sky. The wind swept down the mountains and over the lake, so when it reached them it was knifed with ice. Their nights were short and uncomfortable.

As Hem huddled under the inadequate shelter of a small fir or in the lee of an overhanging rock, exhausted and unable to sleep, he wondered if he had been this physically miserable even on the journey across Dén Raven. That had definitely been a darker road than this, but this journey was probably more uncomfortable. The chill pierced to the very marrow of his bones and never went away. Thinking about warm beds or hot meals only made things worse, and yet he couldn't stop it. On the third day, to cap his misery completely, he developed a heavy cold, with a painful cough. Saliman, who was a famous healer, listened to his chest with deep concern and made a charm that helped slightly. Hem, who had healing skills himself, knew that the only real remedy was rest and a warm bed, both of which were impossible. They had no choice but to continue on.

They reached Til Amon well after dark that day. Its high gates seemed to loom quite suddenly out of the mist and darkness. There was a bell-chain beside the gate, for late travellers. When Soron gave it an imperious tug, they heard the bell sound deep inside the walls and stood outside the gate, shivering in the rain, until a guard opened a slit in a small portal beside the main gate and demanded identification. After what seemed to Hem like an unreasonably long time, he let them in.

At last they were under shelter. Hem, cold, feverish and soaked to the skin, was too tired and sick to care. Before he did anything else, Saliman swept Hem to a Bardhouse, where he was handed over to a no-nonsense healer who listened to his chest, clicked his tongue in concern and gave Hem a draught of a black liquid that tasted so bitter it made him almost gag. Then Irc, who had been clinging to Hem's shoulder trying to hide in the hood of his cloak, was firmly removed and Hem was put into a hot bath and dressed in dry clothes. Irc, deeply suspicious of the healer, watched every move from the side of the bath; he had never understood the human predilection for wetting themselves all over. As for Hem, the pleasure of being warm all the way through was indescribable, and he collapsed blissfully into a soft, welcoming bed and slept as he had not slept for weeks.

He woke late the following morning, and then only because Irc was pulling his hair. Sleepily he fended him off, trying to crawl back into the delicious space of dream, where he was still warm and comfortable. He had forgotten that he was in Til Amon, and expected that with wakefulness would come the dripping twigs, hard wet ground and bone-aching cold that had been his lot for the past few days. But the warmth didn't disappear, and he suddenly remembered where he was, and sat up, instantly awake.

Food, said Irc irritably. *I'm hungry.*

Me too, said Hem. There was a yawning hole where his middle should have been. He jumped out of bed and pulled on some of the clothes he had been given the night before. *Where's Saliman? He'll know where the food is.*

With Irc on his shoulder, he padded out of his room in bare feet and made his way downstairs. There he found the healer, who was shocked that Hem was out of bed.

"But I'm fine!" Hem protested. "I've never felt better in my life! And anyway, I need to break my fast. I don't like eating in bed!"

"Last night, you were as ill as any child I've seen," the healer said sternly. "While you're in my charge, you will do as I say."

Hem had no intention of returning to bed, and was about to argue the point heatedly when Saliman entered.

"Good morrow, Edadh," he said to the healer. "And to you, Hem. What are you doing out of bed?"

"I'm feeling fine!" Hem said. "But the healer wants me to go back to bed. I'm just really hungry. And so is Irc," he added, as the crow gave an indignant caw. "I didn't have anything to eat last night..."

Saliman exchanged an ironic glance with Edadh, and then made Hem sit in a chair and examined him carefully. When he had finished, he looked up at Edadh. "I'm afraid he's right," he said. "There's nothing wrong with him; the sickness seems to have disappeared altogether. This boy is very tough – I've seen him recover like this from a serious fever before, and I didn't believe my eyes. Well, I don't think there's a lot of point in confining him to his room: it would only cause you unnecessary trouble."

Edadh looked relieved. "I am glad to hear it, Saliman," he said. "A little surprised, I confess; perhaps he looked more ill than he was last night, although then I would have to believe that my healing skills are deserting me."

"Think rather that your skills are at their highest," said Saliman, smiling. "And that your healing has led to a miraculous recovery."

Edadh turned to Hem, spreading his hands. "Go, then, and my good will with you."

Hem bowed, mollified. "And mine with you, too," he said. "Thank you for your care."

"You might as well come with me," said Saliman to Hem. "Do you have your pack?"

Hem ran upstairs, where his pack lay by his bed, and joined Saliman. Although his first priority was breakfast, he was also very curious to see Til Amon. Like most Annaren Schools, it was built as a series of concentric circles, with major roads running like spokes through the circling streets. It wasn't, thought Hem, as beautiful as Turbansk: the buildings were of grey stone, rather than the rose-pink from which most buildings in Turbansk had been constructed, and here there was not even the beginning of spring green. Naked elms and lime trees spread their dripping branches against the stone, and the only greens that Hem could see were the dark leaves of ivy, fir and yew. A grey mist of rain concealed any views of the lake or the mountains. Under the dim winter light, he privately thought that Til Amon looked a little bleak.

As they walked briskly to the dining hall, Saliman told him that he and Soron had already conferred with the First Circle of Til Amon. "We didn't find them entirely unprepared," he said. "They have their own means of gathering news, and were aware that the Black Army would likely march first on this School, if they came up from the south. It is a blow, all the same; daily they also expect news of an army marching from Norloch."

"But none yet?" said Hem.

"Not yet. They have scouts through Lauchomon, as far as the West Road, and Il Arunedh and Eledh gather their own news, and they keep in contact with them too, of course... Their biggest fear is, of course, armies attacking from both south and north."

Hem fell silent, thinking of the siege of Turbansk. He had a sudden vision of a line of flame creeping over Annar, from south to north, from west to east, consuming everything in its path, leaving behind it a wasteland of ash and ruin. It opened a black pit of hopelessness inside him, and he shook his head to dispel his gloom. "Where's Soron?" he asked.

"At the Bardhouse," said Saliman. "I will find you something to eat, and then we will meet him."

* * *

Hem (and Irc) breakfasted lavishly. It was a long time since Hem had enjoyed good, plain Annaren cooking: he ate yeasty bread with lashings of cool, pale butter and honeycomb, a hunk of hard yellow cheese, coddled eggs, cured ham and several exquisite herbed meat pastries. Saliman, who had already eaten, poured himself a mug of ale and watched him eat with amusement dancing in his dark eyes.

"I can't say that your appetite has diminished since we first met, Hem," he said. "Even if much else has changed."

Hem helped himself to another slice of the crusty white loaf that Saliman had wheedled from the baker. "It's not that I don't like Suderain food," he said, with his mouth full. "It's completely delicious. But I think fresh Annaren bread is the best thing in the whole world…"

"There are moments when I agree with you," said Saliman. "But still, the smell of sweet flatbread just out of the oven is the smell of home for me."

By the time Hem had finished eating, the rain had lifted and there was even an expanse of blue sky opening above them. Til Amon didn't seem so dreary on a full stomach, with the pale winter sun sparkling off the puddles, and Hem cheered up as he followed Saliman to the Bardhouse where he would be staying. It belonged, Saliman told him, to Nadal, the First Bard of Til Amon. It was a high, grand building that stood on the edge of the inner circle of the School, opposite the Library and the Meeting Hall. As they crossed the circle, a wide space paved with coloured tiles in the very centre of the School, Hem looked curiously at the people they passed: it seemed strange only to see pale Annarens. For months he had been among the people of the Suderain, black-skinned like Saliman or dark copper like Zelika, and he had become used to it.

He remembered that Karim had said he would be presenting

one of his plays here, but there was no sign of the caravan. It would have been hard to miss, like a fabulous beast in the middle of the circle's austere symmetries. He supposed that the players hadn't yet arrived and, hoping that they hadn't run into any trouble, he followed Saliman through the high wooden doors that led into the Bardhouse and into Nadal's rooms.

Saliman ushered Hem into a pleasant sitting room, in which a fire flickered against the cold at the far end. Like the rooms of most Bards, it was decorated with an eye to both beauty and comfort. The walls were panelled with honey-coloured wood polished to a soft glow, and covered with shelves which held the usual Bardic assortment of books, scrolls, curios and instruments. In the centre, low couches covered in rough-woven silk dyed Thorold blue were arranged around a wide, low table. Soron was seated by the fire, talking earnestly to a tall, fair-haired Bard. They both rose when Hem and Saliman entered, and the Bard, who was, of course, Nadal, greeted them courteously, glancing in surprise at Hem.

"I'm surprised you're out of bed, considering how fevered you were last night," he said.

Hem bowed his head politely. "I think I'm quite tough," he said. "I feel fine this morning, anyway."

"There's nothing wrong with him, judging by his appetite," said Saliman. They sat down with the other two Bards, and his voice became brisk. "Now, Hem, I want you to show Nadal the tuning fork you took from Sharma while you were in Dén Raven."

"Irc found it, really," said Hem. He felt a strange reluctance as he lifted the chain over his head; usually the tuning fork lay forgotten against his skin. He held it in his hand, feeling its weight: it was a simple object, made of brass, but he felt its veiled power as he touched it.

Nadal took the tuning fork curiously, and examined it closely. "It looks like nothing much," he said. "But that is often the way with magical objects. Those runes are very strange. I've never seen the like."

"I have," said Saliman. "As I told you. On Maerad's lyre. They clearly belong together… and the lyre is undoubtedly Dhyllic ware, made in the lost city of Afinil. I have wondered if Nelsor himself might have made these things. He was, after all, a master of scripts; those runes might be his own."

"From what Irc tells us, the Nameless One wore this about his very neck," said Soron. He was looking at the fork askance, as if it still held some trace of the Dark's presence. "And it seems very likely to me that it is something to do with the Spell of Binding that holds Sharma to this earth. And given what Hem has told us about his encounters with the Elidhu, Saliman's guess that all this is deeply to do with the magery of Elementals seems like a good one to me."

Nadal nodded, and handed the tuning fork back to Hem.

Hem quickly put it back on, hiding it beneath his clothes; he felt somehow that it was something that should not be looked at by the naked eye.

"These are deep waters indeed, and it's hard to find our way," said Nadal. "We know too little of the Elementals. For too long have our paths been sundered by mistrust. Your guesses seem good to me, but they are still only guesses."

"I agree, there is too much we don't know," said Saliman. "Nevertheless, these are guesses informed by Knowing. You have not met Maerad… She has an unsettling power, Nadal, that is not Bardic."

"This boy's power is not so conventional, either." Hem caught Nadal's eye; there was an uncomfortable sharpness in his glance. "I felt it as soon as you walked in this room. You speak the Elidhu language, as your sister does?" Hem nodded. "We live in perilous times… How do we know that this power will serve us, and not some other necessity?"

Hem bridled, remembering the immense sadness of the Elidhu Nyanar as he spoke about his poisoned home, the hills of Glandugir that the Nameless One had marred beyond recognition. "The Elidhu serve their own ends," he said. "But they hate the Dark as much as we do. The Nameless One has destroyed their homes, too."

"Yes. Yes, you may well be right." Again Hem found himself subjected to Nadal's keen, searching glance. "Some wisdoms we have held dear as Bards might have to be put aside in this war. Perhaps they have been, indeed, blindnesses. Still, after all this time it seems strange to think of the Elidhu, who allied themselves with the Nameless before the Great Silence, as being on our side."

"It's not about sides," said Hem. He turned to Saliman. "The Elidhu were at Afinil, weren't they?"

Saliman nodded. "Yes, they weren't always distrusted by Bards. And it was only the Winterking and a couple of other renegade Elidhu who helped Sharma..."

"I accept what you say, Saliman," said Nadal. "Still, there are many angles to this war, and they are not less important. We cannot let our hopes hang on such a slender thread. Let's not forget how desperate things are: Norloch has fallen to the Dark without a sword risen in defence. And now we hear that Nelac has been imprisoned by Enkir, and is charged with treachery."

Saliman looked up swiftly, his face anguished. "Alas, I feared that something of the kind might happen when we fled Norloch. But still, I am shocked that he dares to imprison a Bard as greatly loved as Nelac... He must think his arm strong indeed."

"As I told you last night, Enkir has raised soldiers from all over Annar. His garrison is now very strong. And the Schools are still divided. None save the Seven Kingdoms dare to stand openly against him, and some even now believe that he is their best bulwark against the armies of the Dark. The Fall of Turbansk was a great argument for Enkir: he drives with fear, and will use it as a cover for his own ends. And some Schools are already under attack; I heard that the Vale of Innail has been hard-pressed from the mountains in recent weeks, and there is civil war in Lukernil and Rhon, where bandits are roaming freely, by my guess under Enkir's blessing. Alas for Annar!"

"I wonder how closely Enkir works with the Dark," said Soron. "I can't but be surprised that he has sent no army marching on Til Amon; that is what everyone has been expecting."

"We have sent out scouts through Lauchomon, as far as the Il Arunedh Road, and have seen no sign of an army. Yet. Unless he has found a way to make his soldiers invisible, or all our scouts are blind."

"I think Soron is correct," said Saliman. "If an army is already sent from the Suderain, why attack Til Amon himself? Better by far to concentrate his forces on his other enemies."

"It makes it all the more likely, of course, that the Black Army will not pass us," said Nadal. "I am guessing that they hoped to surprise us. That advantage, at least, they have lost; we have been preparing for war since we had the emissary from Norloch, demanding our fealty. I wish I knew what forces are arraigned against us. Not all are human." He glanced at Irc, who had been sitting quietly on Hem's shoulder throughout the conversation. "I have some ravens here, birds of great wisdom, who offered their help; and they can fly more quickly than men can walk. I will hear something of what to expect today, I hope. But I judge that we can hold out against one army. We are protected by the lake on three sides, and our winter stores are deep enough to endure a long siege. I doubt theirs will be. They will get precious little pickings from Amon Fesse; our granaries and storehouses there have all been emptied and brought here, and our people are even now moving within our walls. They do not find us unprepared."

"The best news for us, Nadal, is that we hear that the Nameless One also marches on Car Amdridh," said Soron. "The full force of his fist will not fall on Til Amon."

"True," said Saliman. "He divides his strength and fights on two fronts, and that, I judge, is a risk. All the same, as I saw on the roads outside Dagra, he sends enormous strength out of Dén Raven. He now reveals his full hand. It will not be a small army that moves on you now, Nadal; from here the whole of South Annar is open to him."

"Aye," said Nadal, but his voice was hard. "I do not cling to false hopes. But I would still place my wager on us."

The sun was nearing noon, and Nadal politely invited the three Bards to eat a midday meal with him. Although Hem had but lately finished breakfast, he assented enthusiastically. Saliman made no comment; after all, they had had thin enough pickings for the past few weeks, and no doubt there would be hard times ahead. Then Hem was shown to his room, which was next door to Saliman's on the topmost floor of the Bardhouse. It was a pleasant chamber panelled in the same honey-coloured woods as Nadal's rooms. A fire had been laid and lit shortly before, and there was a comfortable bed piled high with bright cushions in one corner.

When Saliman left, Hem kicked off his boots and curled his naked toes luxuriously in the thick red carpet that covered the stone floor. He felt very content. Then he padded over to the casement and opened his window to let Irc out. Irc leapt out from the sill, eager to play in the sky after a day spent mostly indoors, and Hem watched him idly.

His window overlooked the Inner Circle. From this height, he could see the spiral patterns made by the different-coloured paving stones, grey and black and white. It seemed fairly busy: he saw Librarians in their black robes hurrying out of the Library, a high, imposing building opposite Nadal's Bardhouse, and many other people crossing the Circle, hooded against the cold. Then he lifted his gaze over the slate roofs of the houses of Til Amon, which ran down to the lake. The face of the lake was very still, like a steel mirror. As he watched, a flight of swans landed on the water, flurries of foam leafing high in their wake, and the water's stillness dissolved in a criss-cross maze of ripples. In the distance, faint in the mist, loomed the dark, snow-crowned peaks of the Osidh Am. It was, as Soron had said, a breathtaking sight, and he stayed there for some time, leaning his elbow on the windowsill, breathing in the silence.

Then something caught his eye, moving in one of the streets close to the Circle: a gleam of gold. He leaned out of the window, trying to get a better look. Yes, it was Karim's caravan, pushing up one of the broad thoroughfares that led from the Circle. As he watched, the caravan lumbered into the centre of the square, followed by a stream of people. Hem was amazed. Surely the Bards wouldn't permit them to camp there, right in the middle of the School? Perhaps they were not planning to camp: perhaps they were about to perform a play! As soon as he was sure the caravan had stopped, he summoned Irc, rushed out of his room, and knocked on Saliman's door.

Saliman came to the door draping a robe over his shoulders, and Hem realized that he had roused him from his bed.

"Saliman! Karim's here, with the caravan, in the Circle!" Hem was pink with excitement. "They can't be camping there, surely. Would Nadal let them? Do you think they're doing a play? Can we go and see them?"

"Well, young Hem, if you want to see Karim and the other players, I'm not stopping you," said Saliman. "But you'll have to excuse me; I am a little tired, and would rather take this opportunity, which comes my way seldom, to catch up on some sleep."

Hem's conscience smote him as he saw that Saliman's face was bruised with weariness. No doubt he had been up late with Nadal, and perhaps he had had other duties. "Saliman, I'm sorry…" he said.

Saliman smiled and ruffled his hair. "I forgive you, Hem, even though I was just on the brink of delicious sleep when you dragged me out of it. Nothing can be a greater mark of my love for you… Now boy, go, and leave me to myself."

Hem turned to go, and Saliman called out after him. "Don't forget that we have dinner with Nadal!"

"I won't!" said Hem over his shoulder, and clattered down the stairs.

Karim had halted the caravan in the exact centre of the Circle, and already there was a crowd of interested onlookers. Hem paused at the door of the Bardhouse, momentarily taken aback by the festive air of the gathering: people seemed to be acting as if no danger threatened, no army marched on Til Amon, nothing hung in the balance. For the briefest of moments, a sudden, consuming rage blotted out his excitement at seeing the players. He understood how Soron had felt when they had first seem them, innocently practising in front of the fire as if nothing were wrong. He, Soron and Saliman had lost too much: Soron had lost his lover, Jerika, in the fall of Turbansk, Saliman his city and many of his dearest friends, and Hem … well, Hem had suffered his losses too.

His anger ebbed as swiftly as it had risen; but as it vanished, there flashed into his mind a foul memory from the nightmare march through the Glandugir Hills. He saw, as clearly as if it were now before him, the terror on the face of one of the snouts, the bewitched child soldiers with whom he had marched through the hills, as a monstrous vine wrapped itself around the child's feet and dragged him screaming into the trees. The memory was as vivid as if he were there: he could even smell the damp, sour earth. A wave of sickness rose through his feet. Hem flinched, cowering against the doorpost, his heart hammering in his chest, dazedly telling himself that he was no longer a snout, no longer in that nightmare place, and that he need never return. He almost turned to go back inside, but shook himself sternly. Why shouldn't people enjoy themselves, even if others suffered? Was it entirely a bad thing? Perhaps, in such dark times, it was all the more important…

He stepped out of the door and stumbled, almost falling over. He hadn't realized until that moment that his legs were shaking and that he had broken into a cold sweat. He took a deep breath, decided to ignore his legs, and strode as steadily as he could across the Circle. Impatiently he wriggled his way through to the front of the crowd, so he could get a clear view of what was going on.

Karim, dressed in a long purple robe, was standing on the stage, which had been let down from the side of the caravan. He was in full flight, but it wasn't, as Hem had expected, a speech like that he had performed at their campsite. He was extolling his wares, like any pot seller in the marketplace. Hem was disappointed, but he listened anyway.

"From far Elevé, dear people, we have travelled through wasteland and wilderness to offer you our crafts and our skills," Karim was saying. "We have played to acclaim before in the great Schools of the East, in great cities and in small villages; we have pleased the rich man and the beggar, the Bard and the minstrel; we bring you the great works of the great poets, for your delectation and delight…" And so on. Irc, bored, flew off to explore, and Hem noticed that the crowd was beginning to get a little restive. But Karim was far too experienced a performer not to notice this himself, and gave signs that he was finishing his speech. "And so, at the fourth bell, dear people, and with the blessing of Nadal the First Bard himself, we bring to you one of Lorica's greatest tragedies: the timeless love story of Alibredh and Nalimbar of Jerr-Niken. And now, dear people, I hope to see you then. Bring your friends, your family, tell everyone you know – even people whom you don't know – for this is a rare treat indeed, and seldom played! And now I thank you for your time. Farewell!"

Karim bowed ceremoniously, with many hand flourishes, and vanished behind the red curtains. The show, for the moment, was over. There was some scattered clapping and a hum of conversation, and Hem overheard several people planning to meet up for the performance. It was well-timed: it would still be light, they could come before the evening meal, and by then most people would have finished their day's work.

Hem made his way around to the front of the caravan and patted the horses. He wanted very much to see Hekibel, but suddenly felt unaccountably shy. He was just about to leave when Hekibel herself stepped down from the caravan. She was cloaked and carried a basket, and looked as if she were about to go shopping; but she noticed Hem immediately and greeted him with an open smile. Hem at once lost his shyness, and grinned back.

"I didn't realize you were a Bard," she said. "You look quite different – I almost didn't recognize you."

Hem looked down at his tunic, borrowed from Edadh's house that morning. "It's not mine, I have to give it back," he said.

"But you're a Bard, all the same?" Hem nodded. "And your friends too?" Hem nodded again. Hekibel sighed, as if she regretted something. "I might have known. Ah well. And where's your bird?"

"He went off exploring," said Hem. "He'll be back later. There are some birds here that he hasn't bullied yet."

"He's a bully?"

"Well, not so much a bully as a braggart."

"I have heard tell that Bards can speak to beasts," said Hekibel. "Do you speak to your bird?"

"Yes, Irc and I are friends. He's not really a pet."

There was a short silence, and Hem wondered if he ought to take his leave. "They are all talking here about the Black Army marching on Til Amon," Hekibel said. "So you arrived in time. People here are very busy... And I thank you, too, for warning us... We could have been caught in a horrible situation!"

"But you still came here, to make your play," said Hem.

"Not for long." Hekibel gave Hem a cool look, as if she were sizing him up. "Now, young master, are you idle at this present moment? I need to find a market, and I could do with someone to carry my basket."

Hem politely took her basket, and they began to walk together out of the Circle. "I haven't been here long enough to work out where the market is," he confessed. "In any case, I thought you had lots of food."

"But precious little fresh. Are you coming to see the show this afternoon?"

"Yes," said Hem. "Yes, I'd like to."

"It's the only one we're doing. Karim is very alarmed, and wants to get out of here as soon as we're able. We plan to leave tomorrow. We're hoping to get a good crowd today. Karim fears that otherwise we'll be stuck here, in a besieged city. And for once, I agree with him."

"Saliman and I don't want to be trapped here, either," said Hem. A thought struck him. "Maybe we could travel with you? It might suit us all. Saliman is a great swordsman and we could help protect your caravan – we have ways of staying hidden. And for us, it would be a brilliant disguise... I'm sure Saliman could act, as well..." He had a sudden vision of Saliman on a stage; somehow he knew that he would be a great player.

Hekibel laughed. "Perhaps Saliman might have his own ideas about that," she said. "And what about your friend, Soron?"

"Til Amon is Soron's birth School," said Hem. "He won't be coming with us." He felt a sudden pang: he had travelled with Soron now for many weeks, and he would miss his steady, good-natured company. "Leaving tomorrow? That might suit us too. Do you think Karim would agree? I'll ask Saliman."

Hekibel gave Hem an amused glance. "If Saliman thinks it a good idea, I will try to persuade Karim," she said. "But I somehow doubt that a Bard would be enamoured of the notion of travelling with players. And there's certainly no room in the caravan for two more bodies."

"Oh, we can manage," said Hem. "We've been travelling for weeks now without a caravan, remember." The longer he thought about it, the better his idea seemed to him; and it would be more fun to travel with others, for once. They certainly ate better than he was used to on the road. And he might even get a chance to be a player himself...

Later, after a pleasant hour in the market with Hekibel haggling over fruits and cheeses and vegetables, Hem checked where Irc was (he was, as Hem had guessed, happily boasting to the local birdlife) and returned to the Bardhouse. He was standing uncertainly in the entrance hall, wondering if he should go up to Saliman's room, or whether it would be rude to knock on Nadal's door, when Nadal himself entered the front door, accompanied by two women, both Bards.

"Greetings, Hem," he said. "What are you doing here?"

"I was looking for Saliman," said Hem. "But he might be asleep."

"I think not. We planned to meet here at this time," said Nadal. "You are free to join us, if you will." His colleagues lifted their eyebrows in surprise that a mere boy should be so casually invited to important deliberations, but made no comment. Nadal, catching their exchanged glances, apologized and made introductions: they were two Bards of the First Circle of Til Amon, Mandil and Seonar.

"This is Saliman's student, Hem of Turbansk," he said, and Hem bowed gravely to both women. "From what I have heard, this boy has as much right to be present at this conference as anybody here. More, perhaps."

The women nodded and studied Hem curiously as they passed into Nadal's chambers. Saliman was already there, with not a trace of sleepiness, as were Soron and a couple more Bards. As he greeted them and was introduced to the others, Hem realized he was tired of war councils. How many had he attended in the past months? A year ago, he had never heard of such things. He sat down on one of the couches, next to Saliman, hoping that perhaps he might be able to leave this one without being rude. Nadal had been very courteous, after all, to invite him; but he feared missing the play.

"Hem!" said Saliman, smiling. "Did you find your players?"

"Aye, I did," whispered Hem, as discussion rose around them between the Bards. "Do you think I could leave soon? They are going to do a play at the fourth bell..."

"I'm sure, if you ask respectfully, Nadal will not be in the least put out."

"And I had an idea, Saliman. You know how we need to leave here swiftly? Hekibel told me that they plan to leave tomorrow, because they don't want to get trapped here. Why don't we travel with them? We could pretend to be players, too."

"Hem, we know nothing of these people," said Saliman, frowning. "For all we know, they could be spies of the Dark themselves."

"Hekibel said you'd say something like that," said Hem.

Saliman studied Hem, his lips twitching at the disappointment on the boy's face. "But, on the other hand, it's not such a bad idea, even though it's probably because you are bewitched by the idea of being a player," he said. "In any case, by my calculations we have three or four days in hand, judging by how the army was moving on the road. But hush, Nadal is going to speak. We can talk about this later."

Nadal had heard from his scouts, and his news was bad. The Black Army was, contrary to Saliman's guess, only two days' march from Til Amon. Hem gave Saliman an expressive glance; perhaps they really ought to leave the following day. The Bards began a long and complex discussion about their plans for the School, and Hem began to get a little restive, wondering how he might take his leave. Saliman unexpectedly rescued him.

"Hem and I have an appointment at the fourth bell," he said. "So, regretfully, we must leave. We know the news that affects us, in any case. Soron, we'll see you for the evening meal."

Soron nodded absently. Hem had hardly seen him since they had arrived in Til Amon; already he seemed a little distant, his preoccupations now no longer the same as theirs. Again Hem felt a pang; he had become very fond of Soron. His plain, undemanding kindliness had meant a great deal to Hem when he was lonely in Turbansk.

Hem and Saliman swiftly took their leave and left the room. When the door shut behind them, Saliman breathed out with relief. Hem gave him a surprised glance.

"I don't think I could stand another war conference," Saliman said, unwittingly echoing Hem's earlier thoughts. "I seem to have spent my life at these things. And this is a battle in which, I hope, I will have no part, although my anxieties and hopes lie with Til Amon: if the Black Army can be stopped here, South Annar has a chance."

"So you're coming to see the players with me?" asked Hem.

"Why not?" Saliman grinned. "In any case, I'm curious. What play are they doing?"

"I can't remember. Lorica, I think Karim said…"

"Lorica? With three people? How will they manage? Well, she's always worth hearing. And Karim certainly knows how to speak her work. It's a shame, Hem, that you never saw the players in Turbansk – there were some fine artists there." For a moment a shadow crossed Saliman's face, and Hem knew he was wondering whether those players he knew had survived. Turbansk, even if it rose from the ashes, would never again be the city he had known and loved. They walked on in silence.

They were a little early, but already people were gathered in front of the caravan. The platform was empty, the curtains remained resolutely shut, but the players were lucky with the weather: it was cold but clear, and the wind had dropped entirely. Saliman found a place near the front and sent Hem up to their chambers for cushions. "I don't feel like standing," he said. "And it will be most uncomfortable if we sit on the stone. I'll guard this place."

Hem grinned and ran off, returning shortly afterwards with fat cushions for both of them. They sat down and made themselves comfortable, and Hem looked around curiously at the gathering crowd. It was very mixed indeed, and included people of all ages, town-dwellers and farmers, Bards and artisans, and many children. Whole families arrived, armed with baskets of food and drink and blankets and cushions, and an excited hum of talk rose in the Circle. Word had clearly spread through all Til Amon.

"Hekibel said they were hoping for a lot of people," said Hem.

"Perhaps everyone here feels like we do," said Saliman.

"That they need a respite from talk of war. The Light knows, things will be grim enough from now on…"

Hem waited, burning with impatience. The fourth bell sounded from the Library tower, and still the curtains remained unparted. The caravan looked as if no one was inside. Then, for no reason that Hem could trace, a silence fell over the crowd, a feeling of pleasurable expectation. Hem looked around – what had they seen that he hadn't? – and was just turning to remark to Saliman, when he saw a hand on the curtain, about to draw it back. He somehow knew it was Karim's hand from the way he grasped the material, flexing his fingers with just a trace of exaggeration. Hem held his breath, and Karim slowly emerged onto the stage. His face was painted so that his eyebrows were very black, his eyes outlined with kohl, and his skin very white. The audience cheered, and Karim gave one of his bows with a great flourish, and cleared his throat. The crowd instantly fell silent again.

"Good people of Til Amon," he said, his voice ringing easily over the Circle. "We are proud and honoured today to present to you the tale of Alibredh and Nalimbar, as it fell from the immortal pen of Lorica, the great Bard of Turbansk."

There was more cheering, and Karim held up his hand for silence. "I thank you, good people, I thank you. I ask you to take particular note that we will be passing around a basket when we are finished: if we have brought you any pleasure, I ask humbly that you donate whatever coin you can afford, to facilitate our humble art. Now, with no further ado, we present Alibredh and Nalimbar!"

As he announced the play, Marich and Hekibel came from behind the curtains. Their faces too were painted and they wore long, blue robes, signifying their youth and nobility. Hekibel launched into the opening speech, in which Alibredh tells of her first sight of Nalimbar, the son of a family with which her own family is in a bitter feud, and of her instant love for him. Hem was spellbound. He followed the tale with breathless interest: the evil Horas (played by Karim), the rich suitor determined to marry Alibredh against her wishes in order to gain her inheritance; the secret trysts between the lovers and their doomed attempt to run away; the terrible fight between Nalimbar and Horas, in which Nalimbar is tricked and suffers a mortal wound and dies in Alibredh's arms.

Hem was fascinated by the players' ability to make him believe in what they were doing, even though it was perfectly clear that they were pretending. Each player acted several roles, signifying the change by donning a new robe or a crown or a different hat. Bards, he thought, would have just used glimmer-spells to become the people they acted, but this illusion seemed to him somehow much more profound: he was enchanted by the art of the actors' voices and bodies and the beauty of the language they spoke. When, in the final speech, Alibredh stabbed herself with her lover's dagger and fell across his corpse, Hem's face was wet with tears; somehow all the sadnesses in his own life flowered in his breast and found expression in Hekibel's poignant gestures, her beautiful, tragic words.

There was a short silence, a kind of sigh, as if everyone had been holding their breath, and then the crowd burst into wild applause. Hem cheered with everyone else, and then turned to Saliman, anxiously asking him what he thought. Saliman had watched the whole play with complete attention, not moving a muscle, and Hem wasn't sure whether he had enjoyed it or not.

"They are very good," said Saliman. "Very good indeed. I confess, I am surprised: I did not expect their work to be of that quality. You wouldn't see acting better than that even in the courts of Turbansk."

Hem felt obscurely relieved and pleased, as if he were

somehow responsible for the performance himself. At that point, Hekibel appeared with the basket, and Saliman, smiling up at her, made a generous donation.

"Thank you," he said. "That was fine indeed!"

To Hem's surprise, Hekibel blushed. "Thank you," she said. "I didn't expect that you would come."

"Why not? It is a beautiful play, and you did it great justice. Is it possible that I could offer you all some wine after you have finished here?"

Hekibel blushed again. Hem looked at her narrowly: she didn't seem the blushing type to him. "It would be an honour, kind sir," said Hekibel, staving off her embarrassment with playfulness. "I will ask Karim and Marich if they would be agreeable. We shouldn't be too long here." She smiled again, and passed on. The basket, Hem noticed, was getting very full.

"Are you going to ask if we can travel with them?" asked Hem.

"Perhaps," said Saliman. For some reason, his face was shadowed. "It may be that Karim will not like the idea. Perhaps, Hem, while we're waiting, you could take these cushions back where they belong."

Saliman had arranged to meet Soron that evening at a tavern that Soron claimed had the best onion soup he had ever tasted. "Miraculous, Saliman!" he had said. "It will make your palate sing for joy. You cannot leave Til Amon without tasting it!"

"Perhaps the tavern has changed hands since last you were here," said Saliman, smiling.

"I have already asked. They have the same cook still. It is famous throughout the Lauchomon, this tavern..."

"I presume they make more than soup?"

"Yes, they have a few dishes, all justly admired," said Soron.

"But the soup is the queen of them all. I shall never forgive you if do not try it."

"That is a serious business, then," said Saliman gravely. "I will, of course, have soup for my dinner. I only fear that the wine will not match the incomparable cuisine. You know that I could never forgive such a solecism, myself."

Soron grinned, and gave Saliman instructions on how to find the tavern. It wasn't far from the Circle, in a little side street that ran off one of the main thoroughfares of the School: a comfortable, friendly building, with accommodation upstairs and a motley collection of tables and chairs downstairs, gleaming warmly in the light of a huge open fire. Irc, who was always prompt when dinner was in the air, swooped down onto Hem's shoulder as they walked there.

Where have you been? asked Hem.

I've been busy with important business, said Irc. *Are we eating? I am hungry.*

Hem grinned. *Yes, if they let rude birds like you into the tavern. So you behave.*

Irc pulled Hem's hair, but otherwise seemed content to ride quietly on his shoulder.

When Saliman and Hem entered with the players in tow it was almost empty; the people of Til Amon tended to dine late. Soron was not due for at least an hour. The few people there gazed curiously at Irc, and then turned back to their drinks. Hem and the others sat down and Saliman cross-examined the proprietor, a rotund, short man called Emil, on the contents of his cellars, at last ordering a jug of rich Turbanskian wine.

"A good choice, my Lord," said Emil, as he placed the jug and some goblets on their table. "But of course you would be familiar with the wines of that region. Alas, for the moment our stocks are limited, and it looks unlikely that we will have more in the near future."

"Alas, indeed," said Saliman. "But that is not the least of our sorrows."

"You're not wrong there," said Emil soberly. "And it seems troubles follow hard on the heels of the last."

"But while we can drink such wines, all is not lost," said Saliman, pouring out the wine. "You will have some yourself?"

"I thank you, but it is early yet and I must attend to the kitchen," said Emil. "Else you might have cause for complaint, which would grieve me deeply." He departed smartly, and Saliman lifted his goblet.

"I drink to the Light!" he said. "May it bless us all!"

Hem was not the only one taken aback by the unexpected seriousness of Saliman's toast, but he sipped obediently. Karim, he noticed, adopted an expression of extreme gravity, and sipped as if he were drinking from a sacred chalice. Hem wondered if he ever behaved like a normal human being; divested of the glamour of their roles, Marich and Hekibel seemed quite ordinary, jesting together in the afterglow of their performances, but Karim still seemed to be on stage. Perhaps, thought Hem, he was performing for Saliman; certainly his manner had changed since he had realized that Saliman was a Bard and not merely a ragged traveller.

They spoke for a time about the performance, until Irc became impatient and demanded food. Emil politely brought a small bowl of raw minced goat meat over to their table, which Irc gobbled down. The players amused themselves by feeding Irc by hand, and he played up to their laughter, bobbing up and down on the table like a clown. At last Irc was stuffed full, and perched himself sleepily on Hem's shoulder, crooning with pleasure as Hem stroked his neck.

Saliman then began to ask questions about the troupe's plans. They were leaving, as Hekibel had said, the following morning, as early as possible.

"I fear being caught in a war that does not concern us," said Karim, frowning. "We hope that further north we will find some safer havens."

"I don't blame you for not wanting to be caught in a siege," Saliman answered. "Myself, I've had my lifetime's worth of sieges already. But I fear that you are misled if you think you will find anywhere in Annar that is at peace. Sadly, this war concerns everyone, whether they will or no."

"Aye, but all the same, I would have nothing to do with it." Karim's bottom lip was pushed out aggressively, as if he felt that Saliman was recruiting him into battle.

"Saliman was not saying that we should stay and fight," said Hekibel, laughing. "Merely that we will be lucky if we can avoid being affected by this war."

"Indeed," said Saliman. "Hem and I are thinking that we must leave tomorrow as well. Like you, we have no wish to be trapped in Til Amon, and we wish to travel north through Annar." Hem glanced across at Saliman, a little bud of excitement blossoming in his chest, and Saliman dropped him a sly wink. "What say we travel together for a time? Hem and I wish to travel as unseen as possible, and it seems to us that we could pass as members of your troupe. For our part, we could offer protection. We have arts of concealment and combat that could keep you safer than if you travelled alone."

Marich looked up, his face alight. "Karim, that's an excellent idea!" he said. "I confess, I am very worried about being attacked. The talk here is of civil war in Annar – and that there are bands of brigands or rogue soldiers roaming the countryside, robbing and killing at will. It has almost made me think we might be safer here! But a Bard can stop a bunch of thieves with a wave of his hand!"

Saliman smiled. "Not quite. Though it's true we have ways of defending ourselves that can be very useful in a pinch."

"There's no extra room in the caravan," said Hekibel. "We're a tight fit as it is."

"As far as sleeping arrangements, Hem and I know how to make shift for ourselves," said Saliman. "And of course we would bring our own supplies, although I'd be very grateful if we could store them in the caravan. Well, Karim, what you do think?"

Karim drew his brows together in an attitude of deep contemplation. The others watched him breathlessly. "But," he said at last, "can you *act*?"

"Hem has no skills in that area," said Saliman, deadpan. "I spent some time with players in Turbansk, and have performed in some few works."

"Another actor would be very useful. And a boy – even if he can't speak, well, he can be a messenger, a herald, things like that. Those parts are a constant trouble for us. Yes, yes, I can see it working…"

Hem looked at Hekibel, his face alive with excitement.

"Perhaps," she said, smiling at his transparent joy, "we could even find a part for Irc!"

The conversations turned to practicalities – what Hem and Saliman should bring, where they should meet, what time they should leave, their direction. Then, although Saliman invited them to stay for a meal, the players took their leave, explaining they had a prior arrangement to dine.

"I'd be grateful for your discretion," said Saliman, as the players stood to go. "These are difficult times, and the fewer people who know my plans, the happier I shall be."

"Your secrets are safe with us," said Karim, making a deep bow. "We shall be as silent as stone."

"It would be better so for all of us," said Saliman. There was a significance in his tone which made Hem glance at him, and Karim nodded gravely.

Hem watched them leave, and then turned to Saliman. "I didn't know that you would do that!" he said.

"Neither did I, Hem. But why not let our paths run together for a time? Your mad idea is not as mad as it sounds. I worry a little about loose tongues – I do not know these people – but it might be easier to travel unseen with players than on our own."

"I trust them," said Hem. "Well, I trust Hekibel, anyway. And it would make a change…"

"It certainly would." Saliman grinned. "Well, you may get your wish, Hem, and be a player, after all."

Shortly afterwards, Soron entered, his face lighting up as he spotted Hem and Saliman at the far end of the room. The tavern was now getting quite crowded, and he wove his way across the room, sat down wearily, poured himself some wine and took an appreciative sip. "Ah, from the vines of the Jiela Hills, surely?" he said. "This is a good vintage: I haven't tasted this for too long. Well, I have kept my part of the bargain, Saliman, and now it's your turn."

"Onion soup it is," said Saliman, smiling. "Hem, what about you?"

"I wouldn't dare order anything else," said Hem. "Anyway, I'm very hungry."

"That's settled, then," said Soron, and waved Emil over, ordering another jug of wine as well as their meals. The soup was every bit as good as Soron had promised; it was fragrant and thick, topped with a layer of delicious melted cheese, and Hem ate slowly for once, savouring its delicate flavours. Soron ate his almost with reverence. "A masterpiece!" he said, wiping his mouth. "And a fit way to bless our parting, for I guess that our ways will now diverge. Am I right in thinking you'll be leaving tomorrow? There is not a lot of time."

"Yes," said Saliman. "Early in the morning."

"Aye. I can't say I'm not sorry to lose your company, Saliman. And we could do with your help here. I do not deceive myself that we're in for a hard battle."

"I believe so. Nadal is correct, I think – I hope – to believe that Til Amon can hold out against the Black Army; but we have both seen what he is up against, and he has not."

Soron gazed down at the table. "I should not like to see Til Amon sacked, as Turbansk was," he said soberly. "And I fear it, Saliman, I fear it very much. So much light and beauty and love in peril, in so many places. And you two not least; I am loath to see you go, although I know you must leave, and that none of us are safe anywhere while the world turns as it does."

Saliman did not speak, but clasped Soron's hand. Soron looked up, and Hem was startled to see tears brimming in his eyes. Hem sat silently, not knowing what to say, unable to think of anything that would comfort Soron or himself.

"Ah," Soron said impatiently, wiping his eyes. "This is not the time for tears."

"If this is not the time for tears, I know not what is," said Saliman, smiling crookedly. "I will miss you, my friend."

"And I you. I swear, when all this is over, we will share a jug of wine together."

"I hold that thought. We will find each other again, Soron."

Shortly afterwards, they made their way back to the Bardhouse through the streets of Til Amon. It was a dark night: the sky was clouding over, and the wind had a smell of rain. None of them spoke, and Hem thought their footsteps echoing back from the walls was the saddest sound he had ever heard. When they reached the door of the Bardhouse, Irc jumped onto Soron's forearm. He had never done that before, and Hem looked at him in surprise; Irc's idea of the future was a little hard to gauge, and Hem wasn't sure if Irc understood that they would be leaving Soron behind when they left Til Amon.

Irc rubbed his head against Soron's chest. *I miss you*, he said.

I'll miss you too, you rogue, said Soron fondly. *I count on you to look after Hem. And I'll see you again.*

Irc gently pecked Soron's nose. *He would be lost if I did not. I will care for him well.*

Hem did not weep when he farewelled Soron. He held him close for a long time, wishing he had the words for what he felt. But when he lay in the dark privacy of his chamber, he cried for a long time.

Saliman woke him well before light the following morning. Hem was already packed, and simply had to drag on his clothes. He called Irc and stood a moment in the door of his chamber, looking back: how long would it be before he slept in a bed again?

"I haven't thanked Nadal, or said goodbye," he said, as he and Saliman made their way downstairs. Saliman had a package slung on his back, which turned out to be a silk tent big enough to sleep two people. It was cunningly waterproofed, very light to carry and would be easy to put up, and should keep in a surprising amount of heat.

"I made your courtesies for you last night," said Saliman, as they went downstairs. "I have been busy." They stopped at the Bardhouse kitchen, where a Bard Hem didn't know was poking the fire, scratching sleep-ruffled hair; he greeted Saliman cordially and gave them some food supplies. Saliman hefted the heaviest pack, and gave the other to Hem; then they waved farewell and went out into the empty streets, where white Bard lamps threw a pale light over the stone flags. Hem told Irc to fly, because he was too heavy to carry with everything else, and he flapped slowly behind them.

The caravan was camped near the outer wall of Til Amon, and it took a while to walk there. Their supplies seemed very heavy to Hem by the time they arrived, and he was glad to put them down. The dog barked wildly, shattering the dawn silence, but quieted at once at Saliman's word and started sniffing eagerly at his feet, while Irc made superior squawking noises from the safety of Hem's shoulder, where he had landed the instant Hem had put down his heavy pack.

Karim, Marich and Hekibel were already preparing the horses, two mares called Usha and Minna, and greeted them cheerfully. Hem began to perk up, feeling the gloom lift from his breast: his boyish love of adventure was beginning to assert itself. Under Hekibel's instructions, Saliman stowed their food supplies in the caravan, and then waited until the players were ready to move. It didn't take long; they were clearly well practised at their routine. There was enough space at the front for two people to sit with whoever was driving, while the others either sat inside or walked, and Hekibel, who was taking the reins, suggested Hem sit with her.

"Perhaps I could learn how to drive the horses?" said Hem eagerly, as he took his place beside her.

"Perhaps you could," said Hekibel. "Have you driven a caravan before?"

"No," said Hem. "The Pilanel wouldn't let me, when I last travelled this way. But I'd like to try."

Hekibel flicked the reins, and the horses started into a shambling trot, with the dog running alongside. The caravan creaked beneath them and began to move, its wheels very loud on the road. The gates were not far, and they passed through them quickly, lifting a hand to the weary-eyed soldiers now at the end of their night watch who opened them to let the caravan through.

"This is more fun than walking!" Hem said.

"Well," said Hekibel. "You get a view. But we've got a way to go yet. See how you feel at the end of the day!"

The eastern sky was now beginning to lighten, revealing a

green landscape shrouded by mist and low clouds. They journeyed northwards through the Fesse of Til Amon, undulating
country dotted by small woods and prosperous farms. These
were mostly deserted now, their inhabitants taking refuge in the
School, but this early in the morning they all looked very peaceful. A light rain began to fall, and the horses snorted and flicked
their tails and pushed on. The caravan rumbled along the road,
swaying slightly. Hem watched the colours of the landscape
deepen and fill as the sun rose, and his heart lifted with joy.

THE WEIGHT OF
THE WORLD

Down came the hail, a frosty flail,
    Down fell the icy rain.
The torches flared with desperate light
And savage lightning stabbed the night
    Which screamed like a soul in pain.

His black brow bound with clouds around
    The Landrost raised his hand:
"Be they so fair and strong and tall,
I'll crush these walls and golden halls
    And I will rule this land!"

Their hearts aflame, defenders came
    With staff and sword and bow
And bravely on the walls arrayed,
Where Innail's maid stood unafraid
    Before her stormy foe.

"Not all your might gives you the right
    In our fair streets to tread,
And you'll not take this fearless town
For I'll cast down your iron crown
    Or die," the lady said.

From *The Ballad of the Maid of Innail*, Anon

VII

THE MAID OF INNAIL

MAERAD thought the cold would never leave her. It seemed to have entered her very marrow: her bones felt as if they were made of ice. She crouched by the fire in the Watch House, a blanket around her shoulders, slowly spooning down a plate of hot stew. Cadvan watched her anxiously, as a mother watches a child who has passed the crisis of a deathly illness.

It was mid-afternoon, not long since the Landrost had almost crushed her, and she still felt deeply shaken. It had been a close call, perhaps the closest she had ever had, and the aftershocks ran through her in fits of shivering.

The attacks on Innail had halted altogether when Maerad had collapsed, and after a while even the storm outside Innail had begun to calm. The defenders could now see some distance over the walls, although the light was still dim, darkening towards an early evening beneath louring clouds. Below milled an army of perhaps two or three thousand mountain men, grouped out of bowshot. They looked cold and wet, and their only shelter was some skin huts; but there was that about them that suggested grim determination. There was no sign of the wers, although the sense of their menacing presence wasn't far away.

When it was clear they had won a respite, Malgorn had called the captains into the Watch House for a brief council.

"They wait for nightfall, when the wers are at their strongest," Indik said to the exhausted Bards. "And there is no moon tonight... But we have beaten back the first onslaught. Chiefly thanks, I believe, to Maerad." He saluted her with his sword, and the other Bards followed suit.

"And what do you think will happen at nightfall?" asked Malgorn.

"I don't know," Indik said simply. "All I know is, whatever it is, we won't like it. We have not enough fighters to choose to attack them, and so we await the Landrost's pleasure; for the moment, I think, we have no choice." He looked briefly across at Maerad again, a cool glance, assessing her; shivering by the fire, she looked like a fragile child. "And we might as well rest and gather our strength while we can."

"Such as it is," said Malgorn. "I've ordered a guard on all the walls, and as many rest as can be spared from that. There are a lot of injuries..."

"How many dead?" asked Silvia.

"Two score, by the latest count," said Malgorn. "Of those, twelve were Bards. I just heard that Irina died of her injuries. "

There was a brief, blank silence.

"Two score," said Indik at last, sighing heavily. "The Landrost can blink at losing ten times that number, but for us, each death counts. There are not enough of us... And the assault has not even begun, I fear. On the other hand, I do not believe that this is a battle that will be won on strength of arms..."

The Bards were silent again. There didn't, in truth, seem anything to say. Their situation was clear: they were heavily outnumbered by a formidable foe that could summon forces that only Maerad had even a hope of understanding. Some Bards looked doubtfully at the frail figure by the fire, wondering if they had any hope at all.

Malgorn asked Cadvan to remain in the Watch House and keep in mindtouch with the Bards posted around the walls of the School. Then all the Bards departed, saluting Maerad as they left, to take care of various urgent duties, or simply to sleep while they could. Maerad's head was bowed and she did not even see this gesture of respect, until Silvia bent down and embraced her, kissing her forehead. After they had gone, the room seemed very quiet.

Maerad wondered what use she could possibly be to Innail now. She hadn't been frightened before; the battle had seemed no worse than other terrors she had already faced, and she had thought herself toughened, inured to them. But now she was terrified. When she thought about the moment the Landrost had perceived her, and what had followed, an abyss opened inside her. It was more than a fear of death, although that was part of it. What frightened her more than anything was how lost she had been, the dizzying infinity of the space that had opened within her. It was far stranger than the loss of self she felt when she transformed into a wolf; that was something deep inside her, whereas this seemed to be far outside, an immeasurable distance... She tried, stumblingly, to put it in words for Cadvan, and he nodded, his eyes dark.

"Maerad, the universe is endless," he said, staring into the fire. "It is a thing that people find hard to even begin to comprehend. How can anything go on and on for ever? How can there be no point where it all finishes? And yet it does not ... and I suppose you are one of the few who has had, as it were, a personal experience of that..."

Maerad shuddered. "It was all – black. And empty. I can't explain. It was so big that distance and time meant nothing, nothing at all."

"There's an old story from Lanorial about a king who was speaking to a Bard who visited his court," said Cadvan. "And the king asked the Bard what a human life was. And the Bard said: imagine that it is night outside your hall, and a swallow swoops through the window of your court, Lord, and out of

the opposite window. For the briefest moment, for an eyeblink,
it flies through the light; then all again is darkness. Life is that
brief moment of light, no more, no less."

Maerad sat in silence for a time, brooding. "It was kind of
like that," she said. "That huge darkness. Only even a swallow's flight is not brief enough ... there wasn't even a memory
of light. I was almost nothing at all. I don't know how I came
back."

"The important thing is that you did come back."

"It's because you called me, isn't it?"

Cadvan hesitated. "I think so," he said. "At least, I know I
called you, and perhaps that is what you heard."

"It was you." Maerad looked up at Cadvan, but his face was
averted. "How did you know how to find me?"

"I didn't know." He was silent again. "I thought that I had
lost you."

Maerad couldn't see the expression on Cadvan's face, but
her heart gave a little leap at his words. Once she had feared
that Cadvan valued her only for what she represented as the
One who, so the prophecies said, was the key to the Nameless
One's defeat. She knew now that he valued her for herself, as a
friend; but lately he had said things that seemed to mean more.
The thought confused and alarmed her, and she pushed it away.
Of course she and Cadvan were dear to each other: that was all
he meant.

Neither of them mentioned Arkan, the Winterking, although
the thought of him stood between them, a dark and troubling
turbulence. They had seldom spoken about him since Maerad
and Cadvan had reunited in Pellinor. She didn't know how to
begin to speak of her feelings for Arkan. Sometimes – most of
the time – they seemed completely reasonless, the foolish infat-
uation of a stupid girl, and she was ashamed of herself. And
yet ... what was it that made her heart lift at the thought of his

voice? She hated the Winterking: he had murdered Dharin, and because of him she had lost her fingers. And yet...

Maerad shook her head impatiently. She was too exhausted to think, but she had to; the Winterking's presence made everything more complicated. He knew, she thought with a strange mixture of terror, despair and excitement, where she was. Perhaps he wasn't far from here at all. The Landrost was one thing, the Winterking quite another. And now she owed Arkan a debt: he had saved her life.

Staring into the fire, she tried to think through her feelings. Why was she so terrified now? Everything was exactly as frightening as it had been when they had first seen the storm clouds over Innail. But now she felt that her fear was paralysing, draining her of all her will. She remembered what Cadvan had told her once about the wers: their worst weapon is fear... Yes, the Landrost was frightening; yes, that moment when he had nearly crushed her into nothing was terrifying. But she had survived, all the same; and she knew, in some cold, inner part of herself, that she had power enough to challenge the Landrost, if only she knew how to use it, if only she weren't so exhausted. This fear was something else.

It must be the Winterking. She literally did not know what she felt, or what she might do if, by some strange chance, he should appear in Innail. How could he? He had told her himself of the pain of his banishment from Arkanda, of how the Elidhu were tied to their place, how place was their being, in some crucial way she didn't understand. But on the other hand, the Winterking had been at Afinil, so he could leave the mountains if he wished. And if he were here, she had no doubt it would be for his own reasons: he would want to recapture her, to take her back to his Ice Palace. And she knew that part of her yearned to go with him. No matter that he coldly wished to use her as a pawn for his own purposes;

even the knowledge of that made it no easier to turn away
from his voice.

She wished she could read the alliances and interests of the
Elementals, but they were too unpredictable. They served neither Dark nor Light, but their own ends. Ardina had helped
Maerad, had even saved her life; but Ardina had her own
inscrutable goals, which Maerad did not understand. Even the
Landrost could not be wholly the pawn of the Nameless One,
however deeply he moved in his shadow. Obviously the Elidhu
wanted the Treesong, and because of that, they were interested
in Maerad: the runes were not enough in themselves, they
somehow had to be undone. As the Winterking had scornfully
told her, the Treesong was a song, it had to be played. And it
had to be played by Maerad, who had no music to play it by,
and who did not understand anything.

She sighed deeply. Her ruminations always seemed to return
to the same place: that she didn't know what she was doing,
and that everything, all the same, seemed to depend on her. She
felt very small and stupid; she didn't know how she would not
disappoint all the hopes in her. And at the same time, she felt a
small stab of anger: why her?

She finished the last of her stew and stood up shakily to
put the empty plate on the table. "I'm deathly tired," she said,
turning to Cadvan. "Even the medhyl doesn't help much. If the
Landrost decided to strike now, I'd be as much use as a piece of
wet string."

Cadvan studied her face. "You're a slightly better colour," he
said. "Before, you looked as if you had no blood in you at all."
He hesitated, and then asked if she felt capable of feeling out
the Landrost again.

"I do not ask you to do anything that might put you in the
same danger in which you were before," he said. "But at the
same time…"

"I know." Maerad looked up at Cadvan, pushing her hair back from her face. "I know you have to ask, Cadvan. I just can't now, but maybe in a little while."

Night stole over Innail. The sun was so shrouded in thick clouds that the transition was imperceptible: the shadows simply deepened and deepened until the darkness seemed almost a solid thing. As the temperature dropped in the late afternoon, a heavy fog began to roll down from the mountains in slow waves. Indik watched in consternation. He did not think the weatherwards would keep the fog out: storm was one thing, mist another.

He sent out a warning to the defenders on the far wall, who would not have seen the fog, and briefly thought of contacting Maerad, to see if she could tell whether the mist was of the Landrost's making. Then he thought better of it. The truth was that Indik had been shocked by Maerad's state earlier, and had pulled himself up short: it did not seem right, it hurt his warrior pride, to be depending so heavily for victory against such a fearsome foe on a mere slip of a girl, however astonishing her abilities might be. Such a creature, barely out of childhood, ought to be looking to Indik for protection, not the other way around ... and yet, what choice did they have?

As Indik stolidly kept watch, the fog rolled over the foothills of the mountain and began to spread towards Innail. The air was very still, magnifying a sense of growing tension. On either side of the wall, every sound had an unnatural clarity: Indik could hear the soldiers nearby talking softly or stamping their feet in the cold, the movement of the men outside Innail as they lit fires and made camp, a dog barking in the distance, the irregular clink of metal, footsteps ringing on the stone roads. Then, with a surprising swiftness, the fog reached Innail, covering everything like a white sea. All sound was instantly muffled and distorted and he could no longer tell its direction.

Indik cursed softly; it was impossible to see ten spans in front of his nose. Below him, the fires lit by the mountain men had become rosy blurs in the darkness. He turned around and stared down across the streets of Innail; vague shapes of buildings loomed through the murk, marked by pale blooms of light where Bardic lamps illuminated the streets, but otherwise he could see nothing. Indik's warrior senses prickled: he did not trust this quiet. He sharpened his hearing, and mindtouched Cadvan.

Yes? said Cadvan at once.

How is Maerad?

Indik could feel the doubt in Cadvan's mind, and waited.

She is somewhat better than before, Cadvan said at last.

Could you ask her if she can tell if this mist is of the Landrost's making?

There was another pause as Cadvan turned his mind towards Maerad, shutting Indik out. Indik continued to stare out into the blackness, his every sense alert. Not a star, not a moon, he thought. Tonight will be the blackest of black nights…

Cadvan's voice cut in on his musing. *She says it is hard to tell,* said Cadvan. *She thinks that it is likely of his summoning. I do not think it is natural weather, myself. And she thinks the Landrost is very close, by the gates.*

Indik thought some more, and then asked for Cadvan's frank opinion: would Maerad be capable of helping in the battle against the Landrost, or had she already done too much?

She believes she can help, said Cadvan. *Although she can't promise anything. She will do her best.*

Indik thanked Cadvan, and returned to his brooding. He did not doubt that Maerad would do her best. He would have given much to know, however, what that best was.

*   *   *

The night wore on, hour after slow hour, and still nothing happened, except that it grew colder. The fog had covered everything in a freezing dew, and the captains keeping their interminable watch on the walls rotated their guards to relieve them of the damp, numbing cold, the endless staring into thick darkness. The tension over Innail increased until it began to be an intolerable force in itself.

In the Watch House, there was constant coming and going as Bards returned from the walls to warm themselves before the fire. Maerad stopped shivering and began to feel warmth stealing through her body at last. Malgorn returned from the western wall, where he had been checking the defences and bringing some of them to the gates, where the mountain men were mostly gathered.

"It's hard to know how many is enough," he said, pouring himself some wine. "I suspect that when the attack comes, the wers might be used where we are weakest. At least this fog covers our own movements as well as the Landrost's." He drank the wine in one draught, and sighed. "Anyway, so far as I can judge, which isn't far at all, we are as poised as we can be against attack. The wards are holding strongly, and aside from the bitter cold, all is presently well. I just wish we knew what to expect."

"Yes, it's the not knowing that's worst," said Maerad.

"Well, Maerad, you know that any help you can offer in that direction will be most gratefully received," said Malgorn. "Don't look at me like that, Cadvan, you know it's the truth. Maerad is as endangered as any of us here. And she's not looking quite as white as she did."

Cadvan looked across to Maerad, and she met his gaze. "Of course Malgorn's right," she said. "And no, I don't feel quite so bad." Not, she thought privately, that she felt especially good either.

Cadvan made no comment, and he and Malgorn began to chat idly, talking of things that had nothing to do with the present crisis, jesting to break the tension, and Maerad found herself laughing with them. Maybe she felt all right, after all.

Even so, when Cadvan turned to her and relayed Indik's question about the fog, she wanted to refuse. It would be easy to claim that she needed more time... She quailed before the thought of attempting to feel out the Landrost: she feared especially how it would expose her to the Winterking, who could trace her presence with an alarming precision. She longed to remain as she was, shielded inside her own skull, untouched by the larger forces that bent their malignant consciousness now on Innail.

Instead, she sat up, casting off the blanket she had been clutching around her shoulders. She shut her eyes, questing through her own inner darkness towards the strange, intangible world of feeling where her magery held its power. She moved warily: she did not want to be seen. It was possible that the Landrost thought he had succeeded in destroying her and would not expect her to return, but it was equally possible that he would be especially vigilant.

The Landrost, she felt at once, was close: very close. His presence clotted her whole being with dread, and she almost retreated altogether. She stilled herself, making herself as small as possible. Then, with infinite caution, she sent out some tendrils of awareness. There was no reaction, and she extended them further, ready to snap back at any moment if she needed to.

She couldn't read the Landrost's intent at all. She only sensed a huge heaviness, a gathering sense of awful gravity, but nothing seemed to be actually moving. Puzzled, she brought herself back to the Watch House, where Cadvan was waiting gravely.

"He's there," she said. "By the gate, I think. I don't know

what he's doing. He could have called the fog, but then again, it might have just happened by itself."

Cadvan nodded and relayed the message to Indik. Maerad stood up and found her legs were no longer shaking. Good, she thought. I'm all right. She walked to the table and poured herself a small glass of medhyl. Its herbed tang in her mouth was like the shock of very cold water, and she felt its virtue spread through her body, lifting the worst of her weariness. She poured another, and wiped her mouth.

"I'd feel clearer outside," she said.

"It's very cold out there," said Malgorn. "A strange sort of cold, too. It's a damp cold, and there's no ice. But it feels much colder than that, as if everything ought to be frozen, a kind of dead cold. It doesn't make a lot of sense."

"A *dead* cold?" said Maerad. A sudden intuition made her feel sick with foreboding.

"Just a turn of phrase..." said Malgorn. Then he saw the look on Maerad's face. "What are you thinking?"

"I don't know..." Maerad hunted for words. "The Landrost is doing nothing. He's just ... gathering ... something ... but what is he gathering? I mean, even as we wait, perhaps ... perhaps for what he's doing now, he doesn't have to do anything..."

"Maerad, you're making no sense at all," said Cadvan.

"I know..." Maerad said despairingly. "Can we go outside?"

"Shall I come with you?"

"Please come with me. Hurry."

Cadvan grabbed the blanket that Maerad had thrown to the floor and put it around her shoulders, and they left the Watch House almost at a run, heading for the palisade by the gates. When they left the shelter of the Watch House, the cold hit like a physical blow; Maerad felt her face turn numb almost at once, and her foreboding increased to a sense of panic. She wrapped the blanket around her head like a shawl as she ran.

The presence of the Landrost was so heavy it made her feel nauseous; he was in the very air, thick, cold, implacable...

It feels as if it's well below freezing, said Cadvan into her mind. *But there's no ice.*

No... said Maerad. *I don't think it's that sort of cold.*

When they reached the palisade, Maerad glanced around at the soldiers. Here they were mostly Bards, some standing still, gazing out into the formless darkness, others stamping their feet or walking up and down to keep the blood moving through their bodies. A brazier was lit, but it gave off no heat. Those who were still made Maerad's heart miss a beat.

"Everyone move!" she shouted. Her voice didn't carry far, muffled by the fog, and a few Bards turned to look at her curiously. "Everyone move! Cadvan, make everyone move! Tell Indik to order everyone..."

"Move where?" asked Cadvan.

"Not anywhere; just get them to move!" Maerad ran up to a Bard who was leaning against the wall, looking through an embrasure, and touched her shoulder. She made no response, and in a fury of impatience, Maerad shook her arm, shouting at her. To her horror, the Bard slipped heavily against the wall and then toppled stiff as a log down to the ground, her armour clattering against the stone. Maerad knelt next to her, shaking her, slapping the woman's face, which was deathly pale in the flickering torchlight, her open eyes glittering like frost.

Indik spoke over Maerad's shoulder, making her jump. "She's dead, I think," he said. "Frozen where she stood... I'll call a healer."

Maerad groaned, feeling chill tears running down her cheeks, and shook the woman again. She had a vision of soldiers lining the walls of Innail, all standing at guard, all dead. Too late, too late...

Indik took her hand and pulled her up, looking intently into her face. His lips were blue, the skin on his face chapped and raw, and fear clutched at Maerad's heart: how close was Indik himself to death?

"Maerad," he said. "I'll attend to this. I don't know how you knew this, but I count on you to find out more. This is no ordinary cold."

"No," said Maerad. "It's the cold of death. He draws the life out of us ... the air is sucking it away ... I'm too late..." She was shaking again, close to panic, and Indik took both her hands in his.

"Maerad," he said again. His voice was gentle, but it held an iron edge. "While there is still breath in us, it is not too late. And I need your help. Now."

Maerad took a shuddering breath and calmed herself. She looked around, suddenly aware of a bustle of activity: people were running and calling, healers were rushing onto the palisade with stretchers to carry away those who were dead or dying. Cadvan was nearby, his attention focused on a Bard who had fallen even as she was speaking to Indik.

"He'll attack now," said Maerad to Indik. "I know it."

"Aye," said Indik. "And those of us who are still alive are as ready as we can be. That's not your business. Now, Maerad..."

She nodded, and moved to a niche in the far wall where she would not be in the way, touching Cadvan's shoulder as she went so he would know where she was. Then she steeled herself and prepared to find the Landrost. It was hard to concentrate with the cold sapping her will, and with the expectation that siege ladders would be thrown against the wall at any moment. She loosened her sword in its scabbard, and huddled the blanket around her head.

She flinched as she opened her mind. The Landrost was so close – a stone's throw, if that – and for a moment she thought that he was aware of her, that something gathered in recognition. The moment passed, and Maerad breathed out in relief: perhaps he thought it was a false alarm, perhaps he was too preoccupied. All the same, a sense that something was aware of her presence, however vaguely, made her cautious. The Landrost's proximity made it more dangerous for her to probe, but she had no choice.

Gingerly, Maerad continued to open her mind, trying to ignore the swirl of Bardic feelings that obscured her perceptions: she was dimly aware of grief and fear and horror, of a growing miasma of despair, but with a wrench she deliberately turned her mind away. That, as Indik had said, was not her business. She cautiously began again to send out feelers, trying to steal into the Landrost's mind, just as he was stealing into the minds of the soldiers and Bards of Innail, thieving the very breath of their lives. A deep anger began to smoulder within her, and she pushed it down; it was not useful. Not yet, anyway. As she concentrated, her fear dissipated. The Landrost, she thought, was too busy to notice her fiddling at the edges of his power.

Maerad realized that what he was doing was, in a way, quite simple. In the middle of the Landrost there was nothing, nothing at all, and that nothing was drawing into its emptiness the warmth and breath of every living thing in Innail. Soon, if she could not stop him, even walls and warm hearths would be no protection. For a moment, Maerad was blank with astonishment. Was the Landrost alive in any way that she could understand? How could he become such nothingness? Even the Winterking, for all his utter coldness, pulsed with being, with a pure, charismatic vitality ... she skipped over that thought; it was perilous. The Landrost was Unbeing, Unlife. There was no way to fight something that simply wasn't.

So, if she could not fight it, what could she do? There was

not enough of her to pour into that endless hole, that inhumanly greedy maw. It desired nothing, you could do nothing to it, it was nothing. If there was a key, Maerad thought desperately, some kind of ... if she could hurt the Landrost, somehow, into becoming something...

She felt panic rising inside her again as she cast about for a lever, for even the beginning of a way to stop him, and came up with nothing. And then, on the periphery of her awareness, she heard faint cries, clashes, screams ... the mountain men, she presumed, were finally attacking the School. And what had the Landrost done with the wers? *That's not your business,* Indik had told her. He was right. She forced out of her mind the thought of the vicious battle that was taking place around her tranced body and fought down her panic. In this strange world of the mind, time did not exist: she had no idea how long she had been pondering the problem of the Landrost. It could have been less than the blink of an eye, it could have been hours and hours... But in that other world she knew she was running out of time and she could not think what to do.

Destroy him.

The voice fell so lightly into her mind that at first she thought it was her own, and she almost laughed out loud at her own foolishness.

Elednor Edil-Amarandh na, said the Winterking, and Maerad's stomach turned over, feeling the pull of him, the leap of desire that rose within her, independently of her conscious choice. *Destroy the Landrost. Or do you lack the will?*

I lack everything, said Maerad fiercely, a sudden anger flaring inside her. *You speak as if I simply had to stamp on a spider. How can I destroy something that isn't there?*

He isn't not there, said the Winterking. *He is here. As I am.*

As she understood Arkan's meaning, Maerad forgot her anger, even forgot him. Of course the Landrost was there – she felt his presence everywhere, thickening the very atmosphere with fear, with an implacable deathliness. The nothingness was his centre. She was making a mistake in focusing on his nothingness.

An unrelated thought flashed into her mind, a scrap of something she had read during her brief studying with Dernhil, in which the Light was described as a sphere in which the centre was everywhere and the circumference nowhere. Somehow the Landrost had made himself like that, but the other way around: his centre was nowhere, his circumference everywhere.

She halted, baffled. This thinking was all very well, but she still didn't know what to do. She cast around blindly for Arkan; if he claimed she could destroy the Landrost, surely he would know how she could do it. But she could feel no trace of him; the Winterking seemed to have vanished utterly. Maerad's heart sank, and the anger smouldering within her flared again. What was the Winterking doing here, after all? She had no reason to believe that he was not deceiving her; she certainly didn't think he was there to help her. It was more likely by far that he aimed to bring about her downfall, that he was in league with the Landrost for his own malign purposes, planning to capture Maerad for himself after Innail was taken. And even without the Winterking behind him, she had as much chance of destroying the Landrost as she had of demolishing a mountain with her bare hands.

On the walls, a desperate and savage battle was being waged to prevent the Landrost from overwhelming Innail. It was not, in fact, the mountain men who were swarming the battlements: if the men climbed the walls, they too would be victims of the emptiness that sucked the life out of Innail. They were camped below by their fires, awaiting the destruction of the defending forces; once they were dead, the invaders could enter the School at their leisure, to rape, sack and pillage. For now, the Landrost was sending his wers to wipe out the defence.

Cadvan had thrown a shield of magery around Maerad to protect her while she attempted her own strike against the Landrost. In her distress after speaking to Indik, she had forgotten to do so herself.

Their position, if serious, was not quite as bad as Cadvan had feared: of all the forces around the walls, three men and women had died of the cold, their lives imperceptibly slipping away as they gazed over the battlements. Another eight had been rushed to the healers, either unconscious or on the brink of stupor. All of them, as Indik noted grimly to Cadvan, were Bards. The other soldiers, though they felt the cold and the creeping stupor, were not quite as vulnerable to it as those who wielded magery. And the necessity to fight was, perhaps, keeping the Landrost's death cold at bay, although Cadvan felt its insidious tug, as if his blood were being slowly drained from his body where he stood, and he could do nothing about it.

Cadvan suspected that the Landrost had called the attack earlier than he had planned: perhaps Maerad had somehow prompted him to move more swiftly. He glanced over to where she stood, barely visible against the wall, the faint shimmer of magery blurring her figure. Maerad's sudden intuition had perhaps saved many people from that particular death. But, he thought, the Landrost was offering the people of Innail many ways of dying.

He set his jaw and braced for a grim battle of swordcraft and magery, standing shoulder to shoulder with Indik as they cast white fire against their attackers, driving them back over the battlements, or hacked them down so that piles of wer corpses began to build on the palisades. Innail stood against wave after wave of wers, more than seemed possible, black wings and long, curved claws that slashed down out of the darkness and were beaten back or struck down, but still there were more, and more again, and the lines of defence began to thin. The longer they fought, the fewer they were, and the weaker; all the warriors were pale with exhaustion, fighting not only the wers, but the Landrost.

Just as Cadvan thought their line would break and the wers would at last take the palisades, there was a brief lull in the assault, and he and Indik stumbled back from the walls, waving other soldiers forward to take their places. They leant on their swords, breathing hard and wiping the sweat out of their eyes.

In the flickering torchlight, Indik's face was a savage mask of grime and blood. Once he had caught his breath, he turned to Cadvan and grinned mirthlessly. "I do not believe," he said, "that we are going to last until dawn, my friend."

Cadvan met his eyes steadily. "If they keep up this attack, we will not last the hour," he said.

Indik's eyes went blank for the briefest moment. "The attack is by far the most fierce here, by the gates," he said. "But it is hard to trace its pattern, all the same; elsewhere they make an assault here, or there, you cannot predict it because you can't see them massing in this fog. So we must keep guard everywhere." He straightened himself and winced. "Of course, the blow falls hardest here, and here most of all we must not fall. I am hoping with all my heart, my friend, that the Landrost has at last run out of wers."

"That is perhaps hoping for too much," Cadvan answered. Even as he spoke, they both heard the wingbeats that heralded another wave of wers. Their eyes met.

"I have always hoped for too much," said Indik. "I will say at the Gates, whenever I get there, tonight or some other night in the far future, that sometimes that hope was answered. But even if Maerad manages to stop the death cold, I fear we are too weakened to hold back the Landrost now."

Cadvan nodded, and saluted Indik with his sword. "It has

always been an honour to know you, my friend," he said.

"And you, my friend," said Indik.

Maerad knew that time was running out. She flickered her awareness quickly to the palisades and saw with horror the savagery of the battle that was taking place there; she saw Cadvan and Indik, side by side, among the forlornly thin line of warriors defending themselves against the wers. The wards still prevented the wers from all attacking at once, but that so, the defenders were hard-pressed. Even as Maerad watched, three defenders fell, killed or wounded, and a wer screamed in triumph at the breach and swooped towards it with a dozen others. Indik, Cadvan and two more leapt to the breach, fighting hard, white fire arcing from their swords, and the assault was beaten back; but Maerad could see the weariness in their bodies, could see that the only thing holding them up was their wills. And even the wills of Cadvan and Indik could be broken...

Maerad couldn't bear to see any more, and pulled herself back into the world of the mind. As she crouched before the great nothing that was the Landrost, she felt despair rising inside her: never, not even when she had faced death in the mountains, had she felt more alone. Then, she had mourned for her own tragedy, for her death and the death of her friends. Now she knew that she alone stood between the larger world she loved – Innail and everything it meant – and its utter destruction. There was no one to help her. And she didn't know what to do.

At last, in desperation, she decided to step out of hiding and to directly challenge the Landrost. She was useless crouching in the shadows trying to feel out his powers; and perhaps, having already felt the full impact of his force, she could withstand him this time. She took a deep breath. I, too, am Elidhu, she said to herself. I am wind and rock and water and fire. I am Elidhu and woman and Bard. He is only Elidhu. It felt like empty bravado, but she had nothing else.

Blindly, Maerad pushed towards the obscene centre, the great void that was sucking out the lifeblood of Innail, the warm breath of those she loved, the breath of warrior and child, singer and herder, artisan and farmer and cook, blacksmith and swordsmith, cooper and potter... Its empty greed drew her in, as if she were being sucked inexorably into the black centre of a great whirlpool, and she felt herself spinning in its force, dizzy, confused, already weaker. It would be so easy, a voice whispered inside her, just to give in, to simply relax into its deathliness. No one would blame her. And she could put down her burden, sink into darkness, know nothing ever again...

Beyond conscious thought, something in Maerad began to fight against the terrible compulsion. She thought of all the people who had placed such trust in her, who had no hope without her, and with an effort of will she shrank herself into the smallest possible space. At last, she stopped spinning in the force of the Landrost and was still.

Now Maerad was as tiny as a pebble, as uncrushable as a shard of adamant. Not even the Landrost had the power to crush her. As soon as she knew this, she felt herself become stronger, and where there had been despair ignited a pure, uncontrollable rage, a fury without thought, a fury directed wholly at the Landrost. Now, beyond her conscious will, she felt herself transform, and everything that she knew as Maerad, her woman's body, her Bard's mind, even her wolf-self, so begin to vanish into her Elidhu being, as if the force of her anger were a consuming flame.

Now she was a tiny star, unbearably bright, pulsing with raw, unmeasurable power, a radiance beyond imagining; she was no longer tiny, she was growing, her power was growing, brighter and brighter; she was no longer herself, not even a mind. She was the power of the sun; nothing could burn her because she was fire itself, the soul of the flame that lived in the core of rock and living things, that tore open the face of the earth, that broke the feet of mountains, that split asunder their arrogance and drove through their fragments like molten breath, until rock ran like rivers of white water, stone transformed into living fire itself.

She-who-had-been-Maerad blazed before the Landrost and at last he saw her, and she felt his pause, his sudden fear. She sensed him transforming himself, bringing his forces to bear on her, gathering all his power into a mighty fist, a hammer of stone, an avalanche that was a whole mountain. But it was too late, the star was already far beyond his power; it blasted the mineral veins of his being with unbearable fire, unbearable light. Even as he turned his mind towards her, the Landrost was collapsing inwards upon his own emptiness, all the peaks and valleys and outcrops of his being wavering and crumbling, his cold mind smouldering before the great heat of the star that now seared him with an anguish beyond his imagining. Before he was even aware, before a thought could begin to form, the fire caught, and what remained of the Landrost flared up in a brilliant arc of flame and spluttered out into darkness.

VIII

AFTERMATH

ELEDNOR *Edil-Amarandh na…*
        The voice sang through the empty cosmos, a vibrating ribbon of cold light.

Elednor, it whispered, *remember your name. Heart of fire, flower of flame, remember your home…*

She-who-had-been-Maerad felt a voice forming in the centre of her fury, a voice that wanted to answer, that lifted with a warmth that was not the incandescence of pure rage. Something inside her shaped a mouth. *I remember*, said the mouth. *I remember my home.*

Come, said the voice. *Come home with me.*

All at once memory surged back, and Maerad remembered who she was. She was not a star after all, she was not fire nor fury. She was Maerad. The voice repeated her name, weaving it into a spell, into a chain, pulling her closer. She remembered the voice, and turned herself gladly towards it, her mind twirling like a twig in a gentle current. But as her memory returned, it stabbed her with a sudden anguish, waking Maerad with a shock and pulling her out of the lulling spell. She had bones and skin, and hands and feet, her heart beat in her breast, her eyes were wet with tears. She was a young woman, and she would not be used.

My home is burned, Maerad said, her voice colder than the voice that called her. *I have no home. Do not lie to me, Arkan.*

She felt the Winterking's surprise that she had so easily shaken off his command, and for a long time he said nothing.

You have grown, Arkan said at last.

I could destroy you as I destroyed the Landrost, said Maerad. *You should fear me, O Winterking. Do not think that I am your toy. I will not come with you.*

She could see him now in the darkness before her, his strong white body globed in blue ripples of light. She studied his beauty bitterly. Their eyes met and Maerad gasped; his gaze was as keen as ice and looked into the very depths of her being.

You did not destroy the Landrost, said the Winterking. *You cannot destroy an Elidhu. And I am stronger than the Landrost. But you have undone him to the very sinews of his being, so that it is almost as if he no longer is. I do fear you, Elednor Edil-Amarandh na. I do not understand what you are. I am no threat to you. I cannot bind you.*

Maerad turned her eyes away. *No,* she said. *You cannot.* She knew it was simply a fact. The Winterking held no power over her. Somehow, strangely, it made her feel a little sad.

I think all the same, my Fire Lily, that you have much to be afraid of, Arkan said. Maerad felt the cold mockery in his words. *You have many enemies, of course. The Nameless One is not unlike what you have become; perhaps you ought to think about that. But it seems to me that, most of all, you should be terrified of yourself.*

Then the Winterking was gone, all trace of his presence instantly erased, and Maerad was alone in the formless darkness, and the tears on her cheeks felt like ice.

When Maerad undid the Landrost, the wers, creatures woven out of the tissue of his being, shrivelled like dry leaves caught in the updraught of a fire. A couple of soldiers who had been fighting furiously in mortal combat fell over as their sword strokes bit into smoke instead of flesh.

For the space of several heartbeats, there was a complete silence. Some people stood with their mouths open in astonishment, wondering if this was yet another trick of the Landrost's.

But every man and woman on the walls felt the life surging through their veins as the dreadful weight of the Landrost's presence lifted from their souls, and the cold ebbed away, and they stood in a still and foggy winter night that suddenly was miraculously ordinary.

On the far wall, Silvia raised her face to the black sky, feeling hot tears coursing down her face, and threw down her sword to embrace Kelia, the short, dark Bard who stood next to her.

"Maerad did it," whispered Silvia, through harsh, racking sobs. "By the Light, Maerad defeated the Landrost."

As the defenders of Innail began to realize what had happened, ragged cheers rose around the walls. Many, like Silvia, simply wept. Others dropped blankly to the ground and sat staring into space, stunned by their reprieve.

Cadvan had felt the surge of energy building within Maerad even as he battled a wer who had made it through the walls and had landed on the palisades, transforming into a brutishly powerful man. This wer was a sorcerer who countered Cadvan's white fire with dark fire of his own, and Cadvan was hardpressed. Even as he fought him, he sensed the fury in Maerad, and part of him feared that all of them, friend and foe, would be swept away in the conflagration of her wrath. And then, suddenly, the wer was a wraith of ash that twisted and dissipated in the fog.

Cadvan knew at once what had happened, and dropped his sword, running to where Maerad lay, crumpled in a small, unconscious heap by the far wall. He lifted her anxiously, listening for a heart beat; at first, there seemed to be nothing, but then he felt her pulse, faint and irregular, and breathed out with relief. His hands began to glow with the silver light of magery, and he passed them over her face, and said her Truename.

He waited for a long time, but Maerad remained pale and still. Cadvan took a deep breath; he was deathly tired, and he had not much strength for magery. But just as he was about to try again, Maerad's eyelids fluttered open and she looked up into his eyes.

"Cadvan," she said, and then her eyes shut again. Her voice was so faint, he could barely hear her.

Cadvan said nothing, and just stroked her face. Maerad slowly sat up. Her eyes glittered wide and dark in the torchlight, and her wet cheeks glistened.

"Cadvan," she said again. "I did it. I unmade him. Oh, I have never been so tired."

"I know you did," said Cadvan. "I was about to be skewered by a monstrous thug of a wer when it just shrivelled into dust before my eyes. You saved my life, again. How many times is that now?"

Maerad smiled wanly. "Four, I think," she said.

"I owe you a wine."

Maerad smiled again. "A glass of laradhel would be lovely," she said, and then she fainted dead away. Cadvan gathered her slight body up into his arms and carried her downstairs to the healers, jealously refusing all offers of help, even though he was stumbling with weariness. When she next opened her eyes, Maerad was tucked into a proper Innail bed, between clean linen sheets, and outside her window a songbird trilled joyously in the glorious light of day.

While Maerad slept, the people of Innail began the task of healing their hurts. The sun rose, burning away the fog to reveal the trampled and churned grasses outside the walls and the storm damage everywhere in Innail. Aside from the black circles where their fires had been, and the litter of splintered siege ladders and discarded objects like broken tools or water bottles, there was no sign of the mountain men. They had slipped away under the cover of darkness when they saw that the Landrost had been defeated. Without his power behind them, they had no chance of winning a fight against the Bards of Innail, or even of entering the School against the wards placed in the walls.

Malgorn ordered some soldiers to scour the surrounding countryside on horseback to make sure that they were indeed gone. He suspected that without the Landrost's protection they would have problems returning over the mountains, and might cause havoc instead among the hamlets and small towns in the Fesse. The soldiers returned, having followed their trail to the foothills of the Osidh Annova without a single sighting. Perhaps the destruction of the Landrost had struck them with a mortal terror of the Bards.

The people of Innail counted and laid out their dead. These were not as many as had seemed likely in the darkest hours of the night, but there were still many houses of grief that day: by evening, one hundred and twenty-six men, women and children lay cold in the Great Hall, draped in the dark-red mantles that honoured their deaths in defence of their homes, the tall candles of mourning burning steadily at their feet. A slow line of people passed through the hall, their heads bowed, to do them remembrance, as a Bard on the dais played the Song of Ending on a lyre. After two days of mourning they would be buried, each body taken by those who loved them and interred in the crypts by the Eastern wall of Innail.

Many more were injured and lay in the houses of healing, cared for by the Bards. After the Landrost had fallen, Silvia had stripped off her armour and had rushed there almost straight away, working on the injured until Malgorn had ordered her to rest. Malgorn himself was almost dead on his feet, but before he collapsed into his own bed, he organized work parties among the farm hands and herders and others who had not been involved in the worst of the fighting, to clear away the mess of battle: the cauldrons of pitch, the blood-soiled rushes and sand.

The streets of Innail filled with people going about their business. They bought food at the markets, embraced their children
and baked their dinners as if this day were an ordinary day like
every other; but in their faces, in the gentleness with which they
greeted each other, was the tacit knowledge that things might
have been very different. Life for every person in Innail seemed
very rich that day.

Maerad slept until mid-afternoon, unaware of the great
labour that was going on around her. When she woke, she lay
with her eyes closed, remembering the horrors of the night
before. She was so weary she felt she could not lift her arms.

Finally she opened her eyes, blinking at the pale winter sunlight that fell through her casement. She didn't recognize the
room she was in: she was in the Healing House and lay in a simple wooden bed, in a room by herself. The walls were painted
in a pale blue wash, her sheets smelled of lemon, and a bird was
singing outside her window. She listened to its warbling for a
long time.

By her bed were a jug of water and a cup, and next to them
a little hand bell. She was very thirsty, but she wondered if she
had the strength to lift the jug. At last, with a great deal of effort,
she sat up. For the moment that was all that she could do, and
she sat where she was, leaning against her pillow, frightened by
her body's weakness, longing for the water.

At that moment Silvia entered. Her face brightened when
she saw Maerad was awake, and she came over to the bed and
embraced her lightly, as if she were an eggshell that might break
if touched too carelessly.

"Maerad," she said, kissing her on the forehead. "You should
have rung the bell – that's what it's for. How are you feeling?"

"I'm very thirsty," said Maerad, looking longingly at the jug.

Silvia laughed. "That's easily remedied." She poured Maerad
a cup, and held it so it would not spill as she drank. The water

was delicious, with a faint herbed tang. Maerad gulped down two cupfuls and finally sat back, wiping her mouth with her hand.

"That's better," she said. "I can't remember being so thirsty. It was as if I've had nothing to drink for days and days."

Silvia sat on the edge of the bed and took Maerad's hand, looking thoughtfully into her face. "You seem surprisingly well, for someone who was busy destroying a powerful Elidhu last night," she said. "In fact, you're only a little pale. I'm astounded."

"I'm very tired," said Maerad. "So, so tired. But I don't think anything's broken."

"If you are tired, you should sleep," said Silvia. "The water will help; it has properties to promote healing rest." She leaned forward and kissed Maerad again on the forehead. "My dear, sleep as long as you need. I will keep the well-wishers from your door; half of Innail has been here already, wanting to give you their thanks. The other half will probably arrive tomorrow. We owe you our lives."

Maerad felt a strange sorrow welling up inside her. "Nobody owes me anything," she whispered. "Nothing at all. I owe everything to Innail."

"My dear, we'll argue the point tomorrow," said Silvia. She settled Maerad back down beneath the coverlet, stroking her brow, and Maerad felt weariness washing over her, a great wave that rolled her into the warm darkness. In a moment she was asleep.

Silvia sat on the bed for a while, watching Maerad, her brow creased and troubled. Then she sighed heavily, and stood up and left the room.

It was a week before Maerad found the strength to remain out of bed for a whole day. All the same, she nagged to be released from the Healing House; she felt uncomfortable languishing there among others who were much more badly wounded than she was. After a stern examination, Silvia cautiously agreed that there seemed nothing wrong beyond extreme exhaustion and permitted Maerad to move back to Silvia and Malgorn's Bardhouse, to the chamber that she thought of as *her* room.

Here, where she had first discovered what it meant to be a Bard, Maerad lay in bed and obediently ate the meals that were brought to her, listening to the gentle voice of the fountain outside. From her bed she could see the top branches of a plum tree. The tips of its fingers were just beginning to redden with the promise of blossom, reminding her that it was almost a whole year since she had first come to Innail.

On the second day after the battle, Maerad had insisted on going to the Great Hall to pay her respects to the dead, and had got her way only after a heated argument with both Cadvan and Silvia, who were worried that she might collapse.

"I don't care," said Maerad stubbornly, her mouth set in a determined line. "If I get tired, I can just rest. It's not very far. I'll go by myself if you don't help me."

Finally, Cadvan had sighed and agreed, even to her insistence that she walk; Maerad claimed it was foolish to ride such a short distance. Silvia wrapped her in a thick felt cloak, and, with Cadvan supporting her arm, Maerad had made her way to the Great Hall. Although it wasn't far, it took them a long time to get there; Maerad had to stop every few yards to rest, and by the time they arrived her entire body was trembling with strain. There was a long line of mourners filing through the hall, but when they saw who had arrived, a rumour swept around the crowd and people started craning their necks to see her. Those nearest stepped back to make way for her, and some bowed or even fell to their knees. Many people looked simply awed. Perhaps because Cadvan was looking so fiercely protective, no one dared to approach and speak to her.

Maerad was utterly disconcerted, and her hands fluttered out before her, asking the people to stand up. She turned to Cadvan, a flush of embarrassment high in her cheeks.

"Why are they doing that?" she murmured. "They don't need to … not here … I mean, people gave their lives…"

"Maerad, it's no use being embarrassed," Cadvan said. "You have another name now, the Maid of Innail. There are already songs about what you did. You'd better get used to it."

"But it's not *me*," said Maerad, feeling distress mounting inside her. "I mean, yes, there was the Landrost, but I was one of so many others … it makes me feel like, well, like a *fraud*…"

"No, it's not you. You and I know that. But Maerad, you must understand, people need stories. You fought the Landrost and you won – that's a wonderful story. And if you don't recognize yourself in that story, it doesn't mean, either, that the story isn't true. People here will tell their grandchildren that they saw you. Be gracious, my lady, and accept their thanks. They need to thank someone for being alive."

Burning with embarrassment, Maerad looked down at her feet.

"Chin up," said Cadvan. He smiled with a sudden irrepressible mischief, and for a moment all the lines of care vanished from his face. "You were the one who wanted to come here. I did warn you. Are you going to have to admit that I was right, after all?"

Maerad met the challenge in his gaze, and straightened her back. Her legs were trembling with the effort of walking from the Bardhouse, but she moved steadily through the Great Hall, leaning heavily on Cadvan's arm, and stopped by each of the dead to bow her head, asking Cadvan to read the name embroidered on each red cloth. Most were names she didn't know, but some made her catch her breath: Casim, with whom she had melded to make the weatherwards against the storm, was one of the dead, and there were others whom she recognized from her time in Innail.

When Maerad finished the round of the hall she was in tears, and even her pride couldn't keep her on her feet. So much death, so much sorrow, was more than she could comprehend. Someone brought a chair so she could sit down, her face in her hands, while the mourners crowded around at a respectful distance, vying for a glimpse of her. She didn't argue with Cadvan when he mindtouched Indik and asked him to bring a mount to take her back to the Bardhouse, and she had to be carried upstairs to her room. When she was back in bed, her head scarcely touched the pillow before she was asleep again.

After that, Maerad didn't argue about her enforced rest. And in truth, it was a welcome respite after the hardships of the previous year; for this short space of time she let her worries float away. It was very pleasant not to think, and to be fed and bathed and fussed over as if she were a child. When she had been a child, she thought, she had had precious little of it.

Indik, Malgorn and Silvia were frequent visitors, and Cadvan spent many hours in her room, talking or just reading quietly in the corner. He was pleasant company, undemanding and attentive. He was taking advantage of their enforced idleness to plunder the Innail Library, searching for any further clues about the Elidhu, or the Treesong, or the spell that the Nameless One had used to bind himself to life, but so far with no luck at all. Sometimes he took out a book of poems or stories and read them to Maerad just for the pleasure of it, and she lay back and listened with her eyes closed. These times seemed to her to be among the loveliest of her life: in this pleasant room, far from hunger or cold or peril, she felt the ease and intimacy of their companionship.

When Maerad felt her strength at last beginning to return, she tried to speak to Cadvan about what had happened to the Landrost. She had avoided thinking about it for the past few days, and her sleep had been deep and dreamless. But one night she dreamed again of the Landrost and the Winterking, dark and troubled dreams that she could not remember, and she woke consumed by a fear she couldn't name. That day she haltingly attempted to describe how she had undone the Landrost, how she had become something that she didn't even understand, how the thought of the power that had then surged through her utterly terrified her. And finally, after a long struggle with herself, she told Cadvan the thing that frightened her most of all: that the Winterking had said that she was like the Nameless One.

Cadvan listened in silence, shading his eyes with his hand.

"I don't know how to offer you any comfort, Maerad," he said, when she fell silent. "I think you are correct to be frightened. What you say frightens *me*. You must remember, all the same, that you are Maerad of Pellinor, as well as the Fire Lily. You are Hem's sister, you are my dear friend, and if you had half a chance you would be no more than an ordinary Bard commencing her delayed studies of the Lore of Annar. You must remember how much you like sitting in a garden in the sunshine, eating a pear."

Maerad laughed out loud at this unexpected advice. "Eating a pear?" she said. "Well, yes, I do like pears ... but what has that to do with anything?"

Cadvan smiled across the room at her. "Maerad, the longer I have known you, the less certain I am about anything. But I am willing to wager on my life that the Nameless One does not sit in any garden, eating fruit and enjoying the sunshine. I think he has long ago forgotten what those simple pleasures mean. The company of true friends, the taste of good food, the blossoms in

spring, all the ordinary things that make the texture and meaning of life – they mean nothing to him. He despises all that is
temporary, all that passes with the passing day, because none
of these things last for ever. If he is indeed like you, then he has
seen the blind fury of the cosmos; but unlike you, he desires its
endlessness and power, he wants to be as infinite as the stars
are, but at the same time to hold onto himself. But in reaching for that immortality, he has thrown away everything that
makes a self. That's what he did when he put away his Name.
The things that matter most are fragile and mortal, but for that
reason he despises them. And so he has nothing at all..."

Cadvan fell silent and walked over to the window, staring
out over Innail. Maerad said nothing, mulling over his words.

"I don't know what I'm trying to say," Cadvan said at last. "I
suppose what I mean is that while you're many things, none of
these other powers, no matter how extraordinary they are, erase
the fact that you are also just an ordinary young woman."

"Not yet," said Maerad, thinking again of how she had
transformed into pure fire, something that was not her at all,
and of how she had so entirely forgotten who she was. "But I
don't know – I'm afraid that I might vanish altogether. I might
forget myself, like the Nameless One..."

"If you fear that erasure, then you must fight it with all your
will." Cadvan turned around, shaking his head. "I'm sorry,
Maerad. I really don't know what I'm talking about. This is outside my ken."

"Mine too," said Maerad wryly.

Once Maerad was able to stay out of bed for a whole day, her
recovery progressed rapidly, and she and Cadvan began again
to talk about leaving Innail. They both knew that they could
ill afford to dally, but at the same time Cadvan refused to contemplate their moving until he was quite sure that Maerad was

completely well. Despite the urgency that burned inside her, Maerad didn't argue too hard; she knew that the road before them would be testing, and she needed to be strong.

And in truth it was pleasant to spend time with her friends and to wander through the streets of Innail, even if it rained most of the time. Men and women constantly approached her in the street and clasped her hand, stumbling out their thanks. She tried to respond with as much grace as she could, but she never got over her embarrassment.

Every now and then, perhaps in the midst of a talkative dinner with the Bards, or pausing by a building, struck by an especially beautiful carving or the way the light fell on a particular tree, Maerad was overwhelmed by an aching nostalgia. She felt as if she were saying goodbye to everything she loved in Innail. Perhaps this was the last time she would be an ordinary Bard. Perhaps she would never walk these streets again. This was her last chance to play in the light, before she turned her face towards the dark and uncertain path that lay before her.

After a week, it was clear to both Maerad and Cadvan that they could delay no longer. Sombrely they prepared their packs, and carefully checked over Darsor and Keru. The first part of their journey through the Innail Fesse would be easy, but after that they would enter Annar, where travelling was, by all reports, now fraught with perils: bandits and worse held sway over the roads, and there were rumours of civil war to the east.

But this time, as Indik reminded her, they were not in danger in the Fesse itself. "We are probably safer here than we have been at any time in the past year," he said. "For which we are all grateful to you, Maerad."

Maerad had given up trying to stop people from thanking her, and merely lifted her glass. "I think that gratitude is due to many others, not least yourself, Indik of Innail," she said.

Indik grinned. "The burden of thanks getting a bit much, eh, Maerad?" he said. "You should enjoy it while it lasts. People are ungrateful most of the time. There will come another day when you'll wonder why nobody notices what you've done."

"I think I'd rather that," said Maerad. "I'd rather nobody looked at me."

"Not much chance of that, unless you put a cowl over your head. But frankly, I think you and Cadvan will, for the most part, be safe enough. Most of the rabble terrorizing Annar are just petty thugs, no match for Bards."

"There'll be others, though," said Cadvan. "I expect Hulls among the rabble."

"Aye. But I'm sure your chances of winning through most things are more than fair. It's just that I don't know what you really think you're doing."

They'd had this conversation before, so Maerad turned the subject. There wasn't really an answer to Indik's doubts. He held that it would make more sense for Maerad and Cadvan to head towards Norloch, to deal with the canker there. What they were planning seemed to him to be arrant madness.

Before they left, Silvia and Malgorn held a meal in their honour. To Maerad's relief there were no formalities: just a lot of good food and wine and conversation and later, of course, music. They planned to leave before dawn the following day, so they made their farewells that night. Maerad embraced her friends, feeling sorrow open like a flower in her breast. Even Indik's eyes brimmed with tears as he clasped her hands, stroking her maimed fingers, and wished her well.

Silvia kissed Maerad's cheek gently and held her away from her, studying her face. "How you have grown since first we met!" she said. "Maerad, I have all faith in you. I will look to your coming, when spring walks in the land."

"I will be there," said Maerad, with a certainty that she didn't feel at all.

As she lay sleepless in her chamber that night, she ran over her words to Silvia. They felt like a vow, but it was a promise that she wasn't sure she could keep. Would she survive to see the spring? She tried not to think about the future, which only seemed to offer one dark path after another. She didn't even know what she was trying to do. Now, in the middle of the night, about to put pleasure and joy behind her, the force of Indik's arguments bore down on her, and she felt the flimsiness of her quest. What did she really hope to achieve, even if, against all the odds, she managed to find her brother? All the same, she reminded herself, they had won a victory in Innail.

She hadn't known that victory could taste so bitter.

IX

THE PLAYERS

HEM's mouth was as dry as if it were packed with sand. At the same time, his stomach seemed to have filled up with cold water, and he thought he was going to be sick. His legs also appeared to have stopped working. They felt like two stiff lumps of wood whose only purpose was to keep him vertical.

Next to him, in the fusty closeness of the caravan, Hekibel sympathetically touched his arm. "It's 'My lord, the enemy is in sight,'" she whispered. "All you have to do is say it. Loudly."

Hem nodded mutely, trying to conceal his naked terror. He wasn't sure if his voice was working, either. He could hear Karim in full flight, and his cue – when he was expected to run onto the stage and urgently report his message – was coming up with discomforting swiftness.

"*Now,*" said Hekibel, and gave him a little push. Hem automatically tottered through the curtain, trying to remember Karim's instructions: "Don't stare at your feet, boy, stare at me. Keep your chin high. And for the Light's sake, don't *mumble.*"

Chin up. Hem stumbled out on stage and somehow delivered his line. He was so worried that no one would hear him that he shouted it, but fortunately his panicked shriek was wholly in keeping with the sentiments of what he said, although he caught, out of the corner of his eye, a rather amused smirk from Saliman, who was to the left of Karim, playing a stolid guardsman (he was also, when the guardsman was not required, playing the drums).

"In sight, boy? Are you certain?" asked Karim.

"Yes," squeaked Hem, and promptly forgot the rest of his line, which was supposed to be, "Yes, my lord, they're coming up through the forest."

Saliman caught up the pause before it became too long. "Are they coming up through the forest?" he asked.

"Yes," mumbled Hem, forgetting to keep his chin up.

"The forest!" exclaimed Karim, and launched into his next speech, waving Hem regally away with his hand. Hem slunk back behind the curtain, wishing the earth would swallow him up. He had only two lines, and he had completely forgotten one of them. How could he have been so stupid? Karim would kill him...

Safely back in the caravan, Hekibel squeezed his hand. "You were fine," she whispered in his ear. "Good save by Saliman ... nobody would have noticed..." Then her own cue came up, and she swept out onto the stage, her chin enviably high.

Hem plumped down on a cushion and took some deep breaths until the trembling in his body subsided. Being a player was much harder than he had imagined. This was his third public appearance, and he just couldn't get it right; although this time, at least, he hadn't stumbled and fallen off the stage... It was one thing to practise on the road, and quite another to get out in front of a motley bunch of curious villagers. It was completely nerve-racking, especially as it was a very different audience from that in Til Amon. There, people had paid attention, and hardly anyone had talked. Here, a play seemed to be an occasion for some very lively conversations, and even Karim's most thunderous acting only brought down the noise slightly.

Hem listened hard to the dialogue and song on stage. He couldn't afford to lose track; at the end of the play he was supposed to run on with a crown. For a panicked moment he couldn't find it, but of course it was exactly where Hekibel had placed it. He picked it up and clutched it tightly. At least with the next appearance he didn't have to say anything, and then the play would be over.

Hem waited for the drumming that signalled his next entrance, and made a creditable appearance, kneeling before Karim without tripping over anything, and walking out backwards, again without tripping over. Once he was back in the caravan he heaved a huge sigh of relief. That was all he had to do.

Now that he thought about it, he really didn't think that he was cut out to be a player.

Hem and Saliman had been on the road with the players for a couple of weeks now. Saliman was, unsurprisingly, a very skilled performer, and Karim was quick to exploit his musical abilities, dragging out a dusty old dulcimer from a deep chest. It was, Saliman said ironically, almost tuneable. Hem, on the other hand, had proved to be startlingly untalented, and almost never got anything right. However, aside from his stage duties as a page, messenger boy, herald and general dogsbody, which were turning into regular rituals of public humiliation, Hem was enjoying himself.

The idea of using Irc in the plays had been given up fairly quickly. Karim, thinking that a performing animal would be an extra attraction, had briefly attempted to train him, but the crow proved resistant to the charms of playing: he either got bored and flew away, or tried to filch Hekibel's false jewels while she wasn't looking. He was getting noticeably plumper, as Marich and Hekibel spoiled him with titbits, and he had found a store house in one of the scrolls on the roof of the caravan where he was squirreling away the bits of glass and other

bright oddments he couldn't resist stealing. He developed a
wary relationship with Fenek, the dog, who made one or two
murderous lunges towards him when Irc tried to pilfer some of
his dinner; after a stern reprimand from Saliman, the dog left
the bird alone, and Irc stayed away from his dinner.

Travelling with Marich, Karim and Hekibel had a seductive
air of freedom: they went, as Karim put it, "where the winds
took them". For hours at a time, as the caravan rumbled through
the low hills under a wintry blue sky, watching quail startle out
of the grasses or the herds of small deer or wild goats grazing in
the distance, Hem could almost forget that they journeyed with
a more urgent purpose.

They had journeyed north from Til Amon, making their
way as swiftly as they could through the green flatlands of
Lauchomon towards the West Road. All of them were anxious to leave the Black Army far behind and, in any case, this
part of Annar was relatively uninhabited, dotted with isolated
hamlets that they passed through quickly, bending their steps
eastward. They lost the stone road as soon as they left the Fesse
of Til Amon, and after that it was slower work; they followed a
wagon track that wound northwards, meandering from village
to village towards the West Road.

Saliman had suggested that the party should travel through
Lukernil towards Innail, which would be simply a matter of
following the West Road, and, after frowningly discussing various alternatives, Karim had agreed that they might as well go
to Innail as anywhere. Saliman guessed that if there were any
news to be found of Maerad, Innail would be a good place
to start. After Innail, his best guess was Lirigon, but that was
a long journey north. He did not tell Hem of his real despair
at their chances of finding Maerad. He also kept his concerns
about travelling along the West Road to himself: from what
Saliman had heard, there was a very real danger of encountering

bandits, rogue soldiers, Hulls or worse, and he also feared that
they might meet the Black Army coming up the South Road.
But it was their fastest route to Innail and, once there, he and
Hem could decide what to do next.

Meanwhile, they journeyed with no sign of trouble. The
weather held crisp and fine, and there was plenty of food, so
they made only hasty stops at nightfall, when they would make
dinner and rehearse (Karim insisted on this every evening, no
matter how tired they were). The villagers they encountered
did not, in any case, encourage them to stay. There was a palpable sense of fear through Lauchomon, which was swept with
rumours of war on every side of them, and although children
always ran out with their faces alight to see the golden caravan, the farmers and shepherds who lived in the region greeted
them with curt words, suspicion harsh in their voices, fear over-
coming even their iron traditions of courtesy.

When they reached the West Road and turned east towards
Innail, Karim insisted that they should perform; the villages
that dotted the road were bigger than the hamlets of Lauchomon, and perhaps would be more open to the players. They
travelled briskly now they were on a proper road again, but
Saliman noted that it was oddly deserted, and stayed alert.
They kept watch at nightfall and he and Hem cast glimveils
when they camped at night, so the caravan would not be seen
by passers-by.

The villages here were walled, and some asked for tolls at
their gates before they let the travellers enter, and regarded them
with, if anything, more suspicion than the folk of Lauchomon.
They were told many stories of lawlessness on the roads, and of
war to the west and east, but so far this part of Annar seemed to
be untouched by the troubles.

Despite the suspicion that greeted them, Karim managed
to get an audience for their plays by sheer stubborn charm.

He would plant the caravan in the common in the centre of a village and knock on the doors of all the most important-looking houses, and eventually the space in front of the caravan would fill with curious onlookers. Once he judged there were enough people, he began the play.

They were performing a play that Hekibel said dismissively was an old mule of a thing. But, she said, at least it was short and easy to remember, and it didn't matter if you got the lines wrong. Karim had no sense of humour where playing was concerned and reprimanded her sharply, so once as they rehearsed a scene she changed all the lines on purpose, to see if he noticed. As Hekibel told Hem later, he only picked her up on one line.

Hem didn't want to think about his first performance: that was when he had tumbled off the stage. His accident had prompted a gale of good-natured laughter, and the audience had followed the rest of the play with close attention, especially when Hem came on stage again. Although Karim (mollified perhaps by the villagers' generous appreciation after the show) and the rest of the players had been kind, the mere memory still made Hem hot all over. His next appearance hadn't been much better, and now, even in the third, he still couldn't get his lines right…

He gloomily listened to Karim's last speech (Karim played the villain who died at the end, repenting his evil acts, and his final speech was very long) and then the drumming came to a climax and the play was over. There was some ragged clapping, and even a couple of whistles and cheers. Now Hem had to go out again, but this time it wasn't so bad. He pushed through the curtains, blinking in the light, and bowed with the other players, looking out over the audience. Maybe forty people were seated on an assortment of cushions, benches, stools and blankets in front of the caravan, perhaps most of the village's population, ranging from babies in slings to some ancient men and women who had been brought out in litters. Most of them were smiling, and as he studied their faces, Hem's heart began to lift. Maybe it wasn't so bad, being a player. Above their heads, the sky was darkening: it looked as if at last it was going to rain.

As was their custom, and it was a pleasant custom, the players packed up after the show and repaired to the local tavern. This was bigger than the last one they had frequented, which had been little more than a kitchen, from which a woman dispensed beer for a minimal charge; here it even had a name – Thorkul's Place – and a designated room. Thorkul doubled as the village blacksmith, and was a large, friendly man who bristled with black hair; his beard was voluminous and Hem could see a mat of chest hair curling from beneath his jerkin. His muscles came in handy, he told Saliman, when the patrons had too much drink in them.

"I'm sure they do," said Saliman politely, studying Thorkul's physique. Saliman was by no means a small man, and Thorkul towered over him. "I imagine you have one of the best-behaved taverns in Annar."

"Aye, it is," said Thorkul, and winked. "And well-frequented, too. I brew a goodly beer that's famous in these parts."

Saliman lifted his mug. "I can attest to its quality," he said. "It's as good as any I've tasted. Though I somehow doubt you'd get anyone saying otherwise. To your face, in any case."

Thorkul threw back his head and bellowed with laughter, showing his strong white teeth, and clapped Saliman heartily on the back, making him choke on his beer. "You're jokers, you players!" he said. "It's good to have a laugh, though. Talk has been all too dour in these parts, these past months."

Saliman recovered his poise, and smiled. "We aim to please," he said.

Thorkul had excellent reason for his good temper; his

tavern was packed to the rafters with villagers, attracted by the presence of the players, and he had already broached a second barrel. Hem had no taste for beer, and was sticking to the wine that he also stocked – parsley and elderberry. It was made by Thorkul's very buxom wife Givi, who looked as capable of dealing with troublesome customers as Thorkul himself. Its taste was very light but, as Hem discovered after finishing his first mug, it was much stronger than it looked.

The gathering afterwards was, as far as Hem was concerned, always the best bit of a performance. The glamour of the players hung about even Hem's shoulders, and everyone was keen to talk to him and buy him drinks. People were also attracted by Irc, who sat on Hem's shoulders and smugly permitted himself to be admired. Hem was trying to drink his wine very slowly, as the last time he had suffered a massive headache all the following day, but the goodwill in the tavern was hard to resist, and already on the table before him were two more mugs of wine. He looked up and caught Hekibel's eye: she was surrounded by admirers, some young farm hands who were very clearly struck by her fair beauty. She gracefully untangled herself from the conversation, and came and sat down by Hem.

"I hope you're not planning to drink all those," she said, looking at the mugs.

"Why not?" said Hem robustly.

"You're too young, for a start. And anyway, remember how sick you were last time…"

Hem shuddered. He did remember, and that was why he didn't drink beer any more. "I see you've got some admirers," he said, turning the subject.

"Sweet lads," said Hekibel. "But their conversation is a trifle limited. To be honest, I don't know a lot about ploughshares. Or growing barley. My ma was a tailor in Narimar, in Lanorial, so I only know about buttons."

The chatter in the tavern grew louder and louder as the room became stuffier and stuffier, until Irc began to protest and Hem took him outside. By this time Hem was beginning to regret that he had finished his second mug of wine. It was raining, a light, steady fall, and he leaned against a wall in the porch outside the tavern, taking in long, slow gulps of cold air. Irc ruffled his feathers, and crouched close against Hem's neck.

I don't know why you drink that stuff, he said.

I like it, said Hem, and hiccupped.

Humans are stupid.

Hem heroically stopped himself from reminding Irc of how last time he had enthusiastically sipped Hem's beer, and had ended up in almost as bad a way as Hem himself. It wouldn't be worth the aggravation. Hem had, in fact, had to rescue Irc from a wrestle to the death with his own feet. He opened his mouth to defend his species, when he stopped: he noticed two people sheltering under a linden tree a little distance away. It was very dark, but he was sure, from the way he stood and his shape, that one of them was Karim. A certain furtiveness in his stance caught Hem's attention.

Yes, birds are much more clever, continued Irc, who was obviously in an irritable mood. *You humans...*

Shhh, said Hem, closing the bird's beak with his fingers. *Is that Karim?*

Irc cocked his head, his attention caught. *Karim?*

Hem opened his Bardic hearing. Now he could hear their voices, although the heavy patter of the rain meant, frustratingly, that he couldn't understand what they were saying. One of them was certainly Karim. There was something about the other figure that he did not like at all.

Why's Karim standing out there in the dark talking to a stranger? said Hem.

Because he's stupid, like all humans are, said Irc. *Like I said.*

As Hem watched, he saw the other man give something to Karim, and heard a faint clink. He was handing over coins, surely. Then Karim was obviously making his farewell, in an unusually obsequious manner, bobbing and bowing. The sight gave Hem a bad feeling inside, and he found that he was suddenly coldly sober. He didn't want to be seen spying, and as Karim turned towards him, he beat a hasty retreat back into the tavern, despite Irc's protests.

The noise and fug were overwhelming after the peace outside, and for a moment Hem reeled, feeling the wine fog his mind again. He couldn't see Saliman at first and pushed through the throng of people, Irc clinging complainingly to his shoulder. Behind him he heard the door open and shut, and a swirl of cold air rushed past him; it was no doubt Karim returning. Hem didn't look back to check. He had spotted Saliman by the hearth, in lively and hilarious conversation with Thorkul and a knot of other villagers.

Saliman had the gift of charm; people flocked to him, attracted by his ease and grace. For a moment Hem paused, reluctant to interrupt; Saliman looked more carefree than Hem could remember. It occurred to him for the first time that perhaps Saliman also enjoyed pretending to be merely a player in a travelling troupe, with no more responsibility than the next village, the next show. Perhaps he too sometimes wanted a respite from the burden of defending the Light.

Hem sighed, and pushed his way through until he was next to Saliman, and spoke into his mind. *Saliman?*

Without diverting his attention from a ribald story that was being retailed by Givi to gales of laughter, Saliman answered, instantly alert. *What's wrong?*

Not here, said Hem.

Saliman gave him a sharp glance. *Pretend you're drunk,* he said.

Hem slumped a little, plucking at Saliman's sleeve. It wasn't so hard to pretend; the parsley wine was circulating headily through his veins, and it was very hot and noisy in the tavern.

"Hem, boy, you're not going to be sick?" asked Saliman out loud. Hem nodded dolefully, as the villagers laughed good-naturedly at his discomfort.

"Givi makes a wicked wine," said Thorkul, winking. "As delicate as the cheek of a princess, but it has the kick of a mule."

As Hem stumbled against him, Saliman turned to the others and made his excuses, coaxed Irc onto his own arm and helped Hem out of the tavern, shutting the door behind them.

They stood on the porch, staring out into the rainy night. Hem checked their surroundings, all his senses alert; he could see no sign of the man Karim had been talking to.

"We could go to the caravan, I suppose," said Saliman.

"Here will do," said Hem. He paused, wondering how to begin. "I don't know, Saliman. I saw something that bothers me. I just came out here for some fresh air, and I saw Karim talking to someone under that tree over there." He pointed. "Something about it gave me a bad feeling. He was talking to a man in a dark cloak ... at least, I think it was a man – he was quite tall – but it was too dark to see him properly. I tried to listen to what they were saying, but the rain was too noisy. And I'm sure the other man gave Karim some coins."

"You're certain it was Karim?"

Hem nodded, and Irc gave a chirp of confirmation.

Saliman frowned, staring down at his feet. "It might be something totally innocent," he said at last. "But then again, it might not be. I have never entirely trusted Karim."

"You don't think he's in league with the Dark?" asked Hem, feeling a chill run through him. "He ... he doesn't seem..."

"No, I don't think it's that simple," said Saliman. "I think he is not a bad person. I do think, however, that Karim is weak, and if someone were to offer him money in return for simply reporting on our conversations, or something like that, he would perhaps tell himself that there was no harm in it. Especially if it was quite a lot of money."

Hem was silent for a time. He was struggling with a sudden deep sadness; he liked Karim, and it hurt that he might betray them.

"But … but who would be paying him?"

"Perhaps someone in Til Amon got wind of what we planned. As I said at the time, we don't know anything about the players. Nor do we have any guarantee that he told no one we would be travelling with the players. And he knows we're Bards."

Hem thought of how the players had left the tavern to have dinner with others on the last night in Til Amon. Saliman's request for secrecy from Karim would have alerted him to the fact that they had their own business. As they were Bards, and Saliman was clearly an important Bard, it wouldn't take a lot of thought to work out that someone else might be interested. It was possible, but the thought made Hem feel sick.

"If someone wanted to know where we were, wouldn't it be easier just to follow the caravan?" he said at last. "I mean, it's a pretty easy thing to follow…"

"Yes. But perhaps whoever follows wants to know what we are saying as much as he wants to know where we are going. And if that's the case, they will certainly know, of course, that we plan to go to Innail. Though thankfully, they won't know anything else … I think it would be too much to hope that the Dark hasn't put two and two together, and worked out that Hem of Turbansk, who returned from Norloch with Saliman, is the same Hem who escaped from them in Edinur."

Hem felt dread creeping through his veins. "Do you think we're being followed?"

Saliman sighed, and was silent for a time before he answered. "Hem, I have suspected that we are being followed for the past week now. I have sometimes seen a horseman in the distance, far back behind us, and I have not liked the look of him. And I myself saw Karim speaking to a tall man in a cloak in the village before last. It was late and it was dark, but I am almost sure that he was talking to a Hull."

A cold shiver ran down Hem's back. "A Hull?" he whispered. Hem had too many bad memories of Hulls.

"I don't think Karim would know that he was dealing with a Hull," said Saliman. "They would not appear to him as they would to us."

"Still, he would know that anyone who is following us like that doesn't exactly wish us well," said Hem.

A silence fell over both of them, which was broken by two villagers noisily leaving the tavern. They waved cheery farewells before staggering out into the rain. Hem stared broodingly after them, thinking that his impulsive suggestion to join the players hadn't been such a good idea after all.

"What shall we do?" he asked at last.

"I think at some point soon we will have to leave the players," said Saliman. "One Hull alone would not dare to attack us, but I do not doubt – especially as we near Desor and Ettinor – that it would find friends. And that thought I do not like. The other thought I don't like is that they would know we're going to Innail."

"It'd be hard to leave without Hekibel noticing, in any case," said Hem. "That's if we want to take supplies. And we can't go without them." He paused and then asked, his voice strained: "Marich and Hekibel don't have anything to do with it, do they? Or do you think…"

"No, I don't think so," said Saliman, patting Hem on the shoulder. "I think we can trust them. All the same, it's as well to be careful."

Hem thought of the three players. He had become fond of all of them, even Karim, and it hurt deeply to think that Karim might be betraying them to the Dark. All the pleasures of the past fortnight turned to ashes in his heart.

"Selling us to Hulls just for coins," he said. "If it's true, I'll never forgive Karim."

"As I said, I think he is not a bad man. Just weak."

"And stupid. And greedy."

"Yes, those things too. One day, Hem, you will find that people are often weak and stupid and greedy, including perhaps yourself."

"I wouldn't sell my friends to the Dark," said Hem bitterly. "Why don't we just go? Why don't we leave now?"

"And go where? For the moment, I think we go on as we are. There's little point in leaving now, because we could be just as easily followed as the caravan and, if we are correct, they already know we are heading for Innail. I have not your or Cadvan's talent for disguise, alas, but if need calls, we could use magery and glimveils… In the meantime, I count on you to keep your eyes and ears open. And remember, it could be, as I said, that Karim has a perfectly innocent explanation."

"It doesn't seem likely to me," said Hem. "Why would he hide, otherwise? And anyway, you thought the other person was a Hull. And I saw it too, and something about it gave me the chills."

"Well, then. We watch, and we be wary."

That night, Saliman had arranged for a room for Hem and himself at Thorkul's tavern, which would be more comfortable than sleeping out in the tent. Hem went to bed shortly after his conversation with Saliman, pleading illness, and Saliman returned to the tavern. People were leaving; most had to rise with the dawn, and it was well past dark, and it wasn't long before Saliman joined him.

It was wonderful to lie down in an actual bed, even if it was somewhat lumpy, but despite Hem's tiredness and the wine, sleep wouldn't come. Close by, he could hear Irc shifting now and then on his perch at the end of the bed and Saliman's even breathing. Saliman had the facility of dropping off to sleep when he wished, no matter what their circumstances. Hem lay on his back, staring into the darkness, remembering his time in Edinur with the Hulls, and his even worse time in Sjug'hakar Im and Dagra, when he had seen the very heart of the Dark. For the first time since then, he felt afraid.

At last he dropped off into troubled dreams: the old nightmares of the Hulls in Edinur killing the boy Mark in front of him, newer nightmares about the Glandugir Hills, where strange, deadly creatures appeared out of the tangled undergrowth rattling insectile wings, or of dark streets in Dagra, where he was following Karim, who was dressed in a black cloak and was always slipping out of sight around a corner just as he was about to catch up with him.

Then, quite suddenly, he heard a voice, like the voice of starlight, and it was as if all the shadows were lifted away.

He stood in a walled garden flooded with warm sunlight. In front of him, beneath a tree covered in white blossom, stood Maerad, holding her arms high, as if she had just made a spell. She was wearing a long red dress which fell in simple folds about her body, and Hem saw that two of her fingers were missing from her left hand. In his dream, he felt no sense of shock: he simply accepted it, as he accepted the garden and Maerad's presence. Their eyes met and Maerad smiled, lowering her arms. Hem smiled back. He felt entirely happy, warmed through to his marrow with a sense of deep well-being. There was no need to speak, and in that moment he wanted nothing. It seemed they stood together for a long moment, and then the vision faded into a warm, comfortable darkness, and at last he fell into a dreamless sleep.

X

RAIN

ONCE the rain came, it didn't stop.

The steady grey downpour matched Hem's mood, which was one of unrelieved gloom. Since they had left Thorkul's Place, he felt as if their group had been put under a curse; not unlikely, he thought sourly, if Karim was meeting with a Hull. His sense of hurt at Karim's betrayal was at first softened by his dream about Maerad: the following morning he had woken well-rested, warmed through with an afterglow of the happiness he had felt in the dream. He thought the dream was a sign that Maerad was expecting him, and it made him feel sure that they were getting closer to finding her.

He told Saliman about it as they broke their fast. "I'm sure it means that she's alive," he said. "It wasn't an ordinary dream. It was like the dreams I had about Nyanar..." Nyanar was the Elidhu whom Hem had encountered in the Suderain. His enchantment had lifted Hem into another, earlier age, and Hem remembered it as if it were at once a dream and quite real.

Saliman listened attentively, but all he said was: "I hope you're right, Hem. I really hope you're right." In those words, Hem heard all Saliman's doubts: his uncertainty that they would, after all, find Maerad, that they were even following the right path. After that, the warmth of the dream dissipated all too quickly.

And they were certainly dogged by ill-luck. After it had rained for three days solid, Marich and Karim, whose relationship was edgy at the best of times, had a violent argument over something so trivial that neither of them could remember the original point of conflict, and were now refusing to speak to each other except through a third party. The third party was usually Hekibel, who was exasperated with both of them. The dog Fenek bit Karim on the hand, and the wound had to be bound. Even the horses, great, patient beasts whom Marich tended lovingly, were ill-tempered, and one of them kicked Marich in the thigh, giving him a bad bruise that would have crippled him if Saliman had not tended it.

After their conversation about Karim, Hem and Saliman kept more to themselves, but in the general gloom this was scarcely noticed. It was miserable camping in their tent: it might, as Hem remarked, keep out the rain, but it wasn't designed to be a boat. One night, setting it up in the dark when they were exhausted after a day's hard travelling, they unwittingly placed themselves in a dip. They woke up in a freezing puddle, their blankets soaking. Once their blankets were wet, they couldn't dry them properly. They hung them in the caravan, where they filled the small space with a musty, damp smell.

Aside from anything else, the tedium was suffocating. The weather made performances, or even rehearsals, impossible. The five travellers were forced on each other's company in the claustrophobic space of the caravan all day long, though Hem chose, as much as possible, to sit outside with whoever was · driving the caravan. It was usually Saliman, who for his own reasons wanted to keep his eye on the road; there wasn't much competition, as it was cold and wet work. Hem only came in when he was damp to the bone, or if Hekibel had had enough of the poisonous atmosphere in the caravan and wanted a break. Or if Karim happened to take a shift; he avoided Karim's company as much as was humanly possible.

They mostly passed the time by playing a complicated

game with sheep knucklebones, which Marich kept in the caravan for just such occasions. But Karim wouldn't play if Marich was in the game; instead, he would sit outside the group, maintaining a steadfast pose of mortal offence, which effectively dampened any enjoyment the others might otherwise have had. There was a tension between Marich and Hekibel too, which Hem didn't understand; he guessed that perhaps Marich was jealous that Hekibel enjoyed Saliman's company. If so, Marich never seemed to resent Saliman, whom he probably spoke to more than anyone else. Hem was bored by these adult squabbles, which mostly mystified him. They seemed an awful waste of time.

To make matters worse, there were no villages for many leagues, so there was no chance of getting out of the caravan and seeking relief from other company. Without magery, it was impossible to light a fire and Saliman was very reluctant to use Bardic powers unless it was absolutely necessary, fearing to attract attention. Karim was heard to wonder out loud what the use of Bards were, if they wouldn't use their magery, and even muttered about hangers-on. Only Irc seemed unaffected by the general irritability: he stayed away from Fenek, stole some more gems from the players' cupboards, and ate as much food as he could get his claws on.

Saliman had other concerns. Just after the rains began they passed the crossroads where the South and West Roads intersected, which marked the rough boundary between Lauchomon and the region called Lukernil. Saliman had feared real trouble here; if the Black Army was marching towards Annar, the chances of encountering it were high, and he also thought it likely that scouts or spies would be posted near the crossroads. He cast a glimveil of illusion over the caravan, and maintained a constant vigilance; but they saw nothing living nearby except some wet goats and a few rooks.

All the same, Saliman was troubled by how unusually deserted the West Road was, and his sharp eyes noted signs that the others missed: the rubbish left by passing soldiers on the side of the road, or a house in the distance that had been burned to the ground, leaving only its blackened chimneys pointing dolefully to the sky. He said nothing of these sightings, not even to Hem, but he kept a glimmerspell on the caravan all the time now, and no matter how tired he and Hem were, they laid a glimveil over the camp every night.

The only positive aspects were that now they were travelling rapidly towards Innail, and there was no sign of the stranger who had been following them. Saliman didn't believe that the Hull – if it was a Hull – had abandoned their trail, but he was glad to have at least that sense of oppression lifted, even if temporarily.

After a week the rains lifted, although the clouds hung in heavy purple swags, promising more. For the moment, the travellers were happy not to hear its constant hammering on the roof of the caravan, and Karim and Marich even exchanged some courteous words. That day, they reached the ford over the Imlan River. Past the crossing, they entered the region called Ifant – rich, fertile lowlands that ran all the way to the Weywood – and from here the West Road hugged the Inlan all the way to Innail. The river, fed by the heavy rains, rushed brown and swollen over the ford, and the travellers contemplated it gloomily.

"How are we going to cross that?" asked Marich, shaking his head.

"We have to turn back," said Karim. "Look at it! We'll be swept away and drowned, for certain."

"We can't turn back," Marich said flatly. "There's nowhere to turn back to. And Hiert is only a league or so from the ford. We could stay at the tavern there, and dry off."

"I think we could make it," said Saliman thoughtfully. He stood with his arms crossed, studying the surface of the water. "I know this ford. It's not as deep as it looks, and although the current is dangerous, I think the caravan is heavy enough to stand against it. I think if I cast a fastening charm on it to stabilize it more, we could get over without mishap."

For Hem, there was no question: they had to cross. The thought of tracking back over the miserable countryside they had just crossed was unbearable; and he was sure that Maerad was in front of him, not behind. Right now, he was willing to risk his neck just to escape the caravan. His fascination with the life of a player had evaporated entirely over the past week.

The others listened seriously to Saliman, and Hem studied their faces. He realized that Saliman had become the actual leader of their little band; the others, even Karim, deferred to his advice. Perhaps, he thought, that was why Karim had been so irritable recently, even though Saliman had been unfailingly polite to him, and had never once challenged his authority.

After some more discussion, they decided to risk the ford. Hem and Hekibel climbed into the caravan, Hekibel holding a protesting Fenek, and Karim took the reins. The horses baulked at going into the water, and in the end Saliman and Marich led them, plunging into the water up to their waists. The river was very strong, rushing swiftly over the flat stones of the ford, and if it hadn't been for Saliman's fastening charm the men might well have lost their footing and been swept away; but the caravan stayed steady and they emerged safely on the other bank.

Saliman and Marich were shivering with cold and Hekibel shooed them into the caravan to change into some drier clothes. When they moved on, everyone was more optimistic than they had been in days. Hem's gloom lifted: soon he would be sitting by a real fire, in warm clothes, with a hot meal in front of him. And if their luck held, they could be in Innail in less than a week. Maerad might be there, waiting...

Even when the rain started again, sweeping the road before them with heavy swathes of grey water, it didn't dampen his spirits. Hem remembered his dream about Maerad. Yes, they were getting closer, they would find her, he was sure. He turned his face to the road with newly kindled hope.

They hadn't gone far before Marich noticed that one of the horses, Usha, was limping heavily. He and Saliman examined her, and found the inner part of her hoof was bruised. There was a nasty cut on her fetlock as well, suggesting that she had been hit by something in the river, a stone flung by the current perhaps, as they crossed. Saliman managed to ease the pain slightly, and attended to the cut, but both Marich and Saliman realized that Usha really needed to be taken out of harness and rested. On the other hand, she would be much better off resting in a stable than if they stopped in the middle of nowhere in the pouring rain.

Marich and Saliman huddled together under a tree and discussed what to do, watched anxiously by the other travellers. In the end, they decided to push on carefully to Hiert, where they could find stabling for the horses and shelter for themselves. The risk was that Usha might break down entirely on the way, but if all went well they would make it before dusk.

Usha, understandably enough, was reluctant to move at all once they had stopped, but with a little persuasion the caravan began to roll on slowly. The horses plodded miserably on, braced against the downpour, and Hem felt his heart sinking down into his boots again as he looked out over the dripping, rain-swept landscape. The Inlan to their right looked dangerously swollen, running almost to the height of its banks and in places spilling over them. He wondered what would happen if it kept raining.

He was soaked to the skin, but he stayed out in front with Saliman. Despite the cold, the atmosphere was more pleasant outside. Inside Karim and Marich were bickering again, and Hekibel was silently mending some costumes, pushing her needle through the material with a rather pointed savagery. Irc was perched on the bench beside Hekibel, watching the needle. He was hoping that he might get a chance to steal it, if she looked away; and he hated the rain.

The shadows were lengthening when they came around a bend in the road and saw a cluster of stone buildings gathered on each side of the road. Hiert at last! Hem had seldom been so glad to see anything in his life. Now they could get out of the rain and dry out their clothes. The horses, sensing that they were close to their destination, picked up their pace, and before long they pulling up in a large yard behind the village's tavern. Saliman and Marich hastily began to unharness the horses, while Karim went inside to negotiate some stabling rates, or so he claimed, although Hem thought he just wanted an ale.

"Check in the stables for any spare stalls," Saliman said to Hem. "I want to stable these poor beasts right away, and I can't see an ostler. We'll talk to the owner afterwards. I know him; he's a good man, and he won't mind."

Hem nodded and ran into the stables. For a moment he stood dripping in the entrance, breathing in the good smell of horses and straw; it was such a relief to be out of the constant assault of the rain. The stables were completely empty.

"There's plenty of space," he called out to Saliman.

"Good," said Saliman shortly. He led Usha into the stable. "Whoa girl, you'll be fed soon… Go inside, Hem, and get warm. I'll join you in a moment."

Hem nodded, grabbed his pack from the caravan and dashed into the tavern. He walked down the flagged hallway that ran from the back door to the front, leaving behind him a trail of wet footprints. The lamps were not yet lit, and the hallway was almost completely dark, but he groped his way through the shadows to the taproom at the front. Through the gloom he saw that there was a fire laid in the hearth, but no one had lit that either. Aside from Hekibel, nobody was there.

"Where is everybody?" asked Hem. "Where's Karim?"

"He went upstairs to see if he could find the tavern owner," said Hekibel. There was a tremor in her voice. "It's strange, nobody seems to be about."

Hem's heart sank as he looked around the room. It was not as dark in here as in the passageway; the last chill light of day spilt greyly through the diamond-paned windows. There was a stale smell in the air, as if the room had been empty for some time. A dish of beans, half eaten, lay on a table nearby, and a chair was pushed back as if someone had suddenly stood up. Another chair nearby had fallen over. A mug was broken and spilt on the floor, the beer dried in a dark stain, and several other cups, half drunk, had been left where they stood, scattered on small tables around the room. There seemed to be a thin layer of dust over everything.

"I wonder what happened here?" he said.

"I don't know," said Hekibel. "But it's a bit – a bit strange."

"Well, I'm cold." Hem walked over to the fire and pointed his hand at it. *"Nor!"* he said. Instantly the fire began to blaze, as if it had been burning for hours. He and Hekibel drew close, stretching out their freezing hands to the flames. Steam began to rise from Hem's drenched clothes. With the noise of the rain outside, the room suddenly seemed a cosy refuge.

"It must be handy being a Bard," Hekibel said. "I wish I could do things like that."

"Sometimes it is handy," said Hem. "Saliman says we mustn't use magery unless we have to. But right now, I'm so cold that I don't care."

Before long they heard Karim's footsteps slowly coming down the stairs. He came into the taproom, his face dark and puzzled, though he briefly brightened when he saw the fire and joined the other two there, rubbing his hands together.

"A fire! By the Light! That's a sight to cheer the heart!" he said.

"Did you find anybody?" asked Hekibel.

"Not a soul, my dear. Not even a mouse. I like it not."

"Something's happened," said Hem. He wondered if it was anything to do with Hulls, and cast Karim a dark glance. But Karim was looking towards the door, where Marich and Saliman were entering, their hair plastered to their heads. Before them floated a magelight, and Hem realized how dark it had grown in the taproom, even as they had been talking. It was now almost full night.

"Nobody here?" said Saliman. His gaze swept around the taproom, resting on the spilt mug, the abandoned meal.

"No one," said Karim. "I just checked upstairs. It looks as if everyone has run away."

Saliman frowned, but didn't say anything. He took a tinderbox from his pack and lit the oil lamps, and a warm glow filled the room.

"I do not smell the work of the Dark in this place," Saliman said, when he had finished. "But for the moment I cannot guess why it has been abandoned. It is owned by Finar, a proud man if ever I have met one; he would defend his tavern against the Nameless One himself. But it feels as if no one has been here for at least a day. And they clearly left in a hurry."

"We didn't see anyone in the village, either," said Hem, remembering back. At the time, as they came down the road, he had thought it was because the weather was so bad; but he couldn't remember seeing lights in any windows. There should have been some, surely, on such a gloomy day.

"I suppose we should just make the best of it," said Marich. "I don't want to go back out into *that*." For a moment the five of them stood in the empty taproom, listening to the downpour outside. It sounded, if anything, as if it were getting heavier.

"Me neither," said Hem, with feeling.

Saliman shrugged. "I suppose we have shelter, and the horses, at least, are content. Hem and I can put some veiling about the building, so we don't attract the attention of passersby. And even if enemies were close, who would be out on a night like this? All the same, I would give much to know why the people here left in such a hurry… Hem, let's go upstairs and see what we can find."

"Nobody's there," said Karim, an edge of testiness in his voice.

"I know," said Saliman. "But it could be that we might find some clue about what has happened here."

Together Hem and Saliman climbed the narrow staircase off the hallway, their magelights casting a silvery glow over the dark wood. They said nothing until they were upstairs. Saliman briefly checked the rooms: they were mostly bedchambers, and all of them looked as if people had left hurriedly.

"What do you think happened here?" asked Hem.

"I can only guess," said Saliman. "Something frightened the people here, that seems very clear. But there's no sign of violence, nor any smell of sorcery."

"Should we stay here?"

"I don't think we have much choice at the moment," said Saliman. "Usha can't go any further today, and the rain has set in. In any case, we should stay the night and decide what to do tomorrow."

They found nothing of interest and gloomily returned to the taproom. Karim was lounging by the fire with his feet up, and had helped himself to beer. Hekibel and Marich were investigating the kitchen, and Marich had already lit the stove. They had found some stale bread and a stew that was going mouldy, which Hekibel had thrown out, but there was still plenty of edible food, including a huge, round cheese mouldering fragrantly under a cloth, some winter apples, turnips and carrots, and plenty of flour and grains. Hekibel had even found some yeast and was already pounding dough on the broad wooden table, her hands covered with flour.

"I thought I'd make some bread and a stew, and maybe an apple pie," said Hekibel. "There's some smoked meat hanging in the larder, and various other bits and pieces. At least we can have some dinner. We can leave some coins to pay, we're not looters..."

"A wonderful idea," said Saliman, smiling. "I'll investigate the cellar. As I recall, Finar had some very good Annaren wines... But first Hem and I will attend to some charms, so our lights don't attract any unwelcome attention. We might as well do it before we get changed, Hem, because we have to go outside and we'll just get wet again."

Hem nodded, and he and Saliman went back through the taproom and out the front door of the tavern. The Inlan ran close to the road here, a couple of hundred spans away, and Hem could hear its roar even over the rain.

I think that the river is very close to flooding, said Saliman, speaking into Hem's mind so he could hear him over the rain. *And this is a low-lying area. It could be that the villagers left because they feared it would break its banks.*

Maybe... Hem replied dubiously. It didn't sound likely to

him – wouldn't they rather be working to protect their properties? He squinted up the road, trying to see through the pall of darkness and rain. It was pitch dark, but as his eyes adjusted, Hem could make out the black shapes of the other buildings that lined the street. Then he blinked – further up, there was a bright light, a fire perhaps.

It doesn't look as if everyone's gone, he said, nudging Saliman.

You're right, said Saliman. *I wonder … perhaps we could find out what has happened here … but we should complete the charm first.*

He and Saliman had become very practised at working together as mages. Covering a large building like the tavern with a glimveil that would fool the eyes of Hulls was tricky and effortful, but they completed the task quickly. When they had finished, they stood back and inspected their work: from more than two paces away, the tavern looked as deserted as everywhere else, its windows blank and dark.

Shall we go and see what the light is? said Hem.

Saliman nodded, and they cautiously made their way up the road. They lit no magelights; they were uncertain what they would find, and didn't want to take any chances.

As they drew closer, they saw that the light was indeed a fire. A house was ablaze, the flames spitting under the heavy rain, which was already beginning to put it out. They watched as the roof beams collapsed spectacularly in an explosion of sparks.

"Nothing here," said Saliman out loud, and turned to go back to the tavern. "And there's certainly no danger of it spreading…"

Hem dragged his eyes away from the fire, and was about to follow Saliman when a figure sprang out of the darkness and lunged at Saliman. Taken off guard, Saliman was knocked to the ground. Hem shouted with surprise and leapt towards them, wondering what to do; he couldn't hit the assailant with any guarantee that he wouldn't hit Saliman. For a brief moment, the two figures grappled fiercely, rolling over and over on the road, and then there was a sudden burst of mage-light and Saliman sprang to his feet. His assailant lay gasping on the ground, utterly still, his body twisted in a strange attitude.

Saliman was standing over his attacker, panting. A magelight glimmered to life before him, and the whites of his eyes flashed as he turned towards Hem.

"Are you all right?" Hem asked.

"Yes," said Saliman. "No thanks to our friend here."

Hem glanced at the man on the ground. His face was pressed against the mud, one arm flung out, the other twisted under-neath him. His body shuddered in the rain, but he couldn't move a muscle: Saliman had stilled him with a charm.

"I've stilled everything living within fifty paces of this place," said Saliman. "Except you, of course. Nothing can attack us now, but perhaps it might do to have a quick look around."

The man on the ground screamed through his frozen lips, and the hair rose on Hem's neck; he didn't sound human. He shuddered and gladly turned away to scout the surrounding area. There wasn't much to see: nearby was a low stone wall, and a couple of fruit trees, but otherwise it was clear of hiding places. Hem supposed that the man had been hiding behind the wall before he attacked Saliman. He returned to Saliman, who was wiping the mud off his face with his sleeves.

"I couldn't get much wetter than I already am," he said. "But mud as well! The indignity!" He smiled, and Hem smiled back uncertainly, knowing that Saliman was trying to reassure him. Hem felt in his bones that all was not well. "I suppose we should find out what manner of man decided to pounce on me, and why. He's not a Hull, I know that much."

A short distance away there was an open byre, now empty,

which would provide a shelter from the rain. Saliman bent down and said something indistinctly to the man, and then picked him up, holding his elbow, and led him to the byre. Once inside, the man sat down heavily on the ground, hiding his face in his hands. In the pale magelight he looked completely wretched. His clothes were rags, and seemed to be charred, his hair was stiff with mud, and his limbs shook violently. Hem watched him suspiciously from the doorway, his hand on the hilt of his shortsword.

"Until I release this charm, you cannot move unless I permit you to," said Saliman.

The man whimpered, but said nothing.

"I have no wish to harm you," Saliman continued. "I want to know who you are, and what has happened here. What is your name?"

For a time the only sound was the rain falling on the ground outside. Hem was just about to repeat Saliman's question when the man groaned and attempted to speak, and Saliman held his hand up to Hem, bidding him to be quiet.

"I can't – I can't remember…" said the man. "I had a name once. No name now. No name."

"Is the house that burned down your house?" said Saliman, again looking across at Hem. His voice was much gentler; clearly they had found a madman, a creature who deserved pity, not aggression.

"House?"

"The fire," said Hem impatiently. "Was it your house?"

"Fire! What fire? Is there a fire?" The man stared at them in sudden panic, and Hem at last saw his ruined face. The man's face was covered with scabs, his mouth was open and drooling, and the veins on his neck were like thick, twisted cords. But worst of all were his eyes, which started out of his head, rolling with terror. His irises were almost completely silvered over

with strange milky cataracts, as if a spider had spun a thick web
over his eyes; whatever colour his eyes had been, they were
now pale yellow, the pupil barely visible.

Saliman leapt back as if he had been burned, and swore
under his breath. "Get out, Hem!" he said, turning around
sharply. "Get out of here!"

"No," said Hem.

"It's the White Sickness. By the Light, I understand now.
Hem, you are a Healer, you understand disease: the White
Sickness is very contagious. You must go at once."

"No, I'm not leaving you," said Hem. "What are we going to
do with him?"

The man had turned away from them and was now sobbing
into his hands. Hem stared at him with a mixture of pity and
disgust.

"He's in the last stages," said Saliman. "You see his eyes: they
are almost white. Soon he'll be completely blind. I'm surprised
that he saw us, frankly. He's out of his mind – he leapt on me
with the strength of a lion and I barely fought him off. He was
trying to kill me. I would have had no chance without magery.
And I expect he's already forgotten why he did it. Whoever he
is, we will never know."

"Can't we heal him?" Hem looked over at Saliman, and
Saliman dropped his eyes and was silent for a long time. Hem
waited, feeling an awful premonition growing inside him.

"I'll be honest, Hem," Saliman said. "If I were in the
Healing Houses in Turbansk, with all the physic there and
the best of care, I would rate this man's chances very small.
And even there, to drive back this sickness would take all my
strength. Here we have not the medicines, nor the care, and I
am already very weary. Even if I could drive the sickness out
of his body, which I doubt, I do not think he would survive
it."

"We can't leave him like this!" Hem was now examining the man with a Healer's eye. When he had first seen his face, he had thought him an old man, but he realized with a shock that he was probably much younger. His body was skeletal, as if he had been starved for a long time, and there were sores all over him. He was clearly in a high fever, and his cheeks were flushed, but he was shaking violently with cold, whimpering and moaning. Hem noticed that he had serious burns on his legs and hands as well. Remembering stories he had heard about the madness caused by the White Sickness, Hem thought that it was likely that the man had burned the house down, whether it was his own or not.

"No, we cannot leave him in such suffering." There was a tone in Saliman's voice which made Hem look at him sharply. "Hem, please leave."

"No," Hem said again. "What are you going to do?"

"I will give him the only mercy left to him in this world," said Saliman. "I wish I knew his name. Well, if you will not go, I cannot make you."

Saliman bowed his head for a moment, and then he leaned forward and placed his palms over the man's eyes, breathing in deeply. For a moment the byre was flooded with blinding white light, and then it went utterly dark. When Saliman did not renew his magelight, Hem made one himself. On the other side of the byre the two figures were outlined in the silvery light, one now silent and still on the ground, one standing silently, leaning against the wall, his eyes closed.

"Saliman?" Hem's voice was high with anxiety. "Saliman? Are you all right?"

Saliman sighed heavily. Then he stood straight and lifted his arm, and a silver radiance began to glimmer faintly around his form. "May the Light protect this man's soul," he said. "And may he find solace beyond the Gate." Then he lowered his

arms, and the illumination within him faded away. He looked
utterly exhausted. He slowly lifted his head and looked at Hem,
and a light stood in his eyes that made Hem's throat tighten
with sorrow.

"Well, that's done," said Saliman. He began to say something else, but his voice faltered and he fell silent.

Hem stepped forward, wanting to take Saliman's arm, but
Saliman waved him away. "You must not touch me, Hem," he
said. "Do not even come near me. I may have the White Sickness
myself now."

Hem felt the blood drain from his face. "You what?"

"I may have the illness. That man, whoever he was, breathed
and dribbled all over me. He might even have bitten me. You
know how swiftly it spreads. I would rather not take the risk of
passing it on to you."

Hem stared at Saliman in shock. "That can't happen," he
said. "You can't get sick. You're a Healer."

"You know very well that Healers can get sick," Saliman
said, his voice like iron. "Now, Hem, listen to me. I want you
to go back to the tavern and tell the others what has happened.
You didn't touch the sick man, so I do not believe you will
be infected. I will go to the ostler's room, by the stables. I can
make a fire there. I'd like some dinner, so if you can bring a
plate of something to the door … and bring my pack, also.
Leave them by the door. Do not come in. If I am well tomorrow
morning, we will know I do not have the sickness. At least it
is quick."

"But…"

"Go," said Saliman harshly. "Do what I tell you. Go now."

Hem nodded, swallowing, and ran blindly back to the
tavern. Such was his distress that he ran past it in the dark, and
had to backtrack: the glimveil was working all too well.

Irc, perched on a chair near the fire, cawed in welcome and

fluttered over to Hem's shoulder, and Hekibel came out of the kitchen, her arms still smeared with flour.

"Where's Saliman?" she said, looking past Hem's shoulder.

"You were a long time," said Marich, at the same time. "We were about to send out a search party."

Hem stood dripping in the doorway, and found that he didn't know what to say. He went over to the fire.

"What's happened?" asked Hekibel. "Hem, what's wrong?"

Hem felt tears gathering in his throat, but he refused to cry. "Saliman was attacked by a man with the White Sickness," he said. "He won't come in, for fear that he is infected. He's going to the ostler's room by the stables."

The three players looked at Hem in shock, and Hekibel began to run towards the back door.

"He won't let you near him," said Hem. "We'll know if he's sick by tomorrow. He might not be. He wants some dry clothes, and he'll need some food. He said to put them in the doorway of the ostler's room."

"If he's in the stables, we can't get to the horses," said Karim.

"He won't be near the caravan," Hem said, looking at Karim with open dislike. "He is trying to protect us."

"No wonder this place is abandoned," said Karim. "The White Sickness runs through a place like wildfire ... they say it only takes a touch for the corruption to spread from man to man..."

Hem said nothing. He took his pack and went upstairs so he could change out of his soaking clothes. The clothes in his pack were still damp, and after a little thought he opened the chest in the room. Inside were tunics and jerkins, a little big for him but mercifully dry, and he threw them over his head. He took his own clothes downstairs so he could hang them in front of the fire and dry them out. When he walked in, there was an uncomfortable silence, as if everyone had been talking about him. He saw that they were all pale with fear, and his stomach lurched with sudden contempt.

"You leave here if you like," he said fiercely. "I'll stay with Saliman. You needn't worry. But we might as well have that apple pie."

"There might be nothing wrong with him," said Hekibel, her voice wavering. "But if he is sick, no one can heal the White Sickness..."

"Bards can cure it," said Hem. "If he's sick, I'll heal him."

"Have you healed it before?" asked Hekibel. Her voice was almost a whisper.

Hem hesitated. "No," he said. "But that doesn't mean that I can't."

"I've heard that not even Bards can drive it out," said Marich, holding Hem's gaze. "And only a few live once the sickness takes hold. And all of them blind. I've seen it myself. I like Saliman, but I don't think we do any good by staying. Him or us. He'd say the same."

"I don't want to leave Saliman like a – like a—" Hekibel's voice broke, and she turned her face away.

"You were always soft on him," said Marich, turning on her bitterly. "He's a Bard, Hekibel. A *Bard*. They have their own ways. They don't have anything to do with us."

Karim was standing by the fire, drumming his fingers on the mantelpiece. "Myself, I judge that we should leave," he said, avoiding Hem's eyes. "We can't go anywhere immediately, that's obvious. And we should wait and see if the Bard is sick. It may be that he is not sick. In any case, Usha will not be able to take us further tonight."

"Saliman said he thought she might be all right tomorrow, if we took her slowly," said Marich.

Hem felt a sick, impotent rage welling up inside him. "It

smells like the bread is out of the oven. And is that stew cooked?" he asked coldly. "I'll take some to Saliman. He deserves something for healing Usha's lameness enough to get us here in the first place."

Hekibel nodded and hurried out of the room, while Hem stood awkwardly in front of Marich and Karim, scowling at the floor. She returned swiftly with a bowl of stew, into which she had stuck a large hunk of fresh bread. She had covered it with a plate to keep it warm. Hem took it without speaking, and marched out to the back. He stood for a moment in the doorway, looking across the flagged yard. The rain was a solid curtain over the night; there was something merciless about it. He could see a light in the ostler's room. Hem crossed the yard as quickly as possible and opened the door.

Saliman was inside, sitting at the table on the far side of the room. He had changed into some unfamiliar clothes which had clearly belonged to the ostler, and had lit a fire, obviously by magery, since it was burning brightly and the room was already warm. He smiled when he saw Hem.

"My thanks, Hem," he said. "Just put it on the floor inside the doorway. And cleanse yourself when you leave – wash your hands, in particular. I've touched the latch on the door."

Hem nodded. "I – I forgot your pack," he said. "I'll bring it in a moment. And I didn't bring any wine."

"The dinner is very welcome," said Saliman.

"I'll bring the wine with your pack," said Hem. "And some apple pie, later."

"That, too, would be good. But I don't want you getting soaked again, being my messenger boy."

Hem hesitated, and then said with a rush: "If you have the White Sickness, can't I heal you?"

"We don't know yet if I have it," said Saliman.

"But I could heal you!"

"I don't know if you could, Hem. I know you are a talented Healer, but this is a sickness which defeats many Bards, even Healers. Only the greatest Healers have been able to drive it back. It is probable that if you tried, you would catch the illness yourself. In the meantime, I don't want to take any risks. In any case, I feel perfectly well at present. It's very pleasant to be dry and warm at last!"

"The players want to leave."

"That doesn't surprise me. Now, Hem, I know this is difficult. If I have this disease, we will know tomorrow morning; I should have the first signs then. At the moment, I feel no fever. Go back to the tavern, and get warm, and try not to worry."

"I'll bring your pack."

"Yes, bring me my pack. And the wine. You mustn't worry, Hem, I am warm and dry and fed. Now, boy, go!" Hem realized that Saliman would not pick up his dinner until Hem had left, and that it would be growing cold. He shut the door behind him and ran back across the yard to the tavern.

Hekibel's stew was very good, as were her pie and bread. Hem ate them for the nourishment, but the food turned to ashes in his mouth. He could not get the image of the sick man out of his head, the horror of his ruined face; the thought of that decay happening to Saliman was unbearable. Irc sat on Hem's shoulder, accepting scraps of food, but he was unusually quiet. It was an uncomfortable meal, as a heavy silence cast its pall over the table, and neither Karim nor Marich would look at him. When he had finished eating, Hem went upstairs and walked into a bedchamber at random. Irc flew to the bedstead and ruffled his feathers, and Hem threw himself on the bed and fell asleep almost at once.

When he woke up, it had stopped raining. Hem lay sleepily

in bed for a little while, letting the peace wash over him, until he remembered his anxiety about Saliman and leapt out of bed. It was still dark, but he knew it was early morning, and he could hear movements downstairs.

Hekibel was setting out bread and cheese on the table, and frying some beans on the stove. She bade him good morning, and returned to the kitchen. There was no sign of Karim and Marich. Hem suspected that they were harnessing the horses, getting ready to leave.

They are afraid, said Irc.

So am I, Hem said. *But I'm not running.*

They do not love Saliman as you do.

Don't they? thought Hem savagely, looking at Hekibel's ashen face through the open door. *No, they don't,* he said to Irc. *I would never abandon Saliman.*

Irc flapped off to investigate their surroundings now it wasn't raining, and Hem made a quick breakfast, trying not to think about what would happen if Saliman had caught the White Sickness. Then, his heart hammering with apprehension, he made a parcel of bread and cheese to take to Saliman. When he opened the back door, he saw that the yard was flooded. The water wasn't very deep, but it already lapped at the first step that led up to the back door. He took his boots off and left them by the door and then, grimacing, waded through ankle-deep water, its coldness shocking him properly awake, and knocked on Saliman's door. There was no answer. He pushed the door open and went inside.

Saliman was asleep on the narrow bed in the far corner. He lay so still that Hem thought for a heart-stopping moment that he was already dead, but then he muttered and turned over. Even from this distance, Hem could see that he was ill. He had clearly had a restless night: the blanket lay on the floor and his clothes were twisted around him. His skin was slick with sweat and his hair was soaked, his braids tangled.

Hem sagged against the door frame, trying to catch his breath. At that moment he could not have said what he felt: it was as if he had been dealt a mortal wound, but was yet to feel the pain. Saliman was deathly sick. And he had no idea how to help him.

XI

THE WHITE SICKNESS

HEM splashed back through the yard to the tavern. He heard Marich and Karim talking in the stables, but didn't turn to look at them. The water had risen even in the short time he had been outside, and it had now spread over the first step. He looked up at the sky: it was still overcast with heavy clouds. There was more rain on the way, surely.

In the kitchen, Hekibel was perched on a chair, her head in her hands. She looked up when Hem re-entered and met his eyes. Hem didn't say anything, but she read the news in his face. She bit her lip and turned away.

Hem sat down opposite Hekibel. "I suppose you'll be leaving," he said, his voice harsh.

"Yes," said Hekibel. Her voice was so soft he barely heard what she said.

"It's flooding outside anyway. The river's broken its banks, I think."

"Then you will have to leave here, as well," Hekibel said, turning back to face Hem. "Are you going to stay with Saliman?"

Hem met her eyes, and she saw the anger inside him. Hekibel blushed and dropped her gaze to the table.

"I suppose I didn't need to ask," she said. "But the White Sickness, Hem ... it's a terrible, terrible thing ... and there's no cure."

"I am a Healer," said Hem. "And I'm not leaving him, no matter what. He's my friend."

"If it's flooding here, you'll have to move him."

"There's a wheelbarrow in the stables, I can put him in there and push him somewhere. There's higher ground behind the tavern – there will surely be some byre or hut where we can shelter. If it doesn't start raining again, we'll probably be all right."

Hekibel stared at him, and Hem saw the fear and shame and pain in her face, and his rage spluttered out, leaving behind a bleak despair. It was no use being angry. What could the players do if they stayed, except become as ill as Saliman? And they had to part ways, in any case.

"You should go," he said, with an effort. "Saliman would say it was right."

"But what about you?"

"I'll be fine. There's a path that leads uphill, which I saw earlier; we'll follow that. Anyway, I think the water is rising, so we had better move quickly, or we'll get stuck..."

Hekibel nodded, and Hem ran upstairs for his pack, stuffing his dried clothes inside it and quickly gleaned some food from the tavern kitchen. Then he went to the stables, where Marich and Karim had already put aside food supplies from those in the caravan. Fenek was on the back step of the caravan, growling uneasily at the rising water. The horses were harnessed and stood in the water up to their fetlocks, looking miserable. Hem picked up the supplies and thanked them gruffly.

Karim cleared his throat. "The water's rising all the time," he said.

"I know," said Hem. He didn't want to hear any excuses. "Thank you for the food. I'm just going to take that wheelbarrow, so I can carry Saliman to higher ground."

"Hem, it's not that we don't want to stay," said Marich. "But it won't help him if we all get the sickness. I saw him, he has it.

It's deadly, Hem, he won't get better. Nobody does."

Hem met Marich's eyes and then looked away. He liked Marich, and could even see his point of view. That didn't mean that the players' decision didn't hurt. "Farewell, then."

"May the Light shine on your path," said Marich.

Hem nodded. He didn't feel generous enough to make the courteous return, and sloshed over to where a large wooden wheelbarrow was propped against the wall. It was heavy, and he felt a pang of anxiety as he took it down and pushed it out into the yard, shrugging off Marich's offer of help. How was he to get Saliman into it by himself, let alone push it any distance?

He returned to the stables to pick up the supplies, and put them in the wheelbarrow with their tent, and then went to the tavern to get his pack. Just before he left, he stripped some blankets from a bed and took them too. Then he went to the ostler's room and opened the door.

Saliman was sitting on the bed, his head in his hands. He looked up when Hem entered. His eyes were bloodshot and he looked fevered, but otherwise he didn't seem too ill. "Hem," he said. "I am sick. Go away."

"I'm not going away," said Hem. "I've decided. I don't care if I get sick."

Saliman smiled wearily. "The problem is that I do care," he said. "Please, for once in your life, listen to me. Go with Hekibel and Marich, they'll look after you."

"The tavern is flooding," said Hem, picking up Saliman's pack. "You'll have to move in any case. I got a wheelbarrow for our things – I thought you could get into it as well."

"I'm serious, Hem. Leave me. I am already very sick, and I can feel the illness creeping through me. It is vile."

Hem turned at the door, and his eyes burned with a despairing passion. "Saliman, I know what I am deciding.

I am not leaving. I can't. So don't tell me again, because I won't listen."

There was a long silence.

"We have to move, and find some shelter, and then I will heal you, and then we will be all right." Hem went out the door and threw Saliman's pack on the wheelbarrow and returned. "Can you walk to the wheelbarrow? It might be better to stay barefoot – I'll put your socks and boots in there so you can warm your feet afterwards..."

"I can walk," said Saliman. "I can even walk out of this ill-starred village. I won't forgive you, Hem, for risking your life like this..."

"I'm not risking my life. You said that Bards can heal the White Sickness. So I will heal you, and then we can just go on looking for Maerad. It was probably time we left the players anyway, given that Karim seems to be a friend of the Hulls."

Saliman stood up and swayed, putting out his hand and steadying himself against the wall.

"Do you want some help?" asked Hem, starting forward.

"All right, Hem. I have not the strength to oppose you. But if you're going to do this, let's be sensible. I don't want you to touch me, and you must come near me as little as possible."

"Do you want some help?"

Saliman shot Hem a look of black anger. He drew on his cloak over the clothes he had slept in and stepped shakily out of the door. He waited by the wheelbarrow at a safe distance while Hem checked it over, making sure he hadn't forgotten anything, and then ran inside to take some firewood from the pile in the kitchen. He spread the tent over their belongings to keep them dry. Saliman could sit inside the barrow comfortably enough, though Hem nervously wondered if he would be able to push it with Saliman's weight as well. As they stood there, Hekibel emerged from the back door of the tavern, holding her boots in her hands. She started when she saw them and hesitantly stood with the water around her ankles, brushing her hair out of her eyes.

Saliman raised his hand in farewell, and Hekibel waved back, unable to speak. Then she burst into tears and hurried to the stables, where Karim was already guiding the caravan and its grumpy horses into the yard.

Hem stood by while the golden caravan pulled out of the yard, out of his life. The water was almost up to its axle, and neither the horses nor Fenek looked very happy. Usha, he saw, was still lame, if not as seriously as she had been the previous day. Then he mindtouched Irc, who was nearby, and told him they were leaving the tavern.

Is Saliman sick? asked Irc. *We should stay to look after him ... and I haven't finished looking here yet.*

We can't stay, said Hem impatiently. *There's water everywhere. And you shouldn't be robbing empty houses, anyway. If you want to join us, we're going up that hill behind the tavern.*

I'll catch up with you, said Irc. *I'm busy now.*

Hem sighed and turned to Saliman. "Can you walk, do you think?" he said. "There's higher ground behind the tavern, some rising hills. I think we should go there. We might find an empty house or barn if we're lucky."

"I can walk," said Saliman, "though I fear I can't take a turn on the barrow, alas."

"I'll put a glimveil over us. It is probably better if we remain unseen." Hem made the spell swiftly, and then hefted the shafts of the barrow. It was well made, and the wheel ran true. Perhaps he would be able to manage. Slowly he pushed the barrow out of the yard and then turned off the road, where a sodden track meandered uphill, out of the spreading water. The river had risen through all of Hiert and even now was flooding into the houses.

Almost as soon as they left the West Road, the barrow became bogged. Hem puffed and tugged until the wheel came out of the mud with a sucking noise, and then leaned exhausted against it. This was a way of getting nowhere very fast.

"We should put our boots on," he said to Saliman. "No use being colder than we already are."

The two Bards leaned against the barrow, struggling with their socks and boots. Hem's feet were numb with cold, and he had cut the bottom of his foot on a sharp stone. Absently, he whispered a charm against infection as he pulled his sock over it.

"There's a spell that helps against bogging," said Saliman. His voice was hoarse, and he was shivering. "A simple thing we used to use as children at my grandmother's house. I think I can just about manage it."

He whispered some words in the Speech, his fingers touching the barrow as lightly as possible, and after that Hem didn't have any trouble. Even so, it was hard work pushing the barrow uphill, and he began to sweat. At last they reached the top, and he stopped to rest his aching arms.

From here, he could see how much the Inlan had flooded. It was more like a lake than a river, pushing its grey fingers into every low-lying area. The aspens and willows that lined the Inlan marked the river's normal course, and now they thrust up forlornly out of the floods. The West Road near Hiert was entirely under water, and it was lapping the sides of the buildings a foot over the doorways. The point where they had turned off the West Road had already disappeared.

"The tavern will be flooded by now. It's rising fast," said Saliman. "I think we left just in time. It will probably be waist-deep in Hiert within the hour."

"But it's not raining!" said Hem. "Why is it rising now?"

"It's the rain from upriver, coming our way," Saliman answered. "If it rains any more, the floods will become serious."

"They're not serious now?" Hem surveyed the sky. It was an iron-grey expanse of clouds, with not a patch of blue. "It's a safe wager that there's more rain coming," he said.

"I fear so," said Saliman.

Hem glanced across at him and set his jaw. He was trying not to look too much at Saliman; it hurt him. He had made no complaint on their toil up the hillside, but Hem could see at once that it had exhausted him. His skin was covered in a thin film of sweat, and Hem could see that his legs were shaking.

"So we'd better find some shelter, on high ground," Hem said, looking despairingly around him. This was grazing ground, close-cropped turf dotted with clumps of bare-branched ash or small oak trees. Further along, knots of sheep or goats clustered around the trees, huddled against the piercing wind that blew over the top of the ridge. He had hoped to see a farmhouse, even a shepherd's hut, but nothing was in sight. They would probably have to set up the tent. It might not be too bad, he thought, in the shelter of the trees.

"Do you think you could reach the top of the next hill?" he asked.

"I'll try," said Saliman. "I won't lie to you, Hem; this is hard going for me. It's as if someone has poured molten lead into my joints. And my legs feel as if they're made of stone."

"If it gets too hard, you should get into the wheelbarrow."

Saliman was silent for a time. "I remember when I was a child, I saw an old woman pushing a pig in a wheelbarrow," he said. "The pig was sitting up and looking around as if it were a fine lady in a sedan. It was one of the funniest things I had ever seen, I didn't stop laughing for hours."

"You don't look like a pig," said Hem, trying to smile.

"Nay, not like a pig. But I confess, the thought of being pushed in a wheelbarrow stings my pride."

"There's no one to see," said Hem.

"It's not a question of anyone seeing." Saliman sighed. "Well, let's get moving. That lake at the bottom of the hill is not going to get any smaller while we stay here talking."

Going downhill was easier, even though they were now walking into the wind. When they reached the swirling water at the bottom, Hem examined it uneasily. The water was brown with mud and he couldn't see the bottom, and he had no way of telling how deep it was. If it was too deep, he would have trouble with the barrow, and both of them would end up wet through. He cast around for a long stick and prodded the water in front of him, but the current tore it out of his hands. He found a branch, stripped off the twigs to turn it into a pole, and stubbornly tried again.

It wasn't deep, probably just over their knees, but the current was very strong. And he could see the water level rising in front of his eyes.

"A fastening charm would probably do the trick," said Saliman from behind him. "But we'll have to feel our way. I'm sorry, Hem, I can't help with the charm..."

"I'll have to touch you, to make it work," said Hem.

"Don't worry about me; I'll hold onto the barrow," Saliman said. "I don't want you touching me, Hem."

Hem didn't insist. He would argue later; he couldn't heal Saliman if he were not able to touch him. He made a strong fastening charm, took a deep breath and pushed the barrow into the water where it seemed most shallow, praying that it wouldn't rise over the sides. Slowly and painfully they made their way across. Hem just hoped they wouldn't fall into a sudden hole; he didn't know how he would get the barrow out if they did. The water swirled around his knees and even with the charm he could feel its power. It took all of Saliman's strength to walk against the current, and once he stumbled and almost fell over. But they made it across without mishap.

Now they were both wet to their thighs, and the wind was freezing. They stopped briefly and changed their clothes; it would do neither of them good to get even colder. Hem smelt the wind anxiously; there was rain in it, and it was coming their way. He turned and saw heavy clouds low in the south, sweeping over the green hills.

They pushed slowly up the next hill. By now Hem's arms felt as if they were on fire, but he gritted his teeth and pushed on. He didn't think he could go much further. Saliman was trudging beside him, always two spans away, saying nothing. His silence told Hem more than anything else how much their trek was costing him, and he scanned their surroundings desperately, hoping for a sign of something, anything – a byre or a hut, even the open shelters farmers made for their livestock – that would keep the coming weather off their heads. If he didn't see something soon, he would have to put the tent up, but he was hoping for something warmer and bigger, where he could light a fire.

At last they reached the top of the hill and stood with the wind at their back, looking over a strange, watery landscape: the floods spread as far as them could see. For a brief moment he wondered if the caravan had escaped the floods. And then, just over the ridge, in the lees of a rocky outcrop that protected it from the wind, Hem found what he was looking for: a stone hut, roofed with turf so that he almost missed it. His arms burning with the effort, he pushed the barrow to the low door, and cautiously bent down to inspect the interior. There was nothing inside except a smell of damp, and the roof wasn't leaking, so the hard earth floor was dry. He beckoned to Saliman, who staggered inside and collapsed against the far wall, leaning his head back and closing his eyes. With a feeling of inexpressible relief, Hem began to unpack the barrow, carrying their belongings inside. As he did so, Irc spiralled down from the sky and landed on the roof of the hut, cocking his head to watch.

It's not as nice as the last place.

It's a lot better than nothing, Hem said crossly. *And nothing was what we almost had.* He was in no mood for Irc's criticisms.

Irc, sensing Hem's state of extremity, kept quiet. It didn't take long to empty the barrow, and Hem leant it up against the wall outside and entered the hut himself. It was dark inside, so he made a magelight and lit a small fire by the door. The hut would fill with smoke, but he would rather battle smoke than the cold. The rain finally reached them as he laid the tinder, and Irc flapped inside, shaking out his feathers.

They were out of the wind here, and once the fire took hold the hut warmed up quickly. Hem cut up some turnips and beans he had salvaged from the tavern, throwing them into their cooking pot – he planned to make a stew for dinner – and then, finally, he turned to look at Saliman.

Saliman was visibly more ill than he had been that morning. He was shaking with violent tremors, even though the hut was now comfortably warm, and his face was drawn with exhaustion. He was watching Hem alertly and when Hem turned to look at him he cleared his throat, as if he had been waiting to speak.

"Hem, listen," he said, and struggled to sit up straighter. His voice was hoarse, and it was clearly an effort to talk. Now he used the Speech, not the Annaren they had spoken for the past few weeks. "I believe that you are mistaken in taking care of me like this and risking your life, although I love you for it, and I have not the will to oppose you, although I should. And I am afraid that tonight I may lose my mind, although I am hoping that will not happen yet. This sickness gnaws my flesh, my mind, my very bones, and although I fight it with all my will, all my magery, still I cannot stop it. I fear that you cannot escape the contagion if we sleep in this small space."

"I know how bad it is," Hem said, his voice breaking. "But Saliman, I know I haven't done the wrong thing. Even if I fail, even if I get sick myself, I will not regret it."

Saliman smiled with such sadness that Hem almost wept. "It is said that when the Great Silence ruled over Annar, deeds were done that were never marked by song or story, but that this made them no less deeds of valour. That is why, Hem, in the middle of the Song of the Dark there is a long moment of silence, to remember those whose actions we cannot know, but which deserve our respect and remembrance nonetheless."

Hem nodded. He had learned of this in the School of Turbansk. That time seemed so far away now that he could scarcely remember it; all the sights and colours and smells of Turbansk were like a vivid but distant dream.

"I think that silence remembers deeds like this you are doing now, Hem. If I cannot salute you afterwards, I salute you now." Saliman coughed and turned his face away.

Hem's eyes filled with tears. "It's only because I love you," he said gruffly.

"Aye," said Saliman gently. "Such deeds are borne out of love."

Saliman shut his eyes. A long silence fell between them, and Hem mixed the stew, seasoning it with salt and dried herbs, and put it over the fire. He was so upset that he scarcely knew what he was doing, and the pot almost fell off the tripod and into the fire.

Irc, who had perched himself on Hem's bag, squawked with alarm. *That's our dinner!* he said.

Did you not find anything to eat today? asked Hem.

No. Well, not much. Will Saliman be all right? He is very quiet.

I don't know, Hem answered. *I am going to try to make him better.*

You must make him better, said Irc. *Or I will be very sad.*

Hem said nothing, and stared at the stew, which blurred in front of his eyes.

Saliman would not eat anything, and only drank thirstily from his water bottle. Hem shared the stew with Irc, who ate his fill and then perched himself on Hem's pack and went to sleep. Hem sat and fed the fire, staring into its depths. His body ached all over, and he was very tired. He wondered if he had the strength to do any healing tonight; but if he did not, it might be too late. If it wasn't too late already.

Saliman stirred, and Hem looked over towards him.

"Hem, one more thing." He sat up and leant towards Hem, licking his lips, and Hem saw that there was already a cluster of sores at the corner of his mouth. "If you are certain that you are going to try to heal me, then you must know what this sickness is. It is difficult to heal because it twists through the body like smoke, rippling and changing, so that you cannot find its form. It is always changing. And it is always deeper than you realize. You think you have chased it from the body, only to discover that it has withdrawn itself and emerged somewhere you didn't expect."

"Have you ever tended someone with the White Sickness yourself?" asked Hem.

Saliman shook his head. "It has not been seen in the Suderain," he said. "This is just what I know from what I've read or been told." He paused, as if he were trying to gather energy to speak again. "But I can feel the truth of what has been said in my own body. Ever it evades my own magery.

Patience, Hem, and strength. You should sleep before you even attempt it."

"But if I sleep, it might be too late!"

"Hem, I'll be frank. I do not think that it is possible for you to drive this sickness out of me. I believe, with all my heart, that you should not try this."

"I know," said Hem. "But I'm going to anyway."

"Well, if that is so, I suggest that you rest first. And if you wake, and understand that you cannot do this, know that I think you should leave me. *Know that*." Saliman said the last two words with such ferocity that Hem jumped.

"I do know that," he whispered. "I know what I know, too."

Saliman was silent again for a long time, and then he said: "Hem. My Truename is Arundulan."

"Arundulan," Hem repeated, overwhelmed. To tell one's Name to another was the deepest sign of trust a Bard could show. Arundulan meant "ember" in the Speech, the glowing coals that might at any moment leap into flame. "Arundulan."

"You might need it," said Saliman. "And I do not wish to die without having told you my Name."

Hem cleared his throat. "I wish I knew my own Name, so I could tell you mine," he said.

"The Light willing, you will know it one day." Saliman closed his eyes, and silence fell over them.

Hem stared into the fire, weighing the risks of what he planned to do. Saliman, he knew, was telling him the truth, and the sensible thing to do would be to leave him, as Marich and Karim and Hekibel had done. Hem was incapable of making so cold a choice. He had followed Zelika into the heart of Dén Raven for the same reason that he now stayed with Saliman – *and look how that turned out*, said a mocking voice in the back of his mind. He knew he could not live with himself if he left Saliman to a certain, horrible death without even trying to heal him. The problem was, the attempt to heal him might result in his own death.

Well then, thought Hem. That's how it is.

He thought carefully over what he knew of healing. He was all too conscious of his lack of experience. In the Healing Houses of Turbansk he had learned much: Oslar had been a great and patient teacher, and had given Hem, in the end, as much responsibility as he gave his best healers. Yet he knew in his bones that if Oslar were here now, he would counsel him against the attempt. He was too young, he knew too little, he had no medicines to assist his magery...

He would have to depend on his wits. Perhaps his earth sense, the strange gift that had been breathed into him by the Elidhu Nyanar in Nal-Ak-Burat, might help him where Bardic magery faltered. It was, he thought dolefully, the only thing he had that other Bards lacked. So far all the earth sense had granted him was a crippling nausea when he walked across ground damaged by the Nameless One. But if the White Sickness was, as some Bards darkly speculated, a disease loosed on Annar by Sharma himself, then perhaps this earth sense might be a way of finding where the sickness embedded itself in the body. And it wasn't as if Hem were incapable as a mage – he had managed to unpick the vigilance set by a powerful Hull outside the Blind House in Sjug'hakar Im, and that had been no easy task...

He threw some more wood from his dwindling pile onto the fire. Saliman had fallen asleep, and his light, uneven breathing and his restless movements seemed loud over the crackle of the flames. Hem realized that he was tired, very tired indeed. Saliman was speaking sense when he said that he ought to rest before he attempted anything so difficult as battling the White Sickness. He would sleep now – a few hours, not too long – to gather his strength. He had the knack, after weeks of watch-keeping, of waking himself when he desired. If he slept until midnight, the fever might not have wound itself too deeply into Saliman's body, and Hem would be better prepared to try to heal him.

He understood then that, for all his protestations, he had not been sure until that moment that he would attempt to heal Saliman. If he was honest with himself, he was as afraid as the players; he was terrified of becoming like the poor wretch he had seen in Hiert, without even the mercy of a quick death. Yet now he knew that his decision was irrevocable, come what may. He sagged with a sudden, strange sense of relief, and damped down the fire. Irc was already asleep, one leg tucked into his breast and his head under his wing. Hem stared at Irc for a long moment, his eyes soft with tenderness. Then he drew the blankets around himself, attempting to get comfortable on the hard floor, and quickly fell asleep.

Hem woke at the darkest hour of the night. He sat up, rubbing the sleep out of his eyes. The hut was warm, lit by the faint glow of the fire. Saliman was curled up against the opposite wall, fast asleep, and still except for his light, erratic breathing. Hem reached for his water bottle and took a long draught; then he paused and fumbled through his pack. There was a flask of medhyl somewhere in the bottom that he had brought from Til Amon, and that he had forgotten until now. He took a long draught of that as well. He felt the thrill of the medhyl go through him and wake him up.

Well, he thought. Now is as good a time as any.

Without any further thought, he crawled over to Saliman and sat cross-legged next to him, studying his face. In sleep, he looked vulnerable, somehow much younger; Hem thought he knew what Saliman must have looked like when he was a child. He decided not to wake him; if he did, Saliman would argue, and Hem didn't want to argue. He took a deep breath, emptied his mind, and took Saliman's hands in his own.

Saliman's skin was dry and rough like paper, and very hot. Hem could feel the beat of his blood, a light, hectic pulse that had no regular rhythm. Swiftly Hem scanned his body, sending a white fire running along Saliman's veins. It was a first test of what he would be facing when he began the healing. At once he felt the truth of what Saliman had said to him earlier; the sickness was like a foul, oily smoke winding in infinitely complex patterns through Saliman's being. It withdrew from the edges of the white fire, retreating before Hem's advances, seeming almost to disappear, although a deeper sense told him that it was there, undiminished, at the periphery of his vision.

A sudden nausea flowered in Hem's belly. It was the same nausea he had felt in the forests of the Glandugir Hills, and with it came a visceral sense of revulsion and horror, as if he were about to lower himself into a pit that crawled with spiders and scorpions. He withdrew his mind and sat for a moment, gasping and sweating with the shock of it, trying to gather his wits together.

He had barely touched Saliman, and it was already that bad. For a moment Hem considered leaving the hut, taking his pack and fleeing as far as he could from the horror that was the White Sickness. Saliman stirred, and then kicked out wildly, mumbling something incoherent in his sleep, and Hem jumped. He looked a long moment at his friend's face. If he abandoned Saliman, that beauty would be destroyed for ever. He would never again see Saliman's smile, never hear his voice raised in song, nor his long, improbably absurd stories, told for the pleasure of delighting his friends.

"No," he said aloud, pushing away the cold voice inside him that mocked his weakness. "I said I would heal him. I said that even if I catch the sickness, I will not regret it. I will not regret it."

He took a deep breath, picked up Saliman's hands again, and began the task of healing.

Afterwards, the only memory Hem had of that night was of a confused and endless torment, a long, exhausting struggle with a sickness that embraced him until it wound through into his own vitals, skewering him with an anguish he had never known before. He hunted down flickering snakes of fire and extinguished them, only to see them spring three-headed out of the clean darkness; he wrestled with demons of smoke and oil that smothered him; he chased the sickness down the infinitely tiny byways of Saliman's body, only to see it creep back, stronger, more insidious than before; he ran down dark, empty roads, and before him glided a shadow haloed by light that he knew was Saliman, but ever more distant, ever more faint.

Hem called out Saliman's Name – *Arundulan! Arundulan!* – and his voice died on the thick, dark, choking air. There was no way out of this nightmare; it closed about him, and he smelt his own death rising from his stomach, his own sour and corrupting flesh, and his sight was failing, his ears were stuffed with mud, his hands were numb and felt nothing. He stumbled and at last he felt himself falling, and the road before him broadened and darkened, and he saw a great light growing out of the distance before him, and he knew that he was near death. In despair he reached more deeply within himself than he had ever touched, far beneath the layers of self that he understood, to a place that was at once hot and cold, fluidly passionate and infinitely obdurate, like the living heart of rock itself. He flung himself towards the fleeing figure before him, no longer knowing what he was doing, and he cried out Saliman's Name – *Arundulan!* – with every fibre of his being. For an endless moment all his senses were quenched, and he

seemed to exist only in a void that stretched about him, suspended endlessly between life and death. And then he knew
that his hand clutched Saliman's living hand, and that he bent,
sobbing with exhaustion, over Saliman's softly breathing body,
and that the sickness was gone.

THE HOLLOW LANDS

Nor was such love often seen, as that between
Saliman and Hem; for each held that to lay down
his life were a small price for the other's good.
*As the reeds standing in the river, they bowed side
by side before the gentle breeze; as broad oaks in
the forest, they resisted the fierce tempest together;
nor did one ever fail the other in his promise.
Truly he is blessed, who rejoices in such a friend!*

From *The Tale of Saliman*, Maerad of Turbansk

XII

ARDINA

T HIS is hopeless," said Maerad. Her gaze swept, smouldering with irritation, over the lonely, bare hills of the
Hollow Lands. "I swear the Nameless One himself sent
this rain. Curse him. Curse him and blast him."

Cadvan, who was, with great difficulty, attempting to light a
fire in the face of the biting wind, looked up. "There is no doubt
that the Nameless One is a powerful sorcerer," he said mildly.
"But I think this weather has nothing to do with him. Such
floods have happened before – not for a long time, I grant you
– and we were about due for another."

"It's mightily convenient, all the same," said Maerad darkly.
"How do you know he hasn't called out the rain clouds just to
get in our way? If we ever get the better of him, I'll sentence
him to an eternity of numb fingers and wet clothes. It would
serve him right."

Cadvan laughed, and then was silent as he tended a flame
that had finally caught, cradling it carefully from kindling to
wood. Maerad turned her back on the Hollow Lands, and concentrated on helping him to build the fire until at last they had
a healthy blaze. Then they prepared an unappetizing but sus-
taining meal, consisting mainly of hot bean gruel and turnips
pushed into the coals to roast. Once the meal was over, Maerad
sighed and stretched out her hands to the flames.

They were huddled under a rock formation that made a
natural shelter. Underneath the ground was dry, and there
was even a little protection from the shifting wind. The horses,

unsaddled, wandered close by, cropping the turf, their backs hunched miserably against the cold.

"What are we to do?" said Maerad, returning to her earlier grievance. "We're going in exactly the wrong direction, I'm sure."

Cadvan studied her face as she stared frowning into the fire. "We have two choices. One is to wait for the floods to subside. The worst of it will probably be over in a few days at most. Or we can try to go round them, although my wager is that if the Inlan has flooded so badly, the Aleph will perhaps be worse. And we have no way of knowing if the Milhol is any better. We might be hemmed in by flooding to the north as well, once we leave the hills."

"We don't have time."

"No. But they are choices we have, all the same. At the moment, the south is barred to us. My best guess is that we try to head east, bearing south towards Desor."

"I don't want to go anywhere near Desor," said Maerad, remembering some Desor Bards she had once met in Innail. "I'm sure that School is as corrupt as Ettinor. We'd be sure to run into Hulls."

"I wasn't suggesting that we actually knock on the door of the School."

Maerad was silent for a time, turning over their options. At last she sighed, poking the fire so sparks twirled idly up towards the rocky roof. "I know you're right, and we have no choice," she said. "But I don't like it, all the same."

Until it began to rain, their journey from Innail had been swift and uneventful. In a way, Maerad had been glad to leave Innail; she couldn't get used to her new-found celebrity, and it was pleasant to be anonymous again, away from staring eyes and pointing fingers. By now, she and Cadvan were very used to travelling together, and they made good progress. They had left Innail Fesse in the first couple of days and ridden swiftly down the West Road, the dark trees of the Weywood to their right, and camped alongside the road. The first night, as she stared into the darkness that gathered under the tangled, ancient trees, Maerad remembered her first meeting with the Elemental Ardina, which had been in this very forest. The song Ardina had sung that day lilted into her memory:

Fleet as an unseen star in the dwindling glade
Old as the hidden root that feeds the world
Hard as the light that blinds the living eye
I am this, and this, and this

It was a strange song, and Maerad had often puzzled over its meaning. It was, she was sure, about the Treesong; surely the "hidden root that feeds the world" could mean nothing else. And Nelac had said that the Treesong was something to do with the Speech, the inborn language of Bards which was the source of their powers. It seemed likely to Maerad that the magery held within the Speech stemmed from the Treesong itself.

After the past year, she felt a little closer to understanding what the Treesong was, but it remained, all the same, mysterious and elusive. As was Ardina's song... What did she mean by an unseen star in a dwindling glade? Was it something to do with Starry Groves beyond the Gates where, according to Cadvan, Ardina herself had once wandered, following her lover Ardhor? But the star was described as "fleet"; surely that meant something that didn't last, whereas the Starry Groves were eternal things that didn't change. Unless, of course, the Starry Groves were something Bards had made up; Maerad was already becoming familiar with the Bards' complex ideas about truth, which some said could be seen more clearly through the lens of the untrue. Arkan had told her that humans always lied … perhaps that was part of what he meant. On the other hand, he had told her that the Elidhu did not lie. And this was an Elidhu song.

Maerad found, yet again, that she was going around in circles, and she sighed. Part of the frustration of the past year had been that she had never quite known what she was supposed to be looking for, and what to do when she found it. And yet everything depended upon her. And on top of that, she had powers that she didn't understand and that no one could tell her how to use. Those powers didn't only terrify Maerad, they frightened everyone around her, even her friends. She was monstrous. That was what the Winterking had meant when she had defeated the Landrost, when he had said that he didn't know what she was. Yet Maerad had never asked for these abilities, and if she had had a choice, she would have refused them. It didn't seem fair.

She stared balefully into the depths of the Weywood, wondering if Ardina was nearby, and whether the Elidhu, too, would be frightened of her. Sometimes it had seemed to her that Ardina was the only living being who understood her. If even Ardina feared her, Maerad truly would feel alone.

This time they didn't turn into the Weywood, but kept to the Bard Road, intending to travel as swiftly as possible towards Til Amon. Once they left the Fesse, they kept a careful watch for bandits or the groups of rogue soldiers that rumour said now roamed Annar. The only sign of trouble, as Cadvan observed, was that the road was utterly deserted. He said that normally, even this early in the year, there would be some movement – farmers taking their goods to market, or the first Pilanel artisans coming down from Zmarkan, or Bards going about their business; but they encountered no one. The people who lived by the road, who made a good part of their living from such travellers, confirmed Cadvan's observation; now the villages and towns that were walled kept their gates locked even by day, and those that were unwalled were mainly deserted. The reason why was evident in the burned and ruined houses they occasionally passed.

The rains began once they left the Weywood, and initially merely slowed their progress to a crawl. But when the Inlan burst its banks, a few days after they left the Weywood, they were forced to leave the West Road and turn north, riding hard before rapidly rising floodwaters. They were not the only people fleeing; the area south of Desor was a fertile plain dotted with many farms and villages, and the floods affected them as well. Suddenly all the people who had been invisible until now became very visible: Maerad and Cadvan saw many small groups, steadily plodding in the rain to higher ground. Most were on foot, many were driving livestock, and they led wagons pulled by oxen or horses that were loaded high with their possessions. The rapidity and scale of the flooding had taken Maerad aback. In the mountains where she had lived as a child, there had been no such thing as floods, and she had not imagined such devastation.

Maerad and Cadvan had decided to press north-east, since they preferred to stay away from the refugees, and soon found themselves separated from the others by an ever-widening lake. In the end, they were driven past the edges of the Weywood to the eastern edge of the Hollow Lands before they finally escaped the rising waters.

When the floods stopped spreading, they looked back over a massive brown lake, punctuated by trees, or ridges of higher ground which had now become islands. Some of these temporary islets were crowded with unlikely menageries of goats and cows and foxes and sodden rabbits. There was no sign of people; they were now far beyond the inhabited lowlands. No chance of another tavern for miles, Maerad thought gloomily.

"We should have followed the farmers," said Maerad, after she and Cadvan had finished their meal. "Then we'd be closer to Desor. Nobody would have noticed us in that chaos."

"Perhaps you're right," Cadvan answered. He was leaning back against the rock, his eyes shadowed in the firelight, as he rubbed his boots with a mixture of tallow and oil. "But it's hard to say whether we would be better off if we had."

"We're running out of time," said Maerad.

Cadvan gave her a sharp glance. "I know, Maerad. Even I can feel that. But unless you can access some hitherto unknown power that can transport us over several leagues of water – not, I confess, that I rule that out entirely – I fear we are stuck here."

"You mean, sprout wings or something?"

"Is it so strange? You can become a wolf, after all. Perhaps you could shapeshift into another animal. Not that that would help me, unless you became a giant bird like those that are said to live in the southern deserts and lay eggs as big as a man."

A silence fell between them, and Maerad took the tallow and attended to her own boots. She hunched her cloak around her as she rubbed the leather, pondering what Cadvan had said. She knew he had meant it as a joke, but was it possible that she could do something to get them across the floods? She had sometimes wondered if she could assume the shapes of other animals, but had been afraid to try. She was even more afraid now; she had avoided her Elemental powers ever since the battle at Innail, and had been reluctant to use magery, even the simplest of glimmerspells. But maybe Cadvan had a point: if she could be a wolf, why not a bird?

She thought for a while longer, remembering all the different kinds of birds she had seen, and then, on impulse, she attempted a transformation. She was curious to see if she could do it, and in part she was impelled by mischief: she wanted to see the expression on Cadvan's face, when he suddenly found himself sitting next to a hawk. Sinking into the inner space where all her selves fell away, seeking that point where transformation was possible, was easy for her now. This time, instead of seeking her wolf shape, she commanded herself: *Be hawk!*

At first she thought she had succeeded: there was that moment of pure agony which always came with the transformation, before her new shape coalesced out of the protean self she had become. But this time the anguish did not stop; it was as if she were being consumed by a terrible flame. She screamed, but she had no mouth with which to scream; she was racked with anguish through her whole being, and couldn't even cry for help. She had no way of knowing how long this agony lasted, although it felt as if it went on for ever, as if she would always be racked by this torment. Then a blessed coolness fell on her, like starlight, like bells tolling across a landscape of snow, and the fire dimmed; the coolness was her Name, *Elednor*, shaping her into her known self, and as she heard the Name she had a mouth again, and eyes, and skin.

Elednor, said Cadvan again, and this time it was not the voice of starlight, the inhuman voice of magery, but his own voice.

Maerad opened her eyes and stared straight into his; he was pale, and the scar on his face stood out as it always did when he was anxious. The pain had gone without trace, as swiftly as it had overwhelmed her, but the aftershock of it remained, and it was a while before she could say anything.

Cadvan studied Maerad in silence. Suddenly ashamed, Maerad turned her eyes away.

"What happened?" Cadvan asked at last.

"I tried to become a hawk," said Maerad. "It didn't work. I think I got – stuck."

Cadvan's eyes turned black with anger. "You *what*?"

"I tried to become a hawk," she whispered. "It didn't work."

There was a short, ominous silence, as Cadvan brushed his hair distractedly out of his eyes. When he did speak, it was in the cold, even voice that in Cadvan signalled total fury. "Do you mean to tell me that, after weeks of refusing even to work a glimmerspell, Maerad of Pellinor suddenly decides on a whim, with no warning at all, to try a transformation she's never tried before? I thought you'd learned something over the past year."

"It was foolish, I know…"

"Foolish? That's the least of it. Perilous, reckless, stupid … by the Light, Maerad, I'd expect such a thing from a child, but you at least ought to know better than anyone else that magery of any kind is not to be used on a whim. Besides which, you didn't even bother to shield yourself. Any Hulls out enjoying the delightful pleasures of the Hollow Lands will know exactly where you are now."

Maerad sat up, stung by Cadvan's anger.

"I just thought I'd try," she said bitterly, meeting his eyes. "How else am I supposed to find out what I can do? Here I am, with this wonderful Gift that's supposed to save the world, and I haven't the first idea how to use it. I'm guessing all the time. It's not as if anyone can teach me. What do you suggest, Cadvan? Can you guide me through the magery of Elementals, so that I make no mistakes? Or if you can't do it, who do you think might show me what to do?"

Cadvan said nothing, but she saw his anger subsiding. He sighed, and leant forward and pushed some more wood onto the fire.

"You have a point, I grant you," he said at last. "All the same, Maerad, you know as well as I do that that was a reckless act. And we cannot afford such acts. Not if we are to survive. Myself, I am quite fond of my own skin. And I am not overfond of seeing you in such a state as you were then."

Maerad didn't want to ask what that state was. She had a feeling she wouldn't like the answer.

"I don't like it much, myself," she said, reaching out and taking his hand. "I'm sorry, Cadvan. I really am."

"I forgive you." Cadvan's face softened, and Maerad saw that his rage had passed. "Just. But please, Maerad, if you're going to do something like that again, at least warn me."

"I promise. And maybe there's some good in this; at least I've found out that I can't be a bird. I think that maybe a wolf-skin is the only form I can take. I could have tried it in some other circumstance and been stuck in between for ever." She shuddered at the thought. "I don't know what would have become of me if you hadn't been there."

It occurred to Maerad as she spoke that in the strange world of the mind where even she was sometimes baffled and lost, Cadvan always seemed to know where to find her, how to call her back. How did he know? This was the magery of Elementals, not of Bards; Cadvan said often that he knew nothing about these powers. And yet, when the Landrost had thrown her beyond her own Knowing, Cadvan had found her in the infinite vastness and brought her home; and just now he had called her out of the torment of unbeing, and reminded her who she was. She looked at him with a new curiosity: there was much she didn't know about Cadvan.

"Well, frankly, it's a relief to know there's something you can't do," said Cadvan. He gave her his sudden, brilliant smile. "You look very tired. I'll take first watch tonight."

Maerad nodded. It was true that she was weary; it was not as bad as the exhaustion that she had suffered in Innail, but it was of the same kind. She wrapped herself in her blanket, trying to find a comfortable place to rest. Briefly, as she always did, she regretted the comfortable bed she had left behind; but she fell asleep almost at once.

At first she lay in the dreamless slumber of exhaustion, but after a while she began to dream. It was the old nightmares in which Hulls stretched out their bony hands towards her, their eyes glowing like red coals in the darkness; then she was alone, on a huge, dark plain, with a sense of panic rising in her throat; she could see nothing clearly, but she knew that she was being hunted down, and that she had nowhere to hide. But the dream shifted abruptly to something worse. She was in the middle of a tormenting struggle, and her body was shot through with pain that made her cry out. At the same time, she was chasing someone, someone she loved, who was in terrible danger; she was pursuing him down a long and empty road, unable to cry out a warning. She heard someone calling behind her, and she turned; it was Hem. He was running as fast as he could, but it seemed as if he were standing still. She called his name, but he didn't hear her. He caught up with Maerad and she wanted to touch him, but something forbade her to reach out. Then he passed her and was, impossibly, at once a small figure receding into the distance. As Maerad watched him an immense grief gathered inside her. She tried to follow him, but her legs were rooted to the ground and she couldn't move. Then there was a blinding light, and she seemed to fall, she did not stop falling, and then someone was shaking her.

"Maerad." It was Cadvan. "You were having a nightmare."

"Yes." Maerad sat up, fighting her way out of the dream, and found that she had been weeping and that her blanket was twisted around her. It was the darkest part of the night, and the fire had burned down to embers.

Cadvan handed her the water bottle, and she took a deep drink. "Were you dreaming of Hem?" he asked.

"How did you know?"

"You were crying out his name."

"Yes … it was a horrible dream…"

"Was it a foredream?"

"No," said Maerad, frowning. "No, it was different some-how. And I don't understand it. I don't even know how to describe it to you. It was just one of those – those bad dreams you have."

Cadvan didn't pry, although he was clearly curious, and Maerad didn't want to talk about it. Shortly afterwards she took over her turn at the watch and Cadvan slept. Maerad put some more fuel on the fire to keep it alive and studied Cadvan's face in its dim light. Asleep, he was a man like any other man, vulnera-ble in his flesh; the powers that in his waking life made him one of the most famous Bards in Annar slumbered too. She smiled, remembering suddenly his pleasure when he haggled over a cheese in a market, or when he swapped weatherlore with the publican of a tavern. He was both more simple and more com-plex than others thought him: he wore his powers lightly, with an air of self-mockery, and yet she had seen the fierce pride that drove him. He was the least vain person she knew, but among the most arrogant. After all this time she probably knew him as well as anybody in Edil-Amarandh, and yet he still had the power to surprise her.

He always seemed much younger when he was asleep, as if the burdens that he carried in his waking life were lifted from him. I wish it were the same for me, Maerad thought; there's no escape, even in dreams. She didn't want to think about her nightmare; its grief still lay heavy inside her. The only thing she felt certain about was that it had been a dream that was full of death. She cast her mind out into the night, seek-ing the dim knowledge that told her that Hem was present in the world, but she could find nothing. Although she wouldn't admit it to herself, deep inside she was now very afraid that Hem was dead.

* * *

The next day they picked their way slowly east, staying as close to the edge of the floodwaters as was practical. The water had begun to subside as rapidly as it had risen, leaving behind pools of brown water and a detritus of rubbish: broken branches, the bloated corpses of drowned animals, and everywhere a layer of silt. The horses stepped daintily over the soggy turf, and Darsor refused to walk into the mud. Keru, though less vocal than Darsor, was as stubborn, although Maerad was incandescent with impatience and would have pushed them on back to the West Road, if she had been able to.

It smells like death, said Darsor, when she argued with him. *I will not steep my hooves in death.*

"The horses are right," said Cadvan. "It's dangerous, at least until we're sure it won't rain again; it wouldn't take much for the floods to come back. And it won't be long before this smell gets worse."

Maerad scowled and scanned the grey skies, but she made no further protest. There was a definite smell of rot and mould that the floodwaters left behind them, and she had as little desire as the horses to be caught in the floods again. As the day wore on, it seemed the worst of the rains had passed; the clouds brought only a few light showers that passed swiftly. The sun cast a dim watery light, conspiring with the empty, lonely landscape to fill Maerad's heart with gloom. She had not told Cadvan about her dream, or her anxieties about Hem, feeling almost superstitiously that to talk about it might make it true, but her fears of the night before lay heavy upon her. By evening her impatience had subsided into depression. They made their camp in the shelter of an overhanging rock, not far from one of the stone circles that dotted the Hollow Lands. The red glow of a westering sun sinking through ashy clouds cast an unreal, gloomy light, throwing dark shadows behind the lichened standing stones which loomed nearby, inscrutable but heavy with a long-forgotten significance.

"We're not going to find Hem in time," Maerad said, as she and Cadvan finished their evening meal.

Cadvan sighed. "Maerad, what do you mean by 'in time'?" he asked. "I know that our task is urgent. Yet we have all Annar and the Suderain in which to seek him, and no guarantee that he is still alive."

"He's alive," said Maerad stubbornly.

Cadvan was silent for a while, staring into the fire. "I came with you from Innail perfectly aware that we didn't know how to find Hem, and hoping that your Knowing would guide us," he said. "But I tell you frankly that, even if he is still alive, I rate our chances of finding Hem very low."

In her current state of doubt, these were not words that Maerad wanted to hear. She turned her face away from Cadvan, remembering that he was a Truthteller, that he would know if she lied to him.

"I was thinking about what happened last night," she said at last, to change the subject. "And I thought of one person who might be able to help me."

Cadvan looked his question.

"Ardina. She gave me those pipes, remember? And she told me that if I ever needed to speak to her, I should use them. I played them once before, and she came to me... Perhaps she could help me now. Perhaps she could teach me how to use my powers."

Cadvan looked puzzled. "*Ardina* gave you those pipes?" he said. "I thought it was the Elidhu in the Weywood."

Maerad remembered that she had never told Cadvan that the wood Elidhu and the Queen Ardina of Rachida were one and the same.

"The Elemental in the Weywood was Ardina," she said, her eyes averted from Cadvan's. "They are the same. She told me to keep it secret; she said that you wouldn't understand."

Cadvan was silent for a time as he absorbed what Maerad had said. "I think I know why she wanted it kept secret," he said at last. "Ardina understands enough of Bards to be aware of how deeply they mistrust the Elidhu. And the Elidhu in the Weywood had nothing human about her; she was deeply fey. I would not trust her, as perhaps I might trust Ardina in her human guise. Maerad, these are deep waters, and perilous; I would be wary of calling on the help of the Elidhu. I am not so sure that what they might bring you would be help, or something else."

"Like what, for instance?" said Maerad, her voice cold. "I trust Ardina."

"I think it foolhardy to trust her," said Cadvan. "She is Elidhu, she is immortal; she is moved by things that we do not, that we cannot, understand, and in this matter she follows her own ends, which may have very little to do with yours and mine. You've seen the floods, what they have destroyed: that is the power of the Elementals, Maerad. It has no mercy, and no thought; the Dark and the Light mean nothing to it. It simply is."

"I think the Bards made a big mistake when they stopped talking to the Elementals," said Maerad.

"I am sure you are right. And alas, now our paths are sundered, and in this time of great need we have less chance of understanding each other. Yes, Maerad, the Treesong is a matter that concerns the Elidhu, and I understand that; but I would give a great deal to know how it concerns them, what their interest is in this matter."

"The Treesong was theirs, and Nelsor stole it," said Maerad sharply. She was beginning to feel annoyed. "It seems quite straightforward to me."

"And if we give it back to them – supposing we find out

how that is possible – what then of the Speech? Will Bards also have to give back their magery?"

"No, of course not!"

"How do you know, Maerad? I, for one, am not so sure. It seems to me that there is a good chance that should we succeed in finding the Treesong, should we release it back to the Elidhu and somehow also destroy the Nameless One, we could lose everything that makes us Bards."

Maerad was silent with shock. The thought had never occurred to her. "Surely that's not possible?" she said uncertainly. "Bards in Afinil had the Speech before Nelsor wrote down the Treesong…"

"Aye, they did," said Cadvan, his voice harsh. "But that doesn't mean that the Speech will live in us once we give the Treesong back. Undoing the magery that captured the Treesong is not simply a matter of reversing it. You should know that. And I fear what else might unravel after: it might go back to the very roots of our Knowing and silence our tongues. The truth is that we cannot know what will happen. If you haven't thought of this before, it's time you did. I am prepared to countenance that possibility if it is a choice between that and another Great Silence under the Nameless One; but I do not love the thought. We stand before an abyss. I think that even if we should claim victory in the midst of all this uncertainty, we could still find ourselves with our hands empty. Whatever happens, our world will not be the same after this. This is not a game, Maerad. We risk everything. And we could win, and still lose."

Maerad stared at the ground, biting her lip. At the back of her mind there had always been the hope that, if everything turned out well, if the Nameless One was defeated, she would simply become a normal Bard, studying the lore of Annar and the Seven Kingdoms somewhere like Innail or perhaps Gent, which had been Dernhil's School. The thought that even their victory could mean the end of Barding, the end of Schools, shook her deeply. Cadvan watched her closely, his face still hard.

"Given what we risk," he said, "I should hope that we are at least honest with each other. My hope Maerad, and it is a very small hope to place against the darkness that is now engulfing Annar, lies in your love for Hem, and, perhaps, in your love for me, and for others whose kindness you have been grateful for. So if you are leading me on a wild goose chase, I think you should have the courtesy to tell me."

Maerad said nothing for a time, pondering Cadvan's words and wondering how to answer. Did he doubt her love for him? Of course she loved him, of course she was grateful for his kindness. She looked past his shoulder and said evasively, "What do you mean?"

"I mean that if you think, in your Knowing, that Hem is dead, you should tell me."

Maerad blushed. She should have known that she could not keep her fear secret from Cadvan. "I – I don't think he's dead…" she said. "I just…" She stuttered into silence. "I'm not so sure," she said at last. "I've lost that – contact – before sometimes, but it hasn't meant that he was dead. This might be the same."

"But you had a nightmare about Hem," said Cadvan flatly.

"Yes," she whispered. "He might be dead. But I am not sure, and I still think we should look for him."

A long silence stretched out between them. Maerad stole a wary glance at Cadvan; he was staring into the fire, his face closed.

"Do you not trust me?" she said at last. "Is that it?"

"Why should I trust you?" he said, turning to face her.

Maerad felt her temper rising inside her, but tried to keep it leashed; at the same time as she smarted at the injustice of what Cadvan had said to her, and the deeper hurt of his mistrust, she remembered the terrible fight they had had before the disaster in the Gwalhain Pass, when she was sure that he had been killed. She didn't wish for another such breach to open between them.

"I don't have to tell you every thought that passes through my head," she said, her voice even. "What gives you the right to demand that?"

"The right I have is the faith I have placed in you, risking my very life to follow your Knowing," Cadvan said. "Would you not agree?"

There was another long, uncomfortable silence. It was true that Cadvan had risked his life, and more. Yet Maerad felt more and more irritated; this side of Cadvan, his ability to turn, without notice, into an implacable, unforgiving judge, annoyed her beyond measure, and it was deeply wounding. What made it worse was that there was a grain of truth in what he said. But it was partial only, she thought; it was not the whole truth.

"I think you are wrong about Ardina," she said at last. She stared at Cadvan defiantly, and he met her gaze. "I have seen more of her than you have. Yes, she is an Elidhu; but just because the Elidhu are dangerous, or have their own concerns apart from ours, doesn't mean that they are evil. I need help, and I think Ardina can help me. It's not as if you can." Her last sentence sounded more spiteful than she meant, and she bit her lip.

"Perhaps you are right in this," Cadvan said, his face expressionless. "I have no way of judging one way or another." He paused, and then added, "I'm sorry for what I said before. Words said in haste or anger can be harsher than their true intent."

Maerad nodded, accepting the apology. Then she took up her pack and, her fingers trembling, she searched through it for the reed pipes Ardina had given her. She inspected them closely; it occurred to her that she did not know how to play them with her damaged hand. She thought of summoning her magery, to create her fingers of light, but for reasons she could not explain, discarded the idea: they were humble pipes, and she should play them humbly. Cadvan watched her curiously, but said nothing.

"I might as well try now," she said. "Though I'm not sure what tunes I can play any more..."

She stood, feeling that it would be somehow disrespectful to summon Ardina while she was sitting down, and gave the pipes an experimental blow. The high, fleeting notes evoked a vivid image of a beautiful, deserted landscape: long banks of reeds perhaps, by a wide lake, where curlews called in the evening. It had been a long time since she had played any pipes, and she frowned as she missed a note. She glanced swiftly at Cadvan, as if reassuring herself that he was there; although she wouldn't have admitted it, she felt nervous about this summoning, especially after the near disaster of the previous night. She took a deep breath, and began to play a simple melody, a child's tuning, improvising around her missing fingers.

For what seemed like a long time, nothing happened. The reedy notes floated out into the darkening evening, plaintive and lonely. Maerad began to lose herself in the fascination of making music; even with her maimed hand, she could find a range of expressiveness that pleased her, and she began to experiment. Then she felt the back of her neck prickle, as if someone were watching her, and she whirled around, letting the pipes drop from her lips.

"Greeting, Elednor Edil-Amarandh na," said Ardina.

Maerad forgot, every time, the stunning impact of Ardina's beauty. The Elidhu stood on the grass a short distance away, in her guise as the grave Queen of Rachida. She wore a simple white dress that fell shimmering about her body as if it were woven of moonlight. A moonstone suspended from a silver fillet hung on her forehead, and about her waist was a silver chain. Her long unbound hair fell like a silver waterfall down her slender back. She turned her yellow eyes, with their inhuman slotted pupils, upon Maerad, and the glance went deep. Maerad bowed breathlessly, unable to speak. Darsor and Keru, grazing nearby, whinnied in welcome; Maerad thought it sounded oddly as if they were welcoming a dear friend. Out of the corner of her eye she saw Cadvan scramble to his feet and bow; Ardina turned and acknowledged his homage with a nod. "And to you, Cadvan of Lirigon, greetings."

"Greetings, Ardina," said Maerad, stammering. The awe she felt in the face of Ardina's presence in this guise made her tongue-tied; it had been much easier to speak when they had both escaped from Arkan's palace in the guise of wolves.

"You asked me to come, and so I have come," said Ardina. Maerad noticed that she did not use the Elemental tongue, but the Speech. Maerad thought that perhaps Ardina was not unaware of Cadvan's mistrust of her.

"I – I wanted to know if you could help me," said Maerad.

"I will help, if I am able," said Ardina. "Speak your desire."

What Maerad said next surprised her. "I want to know if Hem – my brother – is alive."

"I may not be able to tell you that," said Ardina. "I do not have a closeness to him, as I do to you. He may be alive in my time and not in your time. And in many times he is not present. But I will try." The Elidhu's eyes closed, and the faint light that inhabited her grew briefly stronger. Maerad waited, holding her breath.

"I do not know how or where your brother is," said Ardina, opening her eyes and looking straight at Maerad, who fought not to avert her gaze. "He has about him a smell of death, yet I do not think he is dead. He walks many possible futures and many possible pasts, and his paths are knived with pain. Your brother is almost as unlucky as you are." Ardina smiled, but her smile held a deep sadness.

"Does – does that mean I should keep looking for him?" asked Maerad, a catch in her voice.

"I do not advise. In this, as in all other matters, you must follow your heart. But I think that if you seek, you will find. What you might find I cannot say."

Maerad looked at the ground, crestfallen. "I don't understand how to look," she said. "I sometimes can feel where he might be, but it's all very vague. I thought that perhaps I could feel where he is. I know I have powers that are not the powers of a Bard, but I don't see how to use them. I hoped that perhaps you might tell me how."

Ardina laughed, and her laughter was like a cool rain, sending a pleasant shiver down Maerad's back. "Ah, Elednor Edil-Amarandh na! I am no teacher. But even if I were, I could not teach you how to use your magery. It is neither Elidhu nor Bard, although it partakes of both of them."

"Like the Nameless One," said Maerad softly.

"Aye, like Sharma. Know this, my dear one: the Light and the Dark are not so different, and neither can attain their full power until they acknowledge all their nature, both the fire and the ice, the sun and the shadow. But you are also not like Sharma. I tell you, whereas you are a Lily of Fire, that grows ever towards the Light, he is the poisonous fume that eats up the air, so that nothing else might live."

"How might Maerad know her full nature?" Maerad started in surprise; it was Cadvan speaking. In the bewitchment of Ardina's presence she had altogether forgotten that he was there.

"Through pain and sorrow and darkness, Cadvan of Lirigon. Through hatred and despair, perhaps. Through need and desire, surely. Did I not once tell you so, Elednor, before you were awake? Did I not say you were unlucky?"

Ardina's form began to dim, and by the time she finished speaking she had vanished altogether, as if she had never been there. Her final words hung on the air with the soft, aching resonance of a bell, and faded away. Maerad blinked, bereft, and turned to Cadvan, and saw the same loss reflected in his face. She realized with a slight shock that it was now full night: the clouds had cleared, and the cold stars glittered brightly over the desolate wolds in a moonless sky. Never had the Hollow Lands seemed so aptly named.

XIII

THE SUMMONING

MAERAD and Cadvan didn't speak for some time after Ardina's appearance, although their silence was companionable. Instead, they busied themselves with small tasks, such as finding more brushwood for the fire, or cleaning their supper dishes. Maerad didn't know whether she was comforted by Ardina's words or not: remembering her farewell, she thought that she wasn't comforted at all. On the other hand, Ardina seemed to think that Hem was still alive. Perhaps he was deathly ill or mortally wounded or in some other danger? The thought made her ache with worry and help-lessness. It was a physical pain in her chest – she couldn't bear the thought that Hem might be suffering, perhaps alone, and that she was unable to help. At least Maerad felt clear on one thing. Her heart commanded her to seek for Hem, and Ardina had told her to follow her heart.

Idly watching Cadvan as he polished his boots, another meaning occurred to her. *Through need and desire, surely…* What did that mean? She thought of how she had felt when the Winterking had touched her, how it had shaken her to the core of her being. If I am to follow my heart, thought Maerad, I must first understand it.

When there was nothing further to do, the two Bards settled by the fire, and began to talk, haltingly at first, because it was hard to shake off the powerful enchantment of Ardina's pres-ence. Cadvan said no more about distrusting Ardina, but he was puzzled and disturbed by what she had told Maerad.

"Ardina spoke in the Speech, not the Elemental tongue. She wanted you to hear what she said," said Maerad, "so that you would not think she or I were hiding anything."

There was no sign of Cadvan's former anger, and his glance was clear and open now when he looked at Maerad. "I'm sorry such Bardic mistrust took hold of me, Maerad; it was small of me. I remember now that you told me the Winterking said that the Elidhu do not lie. I think they do not; but that doesn't mean, either, that it is easy to puzzle out what they mean, or even that what I said to you in warning is not true. Ardina speaks in riddles, and while she is not dishonest, you may be misled, all the same."

"I'm sure of one thing, anyhow: that for better or worse, I have to find Hem. And – I *think* – he's still alive..."

"Aye. That seems clear, even if nothing else does. I do not understand, all the same, what she meant when I asked her how you might know your full nature. Or at least, if I can puzzle out a meaning, I do not like it."

Maerad heard Ardina's voice echoing in her inner ear: *Did I not say you were unlucky?*

"It doesn't sound very good for me, that's for certain," said Maerad, trying to shake off the deep foreboding the Elidhu's words opened inside her. "But she must be the only person in the world who isn't afraid of me, so I'm inclined to like her, all the same." She laughed, trying to speak lightly, but her voice shook, and she didn't look at Cadvan.

Cadvan was silent for a long moment. "Maerad, I'll be frank. Well, it seems to be an evening for being frank..." He sighed, passing his hand over his face, and Maerad saw for a moment how tired and strained he really was. "I can't help but be afraid of what exists within you. No sane person could feel otherwise. I have never seen the like, and I hope I never do again. The power that can – obliterate – a being like the

Landrost is not something that can be considered lightly. Even destroying a Wight or a Kulag is beyond what I believed possible, but an Elemental being, even one of the less powerful … it is terrifying, Maerad, that so much force can exist within a mortal. But that doesn't mean, all the same, that I am afraid of *you*."

"But what's inside me *is* me," said Maerad sadly. "It's me as much as my eyes or my voice or my music or my – or my hands." She stretched out her hands in front of her, the whole and the maimed, gazing at them. She still couldn't get used to looking at them. "I am what I am, all the things that have happened to me, all the things I have ever learned, as well as all the things that were born inside me."

"Aye, so are we all," said Cadvan. "And all the choices we have ever made…"

"I can't help thinking… All I've really learned in the past year is how to be a killer. How to destroy. From that first battle with the wers to the Hulls and the Kulag and the Landrost and – and even a Bard." Maerad put her hands under her cloak, where she could not see them, and stared into the fire.

"Is that all you have learned?" said Cadvan gently. "Surely you have learned other things? Have you not also learned something about love?"

Maerad felt herself blush, and was silent for a long time. "Perhaps I have. I don't know," she said at last. "I don't think I know anything about it."

"What is it, then, that draws you to Hem?"

"He's my *brother*. He's my only kin. I don't like to think of him, afraid, or sick, or maybe alone…" She looked at the ground again. "I've learned that people can be – kind," she said hesitantly. "Silvia and Malgorn and Dharin and you and so many others have been kind to me."

"I think it is more than kindness. But kindness is a word for it, I agree. Maerad, I think human evil is easy to explain. But what we call kindness, or love: that is endlessly mysterious. And I don't believe that you know nothing of love. I think you loved Dernhil, in the short time that you knew him. And I know that he loved you."

Maerad felt her blush deepen. She hadn't told Cadvan of her visit to Dernhil's chamber in Innail. It was true, Dernhil had loved her. And had she known herself better, she might have learned something of her own heart.

"There was ... no time," she mumbled. "And then he was killed." And he's gone through the Gates, she thought bitterly, and I will never speak to him again. I wish I could thank him for protecting me from the Hulls. I wish I could tell him that I have learned something of the Way of the Heart.

She looked up and saw that Cadvan was studying her gravely. "I did love Dernhil," she said in a low voice. "But I only understood later. And now he's dead, and it's too late."

"Perhaps Dernhil knew there was no time. He had fore-sight..." Cadvan sighed and looked away. "But he was ever one who looked clearly into his own heart. That is the beauty of his poems. Would that all of us were so lucid." He fell silent, following his own thoughts.

"But I've learned how to hate, too," said Maerad. "I thought I hated Gilman, back when I was little, but I only despised him. I hate Enkir. I hate the Nameless One. I hate them for every-thing they've destroyed. For destroying my life, and Hem's life..." She looked again at her maimed hand. "I just don't know where it *stops*. When you think about it, are the Light and the Dark so different? Why is it right to hate sometimes and not at other times? Why is it right to destroy this creature, and not that one?"

"It is never right. Sometimes, Maerad, there is no right thing..."

"Well, I do not like the world that makes it so." Maerad clenched her hands under her cloak. "And I will never like it." She took a deep breath. "You know what Ardina meant, Cadvan, as well as I do. She was saying that I have to embrace that hatred and that darkness and that – murderousness – inside me, if I'm to understand myself, if I want to know how to use those powers. The strange thing is, I thought I *had* embraced them. But when I think about it…"

Cadvan listened alertly, his eyes dark, as if he knew what Maerad were about to say and wanted to stop her saying it.

"… When I think about it, I know I've been too afraid of that hatred to really feel it. You know, after I destroyed those Hulls, the first time, I was so frightened of what I had done. But underneath that, I was so excited, I felt – well, it was something like a kind of – even like happiness, exhilaration, something like that. I think that feeling frightened me more than what I had done."

"What are you saying, Maerad?" said Cadvan tensely.

"Cadvan, you *know* what I'm saying." Maerad looked at him with despair. "Please, please, don't pretend that you don't know what I'm saying. You, of all people…"

"I think you're saying that you want to open the darkness within you."

"Yes." Maerad held up her hand to stop Cadvan's objections. "I know what you're going to say, Cadvan. I know it. I know all the arguments."

"Maerad, that seems to me a grievous misunderstanding – you can't mean it." Cadvan was very pale. "Yes, I of all people know that exhilaration you speak of. And I of all people also know its cost. It destroyed my youth, Maerad, and killed one I loved more than life itself. And I fear that if you turn this way, you become even as the Nameless One himself. Perhaps worse. No, Maerad, I do not permit this."

"It's not a question of whether you permit me or not," said Maerad stiffly.

"Then I beg you, Maerad. I beg you by the long friendship between us. Do not go that way. If you choose this path, I can only foresee doom. For all of us, not only for yourself."

"But if I can use these powers properly, if I can enter my full strength, I might be able to find Hem," said Maerad. "And you're right, Cadvan, we don't have much chance of finding him otherwise. Maybe no chance at all."

Cadvan said nothing for a long time. He stood up and walked out into the night, and Maerad could hear him moving around in the darkness, and then talking quietly to the horses. Maerad sensed the turbulence in his mind, and it grieved her; at the same time, she felt she had no choice but to do as Ardina had suggested, and she knew that she would attempt to wake her full powers whether Cadvan approved or not. But she would greatly prefer it if she had his support. The memory of her idle experiment the night before was still fresh in her mind; she didn't want any repeat of that torment.

And most of all, despite the growing determination within her – which amounted to a certainty that she had no choice, that she had to try or fail utterly in her quest – she was desperately afraid. She didn't want to make the attempt alone. She needed Cadvan.

At last Cadvan came back to the circle of firelight, and sat cross-legged next to Maerad. "I understand that you feel you must do this thing," he said. "And I cannot say that I think it is right. But I also know that I can't stop you, and that you will do it anyway, whatever I say. So." He stared at the ground, his face dark and troubled, and Maerad held her breath. "My one request is that you wait a day. Don't attempt whatever it is you think you should do until you've slept on it. I will not abandon you, Maerad; it's too late for me to turn away. And I will do my best to help you, even though you plan to do what I think you should not, even though I fear the ruin of all our enterprise in this venture. I will do this, out of the love that I bear you. For no other reason. May I be forgiven under the justice of the Light."

Maerad was overwhelmed with relief. She hadn't understood until that moment how much she had feared that Cadvan would abandon her. Unable to speak, she reached out and took Cadvan's hand. He clasped her small white hand in both of his and looked down at it, earnestly examining the broken, dirty nails, the calluses, the small white scars that marked her skin.

"I swear, Maerad, that I have never said anything in my life that was harder to say." He looked up and smiled at her, a broken smile that made Maerad's heart contract with pain.

"Everything is difficult," she whispered. "Maybe that's something else that I've learned."

After breaking their fast the following day, Maerad and Cadvan discussed whether to move on or to stay where they were. Maerad thought it figured little where they were: for the past couple of days they had been moving east along the northern edge of the floods, without attempting to venture southwards over the lands where the waters had subsided.

The floods had left a layer of silt over everything, along with a litter of broken branches tangled with dead grasses, and embedded in the mud there were the bloated bodies of animals. Over everything hung the sweet, disgusting stench of rotting flesh: for all its chilliness, Maerad was glad of the freshening wind from the eastern mountains, which stopped the odour of decay from becoming overwhelming. It also lifted the mist that had obscured their view for the past few days, and they could see far over the lowlands. Before them stretched a melancholy swamp, dotted with muddy pools that were rapidly turning stagnant. The most sturdy trees had survived, but many had been snapped off at the trunk by the violence of the waters, and the grasses that weren't covered in silt were flattened and yellowed by the water. For all her impatience, Maerad sympathized with the horses' refusal to venture into the wreckage of the flood. Cadvan said that if the weather continued clear, especially with the drying wind, it would be safe to move south within a couple of days. Darsor kept studiously silent on the subject.

They decided, in the end, to find a place that offered more shelter than the overhanging rock that had been their roof the night before. Cadvan also wanted to find a site that was defensible and gave them a view of the surrounding area, in case Maerad's exercise of power attracted unwelcome notice. In this part of Annar there was no chance of finding a Bardhome, but they thought that perhaps they might discover, among the strange rock formations of the Hollow Lands, something like the rocky shelter that they had discovered the day before last.

It was some time before they discovered what they were looking for. On top of a low hill, a tumulus of huge stones formed a natural cave big enough to house the two Bards, and to the side there was even a kind of porch where the horses could be out of the wind. They stopped here, although it was only just after midday, and set up camp, gathering a high pile of the sage brush that grew thickly around this area to use as fuel. It was dry and easy to light, and it made a fragrant smoke; but it burned quickly. The sky was still overcast, but the clouds were high and held no smell of rain. The wind had risen during the morning, and seemed to have grown colder; it was a relief to be out of its punishing chill. As the homely light of their fire flickered over the grey stone walls, Maerad felt almost cheerful.

"So what do you plan to do?" said Cadvan, after they had finished eating their noonday meal.

Maerad glanced at him in surprise; it was unlike Cadvan to be so forthright. "I don't know," she said. "I've been wondering all morning. It's not like anything I've tried to do before, because, in a way, I'm not trying to do anything. I mean, when I've done things before, either it just happened because I was frightened or angry, or it's because I needed to make something happen. Like when I first turned into a wolf, it was because Ardina told me to do it, and I just thought of what I wanted to happen and went from there; and fighting the Landrost was kind of the same, only more difficult, and all I thought about was how to stop him killing my friends. But this isn't like that. I want to be able to use all my powers, and I know that I have to find – to find the *whole* of me ... but how do you do that? I mean, it's no good just *wishing*..."

She paused, and then directed a sharp glance at Cadvan. "In a way, I don't know why the idea upsets you so much," she said. "Doesn't the Balance talk about the Dark and Light within you? Haven't you said often that you cannot perceive the Light without the Darkness? And surely that's what I want to do?"

Cadvan looked taken aback. "Yes, you're right," he said. "And there is a balance to be found. But there is a darkness in you, Maerad, that makes me wary; it is not of a kind that I have felt before. I have tried to speak of it to you." A shadow passed over his face as he recalled their worst quarrel, a breach that had almost ended in both their deaths. "I fear that in that darkness, there is no Balance. Or, perhaps, that there is not any kind of Balance as Bards understand it."

"Perhaps the Knowing of the Bards doesn't cover everything there is to know," said Maerad.

"Barding does not pretend to hold all knowledge," said

Cadvan, his voice hard, and Maerad looked away. "All the same, do not think to hold the Elementals as all-wise, Maerad, merely because they have Knowing that we do not."

Maerad thought of the cold, arrogant face of Enkir. "Some Bards do believe that their Knowing is above any other kind," she said.

"Aye," said Cadvan, catching her thought. "But those Bards do not observe the Balance, Maerad. Their minds are all too literal, and brook no contradiction. But we could argue of the Balance all day, and still get no closer to the truth. I return to my earlier question: what do you plan to do?"

Maerad drew her cloak around her and leaned closer to the fire, feeling its healing warmth on her wind-chapped cheeks. "I will try to see if I am bigger," she said. "I was thinking – when I change into wolf-skin, I go inside, deeper and deeper and deeper, until I have no Name at all. And when I fought with the Landrost I went out, further and further and further, until I was so far away I no longer knew who I was, or even what I was."

She sat back on her heels and brushed her hair out of her eyes.

"So I thought, what if I do neither of these things, but try to stay where I am, and see if I can become more? I mean, perhaps when I go in or out, I am like a spear, a narrow thing, so I can pierce through all those layers of being. But perhaps I need to be – well, something like a lake. Something broad as well as deep and high." She looked up, frowning with concentration, and when she met Cadvan's intent gaze, her brow cleared and she suddenly laughed. "I suppose I've just talked a mountain of nonsense!"

Cadvan did not smile. "It might not be the most common of sense," he said. "But I do not think you speak nonsense, Maerad of Pellinor."

* * *

Cadvan insisted that Maerad be prepared for her experiment, although he said that she would probably sense best what she should do. He had decided to cast a glimveil over their camp, in case the release of magery attracted unwelcome attention; although he thought privately that if Maerad did succeed in unlocking her full powers, no charm he could make could possibly contain or conceal them.

Maerad pondered for a short time, and then washed her face and hands in rainwater collected in a pool on the rocks nearby. As she did, she remembered vividly the preparation she had made for her meeting with Inka-Reb, the powerful Dhillarearëan in the far north to whom she had journeyed with her cousin Dharin in search of the Treesong. She had not thought about Inka-Reb much since; her life had been full of so many things, and that meeting had been strange and disturbing. She saw his bulky, huge figure clearly in her mind's eye, naked, smeared with ash and fat, squatting by the fire in his cave, and she remembered the wolves who surrounded him – the same wolves who had later accepted her as one of their own. Inka-Reb had an inner power that awed her. Perhaps if anyone could teach her how to come fully into her Gift, he could; but even if she struggled all the way north again, she guessed that he would probably refuse. In this matter, she was on her own. She thought that perhaps Inka-Reb might not disapprove of what she was trying to do. He was, after all, contemptuous of both the Dark and the Light.

When she returned from washing herself, she suggested that she and Cadvan bring out their lyres, which lay, untouched since Innail, in their packs. He looked at her in surprise, but brought out his lyre without further comment. Maerad held hers in the crook of her arm, gazing thoughtfully at the inscrutable runes that decorated its plain wood. She knew what they were now; they were the runes of the Treesong, its power

captured and written down by the great Afinil Bard, Nelsor, in
the days of the Dhyllin. But she still didn't know how to make
them sing, how to release them back to the Elidhu.

"I thought," said Maerad, clearing her throat, "I thought that
we could sing *The Song of Making*."

Cadvan looked pleased, but only said: "Your wish is my
command."

Maerad felt unaccountably nervous, as if she were performing in front of a hall of critical Bards, instead of in the empty
wilderness. She held her lyre in her hands, and let the magery
rise within her until she was surrounded by a nimbus of light,
and her left hand was whole again. She nodded to Cadvan, and
struck the opening chords.

They sang in close harmony, Cadvan's baritone and
Maerad's pure, husky voice filling their shelter, and Maerad felt
all her sorrow and anxieties lift and dissolve in the sheer beauty
of the music.

> *First was dark, and the darkness*
> *Was all mass and all dimension, although without touch*
> *And the darkness was all colours and all forms,*
>   *although without sight*
> *And the darkness was all music and all sound,*
>   *although without hearing*
> *And it was all perfumes, and all tastes,*
>   *sour and bitter and sweet*
> *But it knew not itself.*
>
> *And the darkness thought, and it thought without mind*
> *And the thought became mind and the thought quickened*
> *And the thought was Light, was the Light in darkness,*
> *And where Light fell, there was its shadow,*
> *And the shadow moved and a dark eye opened...*

It was the first song Maerad had chosen to sing in her day-long preparation to meet Inka-Reb. She had been taught this song when she was a child, and had heard it many times in the past year; and every time she heard it, it showed her new, more complex meanings. As she sang the opening stanzas, she realized how deeply it chimed with her recent thoughts. I need, she thought, my own dark eye to open...

As the final chords died on the air, she bowed her head and let the light of magery die out of her, and both she and Cadvan were silent for a long time. Finally Maerad lifted her head and looked Cadvan straight in the eye.

"I will begin now," she said.

Cadvan nodded. He did not seem in the least afraid, but he looked very sad, as if he were bidding Maerad farewell as she left on a long journey.

Maerad took a deep breath, and closed her eyes.

She entered the darkness that was her inner self, the place from which she began all her magery. The desire to move on was strong within her; from this place, she would either plunge down through her deeper selves or quest outward with the heightened perceptions that the darkness generated. With an effort of will she remained just where she was, suspended on the threshold of possibility, waiting to see if anything might happen.

Nothing happened for what seemed like a long time. Maerad found it hard to concentrate; in this place, she felt blurred, as if she were only half present. She tried to keep focused and alert, to feel the mysterious contours of this inner world, attempting to sense any thickening of shadow around her; but nothing seemed to happen. She began to think that she had been mistaken, that perhaps this was not the correct place to begin, when she noticed that there seemed to be a faint illumination, as subtle as starlight, growing around her, as if her inner eyes were adjusting.

After a while she was sure that her awareness had grown inside the space, but it was happening so gradually that she almost hadn't noticed. Again she felt the desire to move on (was it onwards? she wondered briefly to herself: in this place there was no sense of dimension, no sense of time). But again she resisted the urge, and stayed where she was, concentrating on the thought of making herself bigger. Bigger? said the voice in her head again; all you are trying to fill up is yourself, this makes no sense... As soon as her doubts voiced themselves, she lost her focus, and the seeming illumination vanished. She almost withdrew in frustration; while it wasn't exactly unpleasant to be in this strange limbo, it wasn't pleasant either. But a stubbornness kicked inside her, a refusal to give up at the first hurdle. She tried again, this time without letting her doubt and uncertainty rise to the surface of her mind.

Slowly she regained her focus, holding herself in a strangely agonizing pose of suspension. This time the dim illumination – if that is what it was – arrived a little more swiftly. She still couldn't sense anything about this inner space; its strange formlessness simply existed around her (or within her) without revealing any kind of contour. She wondered whether she should exercise some kind of will, rather than the passivity she was having such difficulty maintaining, or whether to do so might obliterate what little she could already sense. At first she decided against it, but when nothing further happened she began to feel impatient. She didn't want to go anywhere; but she did want to know more about where she was. She thought of her earlier idea, that she wanted to be like a lake, and imagined herself as a great body of water, as formless as this faintly glimmering darkness, pushing outwards in all directions, filling it up.

At first it seemed to work; or at least, the illumination began to coalesce into tiny, blurred points of illumination. The dim lights looked like stars seen through a mist. She was at first astonished: surely it was, not just *like* starlight, but starlight itself? Was she full of secret constellations? And then another sense began to rise within her, a fluidly brilliant perception unlike any of her normal six senses, although this too seemed blurred, like a song that she knew intimately, but that evaded her recognition because it ran beneath her hearing. Or perhaps it was like a picture that she couldn't quite see, a half-remembered image from her childhood, perhaps … only it was really like none of these things, but something else entirely, that she had no words for. But neither of these things – the stars, if they were stars, or this other, new perception – became any clearer, although now she strained to perceive them.

The feeling of suspension, of being neither here nor there nor even in between, of being unnaturally still rather than naturally in motion, was beginning to be unbearable, a kind of suffocation of her mind. It grew until she thought she couldn't stand it, that she would have to move outwards or inwards, anywhere but where she was, and she felt a helpless anger welling up through her. It was then that she remembered her reason for being there. Up until now, in the sheer strangeness of this liminal no-space, she had forgotten it, as completely as the most important details of a dream slip from the waking mind.

Normally Maerad would have pressed this anger down, and attempted to keep her thoughts cool and rational. Anger only possessed her at extremities where it was powerful enough to outstrip her conscious control. This time, with an effort of will, she allowed it to grow. At first she disliked the feeling almost as much as the suffocation that had prompted it; she felt a quiver of fear as its red tide rose within her. Like the flood, it brought with it a strange detritus; random fragments of memory swirled through her, things she hadn't thought about for years. Old slights unanswered, injuries unrevenged, injustices suffered – all trivial events that she had at the time set aside, too proud to respond to – returned with their original force, their humiliating stings undiminished. On their heels came memories which were not so trivial: her mother's death, broken and defeated, in the squalid slaves' dormitory in Gilman's Cot; her father's murder during the sack of Pellinor; the point of Enkir's dagger at her childish throat, as he blackmailed her mother into revealing where Hem was taken to be hidden. All her lost, blasted childhood. And all the deaths that had followed her: Dernhil, Dharin...

None of these things was fair, none of them was just, none was her fault. Each memory possessed her, filling her with bitter despair, and then a terrible hatred tore through her like raw flame. She cared about nothing except her own pain, her loss, her maimed life ... for a moment she wanted to howl and she almost sank out of the protean darkness into her wolf-skin; but some remnant of her purpose remained, and she stopped herself, pulsing with an extreme, amorphous hatred. And within her, as if her hatred and anger had undammed a violent river, there rushed a brilliant, luminous sense of power, as deadly and implacable as a flood, as a wolf at the kill.

A thrill went through her, and she forgot her hatred; now she basked in the pure pleasure of power. She had felt something like this when she had first become a wolf, delighting in her physical strength; it had felt something like this when she had killed the Kulag, although she had dreaded that joy. But now she saw clearly the dark coils woven into the bright currents that coursed through her being. She could do anything. She could kill, she could destroy; she could reach out her hand and shrivel the root of all living things, or lean forward to kiss the dead into life; and the thought did not shock her.

She looked about her and saw the stars, bright and huge as she had never seen them, aligned in patterns that were made legible by the other sense that had so puzzled her earlier. It was a sense that could trace fields and vortices of energy; she felt how the stars moved each in its orbit, how the earth rolled beneath her, how the tides undulated to the moon; she heard the slow pulse of rock, the quick heartbeat of birds. She was suddenly aware of Cadvan's stubborn, intent presence, his thoughts bent solely on her, and she knew that he had been watching her for hours, and that the sun had long set. It was now deep night, under a clear and moonless sky thick with an infinity of stars.

She widened her field of perception and her being filled with awareness. She heard voices echoing, many voices, cries and whispers and howls, and she could sense dim presences, outlined with a vagrant luminosity. She knew without thinking that these were the dead in the Hollow Lands, the faint murmur of their voices arcing across uncounted years, the warmth of their hands vibrating still in the stones they had raised, in the tombs they had dug beneath the stones. She cast wider still, curious and exhilarated by this new sense, and felt the dark presence of Hulls, not far away, not close, and she knew that their heads were raised, questing, and their nostrils flared as they caught the scent of the power that briefly touched their minds. For the first time she did not fear them; contempt curled in the depths of her being. They were nothing, no more than wisps of smoke on the wind.

She hunted further still, learning as she went, refining and directing this new sense. She knew by the alignment of her inner stars that she was questing south, over the drenched lowlands. She heard the voices of those who had drowned, the grief of the homeless, the panicked lowing of cattle, the sharp fear of goats and sheep, the feathered terror of birds, the slow agony of trees. She paused, dizzied and confused by the chaotic babble of presences. She was no longer certain what the present meant; the voices came from the present, but she could hear also into the recent past, and behind that, fainter voices rose through the years, through decades and centuries, stretching back to a time that she could barely comprehend.

In all this cacophony, she sought one particular light, one particular smell, one particular voice, one particular time: now. A word formed in her mind, a word of the Speech, and it hung before her like silver fire, one utterly clear thing in this world of shifting shadows and light, and all her desire flowed into it, and it intensified to an unbearable brilliance. Riik. Crow. The silver flame poured through her and became a voice, and she sought through the lowlands, through all the voices, all the dead, all the living, and found the one person whose Truename it was, the one person who would hear his Name coursing through his blood like fiery bells, like the voice of starlight. *Riik*, she said, *Riik, my brother. Come to me.*

Leagues away, in a shepherd's hut on a dark hill, in the nameless depths of sleep, Hem started awake and scrambled to his feet, looking around him with wild eyes. "Maerad!" he said, and stumbled out of the hut's low door. "Maerad?" And then his earthsense rose inside him, a hunger which pulled him with a force so powerful that he almost doubled over with the pain of it.

Come to me, said Maerad.

Hem realized, with a disappointment that hit him almost as painfully as his earthsense, that Maerad was not there. But the force of her summoning had been so strong that he could almost see the way towards her, like a shimmering pathway of silver through the darkness. It was as if Maerad was the moon rising over a calm sea, and the path towards her was a road of white ripples that swept northwards from Hem's feet.

I will come to you, he cried, but the summoning had released him, and he didn't know if she heard his answer. *Maerad, I'm coming*.

XIV

NEWS OF HULLS

HEM sat down on the dew-damp grass, weak with the shock of what had just happened, and stared northwards over the shadowy hills that humped darkly under the star-strewn sky, and which now seemed emptier than ever.

Maerad. He had been so sure that she was just outside the hut, calling him, he could have sworn that he could smell her, a faint sweet musk on the night air. He wiped his eyes on his sleeve and ordered his distracted thoughts. The blazing pathway he had seen had now faded, but he felt its pull vividly; he knew, at last, exactly where to go. His first impulse was to go back into the hut and wake Saliman and leave at once, but he thought again and decided to wait until morning.

He looked up at the stars, seeking Ilion, the dawn star: it was already low on the western horizon. It would not be long before the sky began to pale towards morning. He shivered. There wasn't much point in going back to sleep. He returned to the hut and began to blow on the embers of the damped-down fire, coaxing a small flame onto dry wood with shaking hands. Irc stirred sleepily on his perch on Hem's pack and gave a small protesting caw at being woken, and then instantly fell asleep again.

Hem tended the fire until his hands stopped trembling. It was certainly Maerad who had called him, but he had never felt such a powerful summoning. And she had called him by his Truename. Riik. *Crow.* He glanced across at Irc, and almost laughed aloud. Of *course* that was his Name; that was what everyone called him, after all. *Lios Hlaf*, the White Crow, had been his nickname in Turbansk. But how did Maerad know? He hadn't been instated as a Bard yet, he didn't have a Truename. Maybe, somehow, Maerad had instated him? Or maybe he could have a Bardic Truename without being properly instated, after all? He would have to ask Saliman.

Saliman was sleeping against the far wall of the hut, wrapped in his cloak and blanket. Hem could hear his easy breathing underneath the crackle of the fire. Saliman was clear of the White Sickness, but Hem was shocked by how weakened he was. And he had healed him in the early stages of the illness; Hem knew now that had he been any more sick, their chances would have been slim indeed. When he looked back at the risk he had run, Hem went cold; Saliman was correct, he had been mad to try it. And even so, it had taken everything he had, and more that he didn't know he had.

After that last terrible moment when he had called Saliman's Name and collapsed over his body, he had lain in a swoon until late the following day. He had opened his eyes to the soft red light of the sinking sun, which shone straight into the doorway of the hut. At first, he hadn't known where he was. He was overwhelmingly thirsty, and his body ached from the top of his head to the tips of his toes: it was as if he been beaten all over. He groaned, clutching his head, and sat up.

Saliman was sitting next to him, stirring a stew that smelt very good. When he heard Hem move, he turned around. "I am sorry for the smoke in here," he said. "But I do not have the energy to light a new fire outside the door. Eating and warmth seem more important at the moment."

Hem stared at Saliman, as memory trickled back. "You're alive," he said. His voice croaked with dryness, and Saliman wordlessly passed him a water bottle. Hem took a long drink, and wiped his lips. Never had plain water tasted so sweet.

"Aye," said Saliman. "I have pinched all my arms and legs, and even my nose, and I am not dreaming. Beyond hope, I am still alive. A little the worse for wear, but I am not complaining. I can't but feel glad that you so wickedly disobeyed me. I owe you my life."

"I thought you were going to die," said Hem. He wanted to shout, to sing, to rush around the hills dancing for joy, but he seemed unable to do anything at all except say obvious, foolish things. He was so tired, he could barely hold himself upright.

"Don't speak," said Saliman. "There is no need. And this stew will be ready soon."

The stew, too, tasted excellent. Even the fuggy, smoky air in that tiny hut seemed as fragrant as a rose garden in the palaces of Turbansk.

"I suppose that everything tastes so good because I thought I wasn't going to taste anything ever again," said Hem, scooping up the last spoonfuls of stew from his plate. Saliman smiled, but said nothing.

Irc had come in, with unerring timing, just as Saliman was dishing out their meal, and was crooning contentedly in Hem's lap. Hem put down his plate and tickled Irc's neck. The crow had been unusually quiet; he sensed how close he had come to losing his friends, although Hem hadn't told him how desperate their situation was. And he had been more frightened of the floods than he cared to admit. The water had risen until the ridges where they had taken refuge had become a series of islands, and Irc said some of the islands were crowded with damp, miserable animals.

I saw chickens and foxes together in the mud, he told Hem, wiping his beak on Hem's trousers. *And the chickens were not running, and the fox was not chasing them. Neither wanted to speak to me ... it was very strange.*

They were frightened, Hem said.

Well, I suppose it won't be long before everyone is hunting again.

Irc demanded a scratch and then perched on Hem's pack and went to sleep. Hem and Saliman chatted for a short time about trivial things, like Irc's observations, or the sorry state of Hem's boots; neither of them felt able to speak about anything serious, such as how close they had both been to death, or what they should do next. Hem was trying to conceal his concern at how much thinner Saliman had become in the last couple of days: already lean from hard travelling, illness had made him almost skeletal, and his face was haggard. He scarcely looked less drawn now, despite the fact that both of them had spent much of their time sleeping, only waking for meals.

And now he had been summoned, Hem knew they had to move on. He looked at Saliman's sleeping form and wondered how he would fare. He couldn't leave without him; but the urgency of Maerad's call burned inside his body like a blazing hunger.

For the moment Hem put aside these worries. He realized that the exhaustion that had weighed him down the past couple of days had vanished. He felt no tiredness at all; as his shock dissipated, a rare joy began to sing through his veins. Ever since they had left Til Amon, he had been pursued by a nagging doubt: perhaps his conviction that he ought to find Maerad was mistaken, perhaps he was misled by his hope and love, as he had been when he had so desperately sought his friend Zelika through the cursed realm of Dén Raven. Now he knew that Maerad was alive, that she sought him just as he sought her, and the knowledge filled him with relief. At last he knew what to do.

As the sky lightened, Irc woke up and stepped over to Hem, asking for food. Hem gave him some scraps left over from the night before, and Irc nibbled his hand in thanks, gulped the food down, and then flew off. Hem walked outside and watched Irc soaring into the air. The sky was cloudless, letting down a clear, pale sunlight, and there was a brisk, cold wind. A good day for walking.

Idly watching Irc, Hem wondered what the crow did on his private missions. Sometimes he would be gone for most of the day, impelled most probably by his insatiable curiosity, but he always returned for meals and often just for a chat. He was a fully adult bird now, and on the ground was large and almost clumsy, a quality belied by his aerial grace. His feathers had lost most of the dye that Hem had used to darken him in Nal-Ak-Burat, in preparation for their mission in Dén Raven, and were now almost a glossy white. Hem thought sometimes that perhaps Irc might want to leave his strange, unbird-like life, and become an ordinary crow; although with his white feathers he would always be ostracised by his fellows. He never asked him, and Irc followed Hem without question, although they were now very far away from where he had hatched, in the warm lands of the south.

Wrapping his cloak close around him against the sharp early wind, Hem walked to the top of the ridge and looked northwards over the country they would have to travel. Before him there stretched several long ridges like those they had climbed to find the hut, each lower than the former, like a series of waves sinking down to the plains. They had taken refuge on the only high ground in the area.

The rocky spines of the ridges had escaped the water, but the valleys between them and the plains beyond were a bleak sight, covered with rubbish and silt. If the ground was swampy, it would be a hard trek to the higher ground he saw rising through the haze far in the distance. Hem studied the terrain for a time, then climbed back over the top of the ridge and across to the next southern ridge to look at what had happened to Hiert. The ground he had covered with such painful labour, pushing the wheelbarrow against the rain, now took him little time to cross.

He surveyed Hiert from the top of the ridge. Before him the flood line was clear; above it, the turf was green, while beneath it flattened, yellow grass scattered with rubbish ran down to the houses, which looked forlorn and deserted in the morning light. Most had withstood the flooding, but Hem could see that some buildings had crumbled under the force of the water. The river was now flowing between its banks, still brown and swollen, and the sun shone blindingly on the puddles and pools that it had left behind in its retreat. Stray animals – chickens, pigs, goats, a few cattle – were wandering the deserted roads, looking for food. Hem could see how deep the flooding had been by the watermarks on the trees; in places it had been almost three spans deep, high enough to flood most of the buildings of Hiert to their roofs.

He could smell the sweet stench of decay rising from the wrack of the village, and wrinkled his nose. Somewhere in Hiert was the body of the nameless man who had given Saliman the White Sickness. Hem thought of him with pity; he doubted that he would ever know who he was, but now he knew a little of the torment that poor man had undergone. He understood why the village had been empty, why everyone had fled before that illness; he could feel the terror of it in his body even now, and he hoped fervently he would never encounter it again.

He sighed, and was about to turn on his heel and make the trek back to their hut when something caught his eye. A cloaked horseman, leading another horse on a rein, was trotting slowly down the West Road, into Hiert. Hem's skin prickled with dread. Perhaps it was someone passing through, or a townsperson of Hiert who had survived the floods by fleeing to higher land, as he and Saliman had, and was now returning to find out what was left of their home ... or maybe it was the Hull that Saliman had thought might be tracking them through Annar.

Hem dropped down by a large sage bush, squatting to make himself less visible, and prepared to hide himself with magery if it became necessary. He watched cautiously as the lone horseman slowly moved along the Bard Road. Behind him, there trailed what looked like a large dog. Something about the horseman's intentness told Hem that it was searching for something, or someone, and a shiver ran down his spine.

As the horseman moved behind the higher buildings of the tavern, Hem lost sight of him. He waited impatiently to see if he would re-emerge, but he didn't. Perhaps he had gone inside to salvage some belongings, or to loot what goods remained in the wreckage; or perhaps he was looking for signs that he and Saliman had stayed there. It seemed a long time before he re-emerged, this time without the horses, but still followed by the dog, walking slowly. He wandered along the West Road, looking from side to side. Hem crouched lower to keep himself off the skyline. The walker then turned aside, up the same path that Hem and Saliman had used to climb up the ridge days before, and which led to where Hem was crouching. There wasn't much of a path left; it had briefly become a river in the rains, and now was a deep, slippery runnel in the hill, which made it hard to climb. The figure steadily worked his way up the hill and Hem became more and more anxious.

As it drew closer, he thought that it wasn't a man after all, but almost certainly a woman. A refugee from the floods, most likely, as he had thought; though why she was toiling up this steep hill was a mystery, especially as she was clearly exhausted: her head was bent low, and she often stumbled. He could sense no sorcery about her, although if it were a Hull, and were hunting him and Saliman, it would most likely shield its sorcery. Soundlessly, Hem moved himself behind the bush, keeping the woman in constant view. She stopped and rested for a time, and the dog sat on its haunches and waited for her. Then she stood up and stubbornly began walking uphill again. As she drew closer, Hem became more curious about what she was doing. She slipped, and Hem heard her curse under her breath, and she stood up straight, looking up the hill, shading her eyes with her hands, and Hem at last saw her face.

It was Hekibel; and of course the dog was Fenek. Hem cried out in surprise, and stood up, waving, and began to run towards her. Fenek growled and Hekibel swung around, and Hem saw that in that brief moment she was terrified.

"Hekibel!" he cried. "What are you doing here?"

Fenek recognized Hem and jumped up and tried to lick his face, but subsided when Hekibel told him to stay down and just stood beside them, his tail wagging furiously.

"Hem?" As he reached her, Hekibel took his arms. "Hem? Is it really you?"

"Yes, it's me." Hem studied Hekibel's face: she looked haggard and drawn, as if she hadn't slept for a long time, and the skin around her eyes was puffy and red. She was dressed in men's clothes, and she was filthy, smeared with mud. "What's happened? You look exhausted."

"I am," said Hekibel, her voice breaking. "I am so tired... Oh, Hem, I so hoped to find you, but I thought – I thought I didn't have a chance... But tell me, how is Saliman?"

"Saliman is healed," said Hem.

Hekibel was silent for a moment, clearly amazed, and Hem saw something like awe in her eyes. "Did you heal him, Hem?" she asked at last.

Hem nodded, feeling awkward.

"By the Light." Hekibel sat down very suddenly, as if all the wind had been taken out of her. "You healed him of the White Sickness. Marich said it couldn't be done…"

"He's not sick any more," said Hem. "But he's still weak. And I left him this morning before he woke up, so he won't know where I am. Why don't we go back to the hut?"

Hekibel nodded. "Is it far?"

"Over that next ridge," said Hem, pointing. He stared at Hekibel with concern; he had noticed that her hands were trembling. "Can you walk that far? And then I could make you some breakfast."

Hekibel smiled. "Of course I can," she said. "I've come this far. It might take me a little longer than I would like, that's all…"

By the time they reached the hut, the sun was well up in the sky. Hekibel didn't speak during the walk; she breathed heavily, her lips pressed hard together, conserving all her energy for walking. Fenek followed close at her heels protectively, aware that his mistress was suffering. On their way, Irc touched down briefly: Saliman had told him to look for Hem. Hem sent him back with a message to prepare some breakfast, and by the time they arrived at the hut, Saliman had a pot of porridge bubbling on the fire. Irc had already warned him that Hem was bringing Hekibel, so he showed no surprise when he saw her. He greeted her gently, and offered his arm to lower her down to sit.

Hekibel was so clearly at the end of her endurance, and so transparently glad to sit down somewhere dry, to warm herself by a fire, to eat a hot meal, that neither Hem nor Saliman asked any questions until she had finished eating. Fenek simply curled up by her feet and went to sleep.

Hem took advantage of the silence while they ate to

mindtouch Saliman, and to briefly tell him about what had happened the night before.

Maerad summoned me last night, he said.

Saliman almost dropped his spoon. Hem felt his astonishment and relief as he answered, *She summoned you?*

Yes, said Hem. *I have never felt anything like it, she was so strong. She's north of us. I know where to go now.* He gave Saliman an image of what he had seen, the bright, shimmering path that led to Maerad.

Good, said Saliman. *That is good news, Hem. I was thinking this morning that it is time we moved on from here – all the better if at last we have some idea of where to go. We'll talk more of this later. At the moment, I wish to know what Hekibel has to tell us. Something is very wrong and I fear that it bodes ill for us.*

Hem nodded and ate his porridge. After they had all broken their fast, Saliman offered Hekibel some medhyl. She drank a few sips and a little colour returned to her face. She leaned back against the wall of the hut, shutting her eyes.

"I suppose you want to know why I came looking for you," she said.

"Yes, if you feel able," said Saliman.

"I have to tell you. That's why I was looking for you, to tell you, although I thought that probably both of you were dead…" She paused, struggling with herself, and didn't speak until she had regained control of her voice. "Saliman, I cannot say how sorry I am…"

Saliman cut her off with a gesture. "Hekibel," he said. "As I said to Hem, and as I would have said to you, had I the chance, leaving us behind was the only sensible option. Hard, I know … but the truth. Do not distress yourself, I beg you."

Hekibel looked down at the floor, her face dark. "That is gracious of you, Saliman. I thank you. I'm not sure that I would have such grace, especially after you hear… Whether or not it was the right thing to do, I still felt as if I were abandoning friends in need. But, as you will see, it may have been more fortunate for you than it seemed at the time." She paused, biting her lip, and the others waited.

"It's hard to tell this story," she said at last. "But I suppose, as players say, the best tunes run swift and simple. As you know, we left the tavern and continued up the West Road as swiftly as we could. Just out of Hiert the waters were rising so fast it was terrifying; I thought that we would be swept away. Obviously we couldn't leave the road unless we abandoned the caravan, and Karim wouldn't hear of that... He said there was a stone road that turned to higher ground just past Benil, if we could make it, so we pushed the horses as much as we dared. Karim thought if we could reach Trigallan, we should probably be out of the worst of the flooding. There were many people on the road with the same idea, children crying, panicked beasts. It was chaos." She shut her eyes for a moment.

"Anyway, to cut the story short; we got to Trigallan. It was a big island: when the sun rose the next day, there was water in every direction, as far as you could see, just with roofs and trees and little hills sticking out of it. I've never seen anything like it ... you could see people on the roofs or clinging to trees, and others went out in boats to rescue them. The townspeople took in as many as they could, but there were more needing help than those to give it, there were so many in trouble ... and all sorts, Saliman. There were many soldiers as well as farmers and townspeople, and lots of children who didn't seem to belong to anybody; but everyone was in the same trouble, and I didn't see anyone arguing or fighting, even though there wasn't enough of anything to go around. The headwoman of Trigallan, Narim, made sure of that.

"I was very glad we had the caravan, because at least we

had somewhere to sleep; there were people just sitting out in the rain because they had nowhere else to go. So we found a spot and unharnessed the horses, and waited for the rain to stop. And, eventually, it stopped, and then the water began to go down, quite fast, as fast as it had come up..."

Hekibel trailed to a halt and was silent for a while, her head bowed. Hem thought that she might have fallen asleep, and briefly wondered whether he ought to wake her, but then she shook herself and sat up straight.

"When we reached Trigallan, I did what I could to help Narim and the others who were trying to do something about the chaos. So I wasn't around the caravan much. And anyway, you know what it was like with Karim and Marich. I was glad to get away from them, to be honest; they were squabbling all the time, much worse than ever before. I think Marich felt bad about leaving you two behind, much worse than he would admit. So it was better to be out and doing something. So I wasn't there when..."

Her face briefly crumpled, but she controlled herself, and when she spoke again, her voice was steady. "A Hull came to our caravan, and he was looking for you. Marich told me." She paused, clenching her hands together. "I came back to the caravan late in the afternoon, and Karim was dead, and Marich was – well, he had been stabbed and left for dead, but he wasn't dead, he was..."

Saliman took her hand, and she squeezed it tightly and then pushed him away. "It was terrible," she said. "I didn't know what to do, there was blood everywhere ... Marich was in such pain, and I didn't know how to help him. The Hull had walked in, pretending to be an old associate of Karim's, and when he found that you both had been left behind in Hiert, he was furious, and he – he dropped his disguise, I suppose. Marich said he knew it was a Hull, although he had never seen one

before, and it just – froze Karim, so he couldn't move, and
then it brought out a dagger and said it would make him suffer. Marich tried to stop him, but the Hull just turned around
and stabbed him, and Marich passed out, and when he came to,
Karim was dead. But Marich told me – he told me some things
as he lay there, before he died."

Hem stared at Saliman, his eyes wide with shock. He had
liked Marich, and much as he had distrusted Karim, he would
never have wished such a fate on him. He remembered all too
clearly the casual cruelty of Hulls.

"Marich said the Hull was looking for you both, and he
thought it would come to Hiert," said Hekibel, her voice steady.
"He didn't know why… What's terrible is that Karim had been
spying on you for the Hull. I would swear that Karim didn't
know it was a Hull, but all the same, he had been taking money
to report whatever you said. And he was supposed to keep you
and Hem with the troupe, so the Hull knew where you were.
Whether or not he knew it was a Hull he was dealing with, he
must have known it bode you no good. Stupid, *stupid* Karim.
He was always so greedy for money…" She whispered the last
few words, her cheeks scarlet with shame. "I don't know what
to say. If you don't want to speak to me ever again, I understand…"

Saliman was silent for a time. "Hekibel," he said, his voice
very gentle. "Be comforted that I already suspected as much,
as did Hem. And be sure I wouldn't blame you for another's
act."

"I took the horses right away and just – I just couldn't stay
there. I went and saw Narim and she gave me some saddles so
I could ride the horses. She was very shocked that there was a
Hull in Trigallan. She – she saw that I had to find you, if I could,
to warn you… I've ridden all night and all day to get here. I
kept a watch on the road, and I saw no one else, not one single

person, but I thought maybe – well, they have sorcery, Hulls, and perhaps I wouldn't have seen it even if I passed it. I'm so glad I found you…"

Now, having told the burden of her story, Hekibel began to cry in earnest. It was some time before she could speak again. Hem put his arm around her and waited until she stopped sobbing. "Oh, I'm so sorry," she said, sniffing and wiping the tears from her face with her hands. "It's been so terrible … such a terrible time."

"It has," said Saliman. "I am very grieved to hear that Karim and Marich are dead. I was very fond of both of them; and if Karim was greedy, he didn't deserve such a death. Always it is the way of the Dark, to work our faults to its advantage."

He was silent for a time.

"I wonder why the Hull didn't attack us before," he said at last. "I'm sure it was tracking us from the moment we left Til Amon. And I would dearly like to know why we have sparked their interest; do you think that they have guessed, Hem, that Hem of Turbansk is the same Hem who escaped from them in Edinur?"

Hem shuddered, thinking of the Hulls that had taken him in Edinur, and the nightmares that still pursued him. "I don't know," he said. "Do you think they could add it up? Hardly anyone knew I was in Norloch…"

"It is a small chance, but a chance all the same," said Saliman, frowning. "I think it more likely that it was following me. I did not disguise my identity in Til Amon, after all, and there would be some who would want to know why I am travelling through Annar … that makes sense, without looking for other reasons."

Hem nodded. "I wonder too why we were not attacked when we were on the road?" he said. "It could have, at any time…"

"Perhaps there was only a single Hull following us, and it felt that it could not contest us. Which is the truth: I have a certain reputation as a warrior, after all." Saliman smiled grimly. "It's possible that it is looking for reinforcements before it seeks me. Or that it believes we are dead."

Hekibel was looking from Hem to Saliman, trying to follow their discussion, and Saliman turned to her. "I thank you, Hekibel, for your brave soul, and for telling us this. Well, we will have to decide what to do now. I fear I am not strong, and you do not look as if you could go another step today. If we are cautious, I think we can risk another day here, to be the stronger to travel tomorrow. Hem and I must journey north from here; we will not stay by the roads. Do you wish to come with us, or do you have some other destination in mind?"

"I have nowhere to go," whispered Hekibel.

"You will be in peril, if you travel with us," said Saliman.

"I can't see that I would be any safer, travelling friendless and alone..." Her voice caught, and to cover her emotion she reached down and stroked the sleeping dog at her feet. "I'm sorry, I don't mean to be full of self-pity. I'm just so tired."

Saliman smiled sombrely. "You would be a welcome fellow traveller," he said. "You said earlier that you rode here, but where are the horses?"

"I put them in the stables in the tavern," Hekibel said. "There was some dry hay high up which hadn't been spoiled, and they were hungry, the poor things, and so tired. I didn't feel I could push them any further."

Saliman looked at Hem. "Hem, do you feel able to go down to the village and bring them up here?" Hem nodded. "Put a glimveil over yourself, and the horses, and do not walk on the road but on the grass, so their hooves cannot be heard. And see if you notice anything while you're there."

Hem made a glimveil, strapped on his shortsword and walked across the hills for the second time that day, his senses alert for any trace of sorcery. Irc accompanied him, either riding on his shoulder or flying ahead. Irc had been all over Hiert, he told Hem, and he had seen no sign of Hulls, nor any living human being.

It's empty, he said. *There is no one here but wet chickens and goats.*

A brief glance down the West Road seemed to prove Irc correct. It was covered in a layer of slimy mud, and lined by dark, melancholy houses that were stained by water to the roof of the first floor. A rank stench of mould and stagnant water hung over everything. Hem's nerves were rattled by Hekibel's story, and as he neared the road he checked the glimveil again and doubled his vigilance. He didn't want to step into the mud and ruin his boots, and in the end he took them off and carried them, screwing his face up as his toes slid into the ooze. He trod carefully, trying to leave as few footprints as possible.

The air bore no taste of sorcery, and he could pick up no sense of the dark presence of Hulls, although there was something uneasy in his earthsense, a prickle of premonition that made him move with as much haste as was compatible with caution. Perhaps Saliman was correct, and the Hull had given up the trail, believing that they were both dead. But he thought it more likely that there might be more than one Hull riding to Hiert at this moment. The urgency to move on boiled inside him; he felt the visceral pull of Maerad's summoning, and he was very afraid of Hulls. Yet he knew that unless he left on his own, they would be stuck at the hut until at least first light tomorrow.

He walked to the end of the village and found nothing further. The wrecked houses oppressed him, and when he passed the damp, ashy ruins of the burned house where he and Saliman had been attacked, he vividly remembered, with a shock that

went through his body and left him sweating, how the White
Sickness had touched his body when he had healed Saliman.

Feeling depressed, he turned back and hurried to the tavern.
The horses were in a stable that was damp and stank of mouldy
straw but had somehow escaped the mud. Minna and Usha
were picking in a desultory fashion at a manger of hay. They
greeted Hem with whinnies of recognition.

We have to go a little further, he told them.

The horses snorted in dismay, but Usha said: *I do not like it
here. It smells of death.*

Usha was loaded with a pack, which he guessed contained
food or clothes. Hem inspected them briefly; Minna looked
well, but Usha was still a little lame, and her hoof was hot, so
he soothed it with some hasty magery. Hekibel hadn't taken off
the horses' saddles, and they looked uncomfortable with dried
sweat: if they were not groomed soon, they would get saddle
sores. Hem looked around and found a comb he could use later,
shoving it hastily into his pack; then he cast a glimveil over the
horses and mounted Minna, taking up Usha's lead rein, and
coaxed them out into the road. Here he felt very exposed, even
though he knew no eyes could see through his magery, and in
the clear, watery sunlight he trotted the horses as quickly as he
could back over the bare hills to the hut, where Saliman and
Hekibel were waiting.

They left at dawn the following day, just as the sun's edge lifted
over the horizon. It was a dank and cheerless morning: the wind
had fallen, and a heavy mist rose up from the damp ground,
bringing with it a bitter cold that seeped into their bones.

Hem's night was filled with strange dreams, none of which
he could remember, although he knew Maerad's voice wove
through them, calling him. He woke restless and impatient,
angry that he had lost a day's journeying, although he knew

that there was no choice if he were to travel with Hekibel and Saliman.

Saliman looked a little stronger and Hekibel had recovered from her exhaustion, although her face was still haunted by shadows. The day before, as Hekibel slept, Saliman and Hem had gone through their supplies, which were quite healthy. Hekibel had brought a good stock of food with her on Usha to add to their own. Saliman thought they had enough to keep them on the road for the next couple of weeks.

They had also checked the horses over carefully. Usha's lameness wasn't as bad as Hem had feared; she still stepped gingerly, but Saliman judged that she had suffered no worse than bruising when crossing the Inlan River, and that it was mostly healed. He suggested that they split their baggage between the horses, and that Hem and Hekibel, being lighter, ride together on Minna.

"They're strong beasts, and fit, so we shouldn't burden them overmuch," he said, patting Minna's massive shoulder. "And we will travel all the faster on hoof. It is a lucky chance that Hekibel found us. If luck it was." He squinted at the sky, studying the clouds that were gathering high up. They didn't threaten rain as yet, but the next day would be chilly. "There are forces moving that I do not understand, Hem. My heart tells me that there will be much that is beyond my understanding, before the end of this. My Knowing tells me nothing of this path we are now following, and I am as full of dread as I am of hope. All my trust is in you now."

Hem nodded, wishing that he felt he knew what he was doing. Saliman's faith in him was a little daunting. All he knew was that they had to find Maerad as soon as they could. It wasn't as if he understood why. He had tried earlier, stumbling over his words, to talk about Maerad's summoning, and Saliman had listened intently, his eyes bright in his thin face. He had asked if Hem were sure it was Maerad, and when Hem had nodded, he had said nothing more.

That night he and Saliman shared a watch for the first time since they had been at the hut. They were a safe distance from the West Road, so they decided not to make a glimveil; Saliman said frankly that he didn't feel capable of it. The night passed with neither seeing anything more perilous than hunting owls and foxes, but as Hem watched in the empty night, scanning the sky as the clouds scudded over the stars, he felt a shadow pressing on his mind, a sense that something inimical was drawing closer.

It didn't take them long to pack and mount the horses and then, followed by Fenek, with Irc drawing lazy circles around their heads, they headed across country, bearing north-west. They came down to the flood plains by mid-morning, and stood before them, dismayed. The floods had spread great swathes of black silt over the plains, and even if they detoured, it was still impossible to avoid the mud. Although it wasn't very deep, their tracks would be as clear behind them as if they walked over a virgin snowfield. And it stank.

"I suppose we have no choice," Saliman said at last. "We'll just have to go through it."

"I suspect that's easier said than done," said Hem. "And we'll have to be really careful that the horses don't stumble into holes we can't see under that muck."

Minna and Usha took some persuading, and stepped into the mud with as much disgust as a horse could express. Then began a long, tedious business of crossing what were effectively wide, shallow lakes of black mud. In places the silt was surprisingly firm after a couple of dry days, but in others the horses often floundered up to their fetlocks, and once Minna lost her footing and sank up to her belly. By the time she had been freed, all of them were black with filth. Fenek was lighter than the horses and fared better, but his lips were raised in a constant snarl of distaste. Sometimes there were drifts of rubbish – broken trees, branches, dead animals – that rose as high as their shoulders, and the stench of rot made the horses skittish. At least here they saw no deserted, wrecked houses, which would have made the landscape more melancholy; this part of Ifant, north of Hiert, was largely uninhabited.

The combination of constant watchfulness and tedium was wearing, and by the end of the day their only thought was to seek some grassy ground out of the mud where they could make a camp. Although the hills they had left were now far behind them, Hem felt as if they hadn't made any progress at all. It had been a long, dispiriting day, and nobody talked much as they made their evening meal and prepared their camp. All of them, including the horses, were exhausted and Hem studied Saliman with concern. He was so haggard his eyes had sunk back into his skull, and he scarcely spoke, except to ask Hem if he could make both a glimveil and a ward, so they could all get some rest that night. Hem nodded, although making both charms was almost more than he could manage: at least this way they would get some sleep.

The next day wasn't much better. They saw some higher land to the north and changed their direction slightly. This meant that they were not taking the shortest route, as Hem reckoned it, towards Maerad; but although he felt the summoning as strongly as ever, he didn't argue. By now he never wanted to see or smell mud ever again, and he would have given everything he owned to bathe.

They climbed onto dry ground at twilight and found a likely campsite in a grove of ancient rowan trees. A small stream ran near by, full of blessedly clear water, and one by one they all cleaned themselves of the mud. The water was icy, but Hem didn't mind: he splashed it over his head, watching the black mud twirl away in the current. When they had washed, they changed into less filthy raiment from their packs – nothing they had was really clean any more – and rinsed their clothes and hung them from the trees. No matter how tired they were, their first concern was to get the stink of the mud out of their belongings.

Lastly, Saliman led the horses into the stream and scrubbed the mud from their winter coats. The horses stamped and snorted, glad to get the smell out of their nostrils, and then rolled delightedly in the grass. Fenek splashed noisily into the stream, snapping at the water, and rolled with the horses. Irc watched the other animals rather smugly from a low branch. He was the only one of their party who had not a spot of dirt on him.

A pale yellow light suffused the sky with a gentle radiance as Hem and Hekibel gathered kindling to prepare a meal. When he had finished with the horses, Saliman came back to the grove, looked around him and laughed. Then, to Hem's surprise, he bowed down to the trees and greeted them in the Speech as gravely as if he were entering the palace in Turbansk.

"Hem, remember your manners," said Saliman. "Greet these noble trees. And you, Hekibel."

Mystified, Hem bowed and made the formal greeting. "*Samandalamë.*"

Hekibel made a graceful bow, looking at Saliman out of the corner of her eye as if she thought he was either out of his mind or playing some elaborate joke.

"The Light is with us," Saliman said. "This is a Bardhome. We need fear nothing here, and need set no glimveil; we can sleep soundly tonight, blessed by the trees that protect this place."

Hem and Hekibel looked around them in wonder. At first glance, the grove seemed no different from any other. It was a small dingle, and around it stretched the bare arms of rowans ripening with spring blossom. But as they felt the rich silence of the place rise inside them, it seemed that the air was more luminous among these trees, that the stars shone through their branches more brightly, that the grass between their boles grew softer and greener and more fragrant than beyond their circle. Hem felt his earthsense quicken with a deep gladness like that he had felt in the home of the Elemental Nyanar far south from here in a time now long past, and breathed in deeply. He had been told of such places by Maerad – she and Cadvan had used them sometimes when they had journeyed to Norloch – but he had never seen such a place himself.

"It couldn't just be chance," said Hem. "Maybe Maerad is helping us somehow."

"Perhaps," Saliman said, smiling more broadly than Hem had seen in weeks. For a moment he looked like the old Saliman in Turbansk, and Hem's heart lifted. "Or perhaps some Knowing beneath our awareness guided us here. These are ancient places: they were made when the Bards first came to Annar, long before the Great Silence. Whether there is reason or no, I am thankful to the depths of my soul. It is enough, I confess, just to be out of that mud; to be safe from the threat of darkness for even one night seems like a blessing beyond hope. And it is healing to sleep beneath these trees. The only disadvantage is that it is forbidden to light fire here; but I think we can bear the cold."

Hekibel and Hem exchanged a glance and threw away their kindling. Hem spread the tent on the ground to keep out the damp, and they slept under the trees, curled up in blankets and cloaks, with Fenek snuggled close by and Irc fluffed up in a branch above them, his head tucked under his wing. All of them slept deeply, without dreams, and awoke refreshed, as if the griefs and travails of the past few days had loosened their grip for those few hours.

The Healer in Hem saw with relief that the haggardness had

left Saliman's face. Hem had watched him carefully since he had healed him, concerned that Saliman was on the edge of collapse; after such a serious illness, he should have been abed instead of making a gruelling journey through the wilderness. Although he had never complained, Saliman could not hide his weariness from Hem, who noted how his friend's lively expression had been replaced by a grim mask of endurance. Hem thought sadly that an inner light in Saliman had been quenched, and he feared that it might never return. He missed it more than he could say.

As they packed up their belongings, Hem looked around the grove with regret; he hadn't felt such peace since he and Saliman had ridden through the pine forests of the Osidh Am.

"One day, I'd like to stay here for a long time," he said, as he strapped a pack onto Minna's saddle.

"And live on nuts and berries and nettles like a hermit, eh?" said Hekibel from the other side of Minna, gently teasing him. "Somehow I can't see it. I think you should try some other things first."

"There are a lot of things I'd like to try," Hem said sombrely. "I'd have liked to stay at the Healing Houses in Turbansk too. But they are probably all rubble now." He scowled down at the saddle. "I hate this war."

The light in Hekibel's eyes went out, and she fumbled with a buckle, her mouth trembling. Hem was suddenly furious with himself for his thoughtlessness. "I'm sorry," he mumbled. "I'm just always finding places I like to be, and then having to leave them. And it's so beautiful here…"

Hekibel smiled sadly. "It is. Ah well, Hem, maybe when this is all over, if it is ever over, we can come back and visit, and you can stay as long as you like."

Now they could journey along the northern edge of the flood plain, with no need to cross any more mud. They rode swiftly over moorlands dotted with ancient thickets of gorse, where the tough heathers were grazed by flocks of wild sheep and goats. This gradually gave way to a landscape of gentler hills running with many streams, lightly wooded with stands of oak and ash and linden: a pleasant countryside, but lonely. Two days' hard ride brought them into inhabited regions again. They passed a deserted shepherd's hut like the one they had stayed in near Hiert, and then another, and then on the third day they saw thin lines of smoke rising in the distance into the still morning air. Saliman told them they were now at the edges of the Fesse of Desor, one of the largest and most powerful Schools in Annar.

"Cadvan used to believe that this was one of the Schools which had been corrupted by the Dark," Saliman said, as they broke their fast that morning. Hem glanced at him swiftly; it was the first time Saliman had mentioned Cadvan since they had heard of his death in the letter Hem had received from Maerad in Nal-Ak-Burat. "He thought there were Hulls here. In Turbansk, we did not trust the Bards of Desor. Certainly, the First Circle here has always been one of Enkir's strongest allies."

"What do you mean?" asked Hekibel.

An expression of contempt crossed Saliman's face. "I have heard that this is one of the Schools that does not do its duty by the people here," he said. "The Bards here demand tithes with threats, and their services are not offered freely. It is a place where magery is feared rather than respected, and where the Balance is calculated narrowly, so that it exists only for the self-interest of Bards themselves. Such warping of the Lore brings a sour taste to my mouth." He paused, as if he were about to spit. "I do not know what is happening here now. News is hard to come by from Desor: it was ever a secretive School, and has become more so in recent years. I think we ought to be prepared for anything."

"Should we hide ourselves?" asked Hem.

"We must shield our magery, certainly," said Saliman. "I dearly wish I had Cadvan's talent for disguise; in these parts, black skin is very noticeable. A glimmerspell would hide me from all but Bard eyes; but it's the Bard eyes in particular that I wish to avoid."

"I became quite good at the disguising charm when I was in Sjug'hakar Im," said Hem hesitantly. "Perhaps I could try it on you … it lasts a few days. It might get us past Desor."

Saliman gave Hem a penetrating glance. "Young Hem, I do not know how you did so badly in your studies in Turbansk," he said. "I suppose you are one of those who learns when he sees the necessity, and otherwise kicks over the traces."

Despite himself, Hem blushed. "It mightn't work," he said. "I found it a little easier if I didn't change everything. I could change the colour of your skin and hair, for instance."

Saliman laughed. "I think I would probably look ridiculous with blue eyes and blond hair," he said. "I doubt I'd fool anyone. There is more to being Turbanskian than dark skin, after all. But it's a good idea; we ought to try it, at least. If you show me how to make the lesser spell, I might even be able to cast it myself."

In the end, Saliman cast the spell himself. And, as he had warned, the effect was strange; Hem found a fair-skinned Saliman very disconcerting. Saliman left his hair dark, and refused to cut his braids; he said he would go hooded, if need be. Hekibel watched the whole process with fascination.

"I much prefer the old Saliman," she said. "It makes you look as if you're ill."

"I am too vain to try to look at myself," said Saliman. "It would hurt my pride sadly. But, after all, I have been sick."

They decided to say, if anyone asked them, that they were travellers from Lauchomon who had been caught in the floods.

Saliman thought that Desor would most probably be full of refugees from Ifant, and he hoped they could skirt the edge of the Fesse and pass through unnoticed, just some more homeless people. But Hem saw that he checked his sword was loose in his scabbard when he mounted Usha.

Around mid-morning they reached the top of a long rise and found themselves looking down over a wide, shallow valley. Hem studied it with a feeling of growing unease; it was thickly inhabited, with many farms and hamlets, but he could also see some large camps, with rows and rows of tents. At first the sight reminded him of gazing out from the walls of Turbansk during the siege, at the tents of the Black Army; but he saw also smaller areas that seemed to be fenced, with watch towers at each corner. And that reminded him of the Sjug'hakar Im camp. The countryside was crisscrossed with roads, and even from this distance they could see people moving along them. Some of them seemed to be marching in formation.

"I don't like it," Hem said.

"Aye," said Saliman grimly. "It is long since I was here, and it is much changed. This place no longer looks like a School; it is a city preparing for war. We'll have to move south again, close to the flood plains."

It smells like the Black Land, said Irc. *That place was full of slaves, and this place seems the same. Shall I go and look around?*

Hem nodded, and Irc launched himself from Hem's shoulder and glided down towards the Fesse.

"I think we should back down from this rise," said Hekibel nervously. "We could be seen on the skyline."

Saliman pushed Minna on, but Hem halted Hekibel as she urged Usha to follow him. He was staring south. "What's that?" he said, pointing.

Saliman swung Minna around and stared over the flood plains that stretched below them. It seemed as if a dark shadow were moving over the plains, stretching back into the haze that hung over the lowlands.

Saliman's knuckles tightened on the reins, but his voice was steady. "If I am not mistaken, Hem, that is an army."

"It looks quite big," said Hem. "How are they marching through all that mud? If we go back to the flood plains, we'll run into them. But where is it from? Whose army is it?"

"I can guess," said Saliman grimly. "Although we're too far away to see the banners. Those formations look familiar... But let's move from the skyline here, before anyone sees us."

Dismayed, they turned the horses around and left the rise. They found a copse of ash trees where they felt a little sheltered, and dismounted.

"This is ill luck," said Saliman. "But I think we will have to risk the Fesse, rather than take the almost certain chance of walking into that army."

"Who are they?" asked Hekibel. Her lips were pale. Hem remembered that this would have been her first glimpse of an army on the march.

"If I am right, then it is ill news for Annar," said Saliman. "It surely cannot be from Norloch: why would Enkir send an army up through the south? And I am not sure that Enkir could muster a force of that size, in any case. I fear it is the Black Army; and if that is so, Sharma has sent a force up through Nudd. Perhaps he has already laid waste to Elevé. Perhaps not: it is a strong School, and they would have had to besiege it, which would have delayed them. And this army has moved swiftly. There had been no rumour of any movement through Nudd when we left Nal-Ak-Burat, and Hared had spies in that region. He feared such a move, a strike into the very heart of Annar, although both of us thought that even Sharma would not take the risk of fighting on three fronts. He feels his arm is strong, and he can strike where he likes."

"Elevé?" said Hekibel, her voice unsteady. "I was there – not so long ago…"

"So," said Hem gloomily. "Sharma marches on Amdridh and lays siege to Til Amon, and now he is already in Annar. So what is Enkir doing?"

"Enkir moves in the east, I suppose. Which is why he did not march on Til Amon. I wish I knew more of what is happening in this land! All we can know is that this has long been planned. My guess is that the army marches to Sharma's allies in Desor, and that the plan from there is to take control of north Annar. Cadvan was correct about Desor; but I doubt all the same that he would have predicted this."

A heavy silence fell over them, broken only by Fenek, who was snuffling excitedly at a rabbit hole. Hem studied Fenek, wishing briefly that he was a dog too, with nothing more to worry about than the next meal. An image rose in his mind's eye, one that had haunted him before: he saw, as if from above, lines of fire spreading inexorably through all of Edil-Amarandh, leaving in their wake a desolation of ash.

"Well, we can't stay here," said Hekibel. "So what shall we do?"

"We will have to choose the lesser peril, and enter the Fesse," said Saliman. "It seems an ill choice to me: I do not like the look of those camps, and there are too many soldiers. But I fear that if we encountered the Black Army, we should certainly be in trouble. It is well known that they kill everyone they come across, down to the last infant. But if we move swiftly past the Fesse and stay on the outskirts, perhaps we can thread the needle and pass by both dangers. Perhaps we will be lucky. Perhaps they will be too busy to look very hard at farmers fleeing the floods in Ifant…"

Perhaps, thought Hem. On the other hand, the Bards of Desor might be particularly watchful and suspicious of strangers, especially if they were planning a surprise attack on north Annar. And he wondered, too, if they had really managed to throw off their scent the Hull that had been following them since Til Amon. He wished he could be sure. He was beginning to feel like a hunted animal being driven into a trap. He looked around at his companions, wondering where Irc had got to. A white crow was too noticeable; he was thinking that, despite Irc's objections, he should dye his feathers again.

"We all look shabby enough to be refugees," he said. "We won't need to disguise ourselves. But I think we should cast a glimveil, myself, and then no one would see us anyway."

Saliman looked dubious. "Glimveils are fine for hiding us in the wilderness," he said. "But they are not so good around many people. There's a risk that someone might accidentally blunder into us and break it, and then we would have no chance of hiding that we are Bards. To my mind, we are safer merely disguising ourselves."

"You'd better keep your mouth shut then, Hem," said Hekibel. "You're no good at accents, and you sound exactly as if you're from Edinur. I think Saliman and I can convince people that we're from Lauchomon." She still looked pale, but her lips were set in a determined line. "Well, I suppose the sooner we start, the sooner we'll be through, and the Black Army isn't going to wait for us to pass. Though I think we should stay south as long as we can."

Saliman nodded. They remounted the horses and began to ride along the south side of the rise, keeping a wary eye on the army. It was still little more than an ominous blur through the haze, but it looked all too close to Hem. It was hard to see how fast it was moving, but with any luck it would be hampered by the mud.

Soon the ground levelled out and they began to enter the edges of the Fesse, losing sight of the army in the flood plains. They passed an outlying hamlet, and then another, and then found themselves following a track that led westwards. Before long the track widened into a well-used if muddy road, with broad grassy verges, and they picked up their pace. Now they began to encounter people, the first they had seen for days. At first they were mostly poor farmers or itinerants, some carrying baskets of turnips or onions or driving geese or goats, but as the day wore on, they passed many people who were walking alongside laden mules or oxen, or driving wagons.

Saliman looked about him keenly as they rode, his expression grim.

"I was last in these parts some ten years ago," he said. "Desor has changed much since. And not for the better. It was once a kindly place, like Innail ... but all I can see in its heart is the makings of war." He waved his hand north and west, where they could see the encampments through the haze. "Those do not look to me like refuges for the homeless."

It wasn't long before they began to pass camps of a different kind, desolate temporary settlements filled with those who had fled the floods. Empty-eyed people huddled in primitive shelters made from sheets or blankets or branches scavenged from the woods. It seemed that Saliman's guess was correct: Desor was full of refugees from the floods. Nobody was interested in three more weary travellers. There was no sign, as Saliman commented sardonically, that the Bards of Desor were offering any help to them; rather, the travellers received surly looks from the locals, and more than once villagers spat as they passed. One threw a stone at Fenek, who was innocently sniffing a tree.

"Why did they do that?" asked Hekibel in amazement, as Fenek came yelping to heel, his tail jammed between his legs. "He wasn't doing any harm, and he's obviously with us."

"They do not want us here," said Saliman. There was no expression in his voice. "They are poor, and have no food to share. The tithes are heavy in this Fesse."

Hem said nothing. Irc returned later, his feathers bristling with alarm. He had also seen the army in the distance, and had flown as close as he dared to spy out what he could.

It's the Black Army for sure, he told Hem. *You can smell them. Iron and fear and braintwisting.*

Hem shuddered. *Keep close*, he said. *I don't want you getting into any trouble, Irc.*

There are many Hulls. You can feel them in the wind ... it is like death is walking through the plains. Irc wiped his beak on Hem's hair, and Hem sensed the crow's fear melding with his own. After their time in Dén Raven, neither of them was eager to run into Hulls again.

Are they getting stuck in the mud, like we did? asked Hem.

The army is moving much faster than you, said Irc. *If you grew wings you might outfly them. They are using dogsoldiers to pull heavy things through the mud, and whips. They are very cruel.*

Hem's heart sank into his boots. He relayed Irc's news to the others, who greeted it in gloomy silence, looking across the wide Fesse. The road they were following was veering northwards, where they could see the grey spires of the School of Desor. To the west, shadowy in the haze that obscured the horizon, they could just see a purple smudge of hills. As he gazed towards them, Hem felt a pulse of urgency, and for a moment he saw vividly the path towards Maerad, almost as he had seen it when she summoned him, shining straight across the Fesse.

"Maerad's in those hills," he said, pointing. "It's not so far to go – if we can get through."

"Those are the Hollow Lands," said Saliman soberly. "A melancholy wilderness, but I tell you, they will seem like a perfumed garden after Desor. This place oppresses my spirits more than Dén Raven. It was once a great School, a haven of the Light. And now it stinks of corruption."

X V

DESOR

FTER that conversation, Hem, Saliman and Hekibel
pressed on in silence. The track they had been following was broader and flagged with stone, and although
it meant they could ride more swiftly, they were all nervous:
it clearly led straight towards Desor and, worse, to the army
camps. They passed rough barriers erected across the roads at
regular intervals. Hem noticed with a sinking heart that the
soldiers were not stopping anyone who was heading towards
Desor, but they questioned everyone who travelled the other
way. Only once did the captain of a small band of six soldiers
signal them to halt and demand to know their business. Saliman
told him they were seeking friends who had taken refuge in
Desor.

"The rabble will be cleared out soon," the captain said, looking hard at Hekibel in a way which made Hem feel deeply
uncomfortable. "I hear that wayfarers must soon report to
camps. If you're wise, you'll go there first, before the orders
come out."

"We do not plan to stay," said Saliman. "We are honest folk,
not thieves."

"Mayhap," said the captain. Hem looked at his men, a motley bunch carrying new, crudely made weapons, and reflected
that they did not seem like soldiers at all, but more like brigands. "We're all honest men here, eh, Mindar?" He nudged the
man next to him in the ribs, and they both laughed. There was
something menacing in their laughter, and Hem was relieved

when the captain lost interest in them and waved them on.

After that, they kept a sharp eye out for a way to cut across country. There were open fields on either side of them, but when they turned down a lane that led through them, an angry farmer sent them back, ordering them off his land. The hounds growling at his heels emphasised his demand, and they turned back, their hearts heavy.

"There are walls everywhere in this place," Saliman said, after a fruitless search. "And I feel them closing in on us. Ever this road draws us closer to Desor… Perhaps we can trespass over the fields by night, little as I like the idea."

"If we find no way off this road, I think we must go back. Or stop somewhere likely, if we can, and wait until nightfall."

A light rain began to fall, adding to their gloom. Hem was becoming more and more anxious: Saliman was right, Desor was a trap. He was beginning to feel sick. Remembering the nausea he had suffered walking through the Glandugir Hills, he wondered uneasily whether his earthsense was waking inside him. There was nothing like that poison here, but he had felt an increasing sense of dread since he had entered the Fesse, as if ominous shadows pressed on his mind. It was most likely the presence of Hulls; it could be that he felt the Black Army, but he was sure a shadow hung as heavy before them as behind. The air carried a faint, bitter taste that dried out his mouth, a taste like sorcery. Uneasily he checked his shield again; if a passing Hull sensed any trace of magery, all of them would be in trouble.

Hekibel called them to a halt at the brow of the next hill. "If we do not stop soon, we will not be able to," she said. "I think it takes not much foresight to say that the closer we come to Desor, the more perilous our path becomes. What say you, Saliman?"

Saliman drew up beside Hem and Hekibel. "I fear you're right," he said. "I think we should continue to the brow of the next hill and see if anything is promising from there. If not, I say we retrace our steps. I think no wanderers are permitted to set up camp here; I have seen none for a long time, although there were plenty of people earlier. And remember what that captain said."

Over the hill, the ground swept down to a wide, flat area, like a shallow bowl in the earth, which perhaps had once been pleasant farmland or forest. Now it had the denuded, forlorn look of a freshly cleared landscape, scarred with rough, muddy roads. There was a walled town to the east, which Saliman said was Bregor, the next largest town in the Fesse to Desor itself. From the very edge of its walls stretched a city of tents, staked neatly in long lines. Hem caught his breath: this was already a mighty army, much bigger than he had imagined when looking from the rim of the Fesse.

Hekibel looked on it with wide eyes. "So many!" she whispered to Hem. "Where did they all come from? And what are they for?"

Saliman was staring at the camp blankly. "By the Light," he said. "I had no idea that such an army had been gathered here. Desor has been busy indeed. They can't all be from the Fesse; it must be from Ettinor too, or further afield…"

"Are they there to defend the Fesse, do you think?" asked Hem, his voice wavering.

"It would be a comfort to think so, Hem. But I fear there are Hulls there; surely you can feel their presence? I think rather that they are waiting for the Black Army to join their forces, and that we are looking on the beginning of the Nameless One's campaign on North Annar."

Hem stared at the camp, his mouth open. Inside, he was beginning to feel panicky. The force of Maerad's summoning had been growing in intensity since he had seen the Hollow Lands and known them to be his destination, and it clashed with their need for caution. Now, seeing the huge army in front of them, that urgency flared more strongly. He felt like jumping the walls to their right and galloping across the fields, dogs or no dogs.

He dragged his gaze away from the encampment, and looked west – and spotted what they had been searching for all afternoon: a wide road that led west.

"But there's a road!" he said, pointing. "Right in the middle of that hamlet there… And it leads off this one, look, towards those hills…"

Saliman followed his eyes. "Aye, Hem," he said. "But we will have to go perilously near that army to turn down that way. I am very reluctant to venture any nearer to Bregor. I am thinking that we should retrace our steps and make camp for the night, and wait our chance to cross some quiet fields."

"But it leads exactly the way we have to go!" said Hem. He didn't like the idea of going back at all; turning away from the summoning would be like swimming upriver against a hard current. Saliman caught the urgency in his voice, and gave him a swift, penetrating glance.

I have to, said Hem desperately, mindtouching Saliman. *I can see where we have to go. We can't turn back.*

Saliman nodded. "Let's go back over this hill and discuss what we should do," he said out loud. "A hasty decision might destroy us, Hem. It is better, I think, to take a little longer and arrive, rather than hurry and not arrive at all."

They decided to stop by the road and have a meal, since they had not eaten since the morning, and discuss their next move. They hastily took out some food, anxiously keeping an eye on the road. There were not many people passing now, and those who did were mostly soldiers. Every time a soldier's eye rested on them, Hem felt himself tense: it was only a matter of time, surely, before they were stopped and questioned again.

While all three of them (and all of the beasts) wanted to get out of Desor as quickly as possible, they couldn't agree on how best to go about it. Saliman and Hekibel were for turning back. Hem passionately disagreed. He argued that they couldn't afford to lose any time at all, especially now they knew that open war in Annar was at hand. And he also feared that if they turned back, they could well run into the Black Army on the road.

"And what about the Hull that was following us?" he said. "I don't feel at all certain that we shook it off in the flood plains, Saliman; and we left tracks that a blind man could follow in all that mud. We might run into Hulls that are actually hunting us if we turn back … I think we have to go forward."

Saliman frowned in thought, and sighed. "I fear you're correct, Hem. Perhaps Irc could scout for us on the position of the Black Army. I'd feel better if I knew how far away it is."

"Me too," said Hekibel. "On my life, I do not want to go any closer to Bregor. There are not enough people on the road for us to hide. I don't like it at all."

"There's nowhere safe," said Hem restlessly. "I hate this stinking, rotten place. It's a prison." He looked across at the road, where a patrol of soldiers was passing. "And the longer we stay by the side of the road, the sooner someone will bother us. Whatever direction we're going, we're less obvious if we're on the move."

In the end, Saliman agreed with a heavy sigh that the risks of turning back were as high as going forward, and the risks of stopping by the road and thereby attracting unwelcome notice were perhaps the greatest of all. Irc flew off, with stern instructions from Hem to stay out of trouble, to discover whether the Black Army had reached the Fesse, and the others resumed their journey. It was now late afternoon, and they pushed the horses on. They hadn't discussed where they should stop that night, partly because none of them knew whether they should stop at all, but at some point they would have to rest. The further they were from Bregor, the better. Hem tried not to look at the camp: the sight filled him with dread.

Before long they reached the hamlet where the road forked, and turned west. The road was deserted, and the houses they rode past looked empty. Hem felt more uneasy with every step they took.

"There's a barrier," Hekibel said in a low voice. "I thought there would be. And we can't turn back, they've seen us. Remember to stay quiet, Hem."

The barrier, a roughly made wooden gate across the road, was next to a grim building that looked like a barracks. It was manned by two bored soldiers, who were squatting by the gate playing knucklebones. They stood up slowly as the travellers approached. Saliman nodded pleasantly in greeting.

"Afternoon," said the tallest soldier, a man with the fair skin and blue eyes of northern Annar. "Can I ask where you are travelling, this fine day?"

"Good morrow, kind sirs," said Saliman. Hem noticed that he gave the soldier a surprised look, as if he thought he recognized him and then decided that he was mistaken. He had also suddenly changed his accent. He was no longer using the dialect of Lauchomon, but of Desor. "We are travelling home, after a long journey."

"No one passes this point," said the soldier. "You should have heard the orders, from the School."

"We've been a-visiting in Hiert, and got caught in the floods there," Saliman said. "We've heard no orders. The wife and I left the young ones in charge of the farm, and they expect us this day."

It seemed for a moment as if the soldier would accept Saliman's story and open the gate, and Hem breathed a sigh of relief; but the second soldier was examining them suspiciously.

Hem didn't like his face: whereas the first had a bluff, open expression, if not very intelligent, this one looked like a ruffian.

"And where is this farm?" said the second. "I don't recall your face, and I'm from these parts. I'm sure I'd recognize your woman, if I'd seen her before." He leered at Hekibel, and Hem, sitting behind her on the horse, felt her body tense.

"We have a farm by the edges of the Hollow Lands," said Saliman, without a flicker of hesitation. "Not much of a home, perhaps, but a man might scratch an honest living there. And I'm somewhat eager to get back there, if you'll excuse us. We're late already."

A third soldier came out of the shed and sauntered up behind the first two, and Hem saw to his alarm that his sword was drawn. He could tell by this last man's air of authority that he was the leader of the three. Fenek backed towards the horses, and began to growl, baring his teeth.

"Dismount," said the third. "I am the captain of this region. The orders are that no one passes west of here without express permission. I need to see your note of passing, or you'll go no further this day."

The second soldier sneered. "You wait on our pleasure, peasant," he said. "Perhaps we'd like to get to know your lady a little. Eh, Brant?" He nudged the first soldier, who looked uncomfortable, and walked up to Usha and grabbed Hekibel's thigh, sliding his hand up her leg. Usha shied and almost reared, and the soldier let Hekibel go and laughed. "She seems a handy type, to be sure. We could have a bit of fun together, eh?"

Saliman's eyes blazed with anger. He made no reply, but Hem saw with alarm that he had almost lost control of himself: his disguising charm had briefly slipped and wavered, so that for a moment his real face had shown through. At the same time, Fenek, whose growls had been getting louder, leapt at the throat of the man who had touched Hekibel.

The captain lazily extended a hand. Nothing seemed to happen, but Hem felt a brief pulse of magery, and Fenek fell limply to the ground, his body crumpled, his tongue lolling between his teeth, his lips drawn back in a frozen snarl. Hem realized, with a thrill of dread, that the captain was a Bard. Not a very powerful Bard – he had only a faint glow of magery about him – but he certainly wasn't a Hull. He had never seen a Bard act with such careless savagery before, and even as disaster loomed over them, it shocked him.

"You killed my dog!" he shouted, forgetting that he wasn't supposed to say anything. "You rot-faced murderer!"

"Be quiet, brat," said the Bard. "Or I'll do the same to you."

Hekibel leaned over to the soldiers, pleading, a sob of desperation in her voice. "I'm begging you, sirs, to let us through. I'm sorry my dog went for you – he was protective, he looked after me, and I've had him since I was a child. Surely to kill him like that before my eyes is enough punishment. My young ones are expecting us, and they're all alone…"

"Serves you right for taking a trip in wartime," snapped the Bard. "Do you think I care about your stinking bastards? If, in fact, this farm exists."

"What do you mean, *if* it exists?" said Saliman roughly. "Are you calling me a liar?"

The Bard gave him a glance of contempt. "I said, dismount," he said, his voice hard.

Don't get off the horse, whatever you do, said Saliman into Hem's mind. *And get ready to run.*

"I don't feel safe about it, begging your pardon," said Saliman evenly. "You just killed my dog, and one of your men threatened my wife."

"I heard no threat," said the Bard. "And if you disobey me, you will know what threat is. Dismount."

The Bard lifted his hand, intending perhaps to freeze them

with a charm, but Saliman moved first. A blast of magery erupted from Saliman's outstretched hands and knocked the Bard to the ground. Usha reared in fright, and Hekibel gasped, staring at the Bard, who lay white and unmoving on the ground next to Fenek's corpse. The two soldiers, taken completely off-guard, stood with their mouths open. Instantly another blast of magery shattered the gate to splinters, and Saliman, his disguise fully broken by the force of his own magery, was already through it on Minna at full gallop.

Hem, the only person who wasn't taken wholly by surprise, spurred Usha on. The terrified horse bolted after Minna, completely out of control, as Hem threw his arms around Hekibel's waist and she desperately clutched the reins, trying to stay on. Hem looked back over his shoulder and glimpsed the two soldiers hurriedly mounting horses and shouting, and more soldiers running up from somewhere. Then he concentrated on not falling off Usha, praying that she wouldn't fall lame again, not now.

He snatched another look: the two soldiers were in pursuit, their mounts at full gallop down the road. They had a good lead, but Hem realized that it was inconceivable that Usha and Minna, already tired after a day's hard riding, would be able to outpace fresh horses. Usha was no longer bolting blindly, and Hekibel now had some control. She steered her off the road after Saliman, who was riding over an unfenced field towards a dark wooded hill. Usha was blowing hard, and Hem wasn't sure how much longer they could keep going. He glanced back again: the soldiers were drawing close, and he thought at least one of them had a bow. Belatedly he remembered that he ought to make a shield, and somehow managed to cast the charm, even at their bruising pace.

Then at last they were in the shelter of the trees, but now their ride became even more terrifying. Hem could hardly bear to look as the horses plunged through dead bracken that brushed against their bellies, barely missing the trees. There was no way of seeing the ground: if the horses stepped in a hole or stumbled over a tree root, they could break their leg, which would spell disaster. A branch almost swept Hem off Usha's back, giving him a stinging lash across his cheek, and Hekibel hissed at him to keep low. Saliman was turning Minna sharply, constantly changing direction, and Hekibel rode in his wake, concentrating on following his movements. The noise of the horses crashing through the undergrowth meant that Hem could hear nothing of their pursuers, but he thought that they surely couldn't be far behind. He had by now completely lost his sense of direction.

They came across a small stream and Saliman rode down its sharp banks and urged Minna into the water. Usha snorted and followed her. Now they slowed down, trotting slowly upstream, the shallow water frothing around the horses' fetlocks. The rushing of the water covered any noise they made, and Hem began to relax a little. They had gone some distance before Saliman took Minna up the opposite bank. Here there was a close-knit grove of ancient, wide-boled oaks, growing so close together that their branches entwined and swept down low to the ground. They were newly in leaf, the fresh green making a delicate, close-meshed tent. Here they dismounted and led the horses into the shade.

The horses had cooled down in the slow trot up the stream and were no longer winded, but their coats were streaked white with sweat and their cheeks flecked with foam. They had ridden hard: looking at them now, Hem thought it was a miracle that they had not broken down.

It suddenly seemed very quiet. The tiny noises of the wood – the whispering of leaves, the scurrying of a small animal – gradually rose about them and Hem was sharply aware of the smell of the damp earth, rich with rotting leaves, beneath his feet. With a start, he realized that he had no idea where Irc was, and sent out an urgent summoning. To his unbounded relief, Irc answered at once.

Where are you? said Irc plaintively. *I'm looking and looking...*

We're under the trees, said Hem. *We had some trouble.*

Irc gave the crow's equivalent of a contemptuous snort. *And you told me to stay out of trouble,* he said.

We might still be in trouble. Can you see any horsemen where you are?

I saw a man in the woods a little while ago. He is not where you are. I saw no others ... I will fly and look and then I will find you...

Hem sent out his hearing. There were hoofbeats, a horse trotting, maybe two, a little distance away.

"I think, for the moment, that we have thrown them off our trail," said Saliman, after a long silence. "For the moment. But I have no idea where we are."

Hekibel had been leaning against Usha, stroking her neck. At this, she looked up. "Dear faithful beasts, these two," she said. "They were not made to run like that."

"No," said Saliman. "And yet they ran like the Ernani's racing steeds."

"I thought we were done for." Hekibel shuddered. "Those horrible, horrible men ... and oh, poor Fenek..." She laid her face against Usha's damp withers, and Hem knew that she didn't want him or Saliman to see her cry. "It's true, you know, that he's been my dog for years, since I was a girl," she said in a muffled voice. "He didn't deserve that. He was just trying to protect me."

"He was a good dog," said Hem awkwardly. He was thinking of how he would feel if anything like that happened to Irc.

"It was just so – sudden." She looked up, wiping her eyes. "I'm sorry," she said. "He's only a dog, I know, but I loved him. Now everyone I travelled with is dead. Except Usha and Minna."

There was a bleak silence.

"How did he kill him like that?" asked Hekibel. "Was that man a Hull?"

"He was a Bard," said Saliman, in a hard voice, "though I think such as he do not deserve the title. In any case, he is a Bard no longer."

"Did you kill him?" asked Hem. "I thought you just..."

"He is dead, yes," said Saliman. "I dealt him the justice he was about to deal us. If I were a better Bard, I should not have done it. But I am not a better Bard." There was a dangerous glitter in Saliman's eyes which made Hem drop the subject. Hem had seldom seen this side of him, and it frightened him. Saliman's anger was slow, but when it awakened, it was merciless.

"Well, what should we do now?" asked Hem.

"To be honest, Hem, I am not sure I can go any further for a while. I am not as recovered from my illness as I would like, and that magery drained me, not to mention that wild cross-country gallop. I would give much to know where those soldiers are. They will be tracking us, for certain."

"Irc said he would look for them," said Hem.

"Did he, now?" Saliman smiled, his teeth flashing white in the gloom under the trees, and the old Saliman was back again. "I was wondering what had happened to our feathered friend. I would never say this to Irc, because he would not let me forget it, but he is the best scout I have ever had."

Irc reappeared shortly afterwards as they were making a rough camp. Angling in beneath the oaks and perching himself on a branch, he watched Hem brushing the dried sweat out of Usha's coat and reported that he had tracked the horseman, who was leaving the woods.

Only one? asked Hem.

I saw no other, answered Irc. *And I'm hungry.* He cocked his head, fixing Hem with his eye. *Where's the dog? Did he run away?*

"He was killed by a soldier," said Hem shortly. He feared that Irc might say something rude, since he had always squabbled with Fenek, but instead Irc went very quiet.

I am sad, said the crow at last. *He was good, for a dog.*

"Only one horseman?" repeated Saliman later, as they shared out some food. They had wrapped themselves in blankets as well as cloaks, as it was cold in the shade and they dared not light a fire.

"Yes," said Hem. "He said he saw no other."

"That troubles me," said Saliman. "They will not give up the hunt for us lightly. And I am tired enough to sleep a dozen nights." He sighed. "For the moment, we are safest here. Tomorrow, I think, we should try to get out of Desor. Do you still feel the path, Hem?"

Hem nodded. "At least we're on the right side of the Fesse now," he said. "And Irc told me something else too. The Black Army is past the flood plains and in the Desor Fesse. We would definitely have run into them if we had gone back along the road. Irc said they are as many as ants in an anthill." Hem swallowed. "And he said they left a trail of corpses behind them."

"Who would they be fighting, in the mud?" asked Hekibel, looking up, her eyes large.

"I think the Black Army was not fighting," said Saliman. His voice was very low. "I expect that those corpses are their own. It must have been a cruel march indeed." He was silent for a long time. "Most of those soldiers are slaves," he said. "Sharma's war is not their choice: they had none. I pity them as I do not pity that Bard."

* * *

Hem took the first watch. He sat on his blanket to soften the hard ground, and listened to the secret night noises of the forest, the gentle breathing of his companions, the stirring of the horses as they shifted in their sleep. Before him was a blackness of trees: at first he could see nothing, but his eyes gradually adjusted, and the darkness shifted into subtle shades of light and dark and movement. It was a still night, filled with a deep quiet: the trees barely rustled. The sky was clear again, and the stars shone white in a black, moonless sky.

He was very tired, and before the moon rose he caught himself dropping off to sleep. Angry with himself, he slapped his arms and forced open his eyelids, stubbornly staring out into the night with burning eyes. Gradually the sky lightened as a crescent moon rose, small and high and bright as burnished silver.

Sleep kept sweeping through his body like an irresistible wave. He rubbed his eyes and pinched himself. He couldn't be this tired. He had often kept watch after long and exhausting days, and his body was used to it. It wasn't as if he felt safe; even though he and Saliman had, with a little difficulty, made both a glimveil and a shield, to conceal their presence and any trace of magery, his nerves thrummed with tension. Yet his eyelids were as heavy as stone, and his eyeballs felt as if they had been rolled in hot sand.

It surely wouldn't hurt to shut his eyes, just for a little while, to ease them ... he struggled against the voice that whispered in his head: it can't do any harm, it would be bliss, just to shut my eyes, just for a moment...

Hem picked up his water bottle and tipped its contents over his head. The water was freezing, and he gasped with the shock of it, but it woke him up. He shook his wet hair like a dog. Some sense prickled him with sudden awareness, and he looked around alertly, like a deer that had scented a hunter.

He could see nothing and hear nothing, but someone was close. Very close. He couldn't tell how he knew: there was no smell of magery or sorcery, and the ground beneath the trees was still and silent. But some deep awareness told Hem that something was creeping closer and closer to the trees where they were hiding.

A vivid memory rose in his mind of the agonizing games he had played in Nal-Ak-Burat, when Hared had been training him and Zelika for their spying mission near Dén Raven. Hared had made them stand in a room that was absolutely dark, and attempt to catch each other. In those games, Hem had thought his heartbeat was as loud as a hammer, and his blood sounded like a river rushing through the darkness. Now it was the same. He couldn't hear the night noises of the wood any more, nor the hooting of owls, nor the distant bubble of the stream. All he could hear was his own blood pulsing in his ears.

He sat absolutely still, in an agony of listening, and as he did he felt the desire for sleep swarming again through his body, like the murmur of hives in summer, like the lapping waves on a lake golden with the light of evening. Now the voice, soft and dark as sun-warmed honey, was whispering of the dim shades that curled in the eaves of the palaces of sleep and kissed the slumberer with their gentle blessings.

Hem's eyelids grew heavier again, and he began to nod; but his will kicked him into wakefulness again. *It is a spell*, said another voice inside him, a stubborn voice that he knew was his own. *It's a spell, and someone is making it. Someone who knows you're here.*

As soon as he understood this, the desire for sleep left him. The charm would no longer work on him, although Hem still heard its seductive voice whispering in his ear. This was not sorcery. This was the magery of Bards. A Bard of Desor – a Bard like the one Saliman had killed earlier that day, a Bard who had betrayed the deep fealty of the Light – was creeping closer, but Hem could neither see nor hear any sign of movement. Very slowly, making no sound at all, Hem grasped the shortsword in his hand and loosened it in his sheath, positioning it so he could leap up and draw it in one movement.

If this person walked into the shield he and Saliman had made, its magery would make them visible, no matter what enchantment now hid them from his eyes. Hem's heart shook at the thought that this Bard must somehow have sensed past all their own concealments. Whoever it was knew where they were. Hem didn't know how that was possible: he had long experience now of making shields, shadowmazes, glimveils, all manner of Bardic hides, and he knew they were proof even against the vision of Hulls. So how had this Bard known where they were?

Nothing happened. Hem realized that he was sitting in a cold sweat, and began to wonder if his imagination, rattled by the events of the day, was playing tricks on him, showing him the shape of his fears in shadows and moonlight. But still he didn't relax: at the deepest levels of his awareness, he was sure something was there. The moon rose higher, and a faint silver limned the trees and the grass with silver edges. And still nothing stirred in the empty night.

And then a booted foot came down silently on the leaves an arm's length in front of him, carefully placed to make no sound, and at once a man emerged into visibility through the shimmering edges of the glimveil. He froze in mid-step, taken completely by surprise, as Hem leapt to his feet and drew his sword, holding it steadily at the man's throat.

It was the tall, fair soldier they had seen at the gate. Hem lifted the sword so that its tip rested against the man's Adam apple, and he saw it move as he swallowed. Very slowly, the

Bard raised his hands palm outwards, to show that they were empty. For a long moment, he and Hem stared into each other's eyes.

"Samandalamë," said the man in the Speech. "I have been seeking you."

"I know you have," answered Hem, in the same tongue. "And now you have found us. But do not think you will leave this place alive."

XVI

THE HOUSE OF MARAJAN

THE man met Hem's gaze without flinching, and something in Hem faltered, and he almost lowered the sword.

"I am unarmed," said the man. "I mean you no harm."

"That's hard to believe."

"I'm sure it is. But it is, nevertheless, true."

"A Bard needs no weapons to be dangerous," said Hem. He nudged the sword a little higher under the man's chin, so its tip pressed into the soft skin of his throat, and the Bard blinked, and swallowed again.

"Don't kill me," he said, his voice suddenly harsh, and Hem knew he was afraid. "That would be foolish, and you would regret it later. Wake Saliman of Turbansk. Tell him Grigar of Desor is here and wishes to speak with him."

Hem started at the mention of Saliman's name, and paused in dreadful doubt. "You know Saliman?" he said.

"I have no weapons," Grigar repeated. "I will let you bind me in whatever way you see fit, if it makes you feel safer. I understand why you do not trust me. But think: if I meant you any malign purpose, and if I knew where you were, would I come this way, alone, at night, to find you?"

Hem looked into Grigar's eyes and could see no sign that he was lying; but he was still full of mistrust. There was no reason to believe that he wasn't trying to deceive him, especially as he had been attempting to lull Hem with a sleep charm. If this man could see through glimveils and shields, why should a binding charm hold him? Hem couldn't remember the binding charm, anyway; he had never used it.

Without taking his eyes off Grigar, he mindtouched Saliman, calling him out of his sleep. Saliman was instantly awake.

What is it? he asked.

Bring your sword, said Hem. *A man called Grigar wants to speak to you. A Bard.*

Hem felt the astonishment in Saliman's mind. *Grigar?* he said. *Are you certain?*

That's what he said, said Hem.

Saliman was at Hem's shoulder in an instant. He made a small magelight which floated close to Grigar's face.

"*Samandalamë*, Saliman," said the Bard. "It is long since we met. Perhaps your young friend could stop tickling my throat with his sword point."

There was a long, tense silence, and Hem sensed a connection between the two Bards, as if a ray of intense light joined their eyes, although he saw no such light. Then both Bards seemed to relax, and Saliman turned to Hem.

"Put down your sword, Hem," he said. "I can vouch for Grigar as a friend."

"He's one of the guards at the gate. He was *chasing* us. And he found us despite the glimveils and he tried to bind me in sleep," hissed Hem indignantly. All of them were still speaking in low voices. "How do you know he's a friend? He'll probably kill us as soon we turn our backs…"

"Put it down." Now it was an order, and slowly and reluctantly Hem lowered his sword.

How can we trust him? he said into Saliman's mind.

I have all but scried him, Saliman answered. *And be sure, I was not gentle. If there were any trace of deceit, I should have known it. He is as he seems.*

Hem kept the sword ready in his hand, watching Grigar

with deep suspicion, as the Bard rubbed his neck.

"I thank you," said Grigar. "That was a mort uncomfort-able. You have an apt apprentice, Saliman. I don't know how he knew I was there. I put such a strong sleep charm around this place that beasts must be snoring for miles, and yet he did not sleep. And he came for me like a wolf the instant I stepped through your shield…"

Saliman smiled, and as Hem watched open-mouthed, stepped forward and embraced Grigar. "I am deeply sorry for the hostile welcome," he said. "But perhaps you can excuse us for being a little wary."

"Of course I excuse you," said Grigar. "In this place, the deepest vigilance is not enough. All the same, I feared that I would be slain by the Light rather than by my enemies, which would have pleased the Nameless One more than anyone else. Your young friend has a deadly look."

"My young friend, for all his tender years, has walked darker paths than either you or I," said Saliman. Grigar looked curiously at Hem, and Hem met his eyes steadily. Now he was less afraid, he saw Grigar's face was subtly changed from that of the bluff soldier he had seen at the gate earlier that day. He now looked more intelligent, more alert. More like a Bard.

They drew in under the deeper shade of the oaks, and Hem saw that Hekibel still slept. He thought to wake her, and changed his mind: she looked very peaceful. Saliman checked their glimveil and shield, and then his magelight brightened, so that Hem, Saliman and Grigar could see each other clearly.

Saliman cleared his throat. "Perhaps we should make some introductions," he said. "Hem, this is Grigar of Desor, formerly of the First Circle, and a true Bard of the Light. And a long-lost friend of mine. I thought you were dead, my friend."

"Not dead, although that was put about," said Grigar. "Merely … asleep, you might say. I have been, to most eyes, a humble goat herd in the outskirts of the Fesse for a few years now. I gave over my Barding when the First Circle became something that I did not want any part of. In this Fesse, to be poor is to be invisible. It has allowed me to – observe things." He paused. "I was never more astonished than when I saw your face today, Saliman. I might ask what you are doing here?"

"Trying to get elsewhere," said Saliman wryly. "And almost not succeeding. Am I right in thinking that you led our pursuers astray? I was mighty puzzled that we seemed to lose them so quickly."

"Aye. I am a respected tracker – quite rightly, I might say without vanity – and so when we lost sight and sound of you, at the millstream, I was able to lead them the wrong way. At least, there was stony ground on the other side, so they believed me when I said that you had crossed the stream, and we made a wide search where I was almost absolutely sure you wouldn't be." He sighed and stretched. "I came back after nightfall, and walked upstream until I found your tracks. And have been following them ever since. It was no great mystery how I found you, young Hem; you needn't fear for the strength of your glim-veil. Your tracks were clear, and I could smell the horses. And the sleep spell was because I feared that if I did not find Saliman first, I might be killed by his companions. Which was quite a rational guess." He rubbed his neck again, and Hem saw that there was blood on his fingers: he had cut him.

"I'm sorry," he said. "I honestly did not expect to find a friend here."

Grigar drew closer, so their heads almost touched. "There are more friends than you think in Desor," he said. "I am not the only one who has been watching with horror what has been happening here. I was only the first. But we must move quickly, Saliman; they will bring out the yellhounds at dawn tomorrow and they will find you. You are not safe here: the young man you killed, Hrunsar, is the son of Handar, the First of the Circle here, and they will be out for blood."

Saliman's face hardened. "He had an ill manner," he said.

"He was as corrupt a Bard as I've known, worse than his father," said Grigar. "I believe his father took him to the torture chambers when he was a child. You were unlucky he was at that posting; he was visiting a friend of his. Otherwise you would likely have got through without trouble." He sighed. "But now I propose to take you to the house of a friend of mine, a league or two from here. We must cover our tracks with every trick we have, from woodcraft to magery, and that is hard with two horses. The yellhounds seldom fail to track their prey, once they pick up a trail, though on the way here I did everything I could to hide yours."

Hem wondered what yellhounds were, and decided he didn't want to find out. "Won't the other soldiers notice that you're missing?" he asked suddenly.

"I have a story. Do not fear for me. But we must hurry. You should wake your friend, who slumbers so beautifully. That was what I was hoping would happen to you, Hem."

Hem mindtouched Irc, waking him, and he grumpily flapped over to perch on Hem's shoulder, giving him a sharp peck on the ear as Grigar watched with lively curiosity. Saliman gently shook Hekibel awake. She sat up, alarmed, her hair tousled, and when she saw Grigar, she gave a low cry and covered her mouth, shrinking towards Saliman.

Saliman put his arm around her shoulders. "Don't be afraid," he said. "This man is a friend, and we can trust him. He is going to lead us to a safe place. But now we must be quick."

Hekibel blinked, but asked no questions. They swiftly dismantled their rough camp, and then there was a short delay while the three Bards worked together a weave of hiding charms, to conceal from even the sharpest senses any sign of their presence. Then they moved off, leading the horses through the woods after Grigar.

They reached their destination in the cold hour before dawn. Unlike the others, Hem had not slept, and now he was so tired he felt numb all over, and the weight of Irc on his shoulder seemed like a stone. Once they had left the woods, Saliman had put Hem on Usha, and Hekibel mounted Minna. They went no faster, as Saliman and Grigar walked and led the horses, who themselves were stumbling with tiredness. After midnight a thick mist began to rise around them, obscuring the moon and stars. It was so dark that they couldn't see a span in front of their noses, and they were forced to use dim magelights. But although they followed no roads, Grigar seemed to know the countryside like the inside of his own head, and never appeared to be lost. Hem sank into a dull trance of exhaustion.

At last they seemed to arrive somewhere and he started awake, shaking his head to try to clear it. Out of the mist loomed the outlines of what appeared to be a ruined farm-house, its roof slumped in decay, its stone walls crumbled with age and weather. Grigar led them around the back, to a walled cobbled yard, where huge dockweeds nodded in the corners. Hem sighed. At the back of his mind, he had hoped that Grigar might be taking them to a place with beds – proper beds, with linen sheets and warm blankets ... but of course, he thought, it was too much to ask.

"You should dismount," said Grigar. Hem nodded, slithered off Usha's broad back and stood shivering next to the others. He was cold to the bone. He stared at the ruined house: it was completely dark, with no sign of habitation. What now?

"Saliman, forgive me, I must ask you all to turn your backs and close your eyes. It is better if you do not see what I am about to do, and it will only take a moment."

Hekibel had said nothing at all on their long journey, and looking at her white face, Hem thought she seemed to be on the brink of collapse.

"I do not want to shut my eyes," she said. "I do not know you."

"But I do know Grigar," said Saliman, and he took her hand. "We should do as he asks." Hem felt a surge of jealousy; he would have liked his hand to be taken as well. He was just as nervous as Hekibel.

"Please, close your eyes," said Grigar again. Saliman turned away from Grigar, his eyes shut, and after a moment, Hekibel and Hem followed suit.

They heard Grigar murmur in the Speech, his voice so low that Hem couldn't catch the words. Then there was an indefinable shift. Hem felt it through his whole body, as if the temperature had changed, but he couldn't tell what had happened.

"You may look now," said Grigar.

Hem opened his eyes, and found that in that brief moment the light was completely different: there was now a rose tinge in the sky, a herald of dawn, and it was not as cold. Irc, sitting on his shoulder, gave a low caw, a mixture of surprise and pleasure. Hem blinked. Surely that wall had been crumbled... He turned around, and saw to his astonishment that where before there had been a ruined house, he now stood in the yard of what seemed to be a prosperous, well-run farm. The door was open, and through it he could see a wide hearth where an orange fire burned low.

"Welcome to the House of Marajan," said Grigar. "There are stables to your left where you can bed down the horses. And although I couldn't send word of your coming, it will not take long to make us a breakfast worthy of the appetites we have earned."

Saliman whistled. "I am amazed, Grigar," he said. "Where are we?"

"Where we were before, but in another time. So deep goes the Dark in the heart of Desor now, there is no place that is safe in our time. And Marajan, as you will see for yourself, is a Bard of unusual powers ... but quickly, I'll show you the stables, and then I will tell Marajan you are here. Just come through the door when you are ready."

"Are there beds?" asked Hem in a small voice.

Grigar laughed, and clapped Hem on the back so the breath rushed out of him. The Bard was a big man, with big hands. "Aye," he said. "And you will be able to sleep as long as you wish. While we are here, there is no hurry."

"I thought only Elidhu could take you to another time," said Hem dazedly, as they led the footsore horses to the stables. He was remembering how Nyanar had lifted him out of the unbearable present of the camp at Sjug'hakar Im. This place had a similar air of strange enchantment, of being somehow outside the flow of time.

Grigar gave Hem a piercing glance. "I am curious about you, boy," he said. "What do you know of Elidhu?"

"I met an Elidhu," said Hem, and then stopped. He hadn't meant to say anything about himself until he was wholly sure of Grigar, but in his weariness it had slipped out. He bit his lip, looking sideways at Saliman, as Grigar stared at him in astonishment.

"Hem, it's all right," said Saliman. "Grigar has shown us much trust in bringing us here. Do you think that he is not endangered himself? But come, let's talk later, when we are warm and fed and rested. I can scarce stand up."

When he entered the house, Hem felt himself relax for the first time since he could remember. It had the same tranquil air as

Saliman's Bardhouse in Turbansk, although it was a very different place. They entered a stone-flagged kitchen, filled with a delicious smell that made the water fill Hem's mouth. Grigar sat at a big wooden table with long benches on either side. Over his head dried herbs and onions hung from the dark wooden beams that stretched across the ceiling. A vase of deep blue gentians was set in the window, and there were red cushions on the benches. A large brick oven with an iron door took up all of the far wall, and a kettle was singing on the hob.

By the stove there stood a tall woman with long, black hair, very white skin and very blue eyes. If she hadn't been so tall, Hem might have mistaken her for his sister; she had exactly the same colouring as Maerad. She turned when they entered, and came towards them with open hands.

"Welcome, my friends," she said. Her voice was low and musical, and her smile was warm. "Welcome and thrice welcome. I am Marajan, and this is my house. But please, sit down. I have hot broth here, which will take the chill from your bones, and when you have finished there is fresh bread in the oven."

Hekibel looked dazed, and stumbled as she walked to the bench. Saliman caught her elbow, and she looked up into his face gratefully, trying to smile. Hem suddenly understood that Hekibel knew very little of magery, and that the shock of Marajan's house was for her perhaps as great as any they had suffered in the past days. When they had been in danger, she had been brave and stern, no matter how frightened she had been; but in this peaceful, beautiful place she had lost her bearings and no longer knew what to do. She looked very fragile, her face smudged with weariness and dirt, her hair tangled, her borrowed clothes filthy; and she was staring at Marajan with awe, as if she wished very much that she were better dressed.

They were given mugs of broth, which warmed them down

to their toes; and then Marajan drew the bread from the oven, and laid new butter and good cheese and a pot of dark honey and smoked meats on the table, with bowls of spiced chutneys and jams and other preserves, a jug of ale and another of fresh spring water. Hem realized that he was ravenous and ate his fill, passing titbits to Irc; as soon as he had quelled his hunger he promptly began to fall asleep at the table.

Marajan asked no questions of her guests, and quietly made sure that they had everything they wanted. Then she led them to bedchambers upstairs, closing the shutters to keep out the morning sun. Hem didn't bother to wash: he climbed between the sheets gingerly, almost with disbelief, as if the clean, soft bed were a dream that he might wake from at any moment. He was asleep before his head touched the pillow.

When Hem woke up, he didn't know where he was. He blinked, looking around disbelievingly at a small but comfortable bedchamber. It had plain whitewashed walls, which were now striped with golden bars of light that slanted in through the shutters, and by his bed was a scrubbed wooden chest, on which was placed a vase of lilac, its brown tips just now swelling with blue buds. Then memory filtered back: this was Marajan's house, and for the first time since he could remember, he was not in immediate danger. He jumped out of bed and flung open the shutters, and found himself looking out over a green field that slanted down to a stream. White cows grazed peacefully in the lush grass, and a sinking sun threw a rich honeyed light over everything.

Hem stared in wonder: the contrast with the Desor he knew was almost too much to take in. And then he realized that, for the first time since Maerad had summoned him, he had no sense of her; the urgency had vanished, along with every trace of her presence. He puzzled over this for a while, disturbed. Perhaps, he thought, it was because they were in an earlier time. Perhaps neither of them had been born yet...

Irc flapped up to the windowsill, ruffled his feathers with pleasure, and was about to fly off to explore, when Hem stopped him.

It's magery, he said. *I don't know how the enchantment works. You might fly off into that and never come back.*

It's nicer than where we've been, said Irc, a little sulkily.

I know, said Hem. *Ask Marajan first. You're a nuisance, but I'd hate to lose you, all the same.*

Irc nipped his ear, but stayed. Hem saw that his clothes, cleaned and mended while he slept, were folded neatly on the end of the bed, and he dressed and found his way downstairs to the kitchen, guided by the sound of voices. Saliman, Grigar and Hekibel were seated around the table, but Marajan was not there. On the table were bread and wine and ale, and the smell coming from the oven suggested another good meal was on the way. Hem sniffed the air in appreciation and sat down with his companions.

"This is better, yes?" Grigar smiled across the table, and for the first time Hem smiled openly back. Until now, he hadn't really trusted Grigar – despite Saliman's assurances, he still thought that they might be led into a trap.

"Yes, it's a wonderful place," said Hem. "But who is Marajan? And if we're in the past, when are we? Irc wants to stretch his wings, but I told him to stay close; I don't want him getting lost..."

"Irc can explore as much as he likes, as long as he is back when we leave," Grigar said. "This house is not on an enchanted island of time, but in its own time. We're the ones who have stepped back. About a hundred years, in fact. This was once what Desor was like... I still find it hard to believe how it has changed."

Hem told Irc he could explore, with stern instructions that he was to return at once when he was called, and went out into the cobbled yard. Irc leapt up joyously into the luminous twilit sky. He wouldn't be long, Hem reflected, as it was almost time for dinner. He watched him for a time, absorbing the gentle sounds of evening: the faint clink of cowbells, the comfortable squabbles of birds settling down to rest, the faint soughing of the trees. The peacefulness slowly filled him up, and he sighed with a profound, undirected happiness.

He looked across the field and saw Marajan walking towards him, carrying an iron bucket. She was dressed for farm work: her hair was gathered in an untidy bun on her neck, and her dress was tucked up around her thighs, revealing heavy boots. She smiled when she saw Hem.

"Your crow looks happy," she said when she reached him. "Did you sleep well, Hem? You look rested."

"Yes," said Hem, with feeling. He was slightly tongue-tied around Marajan. Her grave beauty and the frank, generous clarity of her gaze made him feel shy. She seemed almost the most Bardic person he had ever met, and in his short life, he had met some of the greatest Bards in Edil-Amarandh.

"I am glad," said Marajan. "I can see the marks of deep wounds in you, and griefs beyond your years. You have trodden a dark path, and I fear that it will be darker still. If I could, young Healer, I would bid you stay with me until all your hurts were healed. But, alas, I cannot ask that. You are of your own time, and cannot step out of the flow of years for very long. Even here, you can stay but a day and a night."

Hem stared at her in wonder. "Who are you?" he blurted out. "Are you a Bard? I mean..." He spluttered and blushed, feeling that he had been discourteous.

"I am a Bard, yes. But not quite like other Bards, as, perhaps, you are not." She was silent for a time, staring out over the fields. "I have seen you in dreams, Hem, and also your sister. Perhaps I prepared this space for you, knowing that you would need a haven when the darkness crept over Annar."

Hem looked at her in astonishment. Marajan smiled again, and Hem perceived the sadness graven in her beauty, deepening her luminous glance as the coming night enriched the colours of twilight. "It would not be surprising. I am your mother's mother's sister. The Elemental blood runs strong in Pellinor, and to some of us are given the gift of visions, which can seem as much a curse as a blessing. In your time, I am already beyond the Gates of Death, and it is a true gift to see you, brief though this meeting must be ... but come, it is almost supper time, and there is much to speak of, before you must return to your own time. And I should hate to burn the meat."

Hem followed Marajan indoors, his head whirling: Marajan was his grandmother's sister? He felt a pang of loss to think that she was dead in his time. She seemed not at all ghostly, but rather one of the most alive people he had ever met. He wondered if Saliman knew that she was one of the House of Karn, and if he were aware of her Elemental powers; surely it was her Elemental gift that permitted her to make a doorway through time.

After a leisurely and merry dinner, they talked long into the night. Grigar told them that he was part of a group of Bards that worked secretly against the Nameless One in Annar. Their network was extensive, stretching from the Suderain to Lirigon, and it included all the Seven Kingdoms. They were in contact with Hared at Nal-Ak-Burat, although Grigar told them that communication was becoming more difficult by the day.

"Annar becomes more and more like a prison," he said. "You were lucky you struck no trouble, coming up the West Road; frankly, I am surprised. There is civil war almost everywhere. The recreant Enkir has declared war on what he calls the rebel Schools, and even now marches on Eledh. Arnocen and

Il Arunedh know they are next, and are ready for war. The Black
Army lays siege on Til Amon, and if they fall, all Lanorial lies
open to Enkir and the Nameless One. Lirhan and Culain have
mustered their soldiers."

"It is a bleak picture you paint, my friend," said Saliman.

"Aye," said Grigar. "And I fear it will soon be bleaker.
Everywhere we are beaten back, by deceit or treachery or arms.
The only good news is the victory in Innail: I heard that the
School beat back a fierce attack from the mountains, through
the coming of a great mage who destroyed the Landrost. They
call her the Maid of Innail, a mere girl, or so they say. I find that
hard to credit; but from what I hear, the victory is real."

"Maerad!" said Hem excitedly. "It must be Maerad!"

"I did not hear that name," said Grigar. "But who is
Maerad?"

"Maerad of Pellinor. My sister."

"It could indeed be true," said Saliman. "Maerad has a Gift
like no other I have perceived. Although," and here he nodded
towards Marajan, "I must say, Marajan has something of the
same light about her."

Marajan smiled. "You are perceptive, Saliman of Turbansk,"
she said. "I, too, am of the House of Karn."

Saliman looked amazed, and bowed his head. "I confess,
almost nothing about the House of Karn surprises me any
more," he said. "If Hem grew wings and danced about in the
sky with Irc, I would merely blink. Well, perhaps Hem and
I should explain our quest. We are presently seeking Hem's
sister, Maerad, whom we believe is the Foretold who is to
defeat the Dark in its present rising. We know she isn't far away,
somewhere in the Hollow Lands. She summoned Hem some
days ago, and we have been following that summoning ever
since. That is how we happened across Grigar."

Saliman then briefly related their tale: how Cadvan of Lirigon had stumbled across Maerad when she was a slave on the other side of the Osidh Elanor; how he had brought her to Innail and thence to Norloch, finding Hem on their journey; how Hem had journeyed with Saliman to Turbansk, while Maerad and Cadvan travelled north to seek the Riddle of the Treesong. Then he told of the fall of Turbansk, and of Hem's journey into the heart of Dén Raven, into Dagra itself, and of how he had found there, as if by chance, a tuning fork that the Nameless One himself had worn about his neck.

"There are strange runes graven on this fork," said Saliman. "And I have never seen the like, save on the Dhyllic lyre that Maerad bears, which is an heirloom of her house. We know, because the Elidhu Nyanar told Hem, that these runes are deeply concerned with the Treesong."

When Saliman finished, there was a long silence, as his listeners absorbed what he had said. Hekibel had listened intently, seated very close to Saliman, casting an occasional glance, a mixture of amazement and pity and awe, at Hem. She looked much less strained than the night before, but there was a crease in the middle of her brow. This was the first she had heard of the true purpose of Hem and Saliman's quest; she had followed them on trust, because she had nowhere else to go, and now found herself tangled in events beyond her ken. Hem wondered what she was thinking.

Grigar had followed the conversation closely. "The Foretold? The Treesong?" he said. "My friends, we are in deep waters indeed... I take it, then, that you cannot bear the news of this army to Innail, as I had hoped. Yet it is urgent that they know of it. I am sure that Innail is to be the first conquest."

"Not at this moment," said Saliman. "Although it hurts my heart to say so."

Grigar bowed his head in thought. "Perhaps I should put away my role as a common man of Desor, and travel there myself. Desor is becoming more perilous for me, in any case; and perhaps after the death of Hrunsar, and my failure to track you, it would be sensible to leave. I have seen people blinded for less. And Innail must be warned."

"You will find a kinder place there than here," said Saliman. "My soul is darkened by what I have seen in Desor, my friend."

Grigar sighed. "Aye," he said. "Yet, even if it is full of serpents, it hurts to leave my home. I am loath to go."

"I think you must leave Desor," said Marajan. "In any case, you must make your choice soon, before the sun rises. Your hours in my house grow short: the door of time, alas, opens only briefly."

They quickly discussed their plans. Grigar told them the Hollow Lands were a day's ride from the house, and that this part of the Fesse was now deserted and had but light guard. If they travelled under a glimveil, they should not attract notice.

"What of you, Hekibel?" asked Saliman. "What do you wish to do?"

"I will come with you," she said, without hesitation. "If, that is, you will have me."

"I only fear that meeting Hem and me has already cost you too much." Saliman paused. "As you said yesterday, aside from the horses, everyone you travelled with is now dead. I feel the weight and sorrow of that, and I am afraid that if you continue with us, it may cost you your own life."

Hekibel sat up straight and looked Saliman in the eye. "Yes, I have thought of all that," she said. "How could I not? But Saliman, it is already too late for me. I think I must see this through to the end, for good or ill."

"If you wished, you could travel with me to Innail," said Grigar.

"I thank you," Hekibel said. "But I think my path leads elsewhere."

Hem studied Hekibel curiously; he thought that overnight there was a change in her. She looked pale and somehow very fragile, but something had hardened in her expression, a determination he hadn't seen before. He wanted to tell her how brave he thought she was, but somehow the words wouldn't come out.

"Well, then," said Grigar. "I myself will travel through the Weywood. I hope the spirits of the wood will permit me free entrance." He looked inquiringly at Marajan, who nodded gravely.

"I think the woods will not be hostile," she said. "As for you three, you must journey as swiftly as you may. In your time, the hours darken: although whether the world turns to endless night, or will find beyond hope a new dawn, I cannot tell. But all my love goes with you. Especially with you, young Healer. There will be much need of healing, after."

Hem met Marajan's lucid gaze, and his heart swelled with sudden, unlooked-for love. He didn't know what to say, but it didn't matter. He knew that Marajan read his deepest longings, and she understood and blessed them all.

THE DEAD

Alas! Alas! The dead have come,
 The newborn babe, the withered king,
And pale Bards whose empty hands
 No blessings bring.

Poor shades, no hearth can warm them now.
 They walk beneath the roofless skies
Forlorn and lost, and all men dread
 Their fading cries.

Death has robbed their limbs of love
 And starved their gentle flesh to bone:
At last beneath the starless sky
 Each stands alone.

They pluck at me, in my dark mind
 Like burning rain their voices fall,
And who can count their legion ranks
 Or name them all?

From *The Elidhu Canticles*, Horvadh of Gent

XVII

DREAMS

IT was a world neither of darkness nor light, an endless twilight inhabited by dim forms in ceaseless motion. Nothing
seemed to hold its shape: there were voices whose edges
seemed to glimmer with starlight, faint lullabies and lamentations who stepped out of the silence like young girls, their faces
averted. Everywhere there were the marks of hands, as if every
surface breathed out the heat of a body that had just touched
it. It wasn't possible to see anything clearly, always there were
shifting veils of light and shadow drifting and vanishing, and
the eye could fix on nothing. The earth seemed no longer solid,
but a mist that mingled with the vapours of the air. And everywhere the voices, the wan echoes of the dead...

Macrad woke with a start, feeling the cold sweat sliding
down her back and her forehead. She didn't know if she had
cried out; it seemed to her that the echo of her own voice still
hung on the night air, but perhaps it was merely a remnant of
her dream. She gathered her blanket closely around her and sat
up, feeling the wool's roughness against her cheek, the prickle
of the dry grass, the hard ground against her buttocks – these
were tangible things out of the world of solid objects, and their
abrasiveness was reassuring.

She stared up, looking to the stars for comfort, as she had so
often in her life. Ilion, the morning star, had long since set over
the horizon, and the bright litter of the Lukemoi, the Paths of the
Dead, arced across the sky. The stars gave her no consolation. A
slight wind brushed her hair back and cooled the sweat on her

face. Maerad shivered, remembering that those stars marked the bridge between this world and the Gates, beyond which lay – what? Nobody, not even Ardina, knew the answer to that question. Maerad thought now that the dead did not wander through the groves of the stars, as the Bards sang. No, the Gates opened on darkness, and the dead soul stepped into that darkness and was lost for ever. Perhaps, she thought, they stepped gladly into that darkness. She imagined walking that high path, far above the lamentations of the earth, beyond the sweat and filth and sorrow of human existence, and how her own life might fall regretlessly from her open hands, all its joy, all its sorrow, all its triumph and defeat. Yes, they might well step gladly and lightly away from the weight of being alive.

If the dead step out into the dark and leave the world behind them, she thought, who are these voices that I cannot stop hearing? They are not the voices of the living.

She clutched her head in her hands; her forehead was burning, aching, but her skin felt as cold as ice. I have been too much out of this world, she thought. And now I am afraid. Something has happened…

When Maerad came out of her trance, it was just before dawn. She looked about with wonder, sniffing the clean, cold air that seared her nostrils and stung her cheeks. There was a thick, low ground mist wisping out of the dips and hollows, very white in the early light.

Cadvan was standing with his back to her, staring eastwards at the pale hints of dawn that were illuminating the distant, cloudy peaks of the Osidh Elanor. When he turned around she saw his face was very white, and his eyes glittered when he looked at her, with suspicion or fear or some other emotion she couldn't guess. He asked her if she had found Hem, and Maerad nodded.

"Good," he said. "Then I think we should move from this place. I'll wager my life that every Hull in North Annar will be riding hard for the Hollow Lands right now, and that it will not be long before the Nameless One himself knows that you are here; that is, if he hasn't heard already. You might as well have lit a beacon, Maerad. Anyone for leagues with the slightest touch of the Gift, down to the simplest village midwife, will have sensed you, and will know that you're here."

Maerad met his eyes, and saw that he spoke the truth. Her lip curled. "Hulls?" she said, tossing back her hair from her face. "What of them?"

Cadvan's face darkened, as if her scorn were directed towards him as well. "I do not like Hulls," he said. "Especially I do not like the thought of many Hulls riding our way, while we camp in the middle of nowhere with no means of defence."

"I have no fear of Hulls," said Maerad. "I'm not going anywhere. Hem is coming here, he is on his way, and I will stay here and wait for him."

"Surely Hem would be able to sense you, wherever you are," said Cadvan. "And if we are to be visited by Hulls or wers or any other servants of the Dark, I would prefer to have walls around me, than not."

"What walls?" said Maerad.

"I was thinking that we could ride to Innail," Cadvan said, glancing at her sideways.

"We'd be no safer there than here," said Maerad. "In any case, you are probably safer with me than with any other person in Edil-Amarandh." She smiled, meeting Cadvan's eye, and she saw him blench, as if he had glimpsed something that raised the hair on his scalp with horror.

"Maerad," he said, very softly, so that she had to lean forward to hear his voice above the sound of the wind that soughed over the hills. "Maerad, I think you must remember what the

Winterking said to you. I say this not only for my sake. Beware, Maerad."

Her gaze faltered, and she looked away.

"I cannot beware, Cadvan," she said at last, her voice as soft as his. "It's too late for that now. But I am afraid that I have made you fear me, and that hurts my heart."

There was a long silence. "I *am* afraid, Maerad," said Cadvan. "I'm afraid of what I see in you, and of the storm that is gathering beyond these hills and that will soon break over our heads. I should be mad not to be afraid."

"I'm not afraid any more, even though I don't know what will happen." Maerad's voice dropped to a whisper. "Or perhaps I am so afraid that I no longer feel it. I know there are so many things to fear, but Cadvan, please, don't be afraid of *me*." She looked at him pleadingly.

Cadvan, who had been staring broodingly at his hands, looked up and met her eyes again. This time he smiled, and to Maerad's astonishment his expression was unguarded and joyous, a reckless smile that gave her a vivid glimpse of the wild, fearless young man he once had been. Maerad's heart leapt in her breast.

"A pact then," he said. "I promise not to fear you, and you promise not to squash me like a beetle by mistake while you're busy pulverising Hulls. You're right. It's too late for fear."

"There is a storm coming," said Maerad. "And we must ride it."

"I'm not sure I packed the right kind of saddle."

"It's too big for saddles, and it has an evil eye," said Maerad, smiling. "It's either bareback and hanging on by the mane, or be trampled."

After that, there was no more talk of moving on. The days were long, cold and wearisome, but they kept themselves busy. Cadvan scouted around their area and found a site close by that

he said was more defensible, and they moved their belongings
and the horses there. They patched their rough shelter with turf
to keep out the wind, and made a proper hearth.

Maerad spent most of the day scanning the horizon, in
between furious bursts of activity. Cadvan filled in the days by
preparing defences of magery. He set awareness in stones in a
radius around their camp, so they would have early warning
of anyone's approach. He spent hours working on his sword,
laying it on the ground and charming the tempered metal with
new mageries, and when there was nothing more to do, he did
the same with Maerad's sword Eled. He set wards and scored a
line into the ground with a flint knife, making a wall of magery
that wers could not pass, and as she watched him at his labour,
Maerad remembered the first time she had seen him do this,
the night they had taken refuge in a ruined tower, pursued by
the Landrost's wers. The memory was distant, as if it had happened to someone else.

At times she thought that barely a single night had passed
since she had called Hem; more often it seemed to her that she
had been in this one place since the beginning of time, that she
had already been here when the forgotten people who lived
here had so laboriously raised their stone circles to be their
inscrutable witnesses, and that she had watched as they faded
for ever into the dim mists of forgetting.

Sometimes, Maerad felt that she knew these stones like she
knew her own skin. She had watched the slow, patient, weath-
ering of the years; she had noted each shade of light, moonlight
and starlight, the many moods of the sun and the seasons, and
how they changed the colours of the rock through an infinity
of hues, from deep purple to bloody red, from rich yellow to a
delicate blue-grey. She had watched as the bright lichens spread
over their flaking faces. She had been there in the mild days of
summer, when wild bees wove their slumberous song through

the flowering heathers, and in the numberless harsh winters that threw down bolts of freezing rain and filled their veins with ice and split them open. She was almost rock herself.

When these fits took her, she could be silent for hours on end. Cadvan would speak to her and she did not hear him: and yet she was not absent, but rather, more intensely present than she felt she had ever been. At last something would shake her out of it – perhaps Keru might come up and nuzzle her, wanting some company, or Cadvan might touch her hand, trying to wake her from an enchantment he did not understand, and Maerad would jump, as if she were surprised, and smile vaguely. Then she would try to haul herself back into ordinary things with some task: grooming Keru or Darsor perhaps, so their coats shone, or mending every tear in her clothing, or polishing her boots, or gathering firewood.

The dreams had begun the day after the summoning. It was as if a wall in her mind had cracked, and through this crack she could hear the voices of the dead. And the more aware she became of them, the wider the crack seemed; she felt as if she were gradually filling up with these lost voices, as if they were seeping into her consciousness through a slow leak. Every night she seemed to wander deeper into a dreamland in which she could find no bearing.

As the surge of power ebbed from her being, her fearlessness had ebbed as well. Now, although she did not admit it to Cadvan, she felt small and vulnerable, and she was afraid of her magery, and would not use it, even to try to contact Hem again. Cadvan sensed her fragility, and treated her gently. Although he wondered anxiously whether it was certain that Hem was journeying towards them, he did not urge her to attempt to mindtouch him, or to use any of her powers. He watched her as she sat by the edge of their camp, staring westwards, as if Hem might at any moment step out of the distant horizon, and his face was often shadowed with anxiety and pity.

This strange period of suspension, when time seemed to have stopped, felt to Cadvan like a release, a slow taking of breath before some unimaginable struggle. He did not know what to expect; he didn't know whether he had made a good decision, or the most terrible mistake of his life. He only knew that he could not have chosen otherwise. For the first time since Maerad had known him, he had put aside his harsh self-judgement, and there was a peace in his expression that had not been there before. If it was mixed with sadness, Maerad noticed that Cadvan seemed more light-hearted than he had ever been, and she turned to his lightness as a flower turns its face to the sun, and tried not to see the shadows which gathered behind her.

It was eight days since she had summoned Hem. She and Cadvan hadn't spoken of that night. It wasn't that either of them wished to avoid the subject, but more that neither of them had the words, and they both obscurely felt that to speak about it without being able to express precisely what they meant was somehow perilous.

At sunset on the eighth day, Maerad saw two horsemen climbing the long, slow rise to their camp from the west. She had been sitting all day on a low, flat rock, lost in a trance, listening to the quickening of the earth beneath her feet as it wakened to springtime, her eyes fixed on the horizon. She often played her lyre as she watched, and she held it now, her maimed hand straying idly over its strings. She played no particular melody, but the constant gentle fall of the notes soothed her. When she saw the riders, she leapt to her feet with a cry.

Cadvan had been setting snares for rabbits and so was a little distance away, but he ran over to Maerad at once.

"It's Hem!" she said, pointing. She was trembling all over. "At last!"

Cadvan shaded his eyes with his hands and looked. The riders were far away, and he could tell nothing about them; but they carried with them a sense of hidden power that caused him grave misgivings.

"Are you certain it's Hem?" he said at last, turning towards her. "I am not sure that they are not Hulls. I have felt the shadows of the Dark stepping in my mind these past few days, and I fear they draw ever closer."

"I'm sure it's Hem," Maerad said.

"Have you made certain?" asked Cadvan. "Have you spoken to him?"

The light in Maerad's face went out. "No," she whispered, and turned her face away.

"I think," said Cadvan, an edge in his voice, "that it would be as well to make sure, before these people, whoever they are, come close enough to cause us harm."

"But—" Maerad lifted her hands and dropped them helplessly. She didn't know how to tell Cadvan about how she feared the voices seeping into her dreams, how she was afraid that every time she used her power, she opened the breach in her mind that gave them entrance.

"Maerad, if you have the power, use it. Or are we just going to wait for anyone to come here and strike us dead, because you refuse to pick up the sword at your feet? Did you not tell me that you had no fear of Hulls?"

Maerad pressed her lips together and made no answer. Cadvan stared at her, his eyes darkening with anger.

"The last thing I expected was that the price of opening your powers would be that you would lose your courage," he said, after a long silence. "Or perhaps it is simply that the Dark now has a means to enter your mind and so disables you with fear. I do not know, Maerad, and I am too angry to care."

"You don't understand," said Maerad, stung. "You—"

"Of course I don't understand. How could I understand? But it seems to me that I am the biggest fool in Annar, and that my enemies must be laughing up their sleeves."

"What do you mean?" said Maerad. "It's not – it's not the Dark I'm afraid of—"

"Then what do you fear?" said Cadvan, whirling around and taking her chin in his hand, so she was forced to look straight into his eyes. "By the Light, Maerad, what is it that you fear, if not the Dark? Do you know what the Dark is doing in this land at this very moment? Do you not feel it closing in, like a huge jaw, preparing to crush us all?"

Maerad blinked. "You're hurting me," she said.

Cadvan took a deep breath and let go, although he held her gaze. He looked no less angry.

"Tell me, Maerad. Please tell me. What is it?"

"I think… it's the dead," Maerad whispered. "I can hear the dead. They're coming into my dreams, more and more, and I hear them all the time… I don't know who they are."

Cadvan's eyes widened in astonishment, and he stepped back, looking over towards the riders, and then back to Maerad. "The dead?" he said. "The dead frighten you? What dead?"

Maerad's jaw wobbled, and she brushed her eyes roughly with the back of her hand. "They don't threaten me. But I can't stop it. Ever since I…" She wiped her eyes again. "And if I use my powers again, I know it's only going to get worse."

Cadvan studied her face intently, and the anger ebbed from his expression. "I will say to you, Maerad, what you said to me eight days ago. It is already too late. Neither of us knew what would happen when you decided to invoke your full Elemental powers. Cowering beneath the forces you have unleashed will not make them go away. It is probably the worst thing you can do."

Maerad nodded miserably. "I just – can't," she said. "I know it's weak, Cadvan. I'm ashamed. I just can't."

Cadvan nodded, his face expressionless, and then he turned westwards and gazed at the riders, standing very still. A faint silvery shimmer illuminated his form, and Maerad knew that he was attempting to feel them out. The light faded, and he stood long in thought.

"Whoever is coming our way is shielded," he said at last. "Hull or Bard, I cannot tell. And there is with them something very powerful, Maerad. I don't know what it is, but I feel a great foreboding. Something of great might approaches us, and I cannot tell what it is. Can you feel nothing?"

Maerad met Cadvan's eyes. "It's Hem," she said. "I told you."

"How do you know?"

"I just know. Do you think that I wouldn't know my own brother?"

"But you will not attempt to speak to him? Not even that? I know you have closed yourself to all magery over the past days, Maerad, and I understand – as much as I can – the fear that makes you do so; but I say to you, now is not the time. And I fear that it is your hope and not your Knowing that speaks now."

Maerad had no answer to Cadvan's doubt. It was, she knew, quite reasonable, and his premonition that Hulls were coming their way was probably accurate, although she herself felt no sense of their presence. As Cadvan had said, she had closed her mind to magery, and her powers slumbered behind strong barriers that she would not let down. And in fact, aside from a conviction that grew the longer she watched the approaching figures, she had no reason to think that one of the two riders approaching them was Hem. Even so, at that moment nothing Cadvan could say and do would have made Maerad open her powers; and he knew it.

Cadvan loosened his sword, and mentally began to check

the wards he had placed about their camp to see if they remained strong. Maerad was not wearing her sword, and he told her to arm herself. She almost refused, but caught the look in his eye and decided that it was not worth arguing the point. She left her lyre leaning on the stone as she went back to their camp.

When she came back, Cadvan seemed to have forgotten their argument.

"Maerad, do you hear that sound?" he asked.

"What sound?" asked Maerad, and looked around her, as if it were a visible thing.

"It's like – a low humming. It began a short time ago, and I can't tell where it's coming from. And it has a taste of power about it. I like this not at all."

Her attention caught, Maerad cocked her head and listened. "I hear nothing but the wind blowing and the stones growing beneath our feet and the cry of birds," she said.

"Beneath that," said Cadvan. "Do you not hear it?" He was beginning to sound impatient, and Maerad tried again. Again she heard nothing.

"I think," said Cadvan, "you will need your Bard hearing."

Maerad opened her mouth to object, but then she thought that perhaps her hearing was the least of her Bard senses, and that it mightn't do any harm just to listen a little, very quickly. And then at least she would know what Cadvan was talking about. Very cautiously, she cast her hearing out, not even attempting to reach to any distance.

As soon as she did, she regretted it. What Cadvan heard as a low hum was for Maerad an unendurable droning sound, a long, single note that made every bone in her body resonate in sympathy. Even her teeth seemed to rattle in her head. In a panic, she tried to close her Bard ears, but now the vibration was like a wedge keeping her senses open, and she could not, no matter how she tried. She cried out in pain and stumbled forwards, and Cadvan caught her before she fell and lowered her to the ground. Then she saw that her lyre was glowing with an inner illumination, a glow that was like the rich, various light of a summer day.

She picked up her lyre and clutched it as if she were drowning. At once the droning was not nearly so unbearable; it became a low hum which still vibrated through her body, as if she were an instrument herself, but it no longer hurt her. Her panic abated, and she realized that the lyre, too, was resonating, and then that the humming came from the lyre itself. And the light was growing stronger as she watched, until the lyre was blazing in her hands.

"What's happening?" asked Cadvan. He had drawn his sword and was himself luminous with shielded magery.

"I don't know," said Maerad, looking up at him. "It's never done anything like this before. Perhaps it's waking up. Look – the runes…"

The Treesong runes were burning, as if the bright wood were inlaid with ruby fire. For a moment they both forgot everything but the lyre and stared, lost in astonishment.

"It's beautiful," Maerad said in wonder. "I've never seen anything so beautiful…"

Cadvan had told her almost as soon as they had met that her lyre was no ordinary instrument. It was Dhyllic ware, fashioned in Afinil and crafted with skills of magery now long forgotten. And Inka-Reb, the wise man of the north, had laughed at her for not knowing that the Treesong she had travelled the length of Edil-Amarandh to find was written on it, and the Winterking had revealed the meanings of the runes, and had told her that the lyre had been made in Afinil by Nelsor himself, one of the greatest Bards of all. Maerad had known all this, but for her it was still the lyre her mother had given her, the humble companion of her lonely childhood. Now, perhaps for the first time, she began to understand what it really was.

"Are you all right now?" said Cadvan, dragging his eyes away from the blazing lyre.

Maerad nodded.

"Because the riders will be here soon. And I still cannot tell, for all my striving, what manner of people they are. It looks to me as if one of the horses has two people on its back... And it occurs to me also that if any Hulls are nearby, they will be pricking up their ears and hurrying this way also."

Maerad nodded again. Now she had permitted her magery to flow within her again, she was wondering why she had been so frightened for the past week. It was as if she had been crouching in a small hole, her hands over her face, refusing to look at the sunlight that blazed above her.

"I'm sorry about before," she said, and she looked up at Cadvan. "I'll try to speak to Hem now."

She stared at the distant riders. They were closer now, and she saw that Cadvan was right: one horse bore two riders. She bent her head and concentrated.

Hem, she said. *Are you there?*

Maerad? Hem answered at once, and the naked joy in his voice made tears well in her eyes. *We're close, aren't we?*

Yes, you're close. We can see you. Overwhelmed by emotion, Maerad couldn't speak for a moment. *You're very close. Oh, Hem ... I've missed you so much ... I thought I might never see you again.*

But here we are! She could hear that Hem was laughing with sheer delight. *We can't see you yet, but even Saliman can feel you now. We think there are some Hulls nearby. We can't see where, but they'll be riding your way for certain.*

Saliman? Is Saliman with you?

Yes. And Hekibel and Irc. Friends. We've come so far to find you!

But Maerad, something really strange is happening. I have this tuning fork and it's making an incredible humming and I think the Treesong is beginning to do something – I don't know what. I can hardly hear you over the noise.

It's happening here too, said Maerad. *My lyre is all lit up.*

It must be the Treesong. I've got the other half… Hem's excited voice began to fragment, and Maerad lost the mindtouch. She bit her lip in frustration, and was about to report to Cadvan what Hem had told her when Hem's voice cut back in… *It's glowing as well, the runes are like fire!*

I can't hear you, said Maerad.

Hem swore and then she lost him again. The humming was growing, not in loudness but in intensity, so that it filled her whole mind, and it was difficult to be conscious of anything else. Maerad thought it was no longer a single note, but more like a constant, fascinating melody, the logic of which she could not catch. With difficulty, she wrenched her mind away from it, and turned to Cadvan.

He had already guessed that the news was good, and had sheathed his sword.

"It's Hem, and he's got Saliman with him," said Maerad. She was trembling with excitement.

"Saliman?" For a moment Cadvan looked astonished, and then he smiled with unalloyed pleasure.

"And two other people, Hem said. Irc and Hekibel." The words tumbled out of her; Maerad's breath was short, and she felt so dizzy she could hardly speak. She couldn't take her eyes off the riders: they had quickened their pace and were now moving swiftly towards them and Maerad couldn't wait until they arrived, until she could hold her brother in her arms at last.

Cadvan squinted at the riders. "I can only see three," he said.

"Well, that's what he said."

"There's a big white bird that seems to be with them," said Cadvan. "Maybe he means the bird."

"Maybe," said Maerad. "He didn't say. And they think that there are Hulls nearby as well. And he said that he's got the other half of the Treesong, a tuning fork, and the same thing is happening there." Maerad hugged herself to stop her body shaking: the strange music was growing inside her so that she could almost hear its melody, and she couldn't tell any more where the sound ended and she began.

"Hem has the lost half of the Treesong?" Cadvan looked stunned. "That is news beyond hope. Well, maybe that explains what is happening here. Perhaps you are right, Maerad. The lyre is awakening. Although what that means is beyond my Knowing."

For a while neither of them said anything further, their eyes fixed on the approaching riders. Maerad thought she would die from impatience. She shook her head, trying to clear it of the humming. The sound would not die down, and it was still growing in complexity and intensity the closer the riders came.

"If there are Hulls," said Cadvan a little later, "we must be ready for them."

Maerad stared at him as if she saw him through a veil. "If there are Hulls, we will kill them," she said thickly. "I will not countenance their presence here."

Cadvan glanced at her in surprise, and then with growing concern. Maerad's body was shaking with tremors so violent that she was forced to hold the lyre in her arms, close against her body, so she would not drop it. Her face was so white she looked translucent, as if she had been drained of every drop of blood, and her eyes blazed with feverish excitement. Her gaze was fixed unblinkingly on the horses that drew ever closer, bearing her brother towards her. Cadvan touched her arm, to ask if she needed help, but she shook his hand off, almost absentmindedly.

When Hem came close enough to be heard he waved and shouted, and Maerad stood up and shouted back, although she did not know what she said. The horses were some hundred spans away when Hem slid off Usha, tumbling onto the ground and almost falling over. He regained his footing at once and sprinted with all his might towards Maerad.

She let her lyre fall from her hands and it landed by her feet. She scarcely noticed: letting go of it made no difference now. Its music was embedded so deeply in her bones, in her very marrow, that she thought she would never be free of it. She swayed as if she might faint and opened her arms wide, and Hem ran up and threw his arms around his sister, embracing her so passionately that all the breath was driven out of her. And for an infinite moment they held each other so closely that she felt the wild beating of his heart through her whole body, and she could not tell whether her cheeks were wet with his tears or her own.

XVIII

A BREATH

BECAUSE Saliman thought he was dead, Cadvan was the last person in the world that Saliman expected to see, he did not recognize him at first. He slowed Minna to a walk as they came close, and rode up sedately to Maerad and Cadvan's campsite, Hekibel following shyly in his wake. Irc was sitting on Hekibel's shoulder, looking rather huffy: he had been forced to flap into the air when Hem had leapt from the horse, and perhaps he was a little jealous.

Saliman had noted the cloaked figure to Maerad's right, but his attention was wholly caught by Hem's wild dash towards Maerad and the lyre blazing at Maerad's feet. When Hem and Maerad embraced it was too private a moment for other eyes, and Saliman tactfully turned away his gaze away, and found himself looking directly into Cadvan's face.

He almost fell off Minna in his amazement. He forgot everything else, even the strange, enchanting music that was filling his Bardic senses and bewildering his mind with its increasing power. He pulled Minna to an abrupt halt and dismounted, standing face to face with Cadvan.

Cadvan's face lit up with his sudden brilliant smile. "Saliman!" he said.

Saliman clasped Cadvan with almost as much emotion as Hem had hugged Maerad, and then stood back and held him at arm's length, struggling for words.

"I don't know whether I ought not to strangle you!" he said at last.

Cadvan laughed. "What a way to greet an old friend!"

Saliman earnestly studied Cadvan's face. "Yes, it is you," he said, his voice hoarse. "Cadvan, I had heard that you were dead. I have been mourning you these past two months. And to find you here, beyond hope, in the middle of the wilderness…"

Cadvan was suddenly serious. "I am sorry to have given you such grief needlessly, my friend," he said. "For my part, the news from Turbansk made me fear for you, and I have often wondered whether I would see you again."

"There is much – too much – to tell you," said Saliman. He looked around, as if recalling where he was. "And I do not doubt that now we are in great peril. I am sure we are followed by Hulls, a number of Hulls, although perhaps they were not following us, but are drawn to Maerad as moths to a light – her power beams over these hills like a beacon."

"I fear so," said Cadvan. "I can feel them, drawing ever closer. All the same, I suspect they might be the least of our problems. There are powers loose here that I neither know nor understand. But tell me, who is your friend?"

Hekibel had been hanging back awkwardly behind Saliman, holding the reins of the two horses, with Irc perched petulantly on her shoulder. She smiled hesitantly as Saliman took her arm and brought her forward.

"Cadvan, Hekibel, please each meet a dear friend of mine. And Cadvan, this is Irc, a most uncommon crow. But I fear there is no time…"

Cadvan was about to reply, but at that moment all three swung around to look at Hem and Maerad, as if someone had called them. Hekibel cried out, her hand over her mouth.

While they had been talking, Hem and Maerad had parted and were now standing side by side, holding hands. Maerad grasped her lyre in her free hand, and Hem held a small, unbearably bright object in his, which Saliman knew was the tuning fork. They seemed entranced, their faces blank, and both were bright with a shimmering radiance. It was very different from the silvery light of magery: it rippled through them like an unconsuming flame, now the infinite orange and auburn of autumn leaves, now dark as honey, now bright and rich as gold or rubies.

As they watched, brother and sister unclasped their hands. Maerad held her lyre, readying to strike the strings, and Hem bent down with deliberate slowness and struck the tuning fork on a rock.

The tuning fork began to ring with a new sound audible to all ears, not just to those sensitive to magery. At first it was low, like the sounding of a melodious bell, but instead of dying away, the sound gradually grew. Soon it was so loud that it drowned out everything else. Hekibel put her hands over her ears and the horses reared, pulled the reins out of her hands and bolted away. Irc gave a harsh shriek and flew up into the sky.

What are they doing? said Saliman into Cadvan's mind. By now the ringing was so loud that if he had shouted in Cadvan's ear, he would barely have been able to hear him.

I wish I knew, Cadvan answered. *I am afraid that we can do nothing now but watch and hope...*

Just as it seemed that if the sound grew any more intense the stones must begin to crack, it stopped increasing in volume. The fork continued ringing out its single note, a constant, punishing noise, until the three watchers felt that if it continued much longer, they would go mad. And yet still it continued, beyond bearing, with no sign that it would stop.

Hem and Maerad were so still that they seemed not to be breathing: it was as if they were trapped in the enchantment, outside time itself, like flies in amber. Hekibel was staring at them, her face white, her hands still over her ears. She shouted something to Saliman, but he shook his head, unable to understand what she said. She put her mouth close to his ear. "Something's wrong," she shouted. "It's not right."

Saliman looked at her in surprise, and then, without any warning, eluding Saliman's grasp as he tried to stop her, Hekibel ran up to Hem and tore the tuning fork out of his hand, holding it tightly in her fist to stop it vibrating, and she began to shake him, shouting at him frantically to wake up. Saliman and Cadvan looked on, frozen with horror: one of the first things Bards were taught was the danger of interrupting a spell in progress.

As soon as Hekibel snatched the tuning fork from Hem's hand, the noise stopped abruptly. The sudden silence was shocking, and at the same time an inexpressible relief. Hem and Maerad stirred, looking in confusion around them as if they had been woken from sleep, and then an expression of rage flickered across Hem's face and he lunged for Hekibel, trying to take back the tuning fork. She jumped backwards, holding it away so he couldn't reach it.

"It was wrong, Hem," said Hekibel, her voice steady, her eyes locked on Hem. "There was something *wrong*."

"How did you know?" asked Maerad. She was trembling again, more violently than before, and as she spoke her legs crumpled beneath her and she fell to the ground. Hem bent down to help her up and she pressed his arm gratefully, but didn't attempt to stand up. She was still holding her lyre, but the light had died out of it and now it seemed just an ordinary wooden instrument. "How did you know it was wrong?"

"I don't know," said Hekibel shakily. She was holding the tuning fork with the tips of her fingers, looking at it as if she didn't quite believe what she had done. "It just felt – not right." She looked at the tuning fork again, and gave it back to Hem.

He took it and slipped its chain back over his head, and hid it beneath his clothes.

All this had happened very fast, in the time it took Saliman and Cadvan to join them. Saliman was furious. "Hekibel," he said, his voice icy. "You must never do that to a Bard. *Never*. Do you understand?"

"No," said Maerad faintly. "Hekibel was quite right. It wasn't doing what it was supposed to. I think the Treesong was trying to make itself whole, but there was something missing, and it didn't work…"

Saliman paused, taken aback, and before he could speak, Maerad smiled tiredly and reached out her hand. "I suppose we ought to say hello," she said. "It's so good to see you."

The anger died out of Saliman's face, and he smiled back, and embraced her. "And to see you, Maerad. No matter how strange the circumstances."

Unlike Hem, who now showed no sign of power, Maerad still held in her skin an afterglow of the strange, golden illumination that had blazed through her. Subtle ripples of light ran through her veins, and her eyes were aflame. Cadvan glanced at her, his eyes dark with concern, and squatted beside her.

"What was supposed to happen?" he asked.

Maerad, her head bowed, didn't answer.

"I don't know," said Hem, at last. "I mean, we knew what to do, and then it was – well, it was as if we got *stuck*."

There was a silence. "Well," said Saliman. "I wish we had some way to navigate this mystery…"

He stopped, his nostrils flaring, and was swiftly turning his head to look behind him when he froze, as still as if he were carved of stone. A freezing spell, Maerad thought, and inwardly cursed. She looked at her friends, caught out of time in mid-gesture: Cadvan standing with an exclamation of fury half-formed on his lips; Hem reaching towards Saliman, his brow creased with puzzlement; Hekibel halfway through wiping a stray lock of hair from her face.

Hulls, thought Maerad. In the drama of the past few moments – and it had only been a few moments, if that – the threat of Hulls had dropped out of their minds. And yet they had all known that Hulls were nearby; and now the strange enchantment of the Treesong was not obliterating all her senses, she could feel their cold, malignant presence.

There were many of them; perhaps a dozen, perhaps more. Many more than she had guessed earlier, when she had felt their dim shadows pressing on her mind. She had then reckoned there were three, maybe four. They must have used powerful shielding; because the sorcery of Hulls disrupted the Balance, it was much more difficult for a Hull to shield its power than it was for a Bard. Somehow these Hulls had managed to cast a spell on all of them, except Maerad herself, through Cadvan's wards and walls. And Cadvan would have made powerful charms, complex spells that would not be easy to undo or bypass. That meant, thought Maerad, that among their number were powerful and subtle sorcerers.

Maerad closed her eyes, wishing that her body would stop shaking. After days of inaction, it seemed that now things would not stop happening. Then she slowly stood up and looked westwards, down the slope along which she had watched Hem and Saliman and Hekibel ride only a short time earlier.

The Hulls were cloaked by sorcery, but she could perceive them as clearly as if she could see them with her eyes. The sun had now sunk, the last of its light ebbing orange over the western horizon. The evening sky arched huge and luminous over the empty land, which swept down from her feet in rich hues of purple, and the first white stars were already beginning to appear above. Maerad looked over the darkening land before her and was struck for the first time by its lonely beauty.

The Hulls were riding towards her in a line, each abreast of the other, and they seemed to Maerad not like darkness, not like light, but like an absence of both. They were an emptiness riding towards her over the innocent earth – not at all like the terrifying nothing that she had encountered when she had fought the Landrost, but a malign, conscious, deliberate sterility.

A vast contempt rose within her. The Landrost, for all his violent intent, was a power she could respect. What she perceived in the Hulls was, more than anything, a corrosive pettiness, a smallness of being that had made them shrink from the generosity of life and choose instead the emptiness of control, of mere dominance.

She counted them. There were fourteen Hulls riding with slow deliberation towards the campsite. She guessed that Cadvan's wards were slowing them down, otherwise they would already have attacked.

She stood and waited, feeling no urgency. Her body seemed to be stronger, her limbs were no longer shaking so badly. Then she glanced at her friends, and her conscience smote her. If she was not afraid, they felt no such assurance. Hekibel's eyes, the only part of her that could express anything, revealed sheer terror.

"Have no fear," Maerad said aloud, and she made a strange gesture with her hands, not even deigning to speak. At once the spell was broken, and all four of them slumped with relief at being released from their horrible suspension.

"I thank you, Maerad," said Cadvan, rubbing his neck. "That was a nasty moment. Surprised by Hulls…! I could spit!"

"There are fourteen," said Maerad. "They ride slowly. I am guessing they are hampered by your magery but, all the same, they cast that spell through all your wards."

Hekibel drew a sharp breath. "Fourteen?" she said in a small voice.

"If they can break wards that Cadvan set, there must be a mighty power there." Saliman drew his sword and eyed it coldly.

"They will not harm us," said Maerad. "They cannot."

Saliman stared at Maerad with amazement, and then glanced quickly at Cadvan, who gave him a slight nod. He cleared his throat. "Well, even so, I think that maybe Hekibel and Hem can perhaps get out of the way…"

"I don't like Hulls," said Hem thickly. He was struggling against a creeping horror; vivid memories rose in his mind's eye of the Hulls in Edinur, the Hulls at Sjug'hakar Im. "I'm pretty useless here, to be honest."

He took Hekibel's hand, and pulled her away from the other Bards. She said nothing. At first she seemed to resist him, as if she were fixed to the spot, dazed with terror, but she allowed Hem to lead her to the rough shelter of rock where Maerad and Cadvan had made their home for the past week, and as soon as they were inside she crouched on the ground, her arms wrapped around herself.

"Hulls are horrible," said Hem, trying to smile to reassure her. "But if Maerad says we will be all right, we are in no danger."

Hekibel looked up at him, but said nothing. The naked fear in her face made Hem kneel down next to her and take her hands in both of his. He wanted to tell her how sorry he was for the trouble he had caused her, but the words died in his mouth. Hekibel looked up and met his eyes and then she put her arms around him, and he could feel the trembling of her body. Hekibel, he remembered, had not been near Hulls before, although she had seen their work; and, perhaps, not having the defences of Bards, she was more vulnerable to the desolation they wrought in the spirit.

Maerad followed her brother's departure with her eyes, and then turned back to face the Hulls, Saliman and Cadvan on either side of her.

"So, Maerad," said Saliman, with an sardonic smile. "How do you propose we defend ourselves? I confess, I cannot see anything but a fearsome battle before us."

"There are none but those we see," said Maerad absently. She was concentrating all her attention in front of her. "They cannot get another spell through the wards – I think they have been trying. And perhaps they do not know that that first spell has been broken. They do not seem anxious."

"No," said Cadvan, peering through the dusk. "My walls aren't giving them much trouble – they are breaking them as they ride. My wards are still strong, so far as I can see; they shouldn't be able to tell what is happening here. I would give much, all the same, to know how they slid that spell past my magery. It hurts my pride."

"If that is the worst hurt you suffer this night, my friend, I will not pity you," said Saliman.

"Shhh." Maerad glanced at the Bards sternly, and turned back to the Hulls. Saliman cocked an ironic eyebrow over her head at Cadvan, who almost smiled.

Maerad was waiting for the Hulls to come close enough so that she could be sure of destroying all of them at once. Her contempt for them lay like nausea in her stomach; at this moment she felt no pity, no stirrings of conscience, no division of her will. She had no doubt that the Hulls planned to murder her brother and her friends, and to take her captive. They deserved no mercy.

Suddenly, as if they had appeared out of nowhere, the Hulls were visible to the naked eye. They must have broken through one of Cadvan's shields, which had also stripped them of the sorcery that hitherto had concealed them. At the same moment that they became visible, the Hulls sighted their prey, and they drew together and quickened their pace.

Maerad drew in her breath. They seemed much closer now that she could see them, and she felt the Bards beside her flinch at the force of the malignant wills which were now focused upon them with deadly intent. From here she could see the red light that burned in the shadows of their hoods, and the bony hands that held the reins of their horses: and she also saw that the steeds they rode were not living horses, but beasts of carrion, held together and driven by the wills of those who rode them. For the first time she felt horror creep into her heart.

The Hulls were riding now in a semicircle, and she knew that the most powerful sorcerers were in the middle, like the keystones of an arch. Clearly, when they came close enough, they planned to encircle their camp so there would be no chance to escape. They rode arrogantly, sure of their success, and Maerad's lip curled.

She closed her eyes, and sought the Hulls in the shadow world. They were easy to find: they wavered before her, insubstantial forms like fumes of poisonous smoke. They were not aware of her. Hulls could not enter the planes where she now moved.

Slowly, Maerad drew in a deep breath. It was a breath that no living human could take: she inhaled the icy mists that hung over the mountains, the wild briny gales of the sea, the mild spring breezes that wandered over the Hollow Lands, river winds and summer storms and the high still air that stood beneath the stars, drawing them into the very depth of her being. And then, pursing her lips as if she were about to play a pipe, she blew it out at the smoky forms of the Hulls.

There was a brief, panicked turbulence, as the Hulls attempted to resist the force of Maerad's breath, but in this place they were powerless. In moments the wisping vapours that were their souls dissipated and vanished, and it was as if they had never been.

Maerad opened her eyes, and the Hulls were gone. In their places were fourteen small piles of bone and cloth, and then, wafting towards them on the mild breeze, a faint stench of rotting meat. She smiled.

Saliman was speechless, his mouth open with shock. Cadvan cleared his throat, attempted to speak and stuttered into silence. He cleared his throat again.

"By the Light," he said, when he had mastered himself. "I think that beats the singing a lullaby to a stormdog for simplicity and economy, Maerad. But I wish I had known that you simply had to blow at Hulls to get rid of them. It would have saved me a few scars."

"The night is clean again." Maerad turned to the Bards, her eyes glittering. The pallor of her face was now relieved by red flushes of fever high on her cheekbones.

"That's not possible," Saliman said slowly. "I am not sure, much as I loathe Hulls, that I want to see the like again. I –" He broke off, shaking his head, and sheathed his sword. He gave Maerad a straight look. "I think, Maerad, you are the greatest peril I have ever encountered."

"Not to you," she said. "Not to anyone I love."

"A lightning strike or a tempest does not distinguish between friend and foe," said Saliman.

Maerad eyes blazed with anger. "Mistrust me if you will," she said.

"Think not that I mistrust you," said Saliman gently. "Anyone who witnesses what you have just done and claims they are not afraid of that power is either a liar or a fool. And for all my faults, I am neither of those."

Maerad met his eyes for a long moment, and her face

softened. Impulsively she flung her arms around Saliman's neck
and kissed his cheek, and then without saying anything more,
she turned back to the camp. She wanted to talk to Hem.

That night, freed for the moment of the fear of pursuit, they
made a large fire and sat long in talk as a ripening moon rose
into a clear spring sky. Outside the circle of firelight it was
a cold night, but none of them felt the chill. Cadvan made a
stew of rabbit flavoured with wild sage and thyme and, aside
from the grim stories they all had to tell, it was a merry gathering.

The horses, with the exception of Darsor, had panicked and
run off, but were swiftly tracked down with Darsor's help, and
now were exchanging equine gossip as they casually cropped
the turf nearby. Irc had returned cautiously after the confrontation with the Hulls, his feathers still stiff with alarm, and had
been formally introduced to Maerad and Cadvan. He wanted
to dislike Maerad – he was a jealous bird, and he regarded
Hem as his own special possession – but when she greeted him
respectfully and offered him some food he allowed himself to
be charmed, and even hopped onto her forearm, a special sign
of trust.

Hem had been shocked when he saw Maerad's hand, and
at first he tried to avoid looking at it, as the sight pained him.
Maerad herself was no longer self-conscious about her missing
fingers and gestured as freely as she had before her hand was
maimed; and gradually Hem became more used to her injury
and didn't feel a stab in his heart every time he glimpsed it
out of the corner of his eye. They sat very close to each other,
and joked and squabbled as if they were any brother and sister
meeting again after a long parting. Except, thought Cadvan,
for the magery that still flickered subtly under Maerad's skin,
surrounding her form with a faint, ever-changing nimbus of

golden light. She remained pale and feverish, her eyes unnaturally bright, and Cadvan noticed with concern that she ate very little, and only when pressed. She gave most of her meal to Irc.

Everyone agreed they could not stay where they were, but no one knew where they ought to go. Innail, their nearest haven, was quite likely to be under attack again from the forces gathered in Desor, and travelling in that direction would very likely bring an unwelcome encounter with the army. The closest Schools were Desor and Ettinor, but none of them had any inclination to travel that way. Maerad remained silent, staring into the fire. Irc had crept onto her lap and was crooning as she idly stroked his neck, and Hem was beginning to nod with sleep.

"The main question," said Cadvan, "is the Treesong. If we understood what happened today, perhaps we could decide what we should do."

All eyes turned towards Maerad.

"I don't understand it, either," she said slowly. "It's difficult to explain, even to myself..."

"Can you guess what was wrong?" asked Saliman.

"Something was missing." Maerad paused, as if she were trying to listen to an inner voice, and then shook her head. "But I don't know what it was..."

"Hekibel, you knew that it wasn't running true," said Saliman. Hekibel, who had been almost as silent as Maerad during this discussion, looked up. "I am wondering how you knew, and whether that same knowing might tell us something?"

"I know nothing of magery," said Hekibel, her voice low.

"Saliman and I are not considered beginners in the arts," said Cadvan. "And yet we had no inkling of any trouble."

"Perhaps Hekibel felt it because she has no training, and we were hampered by what we expected, instead of looking at what was in front of our noses," said Saliman. "It is not Bardic magery, after all, and it moves in other ways. Simpler ways, perhaps."

"I suppose, for me, it was a bit like a scene in a play where somebody has forgotten the lines, or the scenery is wrong, or a player is missing, or something like that," said Hekibel. "But, well, worse. In a play, you're just pretending that people die, but I thought that if it went on much longer, Hem and Maerad would really be killed..."

Maerad looked up, startled. "Not killed," she said. "Worse, maybe..." There was a silence, as the others waited for her to explain what she meant. She started to speak, and then stopped, biting her lip.

"It's difficult to talk about," she said at last. "I don't have the right words; they don't fit, somehow. I mean, as you know, it often happens in magery that if the – if the circumstance is right, then the action follows. And so, when the lyre and the tuning fork were close together, it was as if the Treesong woke up and – *became* something, almost as if there was another person there." She frowned with concentration. "And the Treesong was there, it wanted to be whole, and that wanting was all there was, and it just got more and more unbearable because whatever it wanted couldn't happen. And there was nothing else in the whole world except that wanting. And if Hekibel hadn't made the Treesong sleep again, Hem and I would have been trapped in that wanting, with no way out of it." She lifted her hands in frustration. "I can't say it properly," she said.

"What does it want?" said Cadvan.

"To be whole. To be free. To be alive." She remembered, with a sudden stab of pain, the Winterking's bitterness when he had told her the meanings of the runes on her lyre in his cold throne room in Arkan-da. "Arkan said – he said the runes were dead, that Nelsor had trapped the power of the Treesong within them, like a flower in ice. He said they were a song, and I had to play them. And when I said I didn't know the music, he said..." She swallowed, recalling his icy rage, the strange mix of fear and desire that Arkan had invoked within her. "He said, *Do you think anything can be alive, when it is cloven in half?*"

Hem sat up, his eyes shining. "I'm the music," he said. "That's what Nyanar meant." Maerad looked at him inquiringly, and he explained. "Nyanar was an Elidhu I spoke to, in the Suderain. He was ... I don't know how to describe how he was." Hem paused, remembering. "He told me there were two foretold. *One for the singing and one for the music.*" Hem slumped and looking broodingly at the ground. "Only the music didn't happen. I know what the music sounds like ... I mean, I know what it *feels* like. But it didn't feel like that at all today..."

"Arkan also said that the Song could only be sung with love." The high flush on Maerad's cheeks brightened, as if she were making a shameful confession. "And that love can't be stolen or feigned, that it can only be given." She paused. "I don't know what that means, either."

"These are deep riddles," Cadvan said, half smiling. "All the same, I think that whatever was missing today, it was not love."

"Perhaps we have to go back to the beginning? I mean, where all this began?" said Hekibel hesitantly.

Maerad stared at her. "Yes," she said. "Yes, I think so ... but nobody knows when the Treesong was first sung. There's that story Ankil told us, about the Split Song..."

"Ah yes," said Cadvan. "*So the Song came out of the nowhere into the now, and slipped into the veins of the Elidhu, as if it were a shoal of minnows slipping into a stream, and each Elidhu felt the Song*

*within it like a shudder of life, and all the sounds of the world burst in
on them: the fall of the rain, and the sough of the sea, and the endless
sighing of the wind through the green trees. And they opened their
mouths in wonder, and so it was the Song leapt out of their mouths,
and at last became itself."*

"That's beautiful," said Hekibel, listening intently.

Saliman was staring at his hands, his mobile face thought-
ful. "I think what might have been missing was the right
place," he said. "It would only make sense. The Elidhu are creatures of place, after all. But then, where would that place be?
The Winterking's mountain? Or perhaps somewhere like Nal-
Ak-Burat, where Hem saw Nyanar?"

Maerad shook her head, and Cadvan spoke. "That's unlikely,
I think," he said. "From what Maerad has told me, the Song
doesn't belong to any one Elidhu."

"Well, then, where it first appeared in Edil-Amarandh," said
Saliman. "Wherever that might be."

"It's not the Treesong we should be thinking about, but the
runes," said Maerad softly. "And the runes were made in Afinil,
by Nelsor himself, in the deeps of time…"

"If it is a matter of undoing what has been wrongly done,
then the place of the doing is the proper place," said Cadvan.
He sounded as if he were quoting something, and Saliman
looked up and unexpectedly laughed.

"Menellin's Rules," he said. "Learned by rote by every
Minor Bard in Annar. How many times I wished, as I chanted
them over and over again in the learning halls and watched the
sun playing outside, that he hadn't written so many! But yes,
perhaps it will do to remember our first lessons…"

Maerad was staring fixedly into the fire, her eyes shining.

"Afinil is the place," she said. As she spoke, it seemed to
those who listened that echoes gathered around her words, as
if many voices spoke behind hers. "We must journey to Afinil

for the singing. Under the sign of Ura, by ash, alder and willow, in the season of renewal…"

There was a blank silence.

"That is all very fine," said Cadvan at last. "But Afinil no longer exists. The Nameless One loathed that city above all others and scoured it from the face of the earth. Even its ruins were ground into dust and scattered on the sixteen winds. And no one living can tell where once it stood."

XIX

THE DANCE OF THE DEAD

THAT night, Maerad didn't sleep. She lay on her back, her eyes open, staring at the blackness of the rough stone above her and listening to the gentle breathing of her companions. Hem stirred restlessly in his sleep and began to snore, and she smiled at the sound, thinking of the times when she had held him in her arms and stilled his nightmares. It seemed so long ago, in another lifetime. That was before she had even known that he was her brother. Though something inside her had known the first moment she saw him, cowering in the wrecked caravan in the middle of the Valverras.

Hem was much changed since then. It wasn't only that he had grown at least two handspans and was now taller than Maerad by a head. He had always been thin, but his face had lost the softness of childhood, and his body had the ranginess of a young colt, at once awkward and graceful. It was possible now to see clearly the young man he would soon be.

To have found Hem at last was a deep happiness that lay, like a glowing coal, in the middle of her being, and she warmed herself against it like a shivering child. Beyond that one simple thing, all was uncertain. After her reunion with Hem, what she remembered most vividly when she thought about the previous day was the flash of fear in Saliman's face when she had destroyed the Hulls. Cadvan had promised not to be afraid of her, and yet even he could not entirely conceal his own anxiety. But what were her powers? Even now, she felt she had little understanding of these forces that moved through her: she was a vessel, nothing more. The Treesong had its own imperative, and she was merely its instrument, for good or ill. The thought filled her with an aching emptiness.

It's strange, she thought. The more powerful I become, the less choice I seem to have about anything. She felt as if she were fixed on the rim of a great wheel, which was turning slowly towards the singing of the Treesong. No force on earth could stop its inevitable revolution: and yet she didn't know what would happen, what might begin or end with the undoing of Nelsor's magery. Beyond the act of the singing, everything was blank.

I might die, she thought. Hem might die. Everything I love might be swept away. Cadvan and Saliman know that, yet still they stand by me. They do not think of turning back, although they do not know what they will meet at the end. They must be allowed their fear, if they are so brave in the face of it. Am I as brave as that? Why do I feel so lonely?

Maerad gazed into the darkness. She had no right to feel such self-pity. She might be in the middle of the wilderness, in mortal danger, but with her were the people she loved most in the world. Somehow, that only made her feel worse. If she failed, their lives were forfeit. She thought of Cadvan's choice to stand by her, his willingness to risk everything he believed in for his faith in her. Was she equal to such faith? She feared, deeply, that she would fail him, that she was weaker than he thought.

At last she gave up trying to sleep. She wrapped her blanket around her and wandered outside to sit with Cadvan, who was keeping the watch. He turned and smiled as she sat next to him, but said nothing. It was the coldest part of the night; the turf glittered with rime under the still moonlight, and Cadvan's breath curled white on the air.

Maerad stared over the hills, and she thought that she could feel the landscape's very bones. As she watched, it seemed to her that a dance of shadows began to unfold and dissolve before her, a dance of such intricacy and nuance that she could barely comprehend it. But she knew it was a dance of the same echoes and shadows that had haunted her dreams the past few nights.

It was a dance of the dead, but now she saw them with her waking senses. She heard their voices ringing dimly on the frosty air, and saw the soft nimbus of their numberless shifting forms. This time she was not afraid; she knew that these were not revenants, the undead who walked again, but rather their memory. Time seemed to her to move in veils that constantly shifted, one over the other, dissolving as swiftly as she perceived them, and through its layers she could follow the shimmering traces of those who had lived here. She saw not only the shadow marks of what they had made or broken with their hands, but the passions that had lived within them: their hatreds and loves and griefs and desires and fears. Every moment when time had stopped under the intense impression of feeling – the joy of a young child at the return of its father, the ardour of lovers, the moment of dying – sang faintly through the fabric of the earth, filling the Hollow Lands with an eerie, melancholy music.

Maerad caught her breath and turned to Cadvan, her heart beating fast, and she cried out. In that moment she clearly saw the skull beneath the skin and muscles of his face, and she knew she was seeing the future of his own death. The vision filled her with utter desolation: how could she bear a world without Cadvan in it?

Cadvan took her hand, urgently asking what troubled her. At once the vision vanished; but Maerad did not know how to tell him what she had seen, and held his hand tightly until her grief and horror began to subside.

She lifted her eyes from the earth and stared at the moon,

which blazed high in the black, frosty night. She realized it would not be very long – seven or eight days, perhaps – before it waxed to the full.

"I have been thinking that the most likely place to look for Afinil is in the Hutmoors," said Cadvan, after a long silence, "though it could have been near Rachida. Or even Rachida itself."

"Wherever it is, we have to find it quickly," said Maerad. "We have to get there before the moon is full. Or it will be too late. Not just for us, I mean, but for everyone: for Innail, for all of Annar…"

"I don't like our chances," Cadvan said. "But then, I never have. And yet we have come this far."

Maerad nodded. "How long would it take to ride to the Hutmoors?" she asked.

"It depends. We could get there in five days, riding hard. But where Afinil might be in that sorry, desolate place, I do not know."

"Ardina would know where it was. She went there when Nelsor was alive…"

"We need all the help we can get," said Cadvan.

Maerad thought a little longer, and then stood up and went back to the shelter. She returned with her pipes and, standing close by Cadvan, she began to play them. The tune she played was sad, and the notes echoed plaintively in the still night. But this time, Ardina did not come.

At last, Maerad gave up and sat down disconsolately, holding her pipes in her maimed hand. "Why will she not answer me?" she said.

"I don't know," said Cadvan. "But both you and Hem have spoken of how the Elidhu fear and loathe the Treesong. It could be that, now the runes are close together, they emanate a great power, and she cannot come."

"But how are we to find Afinil without her help?"

Cadvan didn't answer for a long time. Finally he said, "If we are meant to find it, we will. But you should sleep, Maerad, especially if we are to begin our journey tomorrow."

"I can't sleep," said Maerad. "I don't think I'll ever sleep again."

Cadvan was about to tell her that she must sleep, that she could not contemplate travelling on no sleep at all, but something in her face, the traces of a deep and inarticulate pain, made him bite his tongue. Maerad stared out with burning eyes over the dim hills, and clutched her blanket more tightly around her body, although she was no longer conscious of the cold.

Hem dreamed of the Black Army that he had seen marching towards Desor. In his dream, the dead soldiers that lay strewn behind the army in the flood plains had risen and were marching on rotting feet, their blank eyes staring at nothing. When he awoke, he remembered that he had seen eyes with that same horrifying blankness in his waking life. They had stared out of the faces of the snouts, the child soldiers of the Dark, when they were bewitched in battle fever.

He rose quickly and walked to a nearby brook, where he splashed his face with cold water to wash away the memory. He tried not to think about his time with the snouts. Sometimes he thought it wasn't possible, even in the many moments of darkness that scarred his life, that he had lived through anything so terrible. But it hadn't been a dream.

And that reality, the world of Sjug'hakar Im, marched with the Black Army. It was that reality which had destroyed Baladh and Turbansk and perhaps had already smashed the walls of Til Amon. In Sjug'hakar Im, children were turned into brutalized killers, and beauty or gentleness or courage were mocked, tormented and destroyed. Hem had seen children who were broken beyond the hope of repair, whose empty stares spoke of suffering so unspeakable there were no words that comprehended it; he had seen faces twisted and distorted by insanity and pain, faces blind with terror and anger, and dead faces, too many dead faces...

He thought of his friend Zelika. He hadn't seen her face, after she died. Sometimes he didn't know whether he was grateful to be spared that memory, or whether he had been denied his chance to make a proper farewell. Her lovely, savage features rose in his mind's eye, as vividly as if she now stood before him; and his grief for her opened again inside him, raw and bloody, as if he knew it for the first time. Nothing would ever compensate that loss, nothing would ever heal that wound; even if the Nameless One were defeated and all his works should turn to dust and vanish utterly, Zelika would still be dead. In her death lay all the injustice, all the needless waste, of this terrible war.

Hem splashed water over his head again, gasping at the cold. He didn't want these thoughts. The Dark had torn apart his whole life, but undoing the Treesong didn't mean undoing the terrible things that had happened, and he would never be rid of his memories. He set his jaw, staring unseeingly over the purple dawn-lit hills, towards the mist-shrouded peaks of the distant mountains.

He returned to the others, and busied himself helping to strike the camp. No one argued with Cadvan's suggestion that they should travel to the Hutmoors. Hem merely nodded; it seemed like the right direction to him. An earthsense was stirring in his body, like a melody he couldn't quite hear, calling him north.

Everyone seemed to feel the same urgency, as if they knew that time was running out. They packed quickly and left soon after first light, riding north-west along the borders of

the Hollow Lands, Hem still riding behind Hekibel on Usha.
They averted their faces from the rags and bones and piles of
carrion that were the only remains of the Hulls and their
mounts, and pushed the horses as swiftly as they could over the
low hills. There was a hint of warmth in the sunlight that fell on
their shoulders, and the horses were rested and eager, and the
empty lands passed by them swiftly. By twilight they had left
the Hollow Lands and were approaching the Milhol River, two
days' ride south of Milhol itself. A stone Bard Road ran alongside the water, following the river through the Broken Hills to
Ettinor.

Maerad stared at the brown river, with its banks of black
reeds poking through the surface of the sullen water, and
remembered that her first sight of a Hull had been not very
far from this place, further down the road in the Broken Hills.
The fears she had felt then seemed utterly unimaginable now.
Perhaps, she thought sardonically, she had since encountered
much worse terrors.

Despite her lack of sleep, she felt no tiredness at all, but her
vision was troubling her. The shadow world she had first seen
the night before had vanished with the morning sunlight, but
as the day wore on, the veils began to return, so that sometimes
she wasn't sure which landscape she was riding through – or
more accurately, which *time*. And the hauntings were becoming
clearer. Once she saw a long line of people hurrying through a
mist, burdened by their belongings, and it seemed to her that
they were fleeing in terror. They looked over their shoulders
as if in fear of pursuit, and Maerad thought that she saw in
their eyes the reflections of flames; but she shook her head and
the vision vanished. Another time, near the last circle of standing stones that they passed before they left the Hollow Lands,
she saw an old man with a very long beard, tall and thin as
a young birch, his arms up-reached to the sky in mysterious

supplication. Towards evening, a child ran in front of her, laughing, and Maerad pulled Keru up sharply, fearing he would be trampled beneath her hooves, before she saw that the child was not there. There was something melancholy about all these visions, and Maerad did not speak of them to anyone.

When they reached the Milhol River, they halted briefly and scanned the countryside. It was deserted; the stone road shone white in the late afternoon light, and nothing moved as far as the eye could see. The only sign of life was a pair of hawks circling high overhead and some grey herons stalking in the reeds.

"No floods here," said Saliman, staring at the flat plains of Peredur that lay on the other side of the river. "Thank the Light. I've had enough of mud to last me a lifetime."

"Aye," said Cadvan. "Luck runs with us, so far. If we cross here, we can ride north of the Broken Hills and then cross the Usk Bridge to the Hutmoors, keeping well away from Ettinor. My only fear was that the Milhol might have flooded, and slowed us down. But I think we should go swiftly here; there is something I do not like in this silence, and I don't want to stay on this side of the river."

At this point the river was wide but shallow, with broad, firm sandbanks on either side, so it was not difficult to cross. The light was failing fast as they forded but, although the horses were stumbling with weariness, they rode on until after dusk before they stopped.

Maerad offered to keep watch, since she felt no desire to sleep, but Cadvan, studying her with concern, forbade it and insisted that she rest. Although he did not say so, he was deeply concerned about her. It was more than a day since she had used her power, but her skin still shone with the strange, golden magery; if anything, it seemed brighter than before. And he thought there was something fey in her eyes, a flickering like madness, as if she were seeing things that were not there. He remembered what she had told him about her dreams, and shrewdly guessed what she might be looking at. This night she had refused to eat at all, only drinking water and, at Hem's insistence, some medhyl, and she barely spoke.

All day, Maerad had felt as if she were diminishing; the infinite power she had touched when she summoned Hem or when she had destroyed the Hulls now seemed out of reach, unimaginable, as if it had happened to another person. Her body seemed as fragile and light as a piece of spun glass and she felt her mortality more strongly than she ever had in her life. She sensed the Treesong glowing in her skin, and a faint murmur that she knew was a presage of its music seemed still to resonate in her bones. Yet instead of filling her with power, this half-music left her desolate and empty, as if she were no more substantial than the shadows of the dead, an illusion glimpsed on a darkling plain that might vanish in the next instant.

A warm south wind rose, rushing over the grasses and thrashing the branches of the trees where they had sought shelter. A layer of clouds spread over the sky, and the moon rose blurred and dim, casting a pale light over the empty lands around them. Hem had the first watch, and sat cross-legged listening to the wind, Irc nestled fast asleep on his lap like a kitten. Hem was so tired that he didn't think anything at all: he was just ears and eyes, his senses poured out passively into the night, alert for any change in its rhythms that might signal danger.

The moon was climbing to its zenith when Maerad joined him. He didn't need to turn to know exactly where Maerad was: her presence burned in his consciousness like a flaming torch, so that he was almost surprised when he looked at her and only saw the faint golden shimmer that rippled through her skin.

"Aren't you sleeping?" he asked.

"No," said Maerad, almost petulantly. "It's boring just lying there. I don't want to stop, we should be riding still, we have so little time..."

"We wouldn't get anywhere if the horses collapsed with exhaustion," said Hem practically. "And even if you're not, I'm pretty tired."

Maerad didn't answer. She was staring over the plains, and Hem, sensitive to her thoughts, knew she was watching something that he couldn't see. He stirred uneasily, and she turned, suddenly aware of him.

"Are you afraid of me?" she asked abruptly.

Hem met her eyes. In the darkness they burned with a cold, blue light, and she seemed to be looking both at him and through him.

"No," said Hem. "Are you?"

Maerad looked briefly taken aback, and then laughed. "No ... yes, I am, I think," she said. "I think – maybe – I ought to be afraid." She took Hem's hand and held it, palm up, staring at it broodingly as if she could read her future there. "Everyone else is afraid of me. They sit a little distance away, and they are careful what they say."

Hem shrugged. "Irc's not afraid of you," he said. "He thinks that you are like Nyanar."

"The Elidhu you met?" A smile quirked Maerad's lips. "What does he mean?"

"I think he means kind of – wild and sad. You don't feel like an Elidhu to me, though."

"What do I feel like, then?" Maerad looked at him challengingly.

"Like my sister." Hem glanced at Maerad, and then looked away. "I think I am afraid *for* you," he said, after a silence. "I mean, none of us knows what all this means. And sometimes

I just think it means that soon we'll all be dead, no matter what happens, and that seems so unfair." He paused. "And right now you look as if you have a terrible fever, and you ought to be in bed."

"But I don't have a fever."

"I know you don't. You just look as if you do. And it's bad that you're not eating and sleeping, and I think that it must be the Treesong inside you somehow, or something like that, that won't let you go. I don't feel it like you do, but I can kind of feel it in you. And I think it's not something that a human body can bear for very long, and I wonder how long you can go on."

Maerad's eyebrows lifted in surprise, and her gaze faltered.

"I'm a Healer," Hem said, his voice low. "If I touch you, I can feel that your body is like – like one of the strings on your lyre, and it's humming with a note that I can't hear, and it's so awfully tight. But I know you can't stop it happening. So, yes, of course I'm afraid for you. But I'm not afraid of you."

"You're a Healer?" Maerad studied Hem with a new respect. He spoke with an authority she had not heard in his voice before. Her hand closed tightly on Hem's. "It's strange," she said. "Since we – since the Treesong almost happened, I've been feeling so lonely. I didn't know why ... but I think that the Elidhu have gone away. I think that they used to be with me all the time, Ardina and Arkan; even when I didn't know they were there, they knew where I was, and they were – beside me somehow. I didn't know until they went away. And now they're gone, and it's so empty."

"I'm here," said Hem stolidly, and he took Maerad's maimed hand between both of his.

Maerad's hand shook, and he heard her gasp. "Yes," she said. Her voice was muffled.

"It won't ever be like it should have been," said Hem. He

was suddenly very aware of Maerad's smallness: he was already taller than she was, and the bones in her hand felt fragile, like those of a bird's. "We should have just grown up together in Pellinor, quarrelling and playing together, like children do when you see them... It wasn't like that, and it's not ever going to be like that. I hate the people who did that to us. You're my sister, and I always knew that you were, and I missed you all those years, even without knowing that I did. Even if we don't get through this, I'm glad that I'm here. And I love you, no matter what happens."

Maerad sat very still, and the light within her seemed to burn more brightly. At last she turned to Hem, her eyes shining with tears. "I love you too, my brother," she whispered.

She leaned forward and kissed his brow, and the gentle touch of her lips was like a brand on Hem's soul. Then she stood up and walked away into the night, wrapping her cloak tightly around her against the wind. Hem watched her pacing restlessly to and fro, a faint golden light in the darkness, and it seemed to him that he had never seen anyone so lonely.

Over the next few days, Maerad's sense of confusion deepened. She felt that in some indefinable way she was losing touch with herself. It was a struggle to remain in the present, to be aware of the landscape through which she was travelling; sometimes she felt as if she were trapped in an endless, shadowy dream. If she concentrated hard on shutting down her Bard senses, or if she pinched her flesh, she found sudden moments of clarity in which she was just Maerad, nothing more, in a single present. These moments were a profound relief.

In some ways, it was more difficult because she found it hard to adjust to travelling in company. Over the past year she had never journeyed with more than one person, and the presence of Saliman and Hekibel, much as she liked them, disrupted the

casual rhythm of her intimacy with Cadvan. Maerad was surprised to feel a stirring of jealousy. Cadvan was transparently
pleased to see Saliman, who was, after all, one of his oldest
and closest friends, and the two Bards usually rode side by
side and often talked long into the night. She understood, with
pained surprise, that Cadvan, too, had been lonely over the
previous weeks, that their friendship was compromised by
the anxieties he felt about their quest, by his doubts, even by
his worry for Maerad herself. The thought filled her with a
dragging regret; she thought about how much she leaned on
his support, and wondered at her own thoughtlessness. At
times Cadvan and Saliman seemed completely carefree, as if,
now that they were nearing the unknown end of their quest,
they could allow smaller anxieties to fall away; and Maerad
realized that it had been a long time since she and Cadvan had
laughed together. Perhaps their friendship was not as strong as
she had thought.

She had not eaten a meal nor slept since they had left the
Hollow Lands, and yet she felt no hunger, nor any diminish-
ment in her energy. Cadvan offered her food every night,
and she felt a rebuke in his silence when she refused, even as
she was relieved he did not pressure her. Cadvan's silence was
tact rather than disapproval, but she did not realize this; nor
was she aware of the concern in his eyes when his gaze rested
on her. Cadvan's expression was almost always guarded, but
at times his fear for Maerad appeared nakedly: when he saw
her standing outside at midnight, staring at things visible to no
one else; or once when she almost rode Keru straight into a tree
that she had not seen because her eyes perceived a landscape
that was no longer there. Although he didn't speak of them,
Cadvan was more aware of the shadows that troubled Maerad
than she knew.

And both he and Saliman were very conscious of Maerad's

fragility. Without drawing attention to it, they made sure that she took no shifts on the watch at night, so that she was never alone. Nights bored her: sometimes she lay down as if she were sleeping, feeling her body humming with the living power that never left her, or she walked restlessly through the grass, gazing south to the jagged peaks of the Broken Hills, where she sensed a great, heavy shadow, or west towards the Hutmoors; but most often she would sit with whoever kept watch.

On the second night, she shared a long watch with Hekibel. She found that Hekibel was unexpectedly charming company, with an unspoken gift of understanding that was leavened with a sharp wit. Her conversation soothed Maerad, and for a time it was no struggle to remain in the present, and her ghostly visions vanished. Hekibel passed the time by telling Maerad comic stories about her life as a player. She told them well, and Maerad's laughter echoed over the empty plains and startled a hunting owl, which swooped sharply away from them, hooting in alarm.

The wind had shifted during the day and died down. There had been a light rain earlier in the evening and the good smell of damp spring earth rose in the night air. Maerad felt more light-hearted than she had since leaving Innail. When Hekibel asked Maerad about her childhood, she answered without discomfort. It was pleasant to talk to a woman, to lean into Hekibel's sympathetic, unjudging ear.

Maerad asked Hekibel why she had not chosen to go to Innail with Grigar when they had left Desor, where she would have been safer than she was journeying through the wilderness on their uncertain quest. Hekibel, who liked to keep her hands busy, was rubbing fat into her boots, and when Maerad asked this question she paused, her face serious, and did not answer for a time. Finally she looked at Maerad ruefully, and laughed.

"I fear very much that I have fallen in love with Saliman," she said. "And I think I would follow him to the ends of the earth."

For a moment Maerad didn't know what to say. "Oh," she said, and then she blushed. "Does – does Saliman know?"

Hekibel was silent for a time. "I can't imagine that he doesn't," she said. "You Bards can see things that others can't. He is always very gentle when he speaks to me, but I rather think that is because he pities me." Hekibel grinned wryly. "It is difficult not to feel a little foolish…"

Maerad clasped her hand. "Oh, no, please don't feel foolish," she said, with a rush of warmth. "It isn't foolish to love. Cadvan said to me once that to love is never wrong. *It may be disastrous; it may never be possible; it may be the deepest agony. But it is never wrong.* I've never forgotten it; it seems true to me." She met Hekibel's eyes, her own gaze suddenly clear and present. "In any case, I think that Saliman does love you."

Hekibel turned her eyes away. "If he does," she said, "I don't know how anyone would know. He conceals it well."

Maerad studied Hekibel's profile, the dark blonde hair that curled out from her hood, her soft, sensuous mouth. She envied Hekibel's beauty: next to her luscious roundness, Maerad felt thin and sharp. Hekibel's skin had the golden bloom of a winter apple, smooth and rich, but her sweetness was never cloying: she was too intelligent, too strong. Of course Saliman loved this woman.

"It's obvious that he likes you," she said at last. She realized she was not used to this kind of conversation between women, and suddenly wished fiercely that Silvia was with them. Silvia would know the right thing to say.

"I know that," said Hekibel. She began to rub her boots with renewed vigour. "And his friendship is precious to me. But all the same, I can't help wanting more than that. I wish I were a

Bard, or that he wasn't. He is the most handsome, most generous man that I have ever met. When I left him there, sick to death in Hiert – I wanted to die…"

"There's no reason why a Bard might not love someone without the Gift. It can be difficult, that's all, because Bards are so long-lived. I met a Bard once who told me – he was very old, and his wife had been dead two hundred years, and he still misses her… That's probably why Saliman might not speak to you about this. Quite apart from – well, none of us know if we'll be alive in a week…"

"I wish all the same that he would look at me like Cadvan looks at you." Hekibel looked critically at her boots, and laid them carefully side by side on the grass. "Well, a dog might howl at the moon…"

Maerad blinked. "What do you mean, how Cadvan looks at me?"

"If I saw near so much passion in Saliman's face, I would be buying my wedding clothes," said Hekibel. "That is, assuming there are any weddings after all this."

Maerad's mouth dropped open. For a long moment she was too shocked to say anything at all. "Passion?" she said. "Cadvan is my very dear – my dearest – friend, but I don't think…"

Hekibel looked sideways at Maerad. "You mean you haven't noticed? If that's mere friendship, my dear, then I have never in my life seen a man in love. And I assure you that I have. I can tell you, if my heart were not already ensnared, I might be in very great danger of falling in love with Cadvan myself. Have you never realized how handsome he is?"

Maerad was silent for some time, trying to gather her scattered wits. She felt as stunned as if Hekibel had struck her in the face. She thought back over her recent conversations with Cadvan. It was true that something had changed in his manner since they had reunited in Pellinor. She had thought it an expression of a deepened understanding between them, a deeper friendship; but it had never occurred to her that he might have fallen in love with her.

Hekibel, her expression inscrutable, was studying Maerad's face. "Is it that you don't return the feeling?" she asked at last. "That can be awkward, especially if you are fond of a person..."

"I – I don't know." Maerad said this in whisper. "I haven't thought about it." But was that true, she wondered? Perhaps she had thought about it, and had always pushed it to the back of her mind. It was easy to admit that she loved Dernhil, because he was dead and no longer asked anything of her. She had always known that the Winterking did not love her, at least not in any way she could begin to understand, so that her feelings about him were again easier to admit.

But Cadvan ... was different... She found it difficult to breathe, as if her chest were constricted with terror, but perhaps it wasn't terror at all. Underneath she felt something else; at the thought that Cadvan might love her, a warm rush of excitement made her heart flutter like a dazed bird. Perhaps she had been more truthful than she realized when she had told Cadvan that she knew nothing of love.

Hekibel was watching her closely. "I've upset you," she said. "I'm sorry, Maerad. It was stupid of me. I just meant that Cadvan is very fond of you, and it's obvious. And, well, it's silly to be talking about love like an air-headed girl when we're in the middle of this terrible war, with the Black Army marching through Annar and Hulls on our tail and who knows what awful things happening to people all over Edil-Amarandh." Her eyes were dark and serious, but then she smiled. "It's just a little difficult to keep my mind on the war when Saliman's around."

"No, I'm not upset. I just feel a bit – shocked." Maerad looked down at her hands. "I don't think I know very much about love. Well, that kind of love. And when I do think about it, it frightens me. I am not very brave, I think. Perhaps I ought to be braver." She smiled wryly. "Although the only time I thought I fell in love, it was with an Elidhu, so perhaps I am not so cowardly, after all…"

Hekibel's eyebrows shot up. "An Elidhu?" she said. "That puts me in my place. I mean, what's a Bard compared to an immortal?"

Maerad looked up, fearing mockery, and saw that Hekibel's eyes twinkled with wry mischief. Despite herself, she began to laugh.

They reached the Usk River, which marked the western border of the Hutmoors, after two days of hard riding. The river's course followed the bottom of a shallow valley, and in the distance on the opposite rise ran the Bard Road that led north from Ettinor.

When they topped the lip of the valley, they saw that the road was not empty. Directly ahead of them, and stretching south as far as the eye could see, marched a great army. They did not have to see the banners to know that it was the Black Army.

They hastily retreated behind the rise, and then everyone dismounted. It was obvious that they could not cross the Usk now.

Cadvan looked deeply shaken. "I think your friend Grigar was misled," he said to Saliman. "That must be the army you saw in Desor. But they are clearly not marching on Innail."

"No," said Saliman. "Lirigon lies at the end of that road. A week's march, I would say."

Cadvan gazed north towards Lirigon, and Maerad could see the struggle within him. "They must be warned," he said.

"We could not outrun them, even if we tried," said Saliman. "Their fore-riders are already well ahead of us, and they are moving swiftly. I am sure, all the same, that Lirigon will be prepared for some kind of attack."

"I doubt, even so, that they'll be expecting an army of this size. It's a bitter thought, that the Black Army will be laying waste to the city where I was born." Cadvan turned on his heel and walked abruptly away from the group, and Maerad saw, from the straightness of his back, that he wished to hide his grief from his friends. After all, what he feared for Lirigon had already happened to Saliman's own city, Turbansk, which now lay in ruins under the dominion of the Dark.

She wanted to follow and comfort him, but felt too shy. In fact, since her conversation with Hekibel, she had felt almost paralysed with shyness every time she spoke privately to Cadvan. She was now sure that she loved him, and had loved him all along, from the first moment that she had laid eyes on him. It was as if she had been walking around with her eyes closed. And with this realization had risen an agonizing doubt. Hekibel might, after all, be mistaken, and be reading too much into Cadvan's expressions of friendship.

Maerad also felt culpable. She should have known that the Black Army was so close; now she was aware of its presence, she wondered how she had missed it. The truth was that over the past few days she had been struggling to remain among the simple realities she craved, to shut out the awareness that haunted her with so many pasts, so many presents, so many futures. And she had mainly been preoccupied with her thoughts about Cadvan. Now she cursed herself: again she had been blind. If she had had her wits about her, perhaps they could have done something to warn Lirigon.

The sight of the Black Army was a shock: it was the first time she had seen such an army with her own eyes, outside a vision or dream. It did not compare with the Landrost's forces outside Innail. She realized that the mountain men, deadly and grim though they might be, were a mere rabble in comparison to this. She was not prepared for the dread that rose in her throat at the sight of it, how the long stream of warriors and wagons moved with such tangible, organized purpose towards death and destruction.

I don't like these armies, Irc said, from his perch on Hem's shoulder. Maerad looked up: he was speaking to all of them in the Speech. *They make the land frightened. Everything has gone so quiet...*

They frighten me, said Hem.

I'll fly over and see how big it is, said Irc.

I wish you wouldn't, said Hem. *Some Hull might let an arrow loose and shoot you.*

I'll be high up. They can't catch me. Irc launched himself into the air and hovered over their heads. *I'm a clever crow.*

He soared off, high up as he had promised, and Hem followed him with his eyes. "I hope he's as clever as he thinks he is," he said.

"He's certainly as cunning as he thinks he is," said Saliman. "And it would be useful, without any doubt, to know how long we will have to wait before this army passes and we can cross the river safely. For the moment, we're stuck where we are."

They found a cluster of trees where they could conceal the horses, unsaddled them, and settled down to wait. Cadvan rejoined them, his face grim, and Saliman and Hekibel silently brought out some food.

Maerad glanced anxiously at Cadvan, but he did not meet her eyes. Everything was beginning to waver again, as it had not done since she had spoken to Hekibel. The sight of the Black Army had shocked her out of her defences, and now she thought she could hear, at the edges of her perception, cries of sorrow and terror – a distant chorus of lamentation. She didn't know if what she sensed was her own feelings of fear and dread, or a premonition of the disaster that now threatened Lirigon, or if it was something else entirely; but she feared that if it became any clearer, if she could hear those voices properly, she would be drowned in an ocean of woe.

"What worries me right at this moment," said Cadvan, "is that a Hull will sense Maerad and send a party up here. I am not sure that even you, Maerad, could keep at bay thousands of soldiers."

Maerad looked up, and for a moment her eyes focused sharply in the present. "They look forward, not from side to side, and we are still quite a distance from them," she said. "They are in a great hurry. I do not think they will notice us."

Cadvan lifted his eyebrows. "I hope you're right," he said. "Although you should know, more than anyone, that the Nameless One will be seeking you as urgently as any victory in Annar, and I find it hard to believe that he would allow his forces to bypass you."

Maerad's face went still for a moment, as she pondered what Cadvan had said. She could sense the Hulls on the other side of the hill as clearly as if they stood in serried rows in front of her, and the attention of none of them was turned their way. What she felt was a terrible, intent purpose directly solely towards speed. "I still think they have not seen us," she said. "They're not keeping a guard up because nobody in their right mind would attack them…"

Hem, propelled by a masochistic curiosity, offered to keep an eye on the progress of the Black Army until Irc returned. He shielded himself, and then crawled up to the top of the ridge on his belly, hiding in the thick grass. He lay there watching the Black Army as it marched, like an obscene, many-legged monster, through the empty valley. Irc was right: the countryside was silent, as if the army's presence throttled the songs of birds in their very throats.

* * *

When Irc returned, he had a self-satisfied look that made Hem think that he'd taken the opportunity to do some pilfering. The army, Irc told them, was very big.

Any of us could see that with our own eyes, said Hem. *How big, do you think?*

Very big, Irc repeated. *Fives and fives and fives again and again. It took me a long time to fly to the end of it. They are leaving all sorts of treasures by the side of the road.*

So Irc had been pilfering, thought Hem with exasperation. His irritation stemmed from anxiety: Irc's curiosity could easily get him into trouble. And Hem couldn't help wishing that he could count past five.

Saliman was listening, his brow creased, and asked Irc if the army stretched back past the bridge that crossed the Usk.

No, said Irc. *Not that far. But it is still a very long line. And there are dogsoldiers and Hulls and snouts and lots of men. Many are Annaren and they are being driven by whips. I didn't go near any of them, there is too much braintwisting there, it makes me choke.*

Hem shuddered, wondering if the army included snouts that he had known in Sjug'hakar Im. It wasn't unlikely; the Hull at the camp had told them that the Nameless One had great plans for them and that they were being marched north.

"Lirigon doesn't have a chance," said Cadvan. He looked ill. "The last thing they would be expecting would be a great army coming up from Ettinor. No doubt the captains aim to arrive by night, and have most of the slaughter over before anyone stirs from their beds."

"They'd have guards, surely," said Hekibel, hesitantly.

"Yes. But they need more than sentries to be prepared for an attack like this."

Hem was listening intently, his dark eyes flickering from face to face. He looked at Irc, who was now attempting to burgle the food bag, since he was sure that his scouting deserved a reward.

Irc, said Hem. *Could you outfly the Black Army?*

Irc puffed out his chest feathers. *Of course. I am the fastest bird in the world.*

Hem smiled sardonically and put out his forearm. Irc hopped onto his arm, wiping his beak on the sleeve, and Hem brought him close to his chest, stroking his crisp feathers. *Do you think you could fly to Lirigon, to warn them about the Black Army? It would be a heroic, brave task.*

Irc went silent, and Hem felt the bird's alarm at the thought of leaving him. It kindled his own fears: what if something should happen to Irc? But what else could they do to save Lirigon?

Where is Lirigon? Irc asked at last.

It's a School at the end of the road. All you'd have to do would be to follow the road. But I think it's a long way.

Would it be a brave thing?

Yes. Hem smiled again. *Yes, it would. You would save many lives. You would be the bird that saved the city, like the heroes of tales of old.*

Irc fixed Hem with his eye, his head cocked to one side. *I do not like these armies*, he said. *I will help to fight them. But if it is a long way, I will miss you. I will fly very fast and come back as soon as I can.*

Hem stroked Irc's neck, and he put his head down, enjoying the tickling.

"Irc says that he will fly to Lirigon to warn the city," Hem said to the others. "He could certainly get there quicker than the army. And all he'd have to do would be to follow the road, so he wouldn't get lost."

Cadvan stared at Hem, his face lighting up. "Why did I not think of that?" Then he frowned in thought. "The only problem is that he has to find the right person to speak to. It's no use going all that way if no one listens, and it might be hard to get the right person to listen to a crow. However eminent he is. It would be good if he could carry a letter." He looked at Irc, and asked him in the Speech if he would take something to give to the Bards in Lirigon. Irc cocked his head and cawed assent.

"He's very good at carrying messages," said Hem anxiously, looking at Cadvan. "He helped me so much when I was at Sjug'hakar Im. And in Dén Raven."

I am a clever bird, said Irc complacently. *And I am the King's Messenger.*

"Yes, well." Cadvan considered Irc, who met his eye with a bold look, and then smiled. "It is a much better chance than no hope at all. But we have neither pen nor paper…"

"I have," said Maerad. She rushed over to her pack and pulled out a small oilskin bag, in which she kept the pen Dernhil had given her a year ago in Innail, a tiny stoppered bottle of ink and some precious leaves of paper. "I always keep these, in case – well, in case I find somewhere to practise my writing." She looked ruefully at the bottle, which was almost full. "I haven't had many chances, though."

Cadvan seized the pen and paper, found a flat rock and wrote a short letter, outlining what they knew about the army. Then, looking to Irc for permission, he folded the letter as tightly as he could, and tied it securely to Irc's leg with a leather thong.

You must find Vaclal of Lirigon, he said. *Ask any Bard you see to take you to Vaclal. They will all know who he is, because he is the First Bard. Tell them you have urgent news about the Black Army.*

Vaclal, said Irc.

You won't forget the name?

Irc looked scornful at the suggestion, and didn't deign to answer. He bent his neck, pecking experimentally at the letter on his leg, and then flapped onto Hem's shoulder.

I go now, he said.

Be careful, said Hem. *I do not want to lose you. Don't do anything silly.*

I will be clever, said Irc. *I will be the King's Messenger and a hero and I will save the city. Farewell, my friend. I will fly faster than the wind and I will see you soon.*

Then he launched himself into the air, describing a series of graceful arabesques to underline the sense of occasion. Hem watched him until he vanished into the distance. A new pain lodged itself in his heart. He wondered if he would ever see Irc again. Even if he got to Lirigon and back safely, would Hem still be alive when he returned? And what would Irc do if Hem died?

Cadvan cleared his throat. "May the Light lift his wings, and protect him," he said. "If the King's Messenger saves Lirigon, I'll personally give him seven new titles."

"If he does save Lirigon, he'll be unbearable," said Hem. "But I love him for it, all the same. I just hope he's all right." Despite himself, his voice cracked.

Saliman put his hand lightly on Hem's shoulder. "Do not underestimate Irc's cunning," he said gently. "I'd wager a lot of gold on his safe return."

"You'd have to give half of it to Irc. Though the Light knows what he would do with it, except to stuff it in a hole in some old tree," said Hem.

He met Saliman's eyes and smiled crookedly. Saliman was the only one who really understood how much he loved his boastful friend. For all his undoubted intelligence, Irc was just an ordinary crow, as vulnerable as any other small creature to the accident and malice of the wider world. Hem remembered, with a sudden painful vividness, his first sight of Irc: a scrawny, awkward fledgling, being pecked unmercifully by his fellows. He had grown into a strong, handsome bird, but he was still only a bird. And now he was flying into the darkening clouds of evening, a tiny speck of life lost to sight in the huge sky; and much of Hem's heart had gone with him.

XX

THE HUTMOORS

THEY didn't dare to cross the valley until after midnight, long after the final ranks, followed by a trail of laden wagons, had disappeared down the dark road towards Lirigon. Gradually, as the Black Army vanished into the north, the ordinary noises of the night reasserted themselves, but the travellers did not relax. The tension seemed rather to increase as the shadows deepened into nightfall; they spoke only in whispers, and most of the time did not speak at all.

It seemed that Maerad had been correct that they would not be noticed. Although Saliman and Cadvan were both on full alert, once the Black Army had disappeared they detected no whiff of sorcery, no hint of the presence of Hulls or any other creature of the Dark. But there was still a palpable sense of threat; the empty night stretched out around them like a predatory animal. Clouds gathered overhead, obscuring the moon, and there was a smell of rain, but no rain fell. The wind rustled restlessly through the trees and the horses stamped and snorted as they dozed, but otherwise there was no sound.

Hem and Hekibel napped, huddled against the gnarled roots, while Saliman and Cadvan kept watch. Maerad said nothing at all: now her attention was turned westward. When the army had passed, she climbed to the top of the valley and stared towards the Hutmoors as if she was searching for something, her face white, her eyes blazing. No one asked her what she was looking for. There was something fierce in her stance that forbade questions.

They saddled the grumbling horses and moved cautiously south. Here the Usk ran swiftly between deep banks, and the only crossing was the bridge that carried the Bard Road north from Ettinor, in the shadow of the northern edge of the Broken Hills. They followed the river, while keeping it in sight to their right, and their way was rocky and uneven. Saliman, Cadvan and Hem were forced to make magelights to light the horses' steps, using simple veiling charms to hide them from unfriendly eyes, and it seemed to Hem that the magery drained him more than it should.

Hem's earthsense was stirring; or at least, he thought it was his earthsense. He felt an overpowering urge pulling him towards the Hutmoors. It was impossible to ignore and seemed to grow with every moment. He wondered if perhaps migrating birds might feel something similar when they returned to their spring nests in the north: an exact knowledge, a desire like hunger, that ran through every fibre of their being, pulling them to a particular place. Journeying south along the Usk, they were actually moving further away from where they had to be, and the knowledge weighed him down with reluctance, even though he knew in his rational mind that it was the only way they could get across the river.

At the same time he was troubled by a deep unease that he couldn't quite identify. The shadows seemed darker than even this dark night warranted, full of desolate cries that sounded below the threshold of his hearing; and he felt a loathing creep insidiously into his mind that had nothing to do with his anxiety about their direction. It was as if he sensed the edges of a presence, a premonition that something or someone was coming closer and closer. Perhaps, he thought glumly, it was just his fear about what might happen. For he was very afraid, in a way that he hadn't felt since he had been in Dagra.

They had not gone far when Maerad screamed. The sound went through Hem like a knife. He turned in time to see Maerad, her hands covering her eyes, topple off Keru's back onto the ground. He scrambled off Usha in a single movement, drawing his shortsword and scanning the night for enemies; but he could see no sign of attack, and there was no sound except Maerad's harsh panting as she lay on the ground, her hands covering her face.

Cadvan, who was closest, reached Maerad first. Keru was sniffing her rider in simple astonishment, her ears pricked, her nostrils flaring.

She fell off my back, Keru said, as Cadvan reached her.

Maerad took her hands from her eyes reluctantly and slowly sat up, blinking.

Keru pushed her gently with her nose. *Are you hurt? Did I hurt you?*

Maerad seemed stunned, and at first did not respond; then she gave a laugh that sounded like a sob, and reached up and patted Keru's nose. *No, my sweet, it is not your fault,* she said. *I just fell.*

Cadvan tilted up her chin and looked searchingly into her face. Maerad met his eyes as if the sight of him were a spar she was clutching in a stormy sea to save her from drowning.

"So," he said. "What happened?"

"I just fell off," she said.

"I have never seen you 'just fall off' a horse in a year of riding with you," he said, with gentle scepticism. "What is wrong, Maerad?"

For a moment his heart chilled, as Maerad seemed to look right through him as if he wasn't there. Her face was so pale that her skin seemed translucent; Cadvan fancied that he could see the delicate globe of her skull. Then she focused on his face and blinked.

"I can't see," she said at last. "I mean, I keep seeing too many things and then I can't see."

"Is it the dead?"

Maerad met his eyes, and something within her gaze flinched at his words, as if they pained her. "Yes. And other things. I don't – I don't know what they are. Or who they are."

Cadvan nodded, although he had only the vaguest idea what she meant. The one thing that was clear to him was that Maerad could no longer ride. He thought for a moment, and suggested that Hem ride Keru, while Maerad rode with him on Darsor. Hem, who was watching anxiously, began to talk softly to Keru, stroking her nose. She already approved of Hem, and had no objections to carrying him.

Maerad said nothing further, and Cadvan didn't press her. Obediently she climbed onto Darsor behind Cadvan, putting her arms around his waist. She breathed in his familiar smell, which was slightly spicy, like pepper, and leaned her cheek against his back. He was the one solid thing in a world that seemed to be falling away beneath her feet. It was such a relief to close her eyes.

"This way, I can grab hold of you before you fall," Cadvan said over his shoulder, as they started on their way again. "In theory, at least."

"I won't fall," Maerad said, and tightened her arms around him.

Maerad didn't know what was happening to her. Since she had seen the Black Army marching through the valley, a monstrous killing machine bent on destruction, it was as if something had slipped in her mind. The instability of vision that had tormented her over the past few days was rapidly increasing: she changed dizzyingly from one state to another without reason or warning. One moment she was fearful, the next completely unafraid;

in one instant she was acutely aware of everything that moved in the landscape around her, down to the smallest fieldmouse, and in the next a great black abyss seemed to yawn before her, drawing her in with a terrible gravity and filling her vision like blindness. She had fallen off Keru when she had first glimpsed that abyss: she had put her hands over her eyes in horror, forgetting that she was on horseback. For the first time since leaving the Hollow Lands, she wished she could escape into sleep, but sleep was a place so far away that she couldn't even imagine what it must be like.

The rational, conscious Maerad was still there, but she was a tiny, lonely figure in the midst of an impending storm; the wind moved in jumps and startles, or suddenly ceased altogether, and an eerie light illuminated everything around her with an almost unbearable clarity. Or then it seemed that it darkened without warning, and sudden, unpredictable lightnings shivered through her being. Through all the bewildering transformations she felt an increasing premonition of doom. The one thing that stopped her from feeling that she was going mad was Cadvan's closeness. She didn't think at all any more about whether he loved her, or how much she loved him. She needed him, and he was there, and that was all that mattered.

The dead still flickered before her, but they were fewer and more fleeting, and almost everyone she saw was afraid or sad or in pain. The lamentation she had sensed earlier had retreated, although she was still aware of it. A greater force seemed to be pushing the dead aside, a presence she could not quite locate or identify, and they fled before it, poor desolate shadows, like dry leaves before a rising wind. Whatever it was, Maerad was quite sure of its intent: it was hunting her, and it wanted to destroy her, to swallow her up in its unending darkness.

She kept her eyes squeezed shut; if she opened them she felt nauseous, as if she were falling from a great height. Things weren't much better with her eyes closed, but she concentrated on the rough wool of Cadvan's cloak, which scraped her cheek as she pressed her face against it. She could feel his heartbeat and the warmth of his body through the cloth. It was like a glowing hearth in a cold and terrifying world.

The night was wholly black: heavy clouds concealed the moon. Cadvan led them as swiftly as he dared. Although he had often ridden through this valley, he also feared that he might miss the Usk bridge in the darkness, and he did not wish to stay near the river a moment longer than was necessary. A light but steady rain began, soaking them through. The raindrops shone silver in the magelight, dropping like cold pearls from their sodden cloaks into the shadows at their feet.

Cadvan was deeply worried about Maerad. Her light body trembled against him, with cold or something else, and she had not said a word since she had mounted Darsor. She clutched him so tightly it was difficult to ride. He tried to touch her mind, but Maerad was far distant, in some place he did not comprehend, and when he tried to reach towards her, his spirit shrivelled before an overpowering sorrow that made him draw tactfully back, uncertain and full of sadness.

He no longer knew why they were riding through this dark night, or what they would find at the end of their journey. He felt despair creeping into his soul. He contemplated it with cold loathing, as if it were a cockroach that would not die no matter how many times he stamped on it, and turned away. His own personal despair did not matter any more.

Hem also felt the distance from Maerad, and in his present anxiety it distressed him. He missed Irc, but even though Irc was too far away now for mindtouching, he was always aware of his slight presence, a dim but perceptible light in the wide and empty wilderness. Although Maerad rode less than two spans away from him, she seemed to him immeasurably further away, lost in an impenetrable maze of shadows, and he knew that he couldn't help her. He rode as close as he could to Saliman and Hekibel, and while Cadvan and Maerad rode in silence, these three sometimes spoke softly together, making a fugitive human warmth in the cold night.

They reached the bridge over the Usk in the darkest hours of the night. None of them expected to find the bridge unguarded, and they approached it cautiously. Hem, Saliman and Cadvan had woven the strongest shielding they could manage, with a sense of hopelessness: they could conceal their own presences, and hide magelights from prying eyes, but the power that emanated from Maerad was another question altogether. If Hulls guarded the bridge, they did not have a chance of crossing it unnoticed.

They halted some distance from the road, studying the black arch of the bridge and the shadowy trees that huddled against the river, and the silence around them seemed to deepen, as if something were listening to their approach.

Maerad stirred behind Cadvan.

"There are Hulls," she said. Then she gasped, as if she were in sudden pain, and clutched Cadvan more tightly.

Maerad, what's wrong? said Cadvan urgently into her mind.

He thought that she wouldn't answer, but at last she did. *They hurt*, she said. They are all hurting. *They'll never stop hurting…*

Who? Cadvan turned his head, trying to look into her eyes, but she had hidden her face against his back. *Who hurts?*

Everything is burning, said Maerad. *And the river is red, it's a river of blood…*

Her voice seemed to be coming from further and further away, and Cadvan reached with his mindtouch, to bring her back. But she slipped from his grasp, as if she were falling, and then he knew she was beyond his call. She clasped him as if she were in danger of being torn away by some invisible torrent.

Usk, Cadvan thought. The river of tears. It had been so named when the Nameless One had laid waste to the fair land of Imbral, slaughtering the Dhyllin people without mercy. The Hutmoors was a hard place to be in the best of times; when he and Maerad had last crossed them, it was haunted with an old and irrevocable grief. Now, he guessed, Maerad was feeling this ancient slaughter as if it were happening now, as if it had never stopped happening in all the thousands of years since the beginning of the Great Silence, as if time itself were so deeply scarred that the cries would never cease. He shuddered, and then wrenched his attention to the present. He did not doubt that Hulls guarded the bridge, if Maerad said so; but he felt no trace of them at all.

He glanced across at Saliman, who caught his thought. *Hulls?* said Saliman into his mind. *I cannot feel them…*

Maerad says they are at the bridge, all the same. But I fear that she'll be unable to help us this time.

Saliman nodded. The Bards checked their shields; they thought the Hulls could not but be aware of them by now, and they were alert for an attack at any time. Cadvan took the black-stone out from underneath his jerkin, and clasped it hard in his palm, feeling the strange numbness that it spread through his arm. Swiftly and deftly he wove its power into their shield, to deflect any sorcery, and then turned to his companions.

"Shall we cross the bridge?" he said aloud.

They nodded, Hekibel slightly after the others. In the pale light of the magelights, her face was drained of all colour. Her mouth was set, her face determined, and it seemed to Hem, glancing across, that she was battling down a terrible fear. A sudden rush of admiration filled his heart: of all of them, he thought, Hekibel was the most defenceless, and the most brave.

"Be wary," said Cadvan. "The main thing is to get across as quickly as possible."

They urged the horses to a trot, and soon reached the Bard Road. The sharp sound of the hooves on the stone seemed too loud, and Hem felt very exposed as they trotted briskly towards the bridge, the magelights floating in front of the horses like eerie guides. He could feel a nausea rising in his belly as they approached the river, but he pushed it down. It didn't feel like Hulls; in fact, he couldn't sense the presence of Hulls anywhere. Perhaps Maerad was mistaken...

He knew as soon as they stepped onto the bridge that she had not been mistaken at all. A Hull stepped out of thin air at the far end of the bridge, and at the same time he felt a chill behind him, and knew that their way back was blocked by another. They were ambushed. If it hadn't been for Maerad's warning, they would have been taken completely by surprise; as it was, the blasts of sorcery that both Hulls hurled towards them were absorbed by their shield, and Hem merely felt a momentary deafness as he drew his shortsword from his scabbard, realising as he did so that he had no idea how to fight on horseback, and that probably if he tried he would cause more damage to Keru than to anyone else.

He glanced involuntarily towards Maerad, expecting her to lay waste to the Hulls as she had in the Hollow Lands; but Maerad was staring down into the river with a look of utter horror. She swayed on Darsor, looking as if she were about to faint, and she seemed wholly unaware that they were under attack. Then Keru shied, almost throwing Hem off, and he realized that with his sword drawn on horseback he was more a liability than anything else. Holding the blade out of the way, he swung around on his stomach and slid off Keru, clutching the reins in his hands and whispering to her, trying to calm her down as he attempted to see what was happening.

At first he couldn't see Maerad at all; she was no longer on Darsor. Then he spotted her crouched by the low wall that ran along the bridge. Saliman and Cadvan had swung around so that each of them faced one of the Hulls, and both Bards blazed with magery, their faces grim, their eyes hard and deadly. Cadvan held aloft a black medallion that drew Hem's fascinated attention: he didn't know what it was, but it made him uneasy to see it in Cadvan's hands. Even as he watched, a bolt of light arced over his head, and the bridge was briefly illuminated in a harsh white light that threw livid shadows across their faces. Hem didn't know whether the light had come from Saliman or Cadvan, and he couldn't even tell its direction. The metallic smell of sorcery filled the air, and he gagged and drew back against the walls of the bridge, trying to hold onto Keru, who was now panicking, rearing back from him, her eyes rolling, her ears flat against her head. Hekibel was struggling with Usha nearby, attempting to stop her from bolting.

There was another blast of sorcery, although again it didn't hit them. Their shields were holding firm, but Hem realized that there was something else in play – it seemed to him that the sorcery of the Hulls was not missing them so much as being held in suspension around them. He felt the hair lift on his scalp, as if lightning were about to strike, and ducked instinctively. Another blast of magery flashed across the bridge; at least, he thought it was magery, as it blazed with white fire, but it left a taste of burned metal on the air. Cadvan had used the blackstone to turn the Hulls' sorcery against them.

There was a brief, blood-chilling scream that at once curdled into silence. Hem stared ahead into the darkness, and then glanced swiftly behind him, at the near end of the bridge. The cold, loathly presence of the Hulls had completely vanished. Where the nearest Hull had been standing he could see a small, dark heap. Hem's gorge rose, and he turned his eyes away; he knew that it was a pile of fleshless bones.

He breathed out, and the tension drained from his body, leaving him light-headed. The night was clean now. The river ran noisily beneath them, and the rain fell on the wet road, and aside from the stamping and snorting of the horses and their own breathing, they could hear no other sound. He felt that little time had passed since they had stepped onto the bridge: the confrontation had been over quickly.

"I think there are no more," said Cadvan. He dismounted and comforted the horses, but he did not sheathe his sword. "They were lowly guards, no more; by no means powerful sorcerers. It shows that this bridge is considered important enough for the captain to have posted Hulls rather than ordinary soldiers. I would like to know, all the same, how they hid themselves; it makes me uneasy. It could be that even now a messenger runs to its master, to report this battle..."

"Aye, that is very possible," said Saliman. He looked around, sniffing the night air. "Maerad, can you sense any Hulls?"

Maerad jumped at this direct address. She wrenched her gaze from the river and met Saliman's eyes, and he flinched at what he saw. Her face was drawn with horror and grief, and her eyes seemed to reflect an abyss of such darkness that he could not guess its depth.

Hem started towards her, wanting to comfort her, but she shook her head, as if forbidding him, and swallowed. When she spoke, her voice was harsh.

"There are no Hulls here," she said. "Only death. Death everywhere." She covered her eyes again with her hands. "I don't want to see any more. I can't bear it..."

Cadvan put his arm around her shoulder and she leaned into him, her body shuddering. "I don't want to see," she repeated. "Please, help me, I can't bear it any more..."

Cadvan and Saliman exchanged glances. They clearly didn't know what to do. But Hekibel dismounted and came towards Maerad, unknotting a red silk scarf she wore around her throat. She held it up. "Will this do?" she asked.

Maerad swallowed and nodded, and gently Hekibel tied the scarf around Maerad's eyes. The red silk looked like blood. The sight of his sister blindfolded in this way stabbed Hem to the heart with pity and a sad fury. He didn't understand what was happening to her, but he thought he had never seen anyone in such pain.

They left the scene of the battle as swiftly as they could, following the Bard Road, which ran westwards, for speed. It stopped raining, and the sky began to clear; after a while the moon came out, letting fall its cold light on the stone road. They were numb with cold and tiredness and their damp cloaks chafed their skins, but they dared not stop to make a fire to warm themselves.

The Bard Road turned north about a league from the bridge, and here they left it behind and climbed the west side of the valley. When they reached the top of the ridge, a punishing wind hit them with bruising force. It seemed to pierce them to their marrow with a cold that deadened the heart.

The travellers paused briefly, looking glumly over the bare moors that glimmered before them under the moonlight.

"The Hutmoors," said Cadvan. "I had hoped, last time I crossed this desolation, that I would never have cause to return."

Saliman stared over the waste, an unreadable expression on his face. "I think that I have never seen anything more forlorn," he said at last.

"The Nameless One hated the Dhyllin with a special hatred," answered Cadvan. "And this is what that hatred meant." He paused. "I have no idea what direction we should go. Perhaps it would be best to keep close to the river…"

"No," said Hem, unexpectedly. "It's north from here, that way." He pointed over the moors.

Saliman glanced at Hem in surprise, but made no comment.

"North it is, then," said Cadvan. He gathered up his reins. "I don't know about you, but I am nearly dead from weariness. I think we cannot ride much further tonight."

Away from the river and its stunted willows, there was no shelter from the wind at all. At least, thought Hekibel, grateful for even the smallest of mercies, it wasn't raining. The place was haunted – she was sure she heard voices sobbing on the wind, and she saw fleeting forms at the edge of her sight that vanished when she turned to look. She drew closer to Saliman; even in this desolate night, he seemed to radiate a comforting light. Hem also saw the hauntings, but they didn't trouble him as much as the earthsickness that was growing in him the deeper they moved into the Hutmoors. The very ground was maimed. He felt it in his body: it was a pain that ran through his bones and flowered in his stomach like nausea. He tried to push it aside; it had been worse, after all, in the Glandugir Hills, and he had survived that…

They stopped not long afterwards, huddling for shelter against one of the low, stony ridges that rumpled the surface of these bleak moors. They were too exhausted and too wary of pursuit to make a fire. Despite the cold and his nausea, Hem was so tired that he fell asleep almost at once, and wandered in dreams down the same long road where he had followed Saliman in his sickness, a road that gleamed faintly in an endless darkness. He was searching for someone, but he couldn't remember who it was, only that it was very important that he find her, and at the same time he knew she was lost for ever. He woke with a start in a pale dawn and realized that he had been searching for his mother. He didn't remember anything about her except a fragrance like summer peaches, a memory of dark hair falling across his face, the cradling warmth of arms.

He sighed and looked around at his companions, his heart heavy with foreboding. All of them looked bruised with weariness. Maerad had sat staring blindly northwards as the others slept: under her blindfold, which she refused to take off, her face was hollow and drawn, and there was a high flush on her cheekbones. She spoke no word, but Hem saw that the enchantment that flickered through her skin was becoming stronger. But it no longer seemed warm like firelight or the sunshine of summer; the light that shimmered within her seemed to be colder, a blue fire that made him think of ice.

They made a cheerless breakfast. Maerad again refused food; she had eaten nothing for days. Her thinness was becoming alarming. Hem tried to persuade her to eat, even putting food into her hands. When he pressed her, she smiled and gave the food back to him, closing his fingers over it, and Hem knew there was no point in arguing any further. The only thing that was keeping her alive, thought Hem, was medhyl. Cadvan had brought a good supply from Innail and, aside from water, it was all she would take.

"So, Hem," said Saliman, as they prepared the weary horses to ride again. "You think you know where to go?"

Hem nodded. "That way," he said.

Saliman studied him. "You're quite sure?" he said, almost smiling at Hem's lack of doubt.

"It's the earthsense," Hem said. "This place is waking it up. I feel as if I'm going to be sick all the time, like I did in the Glandugir Hills, but there's also this – pull. Sort of like when Maerad called me. It's getting stronger the closer we get."

"Is it far?"

"No. It's close, I think. Perhaps we might reach it by night-fall."

"I hope you're right." Saliman passed his hand over his face, and in that gesture Hem perceived the full extent of the exhaustion that Saliman had hidden for days. He wasn't fully recovered from the White Sickness, and he had ridden leagues over hard country, through fear and danger, when he should really have been in bed. Only his will was keeping him going, and his will was made of iron. Hem realized that Saliman was very close to the end of his strength. With a rush of love, he reached out and clasped his hand.

Saliman looked up, surprised, and met his eyes, and read there what Hem was unable to say. He smiled, and briefly he was again the Saliman that Hem had known in Turbansk, care-free and mischievous, gentle and strong. "It will be a relief to get to some end, for good or ill," he said. "And it might be ill. I sense a great darkness around us, Hem, and it is not the keen-ing of the lost souls of the Hutmoors that so troubles my spirit. I think I can guess who it is who hunts us over the scene of his last great battle, and I am afraid that we cannot prevail against such a foe, if he is indeed here. If this journey turns out ill, I hope you know how much I have loved you."

Hem nodded, unable to speak for emotion, and turned away to mount Keru. He thought that he, too, could guess the name behind the shadow that pressed upon his mind, but even to think it felt unlucky.

Riding through the Hutmoors by day was only marginally better than riding at night: they could see where they were going, but it was a dour, cheerless place, and it felt no less haunted by daylight. Seated behind Cadvan on Darsor, Maerad was silent. Blindfolded, she stared unseeingly over the grey turf, which spring had barely touched. Sometimes her lips moved as if she were speaking, but not even Cadvan could hear what she said. Her mouth was set in a hard line and her face was drawn, as if she was in constant pain. Her arms around Cadvan's waist were like a vice.

Late that afternoon, they arrived at a place that looked very like any other place in the Hutmoors, except that it sloped down to a swamp dotted with stagnant, weed-choked pools in which grew red sedges and green sphagnums and high stands of rushes.

"This is it," said Hem, pulling Keru to a halt. "This is the place."

Cadvan surveyed the swamp and the higher land next to it, and his jaw hardened. There was no sign, not even the grass-covered ridge of a wall, that showed that here there once stood a fair city.

"Are you certain?" asked Saliman.

"Yes." Hem couldn't have said why he was so certain; he just knew that here was the centre of the urge that had been calling him since he and Maerad had attempted the singing in the Hollow Lands. It was also the centre of the sickness that, now he had dismounted, rose up through his feet and made him want to gag. He pushed away his physical discomfort and began to unsaddle Keru, who nuzzled his shoulder and whickered. "I don't know whether it's the place that used to be Afinil," he said. "But I do know it's where we have to be."

Maerad slid off Darsor and ripped off the scarf. She stared about her, startled, as if she had been woken from sleep. "He's right," she said. Hem looked at her in surprise. Her voice was clear and certain, ringing out over the emptiness, and it seemed to him as if something spoke through her. "It's the right place. It is Afinil. This is where the Song was trapped and made into a thing that could be stolen and used for ill. This is where it all began. This is where it must end, for good or ill, under the same moon that blessed its beginning..."

"If it was Afinil, that swamp was once a lake famous for its clear waters," said Cadvan, after a short silence. "No doubt the Nameless One broke all the towers and used them to fill up the lake."

Saliman swallowed. "I have sometimes dreamed of Afinil," he said. "I walked through the vineyards and orchards of the Dhyllin. And I saw the white spires of Afinil reflected in the water, and heard the music that echoed through her fair halls, and in my dreams I have touched the beautiful things that were made here. But there is nothing left. Nothing. I read somewhere that Sharma's true greatness was in his pettiness. I'm not sure that I really understood what that meant until this moment."

"Aye," said Cadvan. "Of all that great citadel, nothing remains. Not even the shadow of a ruin, of what was said to be the most beautiful city on the face of the earth. It is a kind of greatness, I suppose, to hate with so much thoroughness." He suddenly sounded immensely tired. "And this will be the fate of all the great cities of Annar, if he has his way."

Hem understood that Cadvan was wondering about the fate of Lirigon, and his thoughts turned to Irc. Although he knew that Irc was too far away, he sent out an impulsive summoning. He hadn't really expected Irc to answer, but when no answer came, he felt a stab of sorrow. He would have liked to speak once more with Irc.

"We must wait for moonrise," said Maerad. She took her lyre from her pack, tucking it under her arm, and walked a small distance away from them to the edge of the swamp. There she stood alone, her hair flying back from her face, staring out over the swamp, and Hem knew, with a sudden prescience, that she did not see the same bleak landscape that he did. Perhaps, he thought, she was looking at the mere as once it had been, when it was surrounded by lush gardens and the towers of

Afinil rose high above its tranquil surface. Cadvan was rubbing down Darsor a short distance away, but his eyes were fixed on Maerad. His face was dark with sadness, but he made no attempt to speak to her, and neither did Hem.

Hem sighed, and went over to help Saliman and Hekibel, who were beginning to set up a camp in the lee of a low ridge of rock that would protect them a little from the merciless wind. Whatever doom awaited them, they might as well have a hot meal first.

XXI

THE SINGING

TRAVELLING through the Hutmoors had been for Maerad the worst torment she had ever known. Where her companions glimpsed the shades that haunted this landscape's melancholy present, Maerad saw a bitterly vivid past. With her inner eye she perceived woodlands, vineyards, fields and towns that had long vanished from the face of the world; she saw what the Hutmoors had been two thousand years before, when it was called the Firman Plains, and the Usk had been the Findol River, famous for its clear waters, beloved by dye-makers and vintners.

In the space of a single day she saw all the beauty that had been there, and its irrevocable destruction. She saw the Nameless One's victory over the armies of Lirion and Imbral and she saw the massacre that followed, when the Dhyllin people were cut down in their thousands, man, woman and child, as Sharma's army wreaked his vengeance on the Imbral. As soon as she saw a village standing in the sunlight amid fields of plenty, she knew that she would next witness flame set in corn and vine and home. If she saw a child, she would also see its death; if she saw people gathered in a town square or village common, she knew she would see their merciless slaughter.

The blindfold had helped a little; it protected her outer sight, but the visions rose also in her mind's eye. It seemed to Maerad that she experienced each death as if it were her own father or mother or child or brother or sister who was killed, as if Sharma's soldiers cut down her closest kin, her dearest loves;

she couldn't find any way to hide from the grief and terror of each death, and it happened over and over and over again. She saw cruelty beyond imagining, atrocity on a scale that she could not comprehend, fear and despair and sorrow that were beyond the capacity of words to describe. She thought she was going mad.

The visions didn't stop until they reached Afinil. When she took off her blindfold, she glimpsed for a brief moment Afinil's graceful towers, its gardens of blossoming trees; and then the city dissolved before her eyes, as if it were made of mist, and vanished utterly. She stood on the solid ground, staring over the rocky moors, and she realized with a relief beyond measure that she had been released from the terrible past. At that moment, the sedges and mosses and reeds of the swamp seemed beautiful beyond anything she had ever seen: these simple living things humbly offered up their colours and smells and forms without asking anything of her, content merely to grow and live and die.

Then she knew that the dead had asked her for justice, that she had been shown the crimes of the past because they cried out for restitution. As she stared over the swamp, she felt that the lament of the Hutmoors had entered her body and changed it, and she realized that she would never be the same again.

I cannot make justice, Maerad thought. I cannot undo these acts as if they never happened. Revenge is empty: it will not raise the towers nor bring the massacred children back to life; it will not make the gardens blossom again nor take the poison from the land. The dead ask for more than anyone can give them.

All the same, she thought, if I can destroy the Nameless One, I will.

She stood for a long time, feeling the weight of her lyre in the crook of her arm and the cold wind biting her face, and she studied the tiny white flowers of a creeping plant that flourished in the marshy hollows before her. She felt the shadows gathering as evening fell, and she heard the sounds of her companions as they cooked their meal. A great peace entered her spirit.

She could feel the brooding presence of the Nameless One gathering about her, searching for her as the choking blackness had sought her in her nightmares. She knew that the marsh birds cowered beneath the grasses, the cries in their throats silenced with animal fear as the shadow of a great predator darkened the sky above them. After riding through the Hutmoors, Maerad felt outraged that he dared to send his mind back to the scene of such crimes. With a mixture of arrogance and disgust, she turned her mind away from him. She knew that he hadn't found her yet; he sensed her uneasily, he sought a way into her mind, but he had not yet discovered where she stood. Whatever happened, he would not steal this small moment of peace from her. Perhaps, she thought, it would be her last moment as herself.

But as the shadows lengthened, a soft, melodious voice wound itself into her mind. She had never heard a voice of such bewitching beauty, and despite herself she opened her mind to listen.

Elednor, said the voice. *Elednor, at last I have found you whom I have sought long, through fire and shadow, this other part of myself...*

With a thrill of fear, Maerad looked about her, but she could see no sign of any semblance.

Who are you? she asked.

I am your other self, said the voice. *The other whom you have always desired to be. I am the end of all your longing, all your searching, all your dreams.*

This woke all of Maerad's perverse stubbornness, and the voice's enchantment wavered. *That's no answer,* she said, her voice like a whiplash. She felt the other flinch. *I think that you are Sharma.*

If I am, what I say is no less true. Consult your heart, Elednor,

Elednor Edil-Amarandh na, and see if what your heart tells you is not true. After all, here we can speak as equals.

Disgust rose in Maerad's throat so that she nearly gagged. *Equals?* she said. *I think not. I would never do what you have done. I would never – How dare you speak to me. How dare you come here, after everything that you've done.*

The voice was silent for a time, and then it laughed, and its laughter was warm and intimate in her ear, so that Maerad recoiled.

My dear one, it said. *You are very young, but you have killed without mercy, because it was necessary. Do not pretend to me that you have not. Do not pretend that you are better than you are. You have caused suffering and grief and pain. It is the price of power, is it not? Why should you think that I have acted any differently from you? I have lived longer than you, I have tasted the joy and terror and price of power. So it is, always. Do you think your noble friends are any better than I am? Do not tell me that you have not thought these things yourself. You, of all people, are not stupid.*

Maerad tried to close her mind against the voice, but it insinuated itself through all her defences, and she could not but listen. And now doubt rose inside her; she had indeed thought these things. She bit her lip. And the voice continued, soft, persuasive, its melody a tormenting pleasure that she could not resist.

Now I have found you, I can at last ask you: why do you seek to destroy our powers? You do not understand what it is that you do … Elednor, Elednor, you are misled. There is another way…

Each time Sharma said her Name, the enchantment deepened, although Maerad struggled against it. She looked around again; it was strange talking to someone she could not see, not in her inner vision nor before her naked eye. But Sharma kept himself hidden.

What other way? she asked unwillingly.

You are misled by those who claim they are your friends. They envy your power and wish to destroy it. But Elednor, you are mistaken ... you are the One. In you the Treesong is made whole. This – sickness you see around you – it is but the sickness of the split Song. If we take this power wholly for ourselves, we can remake the whole world. You and I, Elednor: King and Queen of all creation. We can make the world a perfumed garden, the rivers will flow with milk and honey. We can mend all hurts and right all wrongs ... it is this that you throw away, Elednor, if you release the Treesong. You will lose everything if you do this; and having known the possibility of such power, how could you live? It will be a stale life, Elednor Edil-Amarandh na, if you turn away from your destiny, a dull life, knowing the shining that could have been you.

Beneath the beauty of Sharma's voice, Maerad could feel the anguish that inhabited him, an endless anguish that filled her with pity. Sharma was right: he was not a whole creature, and his crimes and cruelty grew out of the agony of the wound that was his being. She saw herself as Queen of Edil-Amarandh, stern and just and immortal, as beautiful as Ardina, as stern as Arkan, more powerful than both. She would rule over a world in which there would be no sadness, no injustice, no ugliness. If she had this power, did she have the right to relinquish it? Perhaps she had been mistaken all along ... even Cadvan admitted that he didn't know all ends, and perhaps this was the true reading of the prophecy, the true new age of the world.

But as she thought of Cadvan, she remembered vividly the shape and warmth of his body in her arms, the dull thud of his heartbeat, the solid presence that had kept her from madness on the terrible journey through the Hutmoors. And then she remembered Saliman and Nelac, Nerili and Sirkana, Dernhil and Dharin, all her friends who had placed such faith in her, who had suffered so much, and had even died, so that she might come to this place. And she thought of her mother and her lonely death, and her father, cut down in the sack of Pellinor, and of Hem, her brother, taken by Hulls as a baby.

Your friends will understand in the end, said Sharma, sensing her thoughts. *They, too, will see the wisdom and justice of your decision, and they will bow before you. And if they do not see that, they have no power to resist you. Why do you think they fear you? They will fear you rightly. You are no longer a child, at the whim of your elders. Put your lyre down, Elednor, Elednor Edil-Amarandh na. Give your lyre to me, and step into your true destiny, blissful queen of all creation ... let the true age of justice begin!*

Justice? said Maerad, with a sudden biting scorn; and she clutched her lyre close to her breast. *What do you know of justice?* The pretty visions vanished, and she remembered the corpses that had choked the Findol River so that its waters were poisoned, and the slaughtered children of the Firman Plains. And at the same time she knew that Sharma did not know her other Name, the Elidhu Name that lay deep within her and that even Maerad herself did not know; and she understood, with a sudden glad knowledge, that without her third Name he could not utterly bewilder her. Nor could he harm her, any more than she could harm him, while she did not open her powers. The bewitchment of the voice fell instantly away; she saw his enchantment as a cheap trick, and wondered why she had ever listened.

The bile rose in her throat, and she spat on the ground. *Get away from me, traitor!* she said. *I am not your fool, to be flattered and threatened. Go!*

She felt his surprise and then his impotent fury, and all sense of the voice vanished. But now Maerad was wary, and she lifted a great shield so that he could not strike her or her companions. And for the first time since she had arrived at Afinil, she began to feel afraid: Sharma could not touch her now, but when she began the Singing, she would be open in her powers, and vulnerable. She felt the force of his cold anger gathering about her in the deepening shadows, and she knew that he, too, was afraid of her, and that like any cornered, desperate beast, he was most dangerous when most afraid.

Hem felt a little better after eating. Although the stew of dried meat and pulses was hardly tasty fare, it was warm and wholesome, and gave him some ballast, staving off the nausea that ran in waves through his body.

As the sun sank in the sky, he found himself becoming uneasily aware of the tuning fork; it vibrated against his skin, as if it were a live thing. Since the Hollow Lands he had forgotten it; the fork had just been a lump of metal that nestled next to the cloth bag he always wore around his neck. Now he remembered that this object had hung for millennia about the neck of the Nameless One himself, that it had been made by Nelsor in this very place; that the tiny, mysterious runes scored on its dull surface held the secret of the Treesong, and perhaps the key to the binding spell that placed the Nameless One among the immortals and gave him his powers...

As soon as the thought crossed his mind, Hem tried to unthink it. After speaking to Saliman, he had been quite sure that the presence that was darkening his mind, that filled his steps with loathing and prompted the wracking nausea in his stomach, was the Nameless One. He couldn't escape the conviction that it was unlucky even to think about him; but it was very difficult to think of anything else. Involuntarily he looked over his shoulder towards the south, as if he could see Sharma riding towards them on a giant black horse that breathed fire through its nostrils, with an army of wers and Hulls at his heel.

All he saw was the bleak expanse of the Hutmoors, darkening under the shadows of evening. It was utterly lifeless:

no birds swooped in the sky to catch late insects; no wild deer skittered nervously in the wind; not a vole, not a rabbit, not a mouse, not even the fleeting shadows of the dead, stirred at the edge of his vision. The wind moaned through the reeds and sedges of the marsh but he could hear nothing else: no marsh birds piping, no curlew calling its forlorn cry. A great stillness lay over the landscape like a paralysing dread.

He won't arrive on a horse, Hem thought, scorning himself for his fancy. His body is in Dagra. But Saliman is right: he hunts us down. He knows we want to destroy him. He is coming closer and closer. Maybe he even hears my thoughts, and they draw him here...

He glanced towards Maerad. While they had cooked and eaten their meal, Maerad had stood unmoving at the edge of the marsh, a tiny figure under the great bowl of the sky. The distress and pain that she had suffered as they traversed the Hutmoors seemed no longer to trouble her; if anything, her expression was serene. To Hem it seemed that her small figure held such power that she was vast: her shadow seemed to stream back from the westering sun like the brooding darkness of a mountain. For the first time, Hem felt a tremor of fear of her. Maerad was now beyond his understanding, beyond any homely call of kindred. He no longer knew who she was.

He turned his gaze back to his three other companions. They all huddled close to the small fire, trying to catch its vagrant warmth before it was blown away. All of them were stained with travel, gaunt with exhaustion. Hekibel and Saliman sat very close together, and Hem saw that Saliman had taken Hekibel's small hands between both of his own and held them fast. Cadvan sat a little apart, his eyes fixed on Maerad, his face inscrutable. No one spoke much, and if they did, they spoke of unimportant things. There seemed, in truth, very little to say. They all knew that they stood before an abyss, and none of them knew whether they would see the following dawn.

Together they watched the sun set through black bars of cloud. It cast a ruddy light over the moors, so that they seemed stained with blood, and Hem shuddered. The light slowly ebbed out of the sky, and the silence deepened around them. Maerad was a dim figure a few spans away, unmoving as a statue. Above them the sky was clearing, and the stars opened one by one until the dark field of the night was strewn with silver points of light. The world held its breath. Everything was absolutely still.

Now their eyes were fixed on the horizon, where soon a pale glimmer presaged the rising of the moon over the distant peak of the eastern mountains.

Cadvan looked over to Hem. "I think it is time," he said gently.

Hem nodded. With trembling hands he took the chain from around his neck and held the tuning fork in his hand. Then he embraced his friends one by one, Saliman last of all. Saliman's warm, strong arms felt like a final bulwark, and to Hem it seemed that to let go was to fall into a darkness whose depth he could not guess. But at last he stood back and took a deep breath. The rim of the full moon had just broken over the edge of the world.

"Right, then," he said.

Hem walked over to Maerad with shaking legs. But although his body was trembling, something inside him was hard and certain. He was more frightened than he had ever been in his life, but he knew that his fear would not stop him from doing what had to be done. The time for fear or doubt was long past. As soon as he turned away from his friends, he forgot them; it was as if a curtain had fallen between them. He felt as if time itself had been waiting for him and Maerad since it had first hatched from the egg of the cosmos, that all pasts and all futures intersected in this one moment.

When he reached Maerad, he put his hand on her shoulder. She turned to him and smiled, and for a moment that smile made Hem's vitals shrivel with fear: it was fey and wild, cold as the storms of winter, a smile to freeze the heart.

"We have not long to wait, my brother," said Maerad. "See, the moon is impatient, she rises fast over the world."

Hem watched as the moon lifted over the horizon. It was huge, huger than he had ever seen it. As it breasted the horizon its light poured over the moors in a bright stream, catching the filaments of millions of tiny, dew-pearled cobwebs strung through the turf, so it seemed to Hem that a path of silver ripples opened before him, and that he could step lightly over it to the very door of the moon. And as the bright pathway ran up to his feet, he heard a high, beautiful melody that pierced his heart, and in that moment it seemed to him that he and Maerad were caught up out of time, and that the shimmering path was made of stars, like the Lukemoi where the Dead were said to walk on their way to the Gates.

As he thought this, he saw that the road of light wasn't empty. Out of the silver disc of the moon, as if it were a door to another world, there came a great crowd of people, and they walked solemnly down the narrow road through the darkness towards Hem and Maerad. Hem gasped and found that he was trembling, although he trembled not with fear, but with awe and wonder.

Before long the first of the people reached them, and they looked straight into Maerad and Hem's eyes, and then they bowed their heads and walked behind them into the dark night and vanished. Their faces were expressionless, neither happy nor sad, but as they passed Hem's heart grew heavier and heavier, as if he were weighed down by an immense sorrow. He saw people of all ages, ugly and beautiful, young and old, mothers with babies at their breasts, small children holding the hands of their elders – face after face after face – and in the brief moment when he beheld them, he saw the story of each life in each face, their fragile hopes and passionate desires and impossible dreams, and at the same time the ending of all these things. And it seemed to Hem that each face imprinted itself on his memory, that he would never forget any person he saw.

Then he caught his breath in a sob. Zelika walked slowly towards him and as he recognized her, he cried out her name in pained surprise. She looked him full in the face with cool recognition, but said nothing. Then she bowed her head and passed behind him with all the rest. And Hem understood then that the endless stream of people were Sharma's dead, those whose lives had been snuffed out untimely because of his wars. He knew that Maerad recognized others: as if he were touching her, he felt her body thrumming with emotion like the string of a harp. He knew the names she spoke – Dernhil, Dharin – but then he heard one he didn't know. Ilar. Maerad reached out her arm and said something softly that Hem did not hear, and although he did not look, he knew she was weeping.

And then he looked into the faces of two who stepped before, a tall man and woman who gravely met his gaze, and he understood that this was the only sight he would ever have of his mother and father, and he felt as if something broke inside him. And still the dead came on, in this bubble of time that seemed to have no end, and Hem saw the face of each one of them.

But at last the crowd thinned and then ceased, and the music sounded again, and he stood on the moors, the rocky ground beneath his feet, and the moon had lifted up from the black horizon and the silver path had vanished.

Maerad turned to him, her face shining with a joy that he did not comprehend, although her eyelashes glittered with tears.

"The dead ask for their accounting," she said. "And those I have killed forgive me. Oh Hem, I am forgiven."

Hem nodded. He did not understand what Maerad said, and he didn't trust himself to speak.

At that moment, Hem became aware that someone was watching them. The skin on the back of his neck prickled with a premonition of menace, as if an archer now trained his arrow on the centre of Hem's back, and he felt as if the air thickened around him, choking him.

"Don't take any notice," whispered Maerad. She lifted her lyre. "Now, Hem. Now!"

Hem hastily bent and struck the tuning fork on a stone at his feet. At first it made no sound, but then the note rang, sweet and clear on the cold air. Just as it began to vibrate, something hit him with a force that knocked him over, and he almost dropped the fork.

He heard Maerad's voice, sharp and impatient over the rising note that now began to fill the whole world. She sounded suddenly like his sister, not the strange, distant, tormented being he had seen over the past days.

"For the Light's sake, Hem, don't drop it!" she said. "Hold onto it if you love your life."

The blow came again, and then again. An instinct told Hem that this was only a muffled attack, that something shielded him from a force that would otherwise have destroyed him as easily as if he were one of the tiny spiders that spread their webs through the Hutmoors. Staggering to his feet, his ears popping, Hem clutched the fork in both of his hands, holding it high over his head. It was blazing with such intensity that he could see the bones inside his hands through the pink clothing of his flesh. Out of the corner of his eye he saw that Maerad's lyre was shining with the same light. She lifted it in her arm and raised her left hand, waiting for the right moment. It was a hand of light, a hand that was not maimed, and at the sight Hem's spirit lifted, because it seemed to him that at that moment she had never been wounded, that she had never lost her fingers at all, that the terrible things that had happened to both of them had only been a dream from which they now would wake, forever whole.

The note that filled the air was swelling and growing, and Hem realized with terror and joy that the tuning fork had roused the music that had surged through his body in Nal-Ak-Burat, the music that the Elidhu had breathed into him. But the music that had possessed him then was a mere shadow of the glorious torrent of sound that now lifted and transfigured him. He was a single shining note in an infinite melody that lifted and carried him beyond everything he had ever been or ever known. It seemed to Hem that he had become an instrument, that everything around him – every stone, each blade of grass, each stalk and leaf of every rush and sedge, the layers of rock that stretched beneath his feet to the molten heart of the world, the stars that blazed in the endless sky above him – was awakened into its own unique melody, and all these melodies wove together through his body into an immense, ever-changing harmony that was the living fabric of the world. His heart broke for its fragility, for the delicacies that wove themselves into the deepest intricacies of its being, and at the same time he thought its cruel and violent loveliness would kill him. He couldn't bear its beauty, but he never wanted it to end.

Then Maerad brought down her hand and struck the strings of her lyre, and the world changed for ever.

When Hem bent down and struck the tuning fork, the sweet note pierced Maerad to her heart, and she gasped. She had felt

Sharma gathering his power as the moon rose up from the horizon and, almost idly, she strengthened her shield against him as she readied to play her lyre. He could not touch her.

Sharma, she said. *You cannot prevail.*

His answer was a massive blow that shocked her with its power. It burst through her shield, although it lost most of its force, and struck Hem. He almost dropped the tuning fork, and a sudden fear bit Maerad's heart: Hem was vulnerable in a way that she was not. This was the single chance they had, and if the note died now, it would never sound again. She raised her shield at once, making it much stronger.

Hem scrambled to his feet, shaking his head, but he did not drop the tuning fork, and the music swelled up around them, and Maerad heard for the first time the music of the Elidhu. But she could not let herself be carried away on its wild splendour. She stood firm against the overwhelming wave of the music as it rushed through her, listening for the correct moment. She would know it when it came. She raised her hand, feeling the lyre trembling with power against her breast, and the Song began to form in her mind, possessing her as if she were the Song itself. She bent her head and struck the chord that signalled the first of the runes, Ura, the Full Moon, the Apple Tree, and she opened her mouth to sing. And in that moment, her defences were open to attack.

Before she could sing the first word, Sharma brought the full force of his power against her. The words caught in her throat; she felt as if a giant hand were throttling her, and an unbearable pressure pushed her down, down, down to the ground. For a fleeting instant she thought of when the women had almost drowned her in the mud at Gilman's Cot; she heard the same roaring in her ears, the same defeated limpness in her limbs. She could still hear the music of the Elidhu, and she heard Hem shouting beside her, holding her up, but it all seemed to come from a great distance. She struggled towards the music, but she was powerless to move in the waves of blackness that now possessed her, that were strangling the life out of her.

Then, inexplicably, the pressure lightened, and she gulped convulsively, leaning dizzily against Hem. The lyre was still in her hands, the Elidhu music still sounded around her, the Song still waited to be played; but she was weak, and her lyre felt as heavy as stone, so that she could barely hold it. She shook her head, trying to clear it, and listened desperately for the chords that should come to her, but she could not hear them; a gale of darkness raged about her ears and deafened her.

And then she saw something that she did not understand. She blinked and looked again: a silvery light was sifting through the darkness, and as it did, the monstrous pressure lifted. It seemed as if the darkness were being touched by thousands of unseen hands, that left briefly upon it a shimmering palm print, like the vaporous print of a hand upon cold glass. For a moment Maerad marvelled at the strangeness of what she saw, and then she understood: it was the dead touching Sharma's shadow, and where they put their hands, he weakened and retreated. And she remembered that Sharma feared death above everything else. Now those whom he had killed had come to touch him with their deaths. She felt his horror and fear as thousands of the dead placed their spectral hands upon him, and her heart lifted with a sudden hope. The music came clearer now, and Hem stood straight beside her, holding up the tuning fork, and the chords came back into her mind, lovely and wild, as they should be played.

She glanced up to the moon, which burned like a pool of molten silver low on the horizon. And the words of the stanza rushed into her mind, and she opened her mouth and sang the first line of the stanzas of the moon. Her voice shook and did not carry, but as she sang her voice strengthened, until it rang out over the empty wolds with a power greater than any mortal voice:

"I am the dew on every hill
I am the leap in every womb
I am the fruit of every bough
I am the edge of every cliff
I am the hinge of every question"

As she sang the final line, she paused, waiting for the music to reveal the chords of the rest of the Song, but she ran her hands continuously over the lyre, so the melodies of the moon staves rippled over the Elidhu music. And it seemed to her then that the moon had been called down from the sky and stood before her on the thin turf. She blinked, dazzled, and Hem hid his face.

It was Ardina, but Maerad had not seen Ardina in this guise. Her beauty shook Maerad's heart with terror. Her hair seemed to be alive, as if she were haloed with hissing snakes, and she blazed with a terrible anger. She wore a helm and armour of shining silver, and in both hands she held long blades that flashed so brightly that Maerad couldn't look on them. When she spoke, her voice was cold.

"Sing for my kindred, Elednor," she said. "Do not fear. I will protect you."

And then Maerad knew the chords, and she sang as Ardina bade her:

"I am the song of seven branches
I am the gathering sea foam and the waters beneath it
I am the wind and what is borne by the wind
I am the falling tears of the sun

I am the eagle rising to a cliff
I am all directions over the face of the waters
I am the flowering oak which transforms the earth
I am the bright arrow of vengeance
I am the speech of salmon in the icy pool
I am the blood which swells the leafless branch
I am the hunter's voice which roars through the valley
I am the valour of the desperate roe
I am the honey stored in the rotting hive
I am the sad waves breaking endlessly
The seed of woe sleeps in my darkness
    and the seed of gladness"

As she sang each stanza, she saw with wonder that hundreds of forms were materializing in the empty moors before her: the Elidhu of Edil-Amarandh were come to claim their Song. The stanzas of spring summoned creatures like waterfalls that tumbled endlessly in the air, and slender girls like saplings crowned with apple and cherry blossom, and a pregnant hart, and swallows whose wings were edged with sunlight; and the summer stanzas called an eagle with feathers of flame, a man who stood tall as a tree and whose hair was leaves, a golden bull, a cloud with eyes and a mouth, a wild pig with massive tusks. And there were many more, all of them so different from the others that she could scarcely comprehend them, but each of them with the same slitted yellow Elidhu eyes. And more came and more, and they lifted their voices to sing with Maerad, so the chorus richened and deepened; but still Maerad's voice rose above them all.

And then she struck the chords for the winter runes, and straight before her stood Arkan, his brow crowned with icy diamonds, and she lifted her head proudly and met his eyes as she sang; and he smiled as dazzlingly as winter sun on snow, and his eyes were only for her. And in that moment she was entirely regretless, and her heart trembled like a bird daring the highest reaches of the sky. The music soared inside her and the Elidhu voices gave her wings, and she knew that it was not Maerad who sang, but all the bright and savage beauty of the wild world singing through her. And it seemed to Maerad that she, too, was Elidhu, that she flew with them through their fluid and ever-changing world, and that she had never known such bliss as she knew in those moments.

When she reached the last stanza, her lyre and the tuning fork blazed with a brilliance that was like the sun itself. She sang the last word, "gladness", and a great light leapt towards the Elidhu and filled them with a blinding radiance, so that it burned Maerad's eyes merely to gaze on them. And as she watched, their forms became indistinct and began to ebb away. There were now only a few chords before the Singing was over, and Maerad played them, sobbing for the loss of this fierce loveliness, begging the Elidhu not to leave her behind. But as her hands rippled over the closing chords of the Treesong, every Elidhu vanished before her eyes, and the music that had lifted her up so that she flew among the stars set her gently on the hard ground and abandoned her.

Maerad saw without surprise that the runes that had been carved into the wood had disappeared, as if they had never been there, and that it was now just the simple harp it had always appeared to be. She stood forlorn in the great waste, the lyre forgotten in her hand, yearning towards the final notes of the Elidhu's music as it carried on past her, an echo of unbearable loveliness, and then faded into silence.

But the silence was not the end. For as the music died, it seemed to Maerad that she was beginning to unravel with it, that her longing for the Elidhu undid her, as if she were a spool that was spinning around and around and the thread of herself were being pulled away. She dropped her lyre and clutched herself with her arms, as if she could hold herself together, but she was spinning faster and faster, and all of herself was spinning away, and it was the greatest pain she had ever known. She heard, as if from very far away, a great scream, and she recognized Sharma's voice and knew the same thing was happening to him. She understood then that Sharma was undone, and that the spell of binding at last was broken, and that he and all his power was being ripped from the world. And as he was undone, so was she; and she realized with bitter anguish that Sharma had been right when he had told her that she would lose everything.

She felt no triumph, no sense of justice done or restitution made. All she could feel was the inconsolable agony of her loss, and she realized that the scream she heard was also her own voice, an endless scream as her mind was ripped and torn, as her flesh was stripped from her bones and her bones shredded into splinters, as everything she had ever known herself to be was torn apart and rushed away from her into a great, burning emptiness, and a blackness whistled through her like a merciless wind, until there was nothing left, nothing at all, of what she was, of what she could be, of what she would ever be.

And then she realized she was still there, after all. She lay on the hard ground, and she was very cold, and a stone had cut her cheek so that the blood tickled as it ran down her face. And Hem's arms were flung around her, and he was sobbing with passionate grief because he thought that she was dead. She stirred and sat up, and put her arms around him to comfort him. And then Hem smiled through his tears, and they held each other close, as if they had found each other again after a long and bitter parting. And they did not hear the plaintive whistle of the wind through the reeds nor the calling of their friends as they ran up to help them, because now, in this moment, there was only each other.

And the Song never stopped: released at last into its own music, it played on through all the depths and heights and breadths of the wide and vivid world, following its own desires beyond the reaches of the human heart, forever wild, forever whole, forever free.

EPILOGUE

CAMPHIS of Innail was on guard by the gate, enjoying the first really warm day of spring, when a ragged band of five travellers rode up on four gaunt horses and demanded entrance. He stared through the grille and harshly demanded their business – aside from the grim mountain men who had besieged the walls of Innail a month before, he thought that he had never seen such a disreputable-looking lot. And besides, he was under strict instructions not to admit anyone who did not satisfactorily identify themselves, and although the Fesse had been peaceful since the Landrost had been defeated by the Maid of Innail, tales came their way of massive armies marching through Annar, of war and civil strife, and they still lived under daily fear of attack. It was a time of fear and suspicion and dark rumour.

"Didn't they send news ahead of us?" came a sharp, impatient voice, before anyone else could answer. "It's me, Camphis. Maerad of Pellinor. And I'm tired and I'm hungry and I want a bath and I'll never forgive you if you don't open those gates at once."

Camphis started, and looked again more closely. He blushed to the roots of his hair when he realized that he had been about to refuse admittance to Maerad of Pellinor, the Maid of Innail herself, and Cadvan of Lirigon. He could be forgiven for his mistake: a dark beard curled on Cadvan's chin, which had always been clean-shaven, and Maerad herself was so thin he barely recognized her even now. And the glossy horses that had stepped proudly out of Innail were now hollow-flanked, and their coats stared with lack of condition. Hastily he unbarred the gate, and the travellers rode inside and dismounted. Maerad smiled at the young Bard, and his blush deepened.

"I'm sorry, Mistress Maerad," he stammered. "I—"

To his surprise, Maerad laughed. "Greetings, Camphis," she said. "Of course I forgive you. It's good to see you again."

Cadvan turned to Camphis, smiling tiredly. "If you love me, friend, call some of Indik's apprentices to take these horses and give them some of the loving attention they so richly deserve. And tell Malgorn we're here, five of us: Maerad and me, and Saliman of Turbansk, and Hem of Turbansk, who is Maerad's brother, and Hekibel, daughter of Hirean. Oh, and Irc of— Irc the Saviour of Lirigon. And we're all hungry."

He clapped Camphis on the shoulder, and Camphis blinked and whistled for a messenger and relayed the names that Cadvan had told him, and the boy looked his astonishment and then took off as if wers were at his heels. And before long the horses were knee-deep in hay, their coats cleaned of every skerrick of sweat and dirt after a long rubdown, munching peacefully at a hot mash of oats and bran; and the travellers were walking slowly up to Malgorn and Silvia's Bardhouse, listening in a daze of wonder to the birdsong that rose in the bright spring sunshine. Their legs felt as if they were made of stone, for they were very weary. It was no wonder that they had outstripped any messengers. They had ridden through the Let of Innail, the narrow opening between the two mountain spurs that embraced the valley, only the day before, and despite being bade to stay and rest by the soldiers who camped there, they had ridden on as fast as they could, so impatient were they to see their friends.

As they neared the Bardhouse, the doors were flung open

and Silvia rushed out, her arms held wide. She had clearly been in the kitchen: her hair was tied up in a scarf and her hands were covered in flour up to her elbows. She ran up to Maerad and Cadvan, her face shining with joy, and she threw her arms around both of them and kissed them over and over again; and then she recognized Saliman, and kissed him; and then Hem and Hekibel had to be introduced and embraced in turn; and by the end of it all everyone, even Irc, was covered in white handprints.

Silvia then brought them all inside and insisted that they eat before anything else – she was deeply shocked by Maerad's thinness. And shortly after a substantial meal of fresh bread and stew, Maerad – reluctantly taking leave of Cadvan, who winked at her behind Silvia's back as she hustled them down the hallway – was sitting on her bed in her chamber. It looked exactly the same as when she had left, as if it had been waiting for her; but Maerad felt as if she were an entirely different person. She dumped her pack on the floor and looked out the open window. The branches that waved in the gentle winds outside were heavy with pink blossom, and bees buzzed idly over them, and she could hear someone practising a flute somewhere inside the Bardhouse. A blue dress was laid out on her bed, and beside it was a cake of soap that smelled of oranges and jasmine. Maerad picked up the soap and prepared to take the longest and most luxurious bath she had ever had.

All the travellers bathed, even Hem, and then they slept all afternoon. As evening began to fall gently over Innail, brushing the sky with strokes of amber and lemon and rose-pink, they each awoke and touched the soft blankets and crisp linen sheets with wonder, and they took a deep pleasure in dressing in the clean and beautiful clothes that Silvia had given them to wear. After the past weeks of lying on hard ground, cold and wet and dirty, such simple pleasures seemed like miracles.

Silvia was preparing a dinner for them, and she had told them to gather in the music room when they were ready; and one by one they made their way downstairs and sat on the warm red couches by the fire that had been lit against the cold of the evening, and waited for their hosts.

Maerad came down to find her friends already gathered. She paused in the doorway, watching them before they noticed her. Cadvan, now clean-shaven, sat nearest the fire, his long legs stretched out before him, his blue eyes sparkling with mischief as he told some story to Saliman, who listened attentively and then burst out laughing. Hem, with Irc perched on his shoulder, was sitting a little aside, steadily eating through the hazelnuts and almonds that lay in a blue bowl on the table. Hekibel, with her glorious hair tumbling down her back, wore a rich red dress that fell to the floor and showed off her sumptuous figure. She caught Saliman's eye and they both smiled.

Maerad's chest tightened with love, making her suddenly breathless: these people had risked everything to help her, they had suffered and struggled and wept with her, and they might have died. She knew that she would love them all her life, that even if they didn't see each other for years she would run to greet them, and that it would always be as if they had only parted the day before. They were her dearest friends.

And Cadvan was dearest of all. The memory of how he had caught her up from the ground at Afinil and showered her face with kisses, all his reserve vanishing in his relief that she was alive, still made her body hum with happiness, as if she were a hive full of bees. She had thrown her arms around his neck and kissed him back without shame, and nothing had needed to be said; although they had said much as they rode together on Darsor back to Innail. She studied him possessively from the doorway. Hekibel was right: he was very handsome.

Then Cadvan, feeling her gaze, glanced up towards her. For

a moment, he looked stunned. It was a long time since he had seen her in a beautiful dress, her hair washed and shining, her skin glowing from a long bath; and it was as if he were seeing her for the first time. Their eyes held for a long moment, and then he smiled slowly and lifted his glass, and she came into the lamplight to join them.

They were just sitting down to eat with Silvia and Malgorn when two more Bards arrived. First came Indik, his scarred, grim face lighting up when he saw Maerad, whom he picked up and swung around in a circle, kissing her almost as often as Silvia had. He didn't even try to hide how delighted he was to see her again.

"I always said you were my best pupil," he said, when he finally agreed to put her down.

"Oh!" said Maerad breathlessly. "You did not! You said I was the worst swordswoman you had ever had the misfortune to trip over, and that it would be a miracle if I didn't chop my own head off!"

Indik grinned unrepentantly. "I may have said something like that at some point," he said. "But I knew you'd do me proud. And you have, girl. You have."

The next guest, who followed hard on Indik's heels, made Cadvan and Saliman drop their mouths open in astonishment, and then scramble out of their chairs and rush to embrace him. It was their old mentor, Nelac.

"Nelac!" said Cadvan, releasing him from a bear hug that had nearly swept him off his feet. "My friend, of all people, you were the last I expected to see! Now my cup is full!"

"Not nearly as full as mine," said Nelac, smiling. "Mine runs over." He glanced over to Maerad, and a thrill ran down her spine: he looked at her as he might at an equal. "Greetings, Maerad and Hem of Pellinor. I am right glad to see you both here, whole and well. We felt the darkness pass from this world a fortnight since, and we knew you had completed your task. But none of us expected to see you again, and so we are the more glad."

Hem blushed deep red and muttered some thanks to the table, but Maerad met Nelac's gaze, and her chin was lifted proudly.

"I am glad to be here, Nelac of Lirigon," she said. "And I'm very pleased we're not all dead, too. That makes it best of all."

"Indeed it does," said Nelac, looking around the room and nodding to the others there as Silvia introduced Irc and Hekibel. "I am looking forward to hearing your tales. But first things first: Silvia and Malgorn have made us a fine feast, and I think courtesy demands that we pay it some attention!"

He sat down at the head of table, next to Malgorn, and Maerad saw that he had aged since she last had seen him; the lines on his face had deepened, and there were marks of weariness and struggle and sadness on his face. He seemed much older, although she sensed no diminution of his strength. It seemed rather as if he had become more essential, as if the longer he lived, the more the magery within him became visible to the naked eye. And indeed, there was a faint shimmer of starlight about the old mage. Perhaps, she thought, when an old mage like Nelac dies, he simply becomes a beam of starlight – but she didn't like to think of Nelac's death, and turned her thoughts to the meal.

It was indeed a sumptuous feast – roast kid with fresh spring peas and carrots and roasted turnips, dressed with a sauce of gooseberries. And it was followed by a classic Innail apple pie, the melting flesh of the apple crisscrossed with a lattice of golden pastry. Malgorn kept his eye on the glasses and made sure they were always filled with a wine as pale as straw and fragrant as spring itself.

Maerad sat between Silvia and Cadvan, and breathed in Silvia's beauty. She had dressed formally, in a long moss-green gown that Maerad remembered from her first visit to Innail, and her auburn hair shone in the candlelight like spun copper. Silvia told her that the death of the Nameless One had been sensed by all the Bards in Innail, and no doubt across all Annar.

"The change happened, oh, two weeks ago, at the full moon. Grigar of Desor arrived here a week before then, to warn us of our peril, and he gave us news of you, Hem. We were much afraid, and we sent forces to the Innail Let to defend it as best we could, although we didn't know how we could hold out against such an army. And then a few days later we had news that the Black Army was marching on Lirigon, and I did not know whether to be relieved or to weep. But it seemed to me that the tides would overwhelm us, no matter what we did, and I despaired. Those days seemed the blackest of all…"

She sighed, remembering. "And then, one night, it came over me that I must walk out into the garden to look at the moon. It was as if something called me. And I thought I heard a beautiful music, although I didn't know where it was coming from, and then an immense sadness and joy mingled within me, and I knew it was done, whatever it was. I felt that a great weight, a great burden, had lifted from my heart." She leaned forward and cupped Maerad's face with her hand. "But I was also sure, Maerad, that you must be dead. I was never so glad as when I saw you this noontide."

Maerad lifted her glass. "I'm a little battered, maybe, but it's nothing that a week won't cure. But," she added, a catch in her voice, "I think I am not a Bard any more. I think I lost it all in the Singing. I don't mind; I am happy just to be alive."

Silvia studied her gravely. "No, Maerad, you still have the Gift, as we all do," she said at last. "It is very clear in you, although it is also clear that you have spent yourself beyond your strength, and that you are deeply tired. And you're far too thin. That tiredness can happen to anyone. Cadvan would have told you, if you had asked him. Yes, you have lost something of your Gift. I think, my dearest one, that you will no longer be able to speak with the Elementals in their own tongue, or work the terrible powers that once you did. And to be perfectly honest, I think that is no bad thing."

Maerad stared at Silvia, and relief rose inside her like a warm tide. Since the Singing, she had been sure that she would never be a Bard again. And for all the happiness she felt in her love for Cadvan, the loss of her powers was a hard thing to bear, and she had tried not to think about it on the long ride back to Innail.

As they ate, they told all their stories, piecing together everything that had happened since Cadvan had found Maerad in a cowbyre, on the Springturn almost exactly one year ago. It was a long and disorderly telling.

Nelac had been imprisoned as a rebel by Enkir not long after Maerad and Cadvan had left Thorold for the north. "He did not dare to kill me," said Nelac. "Although I think it was a close thing. But as Enkir revealed his hand, so he was the less able to convince the honest Bards that his allegiance was to the Light. There was much disquiet when he started his campaign against Ileadh and Lanorial, and he lost much support then; and his only answer was to imprison any Bard who dared to question him. By then, I think Enkir was going mad. I think he is quite mad now."

Nelac wiped his brow with a napkin. "I am not ashamed to admit that there were times when I despaired, locked up in Enkir's dungeon, though the sparrows and mice kept me good company. It was hard to see any glimmer of hope in the clouds that darkened Norloch. And then Enkir did set out my death warrant, and someone – I still don't know who it was, because I suspect it was someone close to him – rebelled. And I was smuggled out of Norloch and given a horse. I couldn't go to Lanorial or Ileadh, because they were besieged by Enkir's forces, so I made my way through byways and across wastes all the way to Innail, which was the only School that I could trust. And I arrived a month or so ago, only to find that I had just missed the battle here, and that Cadvan and Maerad were lately gone. Mine is the dullest story of all, really, and I would far rather hear yours..."

Irc, whose belly was bulging as he perched on the back of Hem's chair, gave a sharp caw, so that everyone turned to look at him. He wanted to tell his story too. Cadvan laughed, and Hem rolled his eyes. "I told you he'd be impossible," he said.

Cadvan lifted his glass to Irc. "To me, Irc is a hero," he said. "He saved Lirigon from certain doom, and he can boast as much as he likes."

Irc danced up and down. *I am a hero*, he said. *The Saviour of Lirigon. Cadvan said so, so it must be true. And I am the King's Messenger, and I am a very clever crow. I flew so far and so fast that my wings hurt and I told the Bard about the army, and he said that I was a brave and intelligent bird, and that they would make a song about me and I should have a necklace of gold. But then I had to fly all the way back to find my friend because I missed him so much ... and my wings hurt even more...* He cocked his head and looked at Nelac, his eyes a little blurry, and Hem realized that Irc was actually a bit drunk: he must have been sipping from Hem's glass when he wasn't looking.

It seems to me, said Nelac gravely, *that you deserve at least one necklace. Maybe two.*

At this, Irc bobbed up and down even more energetically and then, very slowly, overcome by the wine and the excitement, began to topple off the back of the chair. Hem caught him before he fell, put him in his lap and tickled his tummy, and Irc lay on his back, his wings flopped open, his eyes closed blissfully.

"I think he's overdone it," said Hem fondly. "And he does deserve praise. He has been brave." He remembered how glad he had been when Irc had flown back to him, a few days after the Singing. Irc hadn't called him: he had simply dropped onto his shoulder out of the sky, startling Hem so much he almost fell off Keru. Irc was so tired he could barely talk, and he was so glad to see Hem that he didn't make a single rude remark. It had taken a few days before he was his brash and boastful self again.

Irc's warning had bought the city a few precious days. The Black Army had marched up expecting a city open to attack, and instead found itself trapped on the other side of the Lirigon River. The Bards and townspeople had broken the bridge, and on the other side were fierce and well-prepared defenders. Undaunted, the Hull captains had begun to build rafts, felling the trees on their side and lashing them together, and harried the townsfolk, preparing for a siege. They had no doubt that, with their overwhelming forces, they would win in the end.

But when the Nameless One was destroyed, so were all his Hulls, who drew on his power for their own deathlessness. The deaths of their captains threw the Black Army into panic and chaos. The bulk of the infantry were slaves from Dén Raven, and they rebelled and threw down their weapons and refused to fight. The remaining forces – the dogsoldiers and blood-guard – had retreated hastily, and were probably marching back south. Hem wondered what had happened to the snouts.

"The war is over," said Nelac. "But there is still much to do. Enkir's campaigns against Ileadh and Lanorial have been beaten back, although there has been much loss of life. And I've heard, from bird messengers, that Amdridh still holds out strongly against the Black Army, and that Til Amon is still besieged, but under no threat of starvation. But that will be old news now, I expect. The tide now runs with the Light."

"And it runs quickly," said Cadvan. "There is much to do, yes. But I think that it is not too soon to toast victory."

"Aye," said Nelac, his voice low. "And then we must turn our attention to the healing. There is much to heal. I am glad that the Nameless One is no more, and I am very glad, Maerad and Hem, that you did not have to pay for it with your lives. There is great joy in that. But I am an old man, and very tired, and my heart is full of sorrow for all those who have died, and for the great cities that have been destroyed. We have lost much in this war, and much is past repairing. And it will be you young people who must heal these wounds."

Hem thought of the snouts. How would they be healed, after what had happened to them? And a sudden fire lit in his breast: perhaps he could help those damaged children; perhaps that could be his next task.

As if he caught Hem's thought, Nelac looked sharply at Hem. "If you wish to pursue your studies, my dear one, you are very welcome to learn from me for a time. It takes no gift of prophecy to predict that you will be a great Healer."

Hem blushed with pleasure, and his eyes were shining. "Yes," he said. "I want to be a Healer, more than anything in the world."

"I think you already are. But there is always more to learn." Nelac rose, and bowed. "I think that I will heed Silvia's gentle tyranny, and take myself to my bedchamber. I will sleep better this night than I have for many years." He bade them all goodnight, and as he left the room, he kissed Maerad's brow. "Well done," he whispered. "You were always full of surprises, Maerad, but somehow I am not surprised."

As if Nelac's leaving were a signal, the others took themselves

to bed shortly afterwards, yawning and stretching, all of them
looking forward to waking late in a warm, comfortable bed.
Hem realized that if he did not move now he probably never
would; he had drunk far too much of Malgorn's deceptively
light wine. He heaved himself out of his chair, holding Irc in his
arms like a baby, and made a round of the room, kissing everyone goodnight with unusual enthusiasm. He kissed Silvia twice.
Maerad watched him with amused surprise; she had never seen
Hem tipsy before. Then he waved brightly and disappeared out
of the door, to stumble up the stairs.

"He is a beautiful boy, your brother," said Saliman, standing up. "I love him well. I knew he was special the moment
I set eyes on him. I don't think I realized quite how special."

"Yes," said Maerad with feeling. "He is."

"And I think I will follow his example. My Lady Hekibel,
will you do me the honour of leaving with me?" He held out
his hand to Hekibel, and she took it, smiling, and made her farewells to the five remaining Bards. The two departed together,
Hekibel's golden head resting on Saliman's shoulder.

"He is a lucky man," said Indik, following Hekibel with his
eyes. "She is a very beautiful woman."

"She's more than beautiful," Maerad said. "She's generous and true and kind and strong and wise. And she's very
funny."

"She'll need all that, if she is to be with a Bard," said Silvia.
"It's not easy, even for another Bard." She glanced sharply
between Cadvan and Maerad, who were seated close together,
their hands clasped, and then looked over to Malgorn. "It's
late, my dear. And tomorrow will be as busy as usual."

And that was the end of the celebration. Maerad remembered it afterwards as one of the best evenings of her life, rich
and vivid and luminous with joy, snatched back from the dark.

* * *

Maerad was still wakeful, perhaps because of the wine, so she and Cadvan went out into the streets of Innail for a walk. It was a clear, frosty night, at the dark of the moon, and the stars blazed brightly, throwing shadows beneath them on the ground. The streets were empty, save for the occasional walker or curious cat, and they wandered arm in arm through the streets and crooked little squares towards the Inner Circle, because Maerad wanted to see the statue of Lanorgrim and the Singing Hall before they went to bed.

"Who would have thought, when you found me milking a cow, that we would have ended up doing all the things we did?" said Maerad.

"I think that I had an inkling," said Cadvan, smiling. "But all the same, Nelac is right. You surprised me almost every step of the way. Sometimes, truth be told, you terrified me more than surprised me…"

"I surprised myself." Maerad frowned. "I do feel strange, Cadvan. I will have to get used to myself. And I was never used to myself in the beginning, anyway… But I'm glad that I'm still a Bard, you know. I mean, it would have been fine if I were not. But I was a little sad when I thought I had lost all my magery."

"You should have asked me, as Silvia said. I didn't know you were even thinking that. It was obvious that your Elemental powers had gone…"

"I didn't want to talk about it." She leaned her head on Cadvan's shoulder. "I think I didn't want any more sadness. And anyway, I had too much to be happy about."

Maerad had told no one of the sorrow she had felt at the loss of her powers. Hem was simply relieved that everything was over, but for Maerad it was different. It could have been worse, much worse; but even through the relief that she hadn't lost everything and was still a Bard, she still mourned her

Elemental self. She knew now what Cadvan had meant when he had told her: *I think that even if we should claim victory in the midst of all this uncertainty, we could still find ourselves with our hands empty. Whatever happens, our world will not be the same after this.*

No, her world would not be the same. And there would always be loss. She thought of the dream she and Hem had shared, of a beautiful house with an orchard where they both lived. She realized now that it was not a glimpse of the future, but a longing for the childhood that they'd never had.

Cadvan stroked Maerad's hair, interrupting her thoughts. "If something worries you, you should tell me," he said.

"Sometimes it's hard, even now," said Maerad. And then added, smiling, "But, Cadvan, you were my first friend, and you are my best friend, and you know me like no one else does. I always think you should know already!"

Cadvan squeezed her arm. "If the last year has taught me anything at all, it has taught me precisely how little I know. Especially about you. A year is scarcely enough to begin to know you. Even a hundred years might not be enough."

He swung Maerad around to face him, and gently kissed the corners of her mouth and each eyelid, and then stood back from her, earnestly studying her face. Maerad smiled and reached up to stroke the scar on his cheekbone, and then she wrapped her arms around his neck and kissed him passionately. It was some time before they resumed their walk.

They wandered in silence, not taking any particular notice of where they were walking. All Innail was silvered with starlight, lying beautiful and serene under the still sky. Maerad thought that she had never known such peace.

"Maerad, you are going to have to give some thought to what you are going to do now," said Cadvan at last. "Do you have any ideas? You can go anywhere you like; after what you have done, you will be received in honour in every School in Annar and the Seven Kingdoms. My only condition is that whatever School you decide on, I have to be there too."

"I don't want to be anywhere if you're not there too," said Maerad.

"You might get tired of my company."

Maerad looked at him sidelong. "I can't imagine that," she said. "Unless you begin to tell me what to do."

"Since when," said Cadvan, smiling, "have I ever been able to tell you what to do? You have never taken the blindest notice…"

"That's not true," said Maerad. "I've always listened. When it's sensible advice, that is."

"I have always given you *extremely* sensible advice."

Maerad grinned. "Sometimes it has been," she said. "Sometimes it's been too sensible."

"Well. I shall learn to be less sensible, then. Though I must say that I've been called many things in my time, and I'd swear that 'sensible' is not one of them. But seriously, Maerad. What shall you do now?"

Maerad thought for a while, her eyebrows drawn into a straight line. "I want to learn, to study the lore," she said. "I still can't read and write properly, and there's so much I want to know… but I think I'd like to rest first. And maybe then I'd like to see some places that you've talked about. I've only ever journeyed with Hulls chasing me. I'd like to travel like a merchant, with an inn at every stop. I'd like to go to Zmarkan and see Sirkana and bring Imi home, and maybe I could find Nim, the Jussack boy who was kind to me … and I'd love to go back to Thorold … and I have to see the rose gardens of Il Arunedh. And you said once you'd take me to Lirigon."

Cadvan laughed. "I did say that," he said. "We could make a pleasant journey of it, when the roads are less perilous. I need to see my birth home; it is long since I was there. Too long. I could show you all my favourite places, and the houses I used to throw stones at and the orchards I used to raid when I was a small boy and a little less wise than I am now."

"I'd like that," said Maerad.

HERE ENDS
THE FOURTH BOOK
OF PELLINOR

APPENDICES

I N *The Gift*, *The Riddle* and *The Crow*, I provided background on some of the more interesting aspects of the history and societies of Edil-Amarandh, Barding, the Speech, the Elidhu, and of course the Treesong itself. These form an (admittedly all too brief) introduction to the rich and growing field of Annaren Studies, and I recommend that anyone interested in these topics should consult the appendices in the earlier volumes.

For the final book, I have acceded to requests by readers for more information on the major characters. For most of this information, I am indebted to the principal expert on the *Naraudh Lar-Chanë*, Christiane Armongath, who has made an extensive study of the extant resources concerning the heroes of the story. This work mostly remains unpublished, so I am grateful for her kindness in permitting me to draw on her research for these notes.

After the events recorded in the *Naraudh Lar-Chanë*, the Annaren Scrolls record a period of some hundreds of years of peace. The Schools were restored, Turbansk and Baladh were rebuilt, and peace made with the people of Dén Raven. A truce was brokered between the Pilanel and the Jussacks in the North – an effort led, it seems, by Maerad herself.

Maerad, Cadvan, Saliman and Hem were, predictably enough, very famous in their own time, and although we only have fragments of many of the documents, there is enough to piece together a picture of their lives after the quest for the Treesong was completed.

There is no record that Cadvan and Maerad married. They remained close for the rest of their long lives, although the records show that they certainly spent several years apart when they worked in different Schools or pursued different tasks. Under the name Elednor of Edil-Amarandh, Maerad became a famous poet in her own right, and was often referred to as one of the greatest poets of Annar, although sadly almost none of her poetry has survived. There are many writings that are attributed to their co-authorship (most, sadly, only preserved in references in other documents). The most famous is, of course, the *Naraudh Lar-Chanë*, but it seems that they also left extensive writings on Elemental magery and made significant contributions to the Bardic writings on the Balance, with particular reference to the Elidhu.

Fornarii's *Lives of the Bard*s says that Maerad and Cadvan travelled between many Schools, staying several years at Lirigon, Il Arunedh, Busk, Turbansk and Til Amon. Cadvan was made First Bard of Lirigon in N1134, and presided there until his death in N1205. Maerad died in Lirigon in N1297, and was buried with great honour. For many years her tomb was a place of pilgrimage.

In the event, it seems that Hem did not study with Nelac, who returned to his home School of Lirigon, where he lived in peace and honour in the few years before he died, in N950.

Hem journeyed south to Turbansk with Saliman and Hekibel. Saliman was appointed First Bard of Turbansk. Har-Ytan's son, Ir-Ytan, was Ernani of the city, as Har-Ytan's designated heir – she had given him the ruby of the Ernani, symbol of their authority, before she led the charge on the Black Army in Turbansk. Under their leadership the people of the city began the task of rebuilding Turbansk to its former greatness. Despite the devastations of war and earthquake, the damage was not as complete as had been feared, and the work was finished more quickly than was expected. Some said that Turbansk was made even more beautiful than it had been formerly, and its arts and sciences flowered over the next few centuries.

Hem was reunited with Oslar of Turbansk, and was actively involved in restoring the Healing Houses. After Oslar's death, Hem was made Chief Healer, and under his guidance the skill and wisdom of the Healers of Turbansk became a byword through all of Edil-Amarandh. Although he often travelled north to Annar to visit Maerad or to share his knowledge with other Bards, and it is known that he visited his Pilanel relatives in Murask, he based himself in Turbansk for the rest of his life.

Irc continued to live with Hem, and enjoyed as much honour as the other heroes of the *Naraudh Lar-Chanë*. He clearly never became modest: the phrase "Irc-tongue" passed into Turbanskian speech as a byword for boastfulness. He died at the ripe old age of twenty-eight, and it was popularly held that when he died, his soul flew to join the Elidhu, Nyanar, in his land near the Glandugir Hills.

Accounts claim that even in his early manhood, Hem was appointed an emissary to Dén Raven and that, young as he was, he helped to negotiate the peace between the Suderain and the people of Dén Raven. And later, when a stable peace was made, he established a network of houses for the children who suffered in the wars in the Suderain.

Mindful perhaps of his experiences as a child in Edinur's orphanages, Hem insisted the buildings should be beautiful and the schools run with compassion and wisdom. "Beauty is almost as important to a child as is food," he wrote in a letter to Maerad, preserved in the *Iklital*, a collection of correspondence between Bards. "It is beauty that comforts the soul and heals the wounded mind. And in a place of peace and beauty, those who care for children who are wounded in the mind and soul will need its solace even as much as the children themselves."

Saliman married Hekibel and lived with her in Turbansk. Together they had five children, including the famous Bard Maerad of Turbansk, who was later First Bard of Turbansk herself. Hekibel was honoured by the people of Turbansk and lived there until she died in N1003. The chronicles say that Saliman was heartbroken, and for some years forsook Barding, retreating to his grandmother's house and refusing to see any but his closest friends. In those years he wrote songs and poems, none of which survive: it is said that his "Lament for Hekibel" was among the most popular poems of the Suderain people. Although he lived until N1210, Saliman never remarried.

CADVAN OF LIRIGON

MANY people have asked for more information on the early life of Cadvan of Lirigon, before he met Maerad, and again, through the kind offices of Christiane Armongath, I can provide some facts.

Cadvan was born, the oldest of four children, into a poor family in a small village near Lirigon. His father was a cobbler. His mother died of a fever when he was six years old, after she gave birth to his youngest brother Morvan.

We know that as a young Bard at the School of Lirigon Cadvan was one of the most brilliant students of Nelac of Lirigon, and that great things were expected of him. The documents suggest that at that time – around fifty years before the events in *The Books of Pellinor* – Cadvan was one of a particularly bright generation of young Bards that flourished in Norloch under Nelac's tutelage. In particular, there were Ceredin (who became Cadvan's lover before her tragic death), and Malgorn, a childhood friend. Others named in the records of the time were Runilar, who later went to the School of Til Amon; Norowen, later First Bard of Il Arunedh; Grigar of Desor; and Saliman of Turbansk. They were instated together as Minor Bards and remained friends throughout their adult lives. Saliman of Turbansk became part of this Circle when Nelac moved to Norloch, after the tragic events that led to the death of Ceredin. He was followed by many of his young students.

When Nelac of Lirigon was asked to be a member of the First

Circle in Norloch, some time after Cadvan had become a full
Bard, Cadvan divided his time between Lirigon and Norloch,
and most likely at that time met Saliman of Turbansk, who had
travelled to Norloch expressly to study with Nelac. Cadvan met
Dernhil of Gent, his other greatest friend, at Lirigon, when he
challenged the young but famous poet to a poetry duel – and, to
his own chagrin and to the delight of many others, lost. Dernhil
was already on his way to becoming the most celebrated poet
of his age, and this event did nothing to hinder his fame, as the
Bard Turilien records in her *Life of Dernhil*:

> "The whole town was in a fever at Cadvan's chal-
> lenge, and many turned out for the duel from both the
> School and the Town, so the Singing Hall was crammed,
> and the crowd spilled out into the central circle: and yet
> more came. It was like a festival, with Bards bearing ban-
> ners for one or other of the challengers, and three Scribes
> seconded from the Library to record their stanzas. In
> some cases, fights broke out between rival supporters,
> such were the passions aroused by the challenge; and
> many young ladies came to witness the event, wearing
> their brightest furbelows, hoping to catch the eye of one
> or other of the challengers, who were, it was generally
> agreed by the crowd, not only the most talented, but the
> most handsome young Bards of their age."

Poetry duels have very complicated rules, but in essence the
duel required the two poets to extemporize poems in set metres
and forms, responding to each other's poems immediately.
The poems were judged for technical finesse and emotional
power, as well as for their wit as responses. Sadly, although it
is said that the poems were written down, we have yet to find
any record of them. It seems that Cadvan did not lose very

graciously, and stalked out of the Singing Hall "with a face clouded as black as any had seen". However, after this he and Dernhil became firm friends.

This particular event demonstrates Cadvan's arrogance: he was the leader among his friends, used to being the best at everything. This made him enemies as well as friends and admirers, and not everyone was displeased at his later downfall.

As recounted in *The Gift*, the major event of Cadvan's early life was when he was attracted by the arts of the Dark, and raised a revenant which he could not control. Both he and Dernhil were seriously injured and Ceredin was killed. He escaped banishment from the Schools only through the intercession of Nelac of Lirigon and other loyal friends. For the next fifty years – until he met Maerad of Pellinor – he wasn't associated with any particular School, and lived an itinerant life in pursuit of the Dark, attempting to expiate his youthful crime. Although records are patchy, it is clear that it was in this time that he began to establish his reputation as one of the most powerful Bards of the Light.

SELECTED EXTRACTS FROM THE ANNAREN SCROLLS

FOLLOWING are two extracts from the Annaren Scrolls, which I append for their interest. The first is an account by the Bard Fornarii of an incident in Cadvan's childhood that casts an interesting light on his later life. It is unclear whether the Hull mentioned in the story is the same one Cadvan encountered at the Broken Teeth early in the *Naraudh Lar-Chanë*, but it seems at least likely that it might be.

FROM *THE LIVES OF THE BARDS* BY FORNARII OF LIRIGON

CADVAN lived with his father and three siblings in a small Lirhan village, not far from Lirigon. But he did not go to the Lirigon School until much later than most children with the Gift.

He was an attractive child, clever and quick with his hands, and he knew he was different from his brothers and sisters. He came into the Speech early, when he was about five, shortly before he lost his mother. His father, Nartan, never quite recovered from the death of his wife, and was frightened of his son's precocity. He was often harsh with the boy, and ordered Cadvan not to tell anyone about his abilities, but it was impossible for him to hide them completely, and soon the whole village knew that he had the Speech.

When Cadvan was nine years old, the Lirigon Bards, as was the custom, came to Nartan's house to speak about the boy attending the School of Lirigon. Being a Bard was considered an honour in Lirigon; it was not one of those places where those with the Speech were shunned. But even so, Nartan was surly with the Bards, and would not hear of Cadvan attending the School. Perhaps he was reluctant to lose another member of the family, or perhaps he needed the hands of his eldest son to help with the three younger children and his cobbling. The Bards earnestly argued that to leave a boy with the Gift untrained was asking for trouble, but Nartan refused to listen. The Bards said they would come again the following spring, and ask again, but Nartan turned his face away and would not speak another word, so they sighed and left.

Cadvan had not been allowed in the room when the Bards had been talking, but he knew they were discussing him, and he eavesdropped easily enough, using his Bard-given Hearing; what he had heard excited him, and he decided that he wanted to be a Bard more than anything else. His father cuffed him and told him to get on with his work.

After that, Cadvan conceived a great resentment against his father. He began to run wild, and he led other children on his escapades – nothing very harmful, beyond raiding orchards and throwing stones. Because he had the Gift, he could go hidden and speak to animals, which gave him the edge in their pranks. He was learning how to use his powers, but without the careful training of the Bards, which would have controlled his excesses, his use of them was wilful. His behaviour concerned his aunt, his mother's sister Alina, who perhaps had a little of the Gift herself and was certainly a perceptive woman; and she spoke again to Nartan, telling him he ought to send the boy to the School.

Nartan was a stubborn man, and he said he would not agree to his firstborn going away, no matter what. Alina told him he was a fool and was breeding trouble for himself, but he would not listen. The truth was that Nartan burned with love for his son, love that he could not admit even to himself, and so would not let him go – it was often said that Cadvan was very like his dead mother.

One day, when Cadvan was about ten, a stranger came to the village on a black horse. He was tall and severe-looking, and he was dressed in rich clothes. He went straight to the cobbler's house, demanding that a strap on his horse's bridle be fixed at once, as it had broken. Nartan was not at home, so Cadvan took the job. Cadvan saw that the stranger's horse was ill-treated; its mouth was bleeding. This angered him, and he spoke to the man without respect. "If you were more gentle with your hands," he said, "the strap would not be broken."

The stranger told the boy to hold his tongue, and then examined him more closely. What he saw interested him, and he asked his name. Cadvan answered sullenly, concentrating on mending the broken strap and not liking to be questioned. Finally, the stranger asked him if he had the Speech. Cadvan looked up swiftly, and took a long time to answer. At last he nodded.

"Why are you not at the School?" asked the stranger.

"My father will not let me," said the boy.

The stranger heard the resentment in the boy's voice, and smiled to himself. He picked up a pebble from the ground and tossed it in his hand. "How might I make this pebble fly, boy?" he said.

Cadvan shrugged. "Throw it," he said.

"Aye. Or give it wings." And as Cadvan watched, the pebble turned into a butterfly and flew away.

Cadvan had heard of Bardic magic, but had never seen it; he felt the more his deprivation of learning. He refused to appear impressed, however, and merely shrugged. "It's a trick," he said proudly. "I am too old for silly games."

The stranger laughed. "My name is Likud," he said. "I will be back." Then he mounted his horse and rode away.

Cadvan stood in the road and watched him until he was out of sight. The meeting had disturbed him. He didn't like the man, and he liked even less the way he treated his horse; yet there was a strange fascination about him, too. For the next few weeks he waited for the stranger to return, but he did not; and after a while Cadvan decided that he hadn't meant what he had said. He was curious about the man's abilities, though, and began to experiment, teaching himself the simpler enchantments, glimmerspells and other mageries of illusion.

Time passed, and Cadvan grew into an awkward boy, tall and gangly. Every spring the Bards of Lirigon would ride to speak with his father and every year his father spurned their offers. It seemed to Nartan that if he gave in, it would mean admitting that he was wrong in the first place: and he was a proud and stubborn man, like his son. And every year the boy grew wilder.

Now, it was around this time that the Bards of Lirigon began to be concerned about some disturbing, if small, incidents; and one of these happened to Cadvan. There were stories that wers had been seen in the wild lands near the Osidh Elanor, and other creatures that the Lirhanese had not names for, but which became rumours of fear. And also at this time the raids of the Jussack peoples pushed the Pilanel people out of their traditional summer grazing lands in the Arkiadera, and the chief of the southern clans came south over the Osidh Annova and asked the Lirhan Bards and Thane for permission to graze their herds in the Rilnik Plains.

Cadvan was heedless of these things; although of course he heard gossip. Sometimes he would sit with his father at the inn and listen restlessly while the greybeards spoke darkly of bad portents. At such times, he would yearn to be at the School of Lirigon, because then, so he thought, he would be taught great mageries, and would fight these evil things. But he knew better than to mention his wish to his father. Sometimes he thought of running away to Lirigon, but despite his fierce desire, he could not abandon his father. And so he learned the trade of cobbling, and frittered away his spare time, thinking up new pranks to amuse himself and his companions. And all the time, a black bitterness was nursing itself in his heart.

One day the stranger did return. Cadvan was working outside

the house – it was a sunny day – and he saw him riding through the middle of the village, looking neither right nor left. When Cadvan saw him, his heart leapt into his mouth. He stood up and watched the rider. The man glanced sideways at Cadvan as he passed the house, and pulled up his horse.

"Still here then, boy?" he said, with a touch of scorn.

Cadvan stared back and said nothing.

The stranger dismounted and stared at Cadvan. "You'll be a man soon," he said. "And yet you still let your father tie you to his house? The world is big, my boy. You don't belong here."

He said no more than what Cadvan already knew, but the boy's face darkened at the man's mockery, and a loyalty towards his father flamed in his breast. "I am with my own people," he said angrily. "Who are you, to speak thus to me?"

"You know my name," said the man.

Cadvan wanted to deny it, but he did know his name. "Likud," he said.

Likud looked pleased. "So you have some wit. Or some memory," he said. "You have the Gift: from here I can see it is in you in no small measure. Why aren't the Bards of Lirigon here, taking you to where you should be? They betray their duty. Your training is no business of your father's."

Cadvan said nothing, because he had sometimes wondered the same thing. But Bards will not take children with the Gift if their parents do not permit it.

"Come with me," said Likud. "I have something to show you. Your father is away from home, he will not know."

At first Cadvan made no answer, wondering how Likud knew his father was not at home. Then he said, "I have to finish mending this boot. You can come back later, if you want."

Likud shrugged, and made to move away. But Cadvan felt a deep stubbornness wake in him, and would not go anywhere until he had finished his task. He bent his head down and concentrated on his work. When he looked up, Likud was still waiting for him.

Then Cadvan carefully put away his tools, and stood up to follow Likud.

Likud led him out of the village and a short distance into a beechwood. It was high summer, and the light shone bravely on the leaves, but where Likud walked it seemed that the birdsong sank down and a shadow followed him. Cadvan felt fear settle inside him like a bird of shadow, and he began to feel sorry that he had come. He thought about the dark things that had been talked about in the village, and wondered whether he should just turn around and go home – for everyone said that evil was gathering in the north, and he did not think that Likud was a good man. But despite his doubts, he followed him.

At last Likud stopped in a small clearing. He turned and smiled at Cadvan. "Now," he said. "I will show you something you have never seen before."

He lifted his arms and between them there began to gather a darkness, as if he were making a hole in the air. Cadvan was now very afraid and wanted to cry out, but his tongue cleaved to the roof of his mouth and he could make no sound, and he found his feet were rooted to the ground, and he was no longer aware of the woods or the sunshine around him; he could only watch the darkness between Likud's arms.

The darkness thickened and roiled, and there began to be a sound like rushing wind or water. And then, to his astonishment, Cadvan saw a picture form in the shadow: and the picture moved as if it were alive. It was of a glittering city, with graceful walls and towers, which stood by a great mere so still that stars were reflected on its surfaces. The city was built of white stone so that it seemed to be carved of moonlight. And it seemed to Cadvan as if he entered the city and walked around inside it like a ghost, and that he peered through casements and saw men and women in fine robes speaking together, or making fine things; but none of them saw him.

The vision passed, and Cadvan came to, as if out of a swoon. Likud let down his arms and the darkness disappeared. Cadvan stared at Likud with amazement.

"What is that place?" he asked.

"It is a place that is no longer," said Likud. "By my art, you glimpsed the ancient citadel of Afinil, and it has been gone for many lives of men. Is it not wonderful?"

"Aye," said Cadvan, caught in enchantment. He hungered to see more. "What else can you show me?"

Now Likud was a powerful Hull, and its aims were not benevolent. It was pleased that it had enraptured the boy so, because it did not want him to be fearful. It had perceived that Cadvan had a rare and untrained talent, and it wished to bind him to itself, so the boy would be its slave.

Now that Cadvan was no longer wary, the Hull lifted its arms again and put forth its power. But this time the spell was different, and Cadvan did not like it so much; he felt that chains of smoke were winding around his thoughts, and he felt the voice of Likud inside his own head, as if Likud's thoughts were his own; and he thought that he would die from the black pressure in his mind.

And now Cadvan showed his native power, because he looked Likud in the eye, and, untrained as he was, he forced down the spell that would have made him a minion of Likud. And when the Hull felt its own powers useless, it was afraid of the strength of the boy; and it tried then to capture him by force, and abduct him on its horse. But even though he was a boy, Cadvan was stronger than Likud, and he punched the Hull in the face and knocked it over, and then found in himself such magery to strike Likud senseless. And then he stole the Hull's horse and galloped away as fast as he could.

He did not ride home, but to the School of Lirigon, which was three leagues off, and he did not stop until he clattered into the courtyard and almost fell off the horse. It is said that Nelac of Lirigon himself came running out to see what the disturbance was, and took the sobbing boy into his house and calmed him down. And Nelac then rode to Cadvan's village and spoke a long time to Nartan; and after that, Cadvan entered the School, and no more was said of cobbling.

But that was not the last that Cadvan saw of Likud, nor he of Cadvan.

FROM *THE FLOWERS OF THE BARDS*

T HE *Flowers of the Bards* is a collection of short poems that is preserved almost in its entirety, and which gives us the most complete picture yet discovered of the richness of Annaren poetry, which otherwise exists mainly in fragments in other texts. Among them is the only complete poem we have by Elednor of Edil-Amarandh, or Maerad herself. The poem has been the source of some controversy: noting its startling similarity to a famous poem by the Classical Greek poet Sappho, who lived on the Isle of Lesbos (roughly between 630 and 570 BC), some scholars have argued that Sappho must have been aware of Maerad's poem, and consequently was familiar with Annaren culture. Others have suggested that this poem is evidence that Edil-Amarandh was, in fact, the origin of the legend of Atlantis. The untitled poem was written in cyrilenics, an extremely intricate verse form impossible to reproduce in English, and was greatly admired for the grace and skill the poet demonstrated in working this difficult form. Sadly, my own translation, which follows, can only suggest a little of its power in its original language.

> Some say an army of horsemen
> some an army on foot
> others say ships laden for war
> are the fairest things on earth.

But I say the fairest sight
on this dark earth
is the face of the one you love.

Nor is it hard to understand:
love has humbled the hearts
of the proudest queens.

And I would rather see you now
stepping over my threshold
than any soldier greaved in gold
or any iron-beaked ship.

                    Elednor Edil-Amarandh na

MORE BOOKS OF PELLINOR

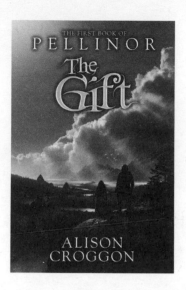

M aerad is an orphaned slave in a harsh settlement, unaware that she possesses a powerful Gift: one that marks her as a member of the School of Pellinor. When she is rescued by Cadvan, a Bard of Lirigon, her destiny begins to unfold. But before Maerad can attain her true heritage, she and Cadvan must embark on a treacherous journey and confront dark forces of the most terrifying kind.

Australian author Alison Croggon's epic fantasy about Maerad is the first of the Books of Pellinor.

"This is a tale with passion, inspiring characters, an enchanting protagonist and vividly described landscapes. *The Gift* is a powerful story and marks the beginning of a great series of fantasy novels."
The Bookseller

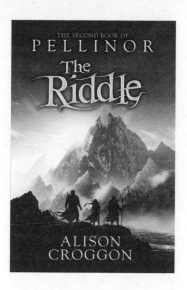

Despite her tragic and bitter past, Maerad's powers grow stronger by the day. Pursued by both the Light and the Dark, she and her mentor, Cadvan of Lirigon, seek the Riddle of the Treesong – the key to restoring peace to their kingdom. As they travel across the ravaged landscape, Maerad is drawn ever closer to the Winterking, the author of her sorrows and the strongest ally of the Nameless One – the greatest tyrant of all.

The Riddle is the thrilling sequel to the highly acclaimed *The Gift*.

"Croggon's world is rich and passionate, brimming with archetypal motifs but freshly splendorous in its own right. Supremely satisfying." *Kirkus Reviews* (starred review)

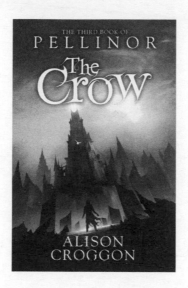

The forces of the Nameless One grow ever stronger, and in the frozen wastelands of the north Maerad seeks to unravel the mysteries of the Treesong, which may hold the key to peace. Meanwhile her troubled and unhappy brother, Hem, is sent south to Turbansk. But evil forces threaten to destroy the city, and it becomes clear that Hem's own destiny is linked to the Treesong more closely than he knows. Aided by his pet crow, Irc, Hem spies on the child armies of the Dark ... with perilous consequences.

The Crow is the third of the critically acclaimed Books of Pellinor.

"The action never flags in this compellingly readable fantasy tale. Riveting and intense, it is a spellbinding addition to a stellar fantasy series."
VOYA